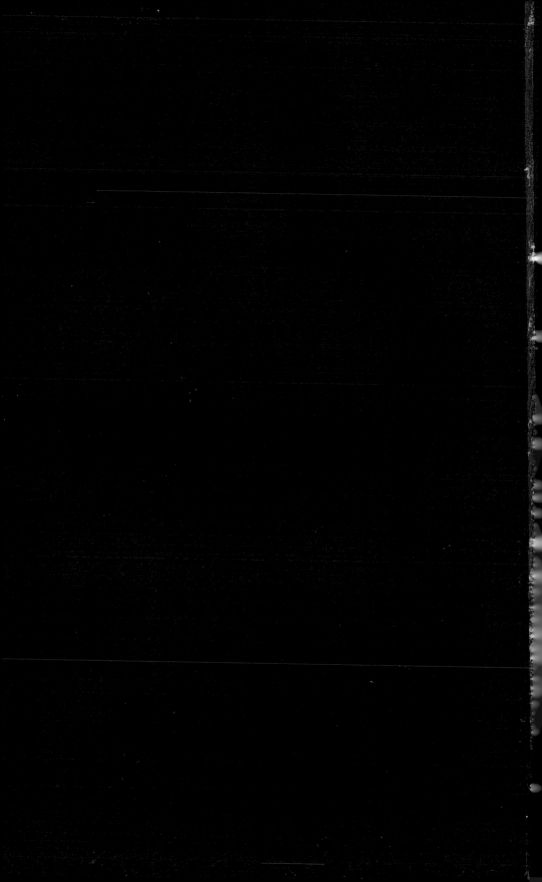

RISING BLOOD

RISING BLOOD

James Fleming

For Holly,
Birthday girl,
from
James

JONATHAN CAPE
LONDON

Published by Jonathan Cape 2011

2 4 6 8 10 9 7 5 3 1

Copyright © James Fleming 2011

James Fleming has asserted his right under the Copyright, Designs
and Patents Act 1988 to be identified as the author of this work

First published in Great Britain in 2011 by
Jonathan Cape
Random House, 20 Vauxhall Bridge Road,
London SW1V 2SA

www.vintage-books.co.uk

Addresses for companies within The Random House Group Limited can be found at:
www.randomhouse.co.uk/offices.htm

The Random House Group Limited Reg. No. 954009

A CIP catalogue record for this book
is available from the British Library

ISBN 9780224091350

The Random House Group Limited supports the Forest Stewardship
Council (FSC), the leading international forest certification organisation. All our titles
that are printed on Greenpeace-approved FSC certified paper carry the FSC logo.
Our paper procurement policy can be found at
www.randomhouse.co.uk/environment

Typeset by Palimpsest Book Production Limited,
Falkirk, Stirlingshire
Printed and bound in Great Britain by
Clays Ltd, St Ives plc

For Sally

One

WHAT STARTS in joy will end in tears, what starts in woe will end with cheers. The best of these sayings, which my mother kept in a brocade notebook with yellow fleur-de-lis on the front, should be written in indelible ink on the palm of every child's hand. When the first truth is revealed, the child will pay attention to the rest of them, that's the idea. But of course it's not how it happens. Experience is the only ink that's truly indelible.

By this point in the Revolution I was still in good health, apart from occasional bouts of malaria, which I'd picked up in Burma when collecting for the Field Museum. If you were a doctor and saw me walking towards you in the street, you'd say to yourself, that man's doing well, just look at his trim, and as I passed you'd eye me with interest. After all, revolutions are famous for promoting famine and disease besides all the rest.

Stripped I weighed 170 lb.

Xenia once decided to measure my chest. Squinting at the tape in the candlelight, she said that thirty-four *arshok* (which is forty-two imperial inches) was exactly the same as her friend Anna, whom she didn't envy one little bit, it had to be so uncomfortable for her – then with a glance at my bare torso she dropped the tape over the side of the bed.

Such eyes she had! Huge and green, like goggles! Ah, Xenia, we had good times together, you and I, until I discovered you weren't the girl you said you were. All the time you were bedding me, you were acting as Glebov's spy. I should have smelt a rat from the circumstances of our very first meeting. But I was too hungry for a woman and didn't stop to think.

I

For the eight months that Xenia and I were together, I was the sucker, the most complete, most gallant, most willing sucker in all of Russia. And when the truth emerged, it was Glebov himself who told me, which didn't help her cause.

So times quickly got less good for her and now she's dead, having bequeathed me Lili during her last moments on the earthly kingdom of Christ, of whom she was enamoured.

Lili, let me add, was her daughter by this very same Glebov.

Here I must introduce another woman – my heart, my treasure, my ever and only love – my wife: Elizaveta née Rykov, whom I always called Lizochka. To make sense of her, I have to bring Glebov into it again. For it was this small, piglike man who – for doctrinal reasons – to ingratiate himself with the Bolsheviks – or to satisfy his sadistic lusts, I never asked him which – led the rape and torture of my woman. We'd been married for exactly seven days.

That was how my chest came down, from forty-two to the forty inches it now is. It fairly hollows a man out carrying a story like that around with him.

Lenin, Trotsky and Glebov, that was the Bolshevik line-up when on behalf of the common man they launched their reign of terror. In this connection, I've noticed that talking of the 'common man' in a fawning and unctuous tone has become a badge of honour with a certain type of person, who is invariably a member of the intelligentsia. Such people are capable of justifying any Bolshevik outrage, however despicable it may be morally. I've never heard one single word of regret from that class of person concerning the disgusting manner in which Lizochka and her family and their servants were butchered.

There are people who whisper behind my back about my own 'morals', hurtful, malicious whispers.

They simply have no idea. One day, when this is all over, I'll confront them. 'You know what it takes to shoot your own wife?' That's what I'll say. And I'll reply on their behalf, since they'll be silent for fear of acknowledging the truth. 'Courage,' I'll say, spitting the word into their faces, 'and I still don't know what it's cost me. The total. When the books are balanced at the end of the day. The grand and final total, not just the last message her eyes held for me.'

Morality, it's a swamp. The tallest stilts in the world won't help you.

Am I such a brute to look at? It's important. Appearances count wherever human life exists. A tear welling from a soft brown eye at the right time can make the difference between life and death. In the matter of Charlie Doig, the blue eyes, the short dark hair that's already showing signs of grey, and the slight stoop (no more than a couple of degrees, but it's there) say one thing. The rugged nose, the obstinate mouth, the wide calf muscles and the six foot two in stockinged feet say something else. Neither aspect is misleading: where they meet is where I am, like a fish swimming at the junction of two currents.

Not just any old fish. If I was that, I wouldn't have survived this long.

My age has helped. I was born in Moscow in 1889, so at almost thirty years old, I'm at my peak. Which is as well. In these terrible times, God help babes and ancients and everyone who's too fat to run away.

My teeth are good, like the teeth of most Russians. You don't want to be a dentist in Russia, we're too poor to afford sugar.

I have a high instep. I lope. The hair on my chest reminded Lizochka of whiskers of ripe barley, both as to colour and flow. My skin is that of an outdoors man.

Other significant considerations: am I clever? Am I sympathetic? Am I principled? A little bit of each, though maybe not enough of the first to get me through this Revolution, which looks like being drawn out. If it doesn't, no one but me will suffer. I have no doting family, no wife, in-laws, lover, not even friends. That's extraordinary, to have no friends. And at the age of thirty, when life should be like a public meeting. But it's how it is throughout revolutionary Russia. There are no relationships left between its citizens, only between them and the state.

I'm certain that somewhere, even though they've held power for only nine months, the Bolsheviks are preparing a dossier on me. Sympintel is how they might describe me, a mixture of sympathetic and intelligent – or some such completely asinine abbreviation. If they had anything in their heads apart from hatred of the bedbug rich, as Lenin calls even the peasants, they'd write the truth: Charlie Doig – hostile, vengeful and lonely.

The most dangerous sort: kill this man on sight. Glebov should have remembered his own words when he had the chance to get me.

One description that's not going to appear in my dossier is 'nice'. No one gets lucky and nice in the same cracker. When I've had luck, I've had it in bold type. To have found a beetle unknown to mankind – to have come through typhus – to have survived the most violent revolution in the history of man, in fact to be in possession, as of this date, 8 September 1918, of far greater wealth than when that squeaky-voiced monster walked up the steps of the Smolny Institute and announced that he was now the owner of all us Russians, these demonstrate the fullness of my luck.

But now it was about to expire. I knew it as surely as I knew anything because that's how luck's always been with me – feast and famine, feast and famine. What happened when Goetz, my fellow naturalist, left me in the lurch? I broke a leg, got bothered for money, caught typhus and on returning to my mother's family home at Smolensk, found that Lizochka, my beautiful, black-eyed, aristocratic girl, was affianced to a famous cavalry officer – to a proper gentleman, let's not beat about the bush.

Then my luck turned: the fiancé was assassinated – blown up by the Bolsheviks, bits of him going right up into the treetops – and I got her. Got her to the altar, got her into bed, got her well and truly – impregnated her first go, I'm sure of it.

No sooner had I come down from heaven than Glebov arrived at our home, riding out of a blizzard, pretending he was a White officer seeking a bed for the night, and everything collapsed again.

Nothing could have been worse, nothing. Until you've been called upon to make the decision, unaided by anyone, as to whether your wife lives or dies, you have no idea how cruel God can be.

It's typical of life's irony that the only time you really need a god is when things are truly awful. Whose god is irrelevant. Call Him just a Being, call Him a Woman if you want. What you're looking for is someone's book of rules to measure your

4

decisions against. God makes the best ones, I think anyone who's suffered will agree with me there. However, the interpretation of them has to be your own. Well and good if there's someone to assist you, but at the end of the day . . . I was lucky here for I had Lizochka to help me – on the floor of the stable, naked beneath the horse rug, her eyes scored with agony, pleading for release.

I refuse to say again how Glebov and his gang tortured her.

It took me a minute to make up my mind and another for us to say our farewells. Not a day has passed since I buried her that I do not hear the thump of my bullet or see the curl of blue pistol smoke rising through the cold, tight air.

No, I'm not your chap if it's nice you're after. But this is a rough world and every man needs some shittiness in him.

Two

MY TANGIBLE assets at this time were a barge stuck on a mudbank on the River Volga and Kobi, a young Mongolian who'd attached himself to me three years before in Samarkand. There were others with me, women included, but they weren't in the same class of asset as Kobi. In fact, they were a long way from prime, being the sort that has to be told things twice.

In the barge were twenty-eight tons of the dead Tsar's gold. Every bar had the double-headed eagle stamped on it. Every bar was numbered and dated. In every bar there were four hundred troy ounces of the stuff that could be turned into cash in every bank of the world from London to Lisbon going the long way round. There wasn't a bullion dealer alive who wouldn't instantly recognise the red flush on the gold that came from the copper content in the Siberian mines.

Fifteen million American dollars, that's what it'd be worth when I got it out of Russia. No one else in the country had anything like that to his name, not any longer. Not a million dollars, not a thousand, not even the possibility of these sums. A single dollar would have been a fortune to most Russians at this time.

On that date in 1918 I was the wealthiest man in Russia, no doubt about it.

Seven time zones, a fifth of the world's surface, 155 million people and Charlie Doig lording it over all comers, flashing his golden smile – that's not too shabby for a man who's never had a penny to his name.

You'd like to know what I could have bought with those

millions? Here's what. For cash, adroitly deployed, no middlemen, I could have bought Estonia. Not just one of its baronies or a large farm with top-grade soil but the entire country. That's an idea to make one stop and think. A *country*. Customs revenue, national anthem, a flag, a foreign policy, bold letters in the index of atlases and a seat at international conferences.

However, this was theoretical. To turn the gold into cash I had to get it out of Russia and even to start to do that I had to get my barge off its mudbank on which we'd grounded during the fight with Glebov. There were Red battleships somewhere on the Volga and when the news got round that the man who'd shot down Lenin's number three was escaping downstream, they were going to come after me like apes chasing a rotten apple. I had to get movement on that barge.

There was no other traffic on the Volga, the boatmen all being too scared to venture out. No one was going to pass us a line and pull us off the mudbank. We were going to have to be dug out by hand.

Or we could wait for a winter flood to float us off. But by the time that happened we'd have been captured by the Reds and flayed and spitted. What was going on around us was class warfare in its purest form, pointless to give it any other name. Men were being led away and executed for no greater reason than they had a resemblance to an oil painting done two hundred years ago of a general or a count in Peter the Great's time. A similar nose or cheekbones, even the cast of someone's mouth, each of these had turned out to be a sentence of death.

If I were caught, my height would be enough. All the Romanov tsars had been tall men. Therefore I had to be a Romanov. That was how the Bolsheviks reasoned. I'd be shot without a second thought.

I called my crew on deck: Stiffy the Englishman, Joseph who'd worked for my Uncle Igor in his St Petersburg palace, the capitalist Boltikov, Shmuleyvich and his big bullying woman, Mrs Davidova – and Lili. Six of them plus Kobi and myself, eight in the party all told. I herded them together and told them how it was: if we weren't afloat within twenty-four hours, we were chopped liver. That got them rattled, you bet it did. Then

7

I waded ashore to gather a labour force to dig us out, local fishermen and the like. They'd have heard Glebov shooting us up, seen his Fokker spinning out of control to the earth. They'd have been curious, couldn't not have been.

I was right. Within an hour I'd got a dozen men and by waving around one of my scarlet thousand-rouble notes had attracted their keen attention. I showed them the problem: I showed them the banknote again, flapped it, flaunted it, tugged it at both ends so that it made a snapping noise. 'Dig,' I said.

Stiffy fetched me a chair and I sat in the bows watching them. Engineer Shmuleyvich threw the engines into reverse whenever I gave the signal, to see if there was any give in the mud's grip.

I drank tea, I strode around shouting at them, I glared and fumed and threatened – I behaved exactly as one of our olden Russian boyars would have, which is to say, like an owner of slaves. It wasn't only my injured shoulder that was making me short-tempered. I really did not want to be caught sitting around on the mud like a stupid duck with Prokhor Fedorovich Glebov lying dead in a swamp somewhere just behind me. He may have deserved it but that wasn't the issue that afternoon.

The issues were my life and fifteen million dollars.

Or my life and Estonia, put it like that if you want.

My father would've seen it as a game with far higher stakes. It was how he saw life, always reaching for the top shelf. He'd have said in that strong Dundee accent of his, 'What's wrong with you, laddie, why just one wee country? Why so timid, why not a continent, why not Africa itself?' He was the most vibrant and lovable man who was ever born. Tears still come welling up when I think of him dying – of the plague, alone in a dosshouse in Tashkent.

I was fourteen when he died, full to the brim with debt of one sort or another. Ever since I've been trying to make up for him. You could say it was in this connection that I was trying to get a barge containing twenty-eight tons of gold off the mud, to prove that I too wasn't a failure.

'Dig, you filthy scum,' I roared. 'Keep your eyes on this and dig.' I filled my tea glass with river water and stood it on top of the thousand-rouble note where they could all see it. 'Think of that as booze. Now think of the women, of the land, of the train rides you could buy with the money' – that's every Russian's secret dream, to wave goodbye to his wife and cow and walk to a railway station and then spend six months cruising round our immense country, chatting and drinking and singing and seeing a fresh view every morning.

The heat started to leave the day. Soon the smell of evening would steal across the river. Even though it was early in September, autumn was already imaginable, that most appalling of our Russian seasons with its fogs and damp cold and limp brown leaves. To my father, man of dreams, it made no difference. But my mother, who had all the melancholy of a Russian aristocrat, dreaded the arrival of October. It was, she said, like the onset of a disease that the books tell you is completely incurable. 'Why should I bother with living?' that's what she used to say, as regular as clockwork, from the end of September until the first proper snows fell in December and people greased the runners on their sleighs.

Leaning on the rail, I called down to them, 'Harder, harder.' They'd uncovered a fair depth of the barge's bows and were now having to heave the mud up onto a raft and float it away.

'What have you got in there, *barin*?' one of them shouted up, his face streaked with dirt and sweat. He slapped at a mosquito. 'Iron ore?'

Of course it was the gold that was the problem, but I wasn't going to tell them that. However, now that one of them had posed the question, they all stopped digging and were looking up at me, every face alive with the question, What's the bastard got in that boat of his? Is it worth fighting for?

A cable almost a foot thick had been run all round the side of the barge to prevent the hull being damaged when wharfing. To board us they'd have to clamber over it. We could pick them off like flies as they scrabbled for a grip. Nevertheless I heard the tone of his voice and saw the greed in those faces. It was time to leave.

I waved to Shmuleyvich. He raised his hand in acknowledgement. I felt the planking vibrate up the 120-foot deck as he moved the lever to Full Astern. One of the labourers exclaimed – the bows were shuddering. I shouted to Shmuley, 'She's moving!'

Boltikov began to jump up and down, saying, 'Away you go, you devil, get floating!' When the barge didn't budge, he took to a swaying, urging motion with his hips. 'Off you go, bye-bye, mud, good evening, Madame Volga, you great wet whore.'

Gassy swirls of air started erupting beside the bows. We couldn't be far from freedom. I looked around: no destroyers, no aeroplanes, nothing on the broad, even expanse of the Volga except the glittering ripples of the evening sun.

Three

KOBI, WHO was with the horse on the far bank of the river, was watching us. The sun had them in its spotlight: the big piebald stallion called Tornado and sitting casually on it, his right foot stroking the horse's neck, in a position known only to someone who has a horse among his ancestors, the young Mongolian. He had one rifle slung over his shoulder and another in his hands. His could have been the bullet that brought down Glebov and his black Fokker. I'd raise a glass to him this evening. He wouldn't respond – I'd never seen him touch alcohol – but that unknowable smile of his would break out and we'd salute each other. He'd captured the white swift for me by climbing up the mosque in Samarkand. He'd nursed me when I had typhus. He'd saved my life more than once. In return I'd given him freedom, adventure and the opportunity to screw Russian girls. They called him Tigerman, because of his diamond-shaped eyes and because that's how he moved, slinking, gliding, on the balls of his feet – and they took him into their beds on account of his lean, hairless body, which fascinated them.

I always thought there was an element of revenge in his pursuit of them. He'd never known his parents, had been brought up by Russian missionaries as their servant. To have Russian women prefer him to their own sort and to have them beneath him all fat and adoring was a way of getting his own back.

Something like that – maybe. He wasn't much of a talker.

As I glanced across at him and Tornado in their sunny halo, who should appear from below decks but the girl who wished to bear my children – Lili, the daughter of my late lover, Xenia, and my late foe, Prokhor Fedorovich Glebov.

Aged about seventeen, everything soft, everything quaking, everything white and moonlike. Legs inclining to stoutness, already a bit puffy about the knees.

She'd changed from her battle costume into a cotton shift – came swaying down the deck with the slight uncertainty of a girl who knows she has a good figure but hasn't yet twigged exactly how good it is.

I said, 'It's no good making frog's eyes at me. I don't think I could even get it up for you.'

She said coolly, 'It was the one thing my mother said you'd be good for.'

I said, 'I'll land you at the first decent town we pass. You can make your own way. Find someone else to father your children.' I had no intention of lying down with her. With the daughter of the man who raped my wife? No thank you a billion times over.

She smiled at me, some pity in there or even contempt. She said, 'Your hair's going grey, Charlenka,' and at the same moment the barge came out of the mud with a vast gurgling belch.

We staggered, I more than her. I grabbed her shoulder to steady myself. Shmuleyvich, letting the barge swing round so that its bows pointed upstream and holding it there in the current, shouted down to me, 'Are you going to pay them?'

I walked to the bows. The leader of the gang was hanging onto the cable fender with all his might, his hands like crabs. The veins in his face were bulging from the effort, like red worms. I said to him, 'Are you touching the bottom with your feet?'

'No. Please, *barin*, our money . . .'

I looked down on him, thinking not about his tiredness but how precisely I was going to exploit the gold now I'd got it on the move.

'Here,' I said, and folding up the thousand-rouble note I bent right down and offered it to his mouth. His teeth snapped at it – vividly white against the scarlet of the note. He let go and swam off to join his comrades, the chopping ripples pasting his beard all over his face. Then I went below to see what twenty-eight tons of gold looked like.

Four

To GET to the hold I had to go through the bargemaster's cabin. That was how the boat was arranged, so that the captain was his own dog, sleeping across the threshold.

I went in, cracking my head on the lintel as I did so. When I'd finished blinking, I found I was looking straight at a shelf of Gogol's works.

I don't suppose I'd seen more than half a dozen books in the last year. And here, suddenly, in the most unexpected of places, was Gogol. No one else, no contamination by lesser authors, just the recessed shelf with a row of uniform maroon leatherette books enclosed between two upright building bricks as bookends – black-painted with a silvered 'V' on one brick and an 'I' on the other, both in a nice ornate script.

My heart began to jerk. I closed the door.

Also in that cabin was an iron stove, a small rectangular table with a vase of withered roses that had shed their petals a long time ago, and two decent chairs. The bed had a loosely woven blanket of a warm brown colour. Various waterproofed clothes and hats were hanging from hooks on the wall.

My heart began to murmur out loud, began to tell me what a homely life the captain and his woman had enjoyed, sitting in front of the warm stove with their books. I said to it, 'Don't finish that sentence, I know what you're getting at.'

But I couldn't stop myself. I was helpless from the emotion within me. I could see only too clearly the captain getting his pipe drawing nicely and plumping up his cushion. Outside's a snowstorm. He's dropped anchor, he'll ride it out with a good depth of water under his keel. That's what he's thinking as he digests his meal of brisket of beef and boiled cabbage.

He puts his feet up. He knows every inch of everything that's going on around him. The snow, the cargo of wheat, the wife, the bill of lading in the chart locker. His barge is twenty foot wide. There are only two rooms in it, the rest being cargo space. It's his world and he's the absolute master of it.

But there is another world besides – Gogol's.

His hand goes up – for which book? Which would have been his all-time favourite?

My eye went straight to it like iron filings to a magnet. I rose from the bed. I took down *The Nose*.

The soft fake-leather cover was stained with candle grease and cup rings. I opened it with shaking fingers, I uncrinkled the onion-skin paper of the title page where it had got folded over and I read the title, even though it could be nothing else than what it said – *The Nose and Other Stories*, by Nikolai Gogol.

Not very long, almost not worth binding as one volume. But that wasn't the thing. The thing was this: it was the story she'd been reading on our last night – on the last night of her life, of her only life. I'd come crashing into our bedroom in my clumsy way and there she'd been, sprawled on the sofa. She was wearing a long day gown with some pink floral pattern in a panel across her chest, was idly flipping a mule around on the end of her big toe.

She looked at me over her spectacles – Parisian, with bright red frames. She laid the book, open at her place, straddling the arm of the sofa. She said, 'Don't tell me it's started snowing again, we'll never get out.'

'Isn't that what you want?' I said.

It was the beginning of our first and only quarrel. Can you guess the subject? It's not difficult. It's fundamental to every man, woman and child whose blood is more than half Russian. It concerns our God (which is the only one in the world as far as we're concerned), our ideas about the motherland, about family, proper vodka, proper snow, the proper ringing of church bells, the proper rituals at burial – every aspect of Russian life and death that can be imagined.

To be more rigorous in this explanation, it is the lack of these things that I'm talking about.

Exile.

That was the subject of our quarrel. Our word for it in this context is *chuzhbina*, meaning life in a country far distant from one's own, which one misses terribly. Not many letters, not many syllables, but those that there are comprise the most detestable word in our language.

I told her for the umpteenth time that there was something about Glebov I mistrusted, that the Bolsheviks were as dangerous as snakes, that we should start for the frontier that very night, that urgent wasn't the word for what I was feeling. She said she wasn't ready, that it was a very different feeling she had. What was wrong with another month? Why was I always in such a hurry? She swept her arm around. 'Charlenka darling, I haven't even *thought* about packing. My whole life and you want it boxed up in a day?'

It wasn't just a tiff. We shouted at each other, made the pictures shiver on the walls, made the buds of candlelight tremble.

The next day, when I was raging through the house looking for her, that was what I saw first: *The Nose*, by Nikolai Gogol, in the same place on the sofa arm.

There'd been corpses throughout the mansion. I'd run from room to room shouting her name. I'd snatched the book up. Her scent, which was Soir de Paris, still lingered on the cover.

I pressed it to my nostrils. 'Lizochka!' I screamed. 'Lizochka! Lizochka!'

Then I tracked her fleeing footsteps through the snow. And found her, ruined, on that stable floor.

The Nose – and here it was again.

Gripping it with insane strength, bending it right over and making a scroll of it, I ran back on deck, to the bows, as far away from the others as I could get. I threw myself down in the coil of mooring cables, almost out of sight.

Dusk was falling. In a while, Shmuley'd take us into the bank where Kobi'd be waiting and we'd tie up for the night. Then everyone'd start thinking about food and I'd be left alone with my misery.

But Joseph had seen me crossing the deck. His dark,

cadaverous face leaned over me. 'Gogol, eh! What a funny name! What small print! Thank God I didn't get further than the alphabet. Here, I'll fetch a lamp for you, *barin*.'

I didn't want to read, I wanted only solitude. The sight of Gogol's name had opened everything up for me again. Was that how it was going to be for the rest of my life? Shadows on the wall forever growing larger? Her voice calling, those low tones as sweet as syrup, was that what would reach me next?

'Damn memory,' I whispered.

'*Barin*?' It was Joseph, still hovering over me.

'Leave me alone,' I shouted. 'Get away from me.'

Then I lay there in the purple dusk, tears of self-pity sliding down my cheeks as unstoppably as if they'd been made of mercury. In my eye was the picture of Lizochka lying on the stable floor the moment before I shot her. In my heart was dread, that the power of memory was so great.

But it wasn't genuine weeping, just a form of maudlin blubbering, and after a while it dawned on me that the only person I was crying for was a version of myself that had been destroyed as surely as Lizochka had. The Pink House, its billiard table, the Konig phonograph on which my cousin Nicholas would play Palestrina's *Stabat Mater* until we begged him to stop, the bearskin on which I'd first made love to her, I could've made list upon list of all the things I was crying for. But they'd gone. Everything had been swept away by the Revolution, and with it had vanished the man I'd then been. What good was grief now? Why waste my time crying when I had twenty-eight tons of gold in the hold and three Red armies after me, what sort of stupidity was that? I wiped my eyes. 'Fuck you, Gogol,' I said, and I hurled the book into the river.

The smell of cooking reached me. I'd get out the last bottle of Vladimir. It was crazy feeling sorry for myself on the day I'd killed Glebov. We'd celebrate and do so in the Russian fashion – swearing eternal love and fidelity, smashing glasses, singing, shouting, falling over.

I stood up and stretched, walked down the deck.

'Ah, there you are, Charlie Doig, I thought you were hiding from me.' It was the Davidova woman, speaking from the pool of darkness formed by the wheelhouse.

Five

S HE STEPPED out of the shadow and advanced on me. Madame Annushka Davidova, who'd always treated me like the smelliest sort of shit even though I'd saved her first from the Bolsheviks and then from her rat-like criminal of a husband, even though I'd fed and watered her for six months, even though I'd procured engineer Shmuleyvich as her lover. Along the deck she thumped in a pair of wooden clogs she must have found below deck. I thought, What more can she want?

She halted a few yards away, a black colossus framed against the sunset. Some distance behind, creeping in her wake, came tremendous-arsed Shmuleyvich.

I said, 'Why are you standing so far away? Are you afraid of me?'

Shmuley said, 'We have a request, *barin*, a-a-a petition . . .' His voice trailed away.

'Out with it, man. We know how to talk to each other.'

But it was she who stepped up and said, 'Our share of the gold, that's what we've come about.'

'Why should you have any?'

'We did the swimming, Yuri and I. It was we who captured this barge. Without us you'd have no gold at all. We must know what our share is so that we can make sensible plans.'

I stood my ground, thinking, did this woman ever have children? Did she strike them if they answered back? So fat, so grasping, so thoroughly unpleasant—

She said, 'How much, then?'

At that moment Kobi shouted something to me. We'd just tied up at the bank. He was coming up the gangplank carrying

Tornado's saddle and bridle. He dropped them beside the wheel-house and padded towards us.

He paid no attention to Mrs D. and Shmuley – said to me, 'This evening I rode through a village where someone had a newspaper. A man was reading it out loud in the square. The entire village was gathered round him. I said, "What's happened?" He said, "The Reds are marching across the steppe. All their armies, all their horsemen, their artillery too. Russia is doomed." Then we had some talk together. It's why I dropped behind.'

Shmuley butted in, 'To the sun! How can it be otherwise? The monsters will always want to move south. That's where the grain is, and the oil and the ships. All the wealth of our country lies in the south.'

'And we'd have to get there before them,' I murmured, drawing in my mind a map showing the huge length of the Volga as it flowed south into the Caspian Sea, and to the west the endless steppes we'd have to cross to get to the Black Sea and thus the Mediterranean – and safety.

'*Barin*, we'd never do it,' said honest Shmuleyvich. 'What is our one horse against a thousand lances? How is a man like me to run away from these Cossack devils?'

Big open country. No rivers to speak of. No railways. No roads. Just the steppe, mile after mile of it until one hit the Black Sea. How was I to get the gold across it? In wagons? And then have to buy teams of oxen to pull the wagons? Then buy feed for the oxen? Then hire men to tend them? And where the hell would I find people to guard the caravan?

And the gold itself, there was another issue. No one in Russia was going to buy it by the ton. They'd seize it all right, but only a cretin would expect payment.

Moreover the gold market was uncompromising, as Boltikov had often told me.

'Charlenka lord of all,' he'd said as we steamed in to attack Kazan, 'are you sure we want this stuff? Were it Turkish gold, the wealth of Byzantium, ancient as can be instead of what these nouveau Romanovs have dug up – I mean, who's going to want ninety-nine per cent purity from us when they can get a hundred in the bazaar? Why get ourselves killed for that, eh?'

The truth was that my sort of gold would only have value at a central bank. And to get to one –

Mrs D. moved in for the kill. Her carnivorous breath swarmed around me. 'A ton would be a fair division,' she said.

I said, 'Lenin himself is drawing only fifteen hundred roubles a month. Are you that much more deserving than Lenin?'

Kobi joined in unexpectedly, from out of the shadows. 'If I'd started a movement like he has, which he says is going to spread to all the nations of the earth, I'd want more money than that. I'd get up and say, if you want my next idea, you must first pay for the last one. Proper pay at that . . . He must be cleverer than fifteen hundred. A decent horse is more than that.'

I said, 'How much should Lenin have then?'

'Ten thousand plus a new horse whenever he wants.'

Mrs D. opened her mouth but Kobi and I were still having a conversation. I said to him, 'Which would be more important to you, the money or the horse?'

'Don't be stupid, Doig,' he said, and with that I made up my mind.

I had Kobi put the saddle back on Tornado and rode off to the village from which I'd hired the men to dig us out. Of course they were all getting drunk now they had my money but I found one man who was sober enough to tell me where the deepest part of the Volga was hereabouts.

By the time I'd got back and unsaddled Tornado, the others had finished their food. I got them on deck, had Kobi shine a lantern upon me so they could see my features and know I was telling the truth.

I spread my arms wide. 'Friends of many miles and many adventures, I've just been reminded by Madama' – I gestured at Mrs D. – 'that part of the cargo belongs to you. How much? she asked, and was right to do so. Times are bad in our country. They are worse than bad, they are worse even than the worst. They would have been unimaginable to our parents, and I hope will be to our children by the time they can tell the difference between good and bad. This is no time for selfishness. So my answer to Madama is this: each of you is free to go below and take away as much gold as you wish. Then you must leave. Yes, this is the parting of the ways. I myself am going and I can't take you with me. I can't say it clearer than that. You've one hour to be off the barge.'

They gulped – except for Boltikov. He narrowed his eyes and said in his shrewd bet-you-a-million voice, 'The gold – carry it in our arms or carry it by any method we choose? What's your meaning?'

I said, 'Glebov is dead. I've avenged my wife. That was always my goal. Now I'm going on a pilgrimage to find my soul. And by carry, I mean carry in your arms.'

The words came out sounding a bit Jesusy. Boltikov smiled derisively.

'Let me come with you, *barin*,' said little Joseph. 'Your family have been my parents, my wife and my children. What shall I do without you?'

I loved this man. He'd stayed true to the Rykovs when he could have bolted, had spied on Lenin for me and been ready to admit that he was a coward, which very few men are prepared to do. 'Leave Russia and you're a goner,' I said to him. He looked blankly up at me. I said, 'There's only one Russia in the world. Anywhere else and we're like fish drying in the sun. Believe me, Joseph, that's the truth. Stay here.'

Again I caught that scornful look on Boltikov's face.

Then Kobi's shoulder was touching my shoulder. Side by side we stood there. Below us gurgled the river, carrying the shit of our miserable history away to wash up on the shores of the Byzantines, the Georgians, the Medes, the Persians and all the other nations bordering the inland sea. With the Bolsheviks in control, modern shit would be produced, tons and tons of it. Plus there'd be all the corpses of the shot, the strangled and the drowned. The Volga would be blocked.

But we'd be long gone, Kobi and I. We were the future.

He suddenly gave one of his deep creaking laughs. 'All of you, you only think of yourselves, of the golden money and how you'll spend it on luxury as soon as you can. You're worthless! No wonder my people conquered you so often and so easily.'

There was no reply possible to that, for it was true, every word of it.

I don't know, but maybe Kobi's words touched a nerve, for

in an instant they were all clamouring to come with me, saying I was their lucky mascot, the only one who could lead them to the promised land, etc., etc. Even Mrs D. came out with a little choking cry. And Lili must have been suddenly seized with apprehension for she flung her arms around my neck and in a girlish whisper reminded me what her mother had said about bearing my children. I put her from me. With her beauty and figure she'd soon get a man to protect her. I told her so, told her to go only for the best, and when she asked how she'd know, told her to keep her eye on who obeyed whom and when she found a man who had to obey nobody, to look no further.

I jumped onto the coil of cable. 'Take as much gold as you can, I don't care. Take it, and go out into the night. Trust in God. Multiply. Live to the age of ninety. Do what you want, but go before I change my mind.'

Of course they all rushed down to grab what gold they could – except for Boltikov and Kobi. Alexander Alexandrovich folded his arms across his chest and put on a surly, obstinate look. He said, 'What's astonishing is that you appear so unalterably Russian. Your high blue cotton shirt, the wide leather belt, the trousers so extremely loose-fitting you could be keeping a python down there. So like our late Lev Tolstoy. It's you, your family, your breeding, your history. Yet now you deny it. You want to change your nationality and show the only friend you've got left that you can be as faithless as any Englishman. You are one capital shit, Doig.'

I said, 'As much gold as you can carry is not to be despised.'

He said, 'You know what I mean. We were in this together, you and I, dividing the spoils evenly. *Tak na tak.* Fifty-fifty.'

There was no point reminding him who'd been carrying the can for the whole enterprise from start to finish. He wanted more gold than I was ever going to give him, that would remain the heart of the matter even if a thousand words were to pass between us. So I just said, 'Alexander Alexandrovich, take what you can and count your blessings. I could have given you just a bullet in the head.'

He didn't go down to the hold where the others were hauling gold bricks out as fast as they could but made straight for the gangplank muttering that I hadn't seen the last of him.

They went as I'd said they should, staggering ashore with their gold bars. I cried to see the last of Joseph. He handed the one ingot he was taking to Stiffy, told him not to run away with it, then going up on tiptoe kissed me on the lips and snuggled into my arms, laying his head flat against my chest like a woman. But he'd never have lasted where I was going: he was truly better off taking his chances with the Reds. As for the others, I didn't give a damn. It was true what Boltikov had said: I was in the process of changing. Russia held nothing for me any longer. I'd take myself to Vladivostok, board a ship and build a new life somewhere in the outer world.

Goodbye, I said, standing at the foot of the gangplank to make sure none of them stole the horse. Goodbye, goodbye – good luck with everything. Then I led Tornado up the gangplank, Kobi and I pulled it aboard and we sailed the barge to the other side of the river, that which faces Siberia and the Orient.

Six

I HUNG a storm lantern from a bracket on the wheelhouse so that Boltikov could find us easily. I knew he'd come. He wasn't the sort of man to surrender a claim before he had to. And he was a problem I wanted to be done with. I spent an hour fixing things up with Kobi. Then I lay down on deck and dozed.

You can't do anything quietly in water. It reflects and magnifies noises. A river has its own pattern of sucking and gurgling in which any changes are instantly apparent. Even in my half-sleep I heard them approaching, a boat with muffled oars or sweeps, crabbing sloppily across the current with perhaps another two or three boats being towed behind, to hold the spoils.

They came quickly over the side, Boltikov at the head of the three roughs he'd hired. He glanced at me and at the bundle lying beside me under a cloak. It was the moment of greatest risk. Who was to say he hadn't decided that with his boarding party he'd be strong enough to kill us and take all the gold? I had my Luger ready if it began to look like that. But my betting was that he'd settle for what he considered to be his rightful share because he was afraid of getting into a fight with Kobi. Everyone was afraid of Kobi and his knife.

One of the men was left in the wheelhouse to guard Boltikov's back. Then he slipped down the companionway with the other two.

Three minutes' grace was what I'd agreed with Kobi. I counted them off. By the end, the guard hadn't budged. I began again – and at twenty seconds the shout came for him from below. He pushed himself off the wheelhouse wall and grasped the rails of the companionway. His head disappeared – I threw off my blanket and went swiftly after him.

The four men were jammed round the low bulkhead behind the skipper's cabin. Slivers of lamplight from the cargo space were escaping through the chinks round their bodies. I could see nothing of Kobi. But it had to be as we'd planned, or they wouldn't be there.

I coughed and said, 'Glad you're paying attention. Anything less and he'd have blown you away.'

They rounded on me, barging and jostling each other in the squash – and there was Kobi crouching in the middle of the gold, head and shoulders poking out of the chamber we'd made by restacking the ingots. The two black nostrils of our Maxim 7.62mm machine gun were pointing directly at Boltikov's chest. The belt of ammunition lay sprawled over the bricks of gold.

Kobi grinned at me. 'I was a surprise for them.'

I said to Boltikov, 'When the curtain falls, the fun ends, wouldn't you say that's how it is in life, Alexander Alexandrovich?'

'I'll get you somehow.'

'Maybe. But in the meantime, you stay here and I'm going to climb down into your boats and throw all the sails and oars into the river. Then I'll tow you into the middle and cast off. And then you're free to drift wherever you want until the current casts you upon the shore, which may be in five miles or in five hundred. Perhaps Trotsky'll get you first, with his torpedo boats. Or some other Bolshevik ogre . . . A man of your build could have carried away five or six gold bars from this vessel by himself. Now you'll get none. It was the chance you took.'

There was some shuffling among them: they couldn't decide whether to face me or Kobi. So I left them there, and the plan worked as I'd intended, and in the morning fog, when everything was dead quiet except for the creak of the heron's flight and the whistle of wings as the duck set off for the day, I tossed the rope to Boltikov, thanked him for the gift of one of his boats, and waved him goodbye – two quick flat passes of my hand. I'd never trusted him.

He called up, 'I don't forget, I never forget,' and then they were gone, spinning away into the fog as one of them sat himself on the stern thwart and tried to steer by putting his leg over the side.

I said to Kobi, 'If they'd had a sword, they could have steered with that.'

He said, 'A sabre would have had a wider blade.' He yawned. 'I left mine on the train going into Kazan. Find me another, Doig.'

'Right now?'

He smiled, or what passed for a smile with Kobi. 'Wherever we're going.'

We made tea, we put the gold back as it had been to balance the barge, watered the horse, and then we slipped down the river and after two full days, only once seeing Boltikov and his merry crew, when we ploughed serenely past them right at the start, we came to the large buoy, painted in wide blue-and-white stripes, that I'd been told to look for. Deep water was a hundred yards below the buoy. I'd recognise it by its dark colour and its sinister quietness, that's what the man had said, and if the river was in flood, I should avoid it like the plague. An undertow developed that made fishing boats vanish as quickly and neatly, he said, as a tart pouches the purse of a spent man. It was why it had been buoyed.

We made our camp on the left bank. Before it was properly light, leaving Kobi and Tornado behind, I slowly fiddled the barge out until I reached the oily Stygian glide below the buoy.

I turned her into the current, cut the engine to Slow and dashed below. The valve on the seacock was stiff, but, when I put a lever on it, the locking nut eventually turned, grating horribly as if it knew its fate. I waited until I could hear the water swilling into the ballast. Then I rowed myself to the bank in Boltikov's spare boat and rejoined Kobi, who was waiting with a scarf round his throat on account of the fog, which was bitter that morning.

Tornado threw back his piebald head and whinnied when I stepped ashore. Kobi said, 'He's saying he's happy you didn't go down with the boat.' Then we said nothing as between flitters of fog the barge sank in front of us. For the first time I saw its name – the *Vera Ingrid*. The 'V' and the 'I' were wonderfully graceful, the limner's brush trailing off in long golden adventures, identical to the decoration on the bookends.

So that was the woman who'd dusted the books in the

bargemaster's cabin or done a spell at the wheel for him when Gogol was calling. Vera Ingrid – nice, but not for me. No more women for me.

The barge took its time going. 'Come on, come on,' I whispered, for it was growing lighter with every minute and fishermen are about early. Then suddenly the gold had its way, her stern tipped up into the air and she slid gracefully beneath the water with none of the exploding boilers and whirlpools one reads about. Some debris, bits of timber smashed during Glebov's attack, floated quietly away, that was all.

I saluted her, I saluted the gold, Lili, Joseph, all of them gone. I saluted Russia, which was going.

'The buoy's the landmark,' Kobi said.

'It could move,' I said.

So we got out of sight and waited until the sun burnt the fog off and then we took proper cross-bearings – to the west, the gold and glinting dome of a church; to the east, a steep gully, maybe a ravine, between two low, rounded hills. Having thus made our baseline, we added various refinements, making allowances all the time for objects and buildings that might have disappeared by the time we returned. When we'd agreed on all our marks, we committed them to memory – wrote nothing down. Shaking his head, Kobi said, 'But you'll never come back.'

'I might,' I said. 'Or my children.'

'I'll have got here first,' he said with a leathery smile.

I said, 'You can't swim.'

He agreed. 'No one in Mongolia knows how to swim, why should they? So I'll be the first.'

'Think the Reds'll give you papers?'

'Who needs papers? What are frontiers to people like us? We go where we wish, we always have. So I'll come to this place, I'll swim out and I'll take what gold I need.'

'How many horses would make you a hero in Mongolia?'

'Five hundred minimum.'

'How many women?'

'One good one is enough. You need one as well, to have your children.'

I said, 'Tell you what, we'll wait till we get clear of the Reds before we think about women. Maybe that won't happen till we're in a different country. Russian women have been a disaster for me.'

Tightening Tornado's girths, he said over his shoulder, 'I wonder how far the river'll take Boltikov before it puts him ashore.'

That woke me up all right. In a silly sentimental way, I'd sunk the gold for the kids I still didn't have. Who could say what the future would bring? It could turn out to be the greatest inheritance for them ever. But what I didn't want was for them to labour across rivers and wide continents with their hopes bubbling like warm springs only to find the cupboard was bare because, all the time Kobi and I had been watching the barge sink, Boltikov had been spying on us.

'That's enough, *paidyom*, let's go,' I said testily.

'OK,' said Kobi, and we mounted the piebald stallion that had been presented to me by the Governor of the prison at Strabinsk because he'd known and loved my irrepressible father and wanted to give me a better chance in these perilous times. Such are the strands that flow between generations and families and between those vague extensions of families that we loosely call friends.

Seven

As we climbed out of the Volga valley, Kobi, who was riding pillion behind me, said in my ear, 'That was a good decision, Doig. This country's ruined. You can smell it on the people.'

I agreed wholeheartedly with him, and that was what I meant when I said that things usually turn out the opposite from what you expect. The night before I'd been laden down by the gold, by Gogol, by a sense of responsibility for my small army and by the futility of my existence.

And now? The troop had been disbanded. The gold had been stashed. I was heading out, a free man.

'No women ever again,' I growled. 'They're just trouble, for me and them. You remind me of that when you see me tempted.'

'Men are different,' said Kobi. 'Different muscles, different things in the mind.'

We halted on the ridge and took a last look back. Beneath us the Volga, huge, greasy, turbid, unstoppable, the bearer of food and fertility through the heartland of Russia, a species of god; in a hundred yards, it would've disappeared from sight, but from our minds, never.

Kobi sighed deeply and said, 'So this is what escape feels like.'

I swivelled in the saddle and stared at him.

He said, 'We're escaping. The Red swine have beaten us. It's a fact.'

I jabbed my finger at his chest. 'Don't talk like that. No one's beaten us. Haven't we killed Glebov? Haven't we hidden away a fortune? Aren't we alive and kicking?'

'But we're not riding into Moscow, we're riding away from it. What's that if not escaping?'

'Trying a different tactic,' I said roughly, though tears were prickling at my eyes, 'that's what we're doing. Use that escaping word again and you can get off and walk.'

The man had been born on a horse and hated even the idea of walking, so my threat kept him quiet for a bit. We rode on, deep in our separate thoughts. But the calm didn't last long. He was accustomed to being in the saddle itself, not having to sit on the horse's spine. He got restless, began to put Tornado off his pace by shifting around or by fumbling with his balls, which he said were rucked up in his trousers and getting twisted. It was like the night we'd shared a horse when searching for Glebov, after Zeppelins had attacked the hospital wagon and he'd disappeared. The difference was that then it had been for only a few hours: now we were in it for the long haul.

Three thousand, seven hundred and fifty miles, that's what I mean by the long haul, the distance between Kazan and the port of Vladivostok. From there to Japan – seven hundred and fifty. From Japan to the United States – a short voyage, nothing more.

It was the last part of the land journey that'd be especially tricky, between Irkutsk and Vladivostok. For the fugitives from Bolshevism the port had achieved the status of a magical city, like one of those descriptions of paradise you find in the Bible, where the apples are all golden and everyone has a flock of sheep. Hundreds of thousands of Russians were heading that way. And once you started going east from Irkutsk there were no roads, just the railway and that was single track.

Whether it was in fact operational depended on whether a gentleman called Ivan Pavlovich Semyonov, Ataman of the Ussuri Cossacks, had pulled up the track. That in its turn depended on the progress of the Czech Legion. These men, who hadn't seen their homes for three years, were desperate to get to Vladi, to smell the brine and see the smoke billowing from the transports they'd been assured were waiting to take them to America and thus back to Europe – and their villages. Everyone knew they were the toughest and most determined soldiers in Russia, tougher even than the Reds. No one messed about with them out of whimsy.

Everyone also knew that somehow or other they'd managed to get their hands on all the Tsar's gold that had been in Kazan except – so I was told – for a boatful that the notorious adventurer, Charlenka Doig, had spirited away in the company of a ravishing gypsy woman.

The Czechs' gold was travelling eastwards with them, in boxcars guarded by wagons bristling with machine guns and flatbeds carrying heavy artillery. There was no point in trying to put a value on it, for in a country where not even the state had any money, it was beyond value. If I could have bought Estonia with my boatful, the Czechs could have bought America with their trainful. Which was why Semyonov was lying in wait for them. Whenever he heard a rumour they were coming, he tore up the railway track and loaded his cannon. Men's lives meant nothing to him if, when the smoke cleared, it transpired that the Tsar's reddish gold had popped out on his side.

This man, whom you would have thought from his sadism and love of killing must have been bitten by a viper as he emerged from his mother's womb, was dark and stocky, had tawny Cossack moustaches and darting black eyes. Fearless, totally uneducated and excelling at his business. He used a number of armoured trains with names like *Merciless*, *Horrible* and *Destroyer*. In one of them he kept the twelve most beautiful women in all of Russia.

The age of this tyrant? He was younger than I. He was twenty-five. Russia in 1919 was a land of opportunity.

In telling you this, I'm only telling you what we discovered was public information as soon as we reached Pychas, a small, muddy town in the centre of Russia through which the Trans-Siberian Railway ran.

It had taken us ten weeks to get there, mainly on account of Tornado showing his age. I'd bought a second horse, a strong young animal, before we left the Volga region, to take the pressure off the old fellow. But it made no difference. The moment we entered the forest, his morale declined. Everything spooked him, the darkness, the smell of bears and wolves, the flies, the miasmas arising from the stagnant pools. Like Kobi, he was a citizen of the steppe at heart and ached for high blue skies and scudding clouds and herds of wild mares, wonderfully scented. He began to lose condition. Kobi refused to burden him but walked at his side, not bothering to hold the reins and chatting to him in a language of their own about Utopia.

So it was winter by the time we found ourselves wading through the slush and shit of Pychas's main street, from which the raised wooden pavements had long since been ripped out for fuel. One look at the track and the points was enough to tell us that no train had passed in either direction for a long while. It was in this way that I was again led to appreciate the significance of one of the iron laws of revolution, that their first victims are a nation's timetables.

Eight

How many people were already there? We walked among them when we arrived, slugging through the mud and snow around the tents, the latrines, the makeshift bathhouse, the knocked-up cabins in the trees, the pathetic buy-and-sell booths. Were there three thousand? Were there eight thousand? Could there be as many as twenty thousand when one took into account everyone hiding in the forest? It was impossible to say. Estimating crowd numbers is a branch of poetry. All that was certain was that a hundred trains wouldn't clear the people trying to escape, maybe not even a thousand.

And between Pychas and Vladivostok there'd be identical stations with many more thousands of people who wanted nothing whatsoever to do with the teachings of Karl Marx.

We had two horses, two rifles and my Luger Kriegsmarine. I had wealth sewn into my boots – Shansky's diamonds, a bit of jewellery, a bit of gold, and the last of my Tsarist money, those big scarlet thousand-rouble notes. We could defend ourselves. We had the money to buy whatever was available. We were better equipped for getting out of Russia than every other person in Pychas. But how?

I said to Kobi, 'Shall we have to walk to Vladivostok, is that what it's come to?'

He said, 'Are we pilgrims that we must walk for three thousand miles? Let us ride it if there are no trains.'

I said, 'What would we feed the horses on? Look at Tornado.'

He said, 'It'll be easier in the summer. We can buy hay as we go along.'

I said, 'Easiest of all would be if we were dead. Which we

32

soon could be. Have you noticed how these people are eyeing our horses?'

In this way we went round and round the subject. In the end we agreed there was only one practical way to get out of Pychas and that was by train. But there was no question of buying one as I'd done before, in the hunt for Glebov. Anything local that could get up steam had been removed long ago by the Czech Legion. We were going to have to wait for one of the refugee trains. The last had gone through five weeks ago – without stopping.

'We must have patience,' I said.

He looked at me with contempt and spat, with such force that the pellet of phlegm raised a puff of snow.

'The Bible is full of examples,' I said stolidly. 'In fact, our entire culture is built upon patience. How otherwise would Kutusov have defeated Napoleon? We shall make camp here and in the end a train will come along and we shall stop it. It has to happen. Here are the tracks. Somewhere is the locomotive waiting to use them. One day the two will make an alliance. It is inevitable, it is how the world works.'

He looked at me, he looked towards Vladivostok with his far-seeing Mongolian eyes and he visualised each one of those three thousand miles. I saw it happening, I swear it. Then he grunted, said something to Tornado in tones of great sadness, straightened out a bit of mane that was hanging over its one good eye, and we walked with our horses up the slope to a clapboard hovel I'd noticed and there we established our authority.

Conditions in the camps were horrible. Typhus, dysentery, stuff like lava coming up from people's lungs, tuberculosis, scurvy, lunacy – yes, people were actually going mad, invariably well-off people who'd lost everything, their houses, their jobs, their wealth, their security and as likely as not their children.

Winter's no time to go out of your mind. The scenes that I witnessed were terrible. I often thought of Lizochka. She'd never have lasted. Just watching her dwindle would have made me do something stupid. And Pychas was no place for stupidity. All these thousands of waiting people had nothing else to do but keep their neighbours under observation and pray for weaknesses to appear in them – cracks, then fissures, then the total dissolution of reason, which by that stage one could be certain would be their very last possession.

It took me a morning to figure it out, sitting outside the hovel and watching, listening, estimating distances. Early afternoon Kobi turned up to enquire if I had the answer, Tornado plodding at his heels.

I nodded towards the bathhouse below us. Behind it were a group of kids with others spread out around as lookouts. '*Besprizornye*. Those are the ones whose parents have died, or they've been abandoned, or they've walked out on their families – gone feral. Right now they're ganging up to steal the clothes of the people in the baths. They'll do anything, those brats.'

He looked at me, waiting for the plan. 'Anything to get out of here, anything.'

So I told him. He didn't like it one little bit – sulked, blubbered, would have hollered if it'd just been the two of us alone. In the end he agreed, as of course he had to, there being no room for personal feelings in that kind of situation.

I went down to have a word with the kids. He led Tornado into the forest. When he returned he was alone.

I said to him, 'You did the right thing.' I sighed. 'He was a character all right. I never knew a horse that was so like a crusty, sex-starved old man.'

Kobi was sitting on the sawn butt of a tree, hands dangling between his thighs. He was looking at them vacantly, glooping and moping. Not raising his head, he whispered, 'I loved him. He was a brother to me.'

I said, 'Did you skin him?'

'How could I skin my brother?'

'To get out of here, that's how. So go and do it while there's still light.'

After dark we took the leader of the *besprizornye* up there and showed him the body. Kobi had scraped all the fat off the skin, which he'd rolled up and buried in a pit, beneath a sprinkling of leaves.

Throwing it down like a man selling a rug, he said to the boy, 'That's pure money, that is.' He flapped it a couple of times, seeming to make it float in the air. 'How many boots'd you get out of that?' No teariness in him by then. He'd set his mind on getting out.

The boy nodded. There was another dozen of them hanging back in the trees with hot red eyes like wolves. But they were no danger to us. We were in it together, like criminals, it was how things worked in the camp. Besides, they knew we were better armed than they.

Kobi said, 'There's a tub of fat as well.'

Then he pulled the branches away and showed the kid Tornado.

We did the deal by the light of a single candle, standing over the poor animal, once so noble and horny, now a wasted cadaver with a few streaks of dingy yellowish fat between his ribs that Kobi hadn't been able to get at.

The kid said to me, 'We saw the Chinaman take him away and return alone. But we looked in the wrong part of the forest' – which made no difference to us, in fact I don't know why the boy said it.

Kobi and the juniors butchered the old horse. Then they dragged away their half while the kid and I did the rest of the business out of their sight, which was what he wanted. He personally was to get my young horse plus its bridle and saddle as soon as we boarded a train. I'd say his idea was to gallop away before the pack realised what he was up to. The gang was to get money plus the skin and the tub of fat.

Later that night, over our fire, as we chewed at the meat, Kobi looked up and said, 'He would never have left here alive. It was better that he went where I took him, to be among the spirits of the forest. They'll look after him.'

The firelight flickered over his face, making his cheeks ruddy and turning his eye sockets into black holes. He wore an expression that I'd never seen before, that was somehow vacant, as if his soul had quit, or gone to sleep – at any rate was in abeyance. I thought, Did the missionaries who brought him up stamp their imprint on him after all, somewhere I couldn't see? Have I got a holy man in disguise with me?

He went on, 'Sometimes, when we were journeying through the forest, I heard voices.'

'Calling to you? Real words?'

He looked embarrassed. 'I'm not stupid. It wasn't the wind in the trees, if that's what you mean. Tornado heard them as well. He heard everything that I heard.'

I said, 'So what did the voices say?'

'They spoke to me in their own language.'

'You couldn't make anything of it, is that what you're saying?'

He said, 'You're starting to mock me. You have that look on your face.'

'What do you expect? You and a horse hearing voices from up there? Boils on your arse, Kobi, that's what I say to that. You ate too many mushrooms.'

'It's not like that,' he said, 'but what do you care?' and he turned away from me, a slight, hunched figure in a woollen hat, jaws pounding away at the horse meat, the surges of firelight sending shadows shaped like thistles racing across his cheek.

When he'd finished eating he turned back to me. Referring to Tornado, I said, 'There's another friend gone. We started as two, looks like we'll finish as two.'

'I'm leaving you at Irkutsk,' he said flatly. 'My people live in Siberia, I'm sure of it. The voices were theirs. I must go to them.'

I said nothing, least of all about the voices. (I was concentrating on getting at the marrow in a shin bone by poking it out with a long twig.) Kobi had only once carried out a threat to leave me and had soon returned.

'How far away is it?' he demanded.

'Irkutsk? A week, once we get on a train.'

'A week,' he repeated, 'a week . . . Then you'll be on your own, Doig. You won't last long.'

I thought that come the morning he'd have lost interest in his folk tale. Not so: he'd had 'dreams'. Thereafter I could neither get him to stop talking about his so-called ancestors nor discover how he'd picked up the snippets of information he produced about the various Siberian tribes. Soon it got so that I was listening with only half an ear. Then a few days after the deal with the *besprizornye* the subject of Kobi leaving me came to a close of its own accord when we got the signal, a mirror winking in the frosted sunlight, that an eastbound train had been sighted.

This was how the kid had worked it – he'd organised a relay, day and night, alongside the track, starting ten miles away in the forest. By mirrors or runners, that was how the news was to reach me, whichever way would attract no attention in the camp. The problem was my young horse. Everyone had their eye on it, to eat or ride, maybe both. The kid was no different, but we were going to get something in return.

We mounted, Kobi pillion as usual, and rode east out of the camp as a diversion. One of the kids trotted on either side as a guard.

Once clear of the camp, we looped round behind Pychas and made a wide semicircle back into the forest. There were children posted every quarter-mile in case some of the refugees got curious on seeing us leave the camp and followed. Silently they fanned out behind us, armed and alert.

The train was waiting, panting reproachfully, its buffers touching the branches of a fir tree they'd felled across the line.

More of the young thugs were patrolling the line to prevent any of the passengers dismounting. It had been one of my conditions. I didn't want them spilling out onto the track and crowding us. I wanted to get possession of that train quickly and efficiently, without any of the usual Russian hubbub. If the multitudes at Pychas got wind of what was afoot, they'd come swarming down the line and do for us, however valiantly the kids fought back.

I shouted up to the train driver, 'This a fever train?'

He said, 'That's for you to find out.'

I said to one of the kids, 'Stick your nose inside and tell me what it smells of.'

Sweet yet stinky, like the water at the bottom of the vase – that was the smell to run from. The Reds had had the good idea of tipping the typhus and cholera patients out of the hospitals they captured and sending them by train into White territory to spread their diseases around. Anything to do with lice and anything infectious, even syphilis, went on a fever train.

He said, 'Stick your own nose in.'

I said to the train driver, 'What's your name?'

'Koltsov,' he said.

I pulled my Luger on him, at which he said, 'Would I be here

37

if this was a fever train? Gentry and such like, that's what I've got, and they're paying me five thousand proper roubles to get them to Irkutsk. So are you getting on or aren't you? I don't care to be stopped with louts like these around.'

I had the kids clear the tree off the line. I'd expected last-minute demands, but they were good, they kept to the bargain. I stuffed the matching half of the thousand-rouble note into the head kid's hand. I said, 'A dozen more trains like this and you'll be a wealthy fellow.'

'If I remain alive,' he said, and whistled up his gang. They stood and watched as Kobi and I shinned up the ladder into the driver's cab. By the time I turned, they'd vanished into the woods, my horse with them.

Koltsov was the same build as Shmuleyvich – terrific arse, forearms like Belfast hams. He said, 'I'm not stopping in Pychas, nor anywhere else, come to that.'

'Nor you are,' I said.

He wiped a sleeve across his forehead and tapped the water pressure gauge. 'You've no idea how many hours I've been at this all by myself. If I told you, you wouldn't believe me. In fact, I'm completely shagged out. What's a man to do?'

'Pray hard and keep going. Now start shovelling.'

'No, you do the shovelling, you or your man, I don't mind which. Here, whatever your name is, Johnny Chinaman, spread it well out, into all the corners, burns more evenly like that, and we'll go through Pychas like a messenger with dispatches – or an arrow, whichever is faster. When we get to a nice open stretch of country where we can't be jumped by bandits, we'll stop. And when I've slept for ten hours, we'll continue. I need my sleep if the train's to keep going. There's big trouble all around. We railwaymen know everything that's happening from Peter to Vladivostok –'

'Stop babbling and get on with it,' I growled.

'Hold on, *barin*, I'm going to rack up some speed on her now. We're pegged for the main line, I'm really going to make the bastards jump.'

It was as I expected. As soon as our light grey running smoke rose above the forest canopy, crowds appeared from every corner of Pychas. Out of the forest they came, out of the shanty town, across the snowy fields, men dragging their women, their families, even a cow. People flumped into the drifts, throwing up their arms as they pitched forward – somehow managed to scrabble out of the snow and continue, crawling if it was the only way, like bears in their dark bulky clothing. For some it was too much well before it became obvious that we had no intention of halting. I saw whole families give up: granny couldn't cope, someone had diarrhoea, an icon had been left behind, who could say why but they did – their efforts petered out, they dropped their belongings and just stood there watching us.

To see innocent people surrendering before the onslaught of a remorseless fate that I had myself evaded nibbled at my sense of probity. I felt shame, and I seized the shovel from Kobi so that I didn't have to see the poor devils jumping for their lives as we rocketed past them with the loco swaying from side to side and Koltsov yanking at the whistle cord.

Nine

You'd think it a primary law of human mathematics that for every unhappy person in the world there exists a happy one. Not so, very much not so. Someone has rigged the pack and not in favour of happiness.

My father was the only truly happy person I've known. I'm glad he died before the Bolsheviks took over. Happiness, glee and optimism were so abundant in him that I believe he'd have killed himself merely to think of Lenin in the Kremlin. The rest of mankind clings to its gloom as tightly as a cat does to its fur, that's how it seems to me, and that's how it was on that train.

On probably every single night most of the passengers wished they were dead. At around 4 a.m., which fell into my spell of guard duty, the train hummed with their prayers that God might soon take them to the cold place and dump them there for ever and ever without any chance of returning to His earth in any shape or form whatsoever. So fervent were the prayers that the train probably glowed with a spectral blue light at around that hour.

It got to me, this attitude, it really did. Weren't they a million times better off than the poor devils we'd abandoned in Pychas? Had they gone to all the trouble and expense of buying a train just so they could wallow in misery? Did they honestly believe that God would see their plight and come to the rescue, that His power was greater than Lenin's?

I'd pick on a person, man or woman it made no difference, the sexes were equally unhappy peering out from under their shawls and cloaks, and standing bang opposite him or her so that I could kick the soles of their boots if I felt like it, I'd say, 'You know what, if that's the way you feel, you should end it here and now so that someone more deserving can take your place.'

'End it?' – which was invariably said with astonishment, as if the idea of suicide had never, ever occurred to him.

'Shoot yourself – I don't care, borrow a pistol, then.'

'But something might happen. Our generals might defeat them, someone might assassinate him' – him of course being Lenin.

And I'd want to scream, 'If that's how you think, then be positive, don't just sit there fingering your icon and hoping for death. Do exercises, improve your breathing, do *something* for Christ's sake. Think good for a change.'

It drained me to hear their moaning. Lumps formed in my brain where previously everything had flowed like cream. 'What you think, you are,' that's the truest thing anyone ever told me. And here I was, cooped up with people who could think only of the past and its glories, how beneficent, cheery, orderly, peaceful and prosperous it had all been. If that was the life they desired, they should go somewhere where it was still possible. They should prepare themselves and think to the future. The men should be reading books about engineering, the women about lace-making. They should be learning English or Mandarin, should be throwing aside their despair and adjusting their way of thought to new cultures.

There was an old man I bumped into all the time. A few strands of hair laid carefully across his bald skull, blotchy cheeks, a dropping nose, watery eyes – I had the idea it had been a long time since he'd wished anyone well. He wore black silk knee breeches, used a cane and would have made an ideal grandfather to one of Chekhov's intricate young ladies.

On this occasion he had a rug across his knees and was smoking a cigarette through an amber holder. Between him and the man opposite was a card table on which two packs stood waiting. Stabbing his cigarette at his opponent, the old fellow said, 'It's no good, we have to compare like with like. Martin Luther was a finer man than this Lenin, a hundred times finer – no! a thousand times finer. This is a saying of his that I shall always remember: *Hier stehe ich. Ich kann nicht anders.* "Here's where I stay. I can do nothing else." That's what that means in case you don't have any German, and that's my motto as well. Look what happened to Luther, still going strong. But Lenin – no sensible person can believe in equality if he thinks about it for longer than an hour. The man's ideas will never stick. We'll have nothing to fear in the end.'

'You'll be bones by then,' said the other.

'Poppycock. People must be able to see some advantage for themselves in what they do or they'll stay in bed all day like Oblomov. Why do women blow their noses? Because if they don't, they'll never get kissed. Self-interest, it's what makes us tick.'

'Irkutsk for you?' I butted in, leaning against the door jamb.

'I've a suite in the Central, right next door to the Obolskis. My family got there a month ago. It's Siberia so one can expect cold. But that's the worst. The city is absolutely peaceful except for the usual harum-scarums one gets when people are shifting around. The elders are sensible enough not to be fooled by this craze for soviets, whatever the word means.'

The other man, who was one of those smooth, quiet, lawyerly types who never profess a firm opinion about anything, said to me, 'What do you think?'

'Me, I'm getting out, I'm going to America.'

Picking up one of the packs and tapping it on the table, he said calmly, 'What you're really saying is that there's no hope for people our age, isn't that it?'

I said roughly, 'Get on and deal, help yourself to an ace, of spades if you can find it.'

He said in exactly the same monotone as before, 'That went from the pack a long time ago, when serfdom was abolished.'

Most of the people on that train had sold or hidden their jewellery but this quiet lawyerly man had on the little finger of his left hand a large, very dark ruby in a fine gold setting. It stuck out like a carbuncle and glittered the whole day long. Everyone began to covet it and at the same time to be annoyed by what they thought of as his posturing. A dandy could have carried it off. But he was too suave and silent. I reminded him more than once that this was a revolution based on hatred of wealth, told him he should stop showing off and hide the jewel. But he paid no attention.

I'd told Kobi it would take us a week to get to Irkutsk. After ten days we'd covered no distance to speak of, and on the eleventh we ran out of coal.

Without it the carriage stoves couldn't be lit and nothing could be cooked. Old people need heat. They're more afraid of the cold than they are of death.

For day after day the train stood in the desolate immensity of Siberia, not putting up even one tiny puff of smoke. Unhappiness assumed the proportions of a giant statue carved out of granite.

With time on their hands, people began to concoct the most unpleasant outcomes they could. Scraping the frost off the window, they all too easily imagined their foes charging across the plain with lances levelled, plucks of snow rising from a thousand eager hooves. White or Red, it didn't matter which. Men with lances are always hostile in the minds of the educated.

In the next stage food took over as the chief worry. As I knew they would, they had supplies squirrelled away that would last at least three months on short rations. I took charge of it all and made a central store cupboard, which I kept locked. With envious eyes they watched the portions of bread, cheese and dried fish getting smaller and harder with every day that passed. I said, 'But this is in the nature of bread and cheese. That's why we're eating it first.' It didn't impress them. Everyone knew we were down to the last bottle of pickled gherkins, that the last tin of ham went yesterday, that starvation was a certainty.

It was natural that once people had descended to this level, it would occur to them that their money was useless. How do you survive when you have riches concealed in your underclothes but there's no food to buy? The wealthiest man in the world could have been on that train and he'd have had to go hungry with the rest of us. It was an unfamiliar and deeply worrying perversion of their normal standards. If money was pointless, wasn't life also pointless?

One of the passengers was a baker, an odious man with round red cheeks and a fat neck. His pleasure was to force his

43

conversation onto others and tell them what the price of women had dropped to in his district of Moscow.

'Fifteen roubles, but for that you get the whole thing, no messing around with price per pood, not like flour, what! Between fifteen and twenty for a woman of medium age in good health, that's what I'm telling you, sirs and madams. For an unused woman, who can carry big weights, you may have to go as high as forty. That's Bolshevism for you, that's Mr High-and-Mighty Lenin's idea of citizens having a good time.'

Had it reached that stage when women were being bought and sold like animals? That really scared people. Hardship – frugality – children first – they knew something about that sort of life. But the complete breakdown of civilisation – what was a body to do?

Doubt was everywhere, growing like the most vigorous tree in existence. On every branch was a dangerous red fruit, incised with a hammer and sickle and ripe to the point of falling. The branches were so intricately woven that if one fruit dropped, four more would be pulled down with it. For instance, if society were to be as egalitarian as Lenin promised, what would happen to their savings held by the banks? Were they to be 'looked after' by the state? Were they to be confiscated and given to the poor? Where then was any money to be kept if it were to be safe? Who could be trusted?

Who could be trusted?

That was the most insidious question of the lot. It was also the point at which the minds of these elderly people invariably arrived. Among them I include the man with the ruby ring.

On our twentieth day of helplessness, in the middle of the day, without saying anything to anyone, he clambered down onto the ballast, walked a hundred yards and while we wondered what he was up to, took out a pistol and shot himself through the mouth.

The plain; the locomotive motionless; the fourteen carriages with linen being aired from the windows; the quiet man with his beard bent sideways by the wind; the shot.

Of course everyone was watching. Someone going for a walk in Siberia was a novelty. How were we to have known that his purpose was to shoot himself?

I took charge of the burial party. The sight of his head was horrific. I couldn't help but remember how it had been with Lizochka. I took myself off for a walk while Kobi and another man dug a grave beside a tiny stream, which was the only soft ground we could find. They lowered him in. There was a shout from the train and a woman came running to us with a sheet. She herself draped it over him, apparently not wanting anyone to help her with it. Then Kobi called me and I said a prayer for his spirit. The woman knelt and prayed while Kobi and the man shovelled the soil back.

Walking to the train, Kobi said to me, 'Who do you think has the ring? It wasn't in his pockets.'

Nor was it among his belongings. Had he thrown it away in disgust at the failure of the political system that the ruby stood for? Had the man with the malacca cane stolen it? Did the mysterious woman have it – had she been secretly affianced to him or something? It remained a mystery.

Two days later another refugee train took pity on us. It was now found that money did after all have its use, to pay for the coal, to pay for some of the younger passengers to bag it up, and to pay for others to porter it down the line and hoist it into our tender.

I'd told Kobi it'd take us a week from Pychas to Irkutsk. In fact, it took exactly two months from the day the young thugs stopped the train for us. But at least we got there.

Koltsov damped the fire, wiped the coal dust and grease off his hands with an old shirt, slung his leather railwayman's satchel over his shoulder, explained to me how to get across the river to the city and walked away down the bleak platform. No goodbye, no proposal for a drinking tryst, nothing.

I called after him, 'Are you abandoning it?'

He shrugged, turning but not stopping.

I said to Kobi, 'We could drive it to Vladivostok ourselves.'

With a sneer, he said, 'At the same time as fighting off Semyonov and all the other cunts?'

'All right, Genghis,' I said – and as we leaned out of the cab and thought about it all, our fellow passengers began to shuffle past. The only way of life they'd known had failed them and they lacked the spirit and the health to seek another. Deprivation and bewilderment were about to become the most lenient of their daily companions. Cowed, bowed, lost, they straggled along the platform.

'But we are made of stronger metal,' I said to Kobi, and we climbed down from the cab.

Ten

IN IRKUTSK I saw, one after the other, my first American soldier, my first French soldier and my first Japanese man. I went into a bar and asked what the hell was going on.

'Where've you been? On the moon? They say they're here to help us defeat the Bolsheviks. But I'd say they're after what they can get. Organised looting, that's what their game is.'

'Looting us?'

'Us. Russia. Whatever takes their fancy.'

'The Nips are at it too?'

'More than the rest put together. What they don't want isn't worth ten kopeks.'

A little further down the same street, I learned from a pie man (who sold me my first piroshki in over six months) that British and Canadian troops were also involved. 'Over a hundred thousand Japanese troops are waiting to land at Vladivostok, that's what people are saying. What do they want? To conquer us, nothing plainer. Here, take your pie and stop reminding me of our troubles.'

The hotels were full of either the officers of foreign armies or rich families in exile. A bed wasn't to be had anywhere. Kobi fell in with another Mongolian. We settled on a meeting place for the next morning, then I went and got horribly drunk, out of sheer loneliness, and when I could take no more, staggered off to the cemetery. One can always get a good night's sleep among the dead.

I awoke beneath a grey pelt of early-morning mist that had drifted up from the river. I was cold and angry. The long train ride, the lack of love, the absence of both stability and the comfort of employment – these were poor excuses: the fault was mine for lacking a positive and healthy outlook, the very disease I'd preached against on the train. I rose and pissed my anger away in a hot whistling stream. Then I lay down again to help the blood spread evenly through my body.

Mulling things over with my fingers laced behind my head, I became aware of a man walking around in search of something. He was quartering the ground between the graves about eighty yards away, steadily, slowly, his head weaving from side to side. He was joined by a second man. From time to time both were transformed into giants by the fog, which was sliding through the cemetery like puffs of cannon smoke and magnifying everything, both as to sight and sound.

They halted – looked down – conferred. What could it be?

Poof, suddenly the fog was stripped away and I saw that the mound they were bending over was a man, as asleep as I had been fifteen minutes ago. They began to go through his pockets, slyly at first. When he awoke and shouted out, they wrenched wildly at his coat, not trying to pull it off his shoulders but as if they were looking for a secret pocket.

He sat up in a rush, bolt upright from the waist. 'Get off me! Thieves! Help!' He cast round for a weapon – a stick, a stone lying handy – went on with his shouting, calling them by their individual names: expostulated, flailing around with his arms as he tried to beat away their hands. 'Pyotr, I don't have any, I was making it all up. I swear it on the Virgin – why are you doing this to me?'

For a second he won a respite. He managed to get onto one knee, was tensed to spring up. Then one of his assailants produced a thin-bladed skinning knife, pushed him back and, as he fell, stabbed upwards into his ribcage – with a quick hard forearm – straight up the gully of life.

A shred of fog clung to the scene. For a moment they were still-framed – the murderer crouching like a man slipping a greyhound while his victim slid slowly off the blade and slumped, twisting, to the ground, into the lair in which he'd enjoyed his last dream on earth.

Seeing me jump up, the murderers scuffled the body around, hunting for whatever it was. They spoke – 'Let's get out of

48

here,' or something like it. They dashed their bloody hands up and down his coat, wiping them – spoke again – then upped with his legs, pulled off his boots and ran away, jumping over a low part of the cemetery wall.

Had it been me they'd discovered first and had it been my boots they'd gone off with, clanking with diamonds – it would've been the end. I'd have become an ordinary refugee like the rest. I couldn't feel angry any longer after an escape like that.

The man raised his arm and called out. I went to him, striding in my lucky boots.

His foot wrappings had gone with the boots. His bare feet were such a brilliant white they could have been mistaken for seagulls. By contrast he had long, brown, curling toenails.

He was leaning on his forearm, staring at the pattered grass. I could smell the drink on him. He'd have slotted home his last flask of vodka, wistfully cuddled the waitress's bosom and been shoved, tottering, into the night. Now he was dying, not realising that his boots had been the best part of him.

Already his cheeks were emptying. Even as I watched, they collapsed a little more, pulling down on the skin around his mouth.

He raised a bloody hand, wanting someone to stay with him and see him to the end. Jutting out his lower lip, he strained to speak. He snatched my trousers at the knee and held me fast. Then his life began to ebb more quickly. His hand slipped onto my boot. He left it lying there, red and scaly, like something from the tidal wrack.

I crouched beside him. 'Old man, there's nothing anyone can do for you. You've had it.'

He glared up at me. His throat buckled. He said, 'Then shoot me. I'd prefer a bullet to this pain.'

I reared up. My whole blood churned within me. How could it have happened that fate had picked on me, out of all the people in Irkutsk, to put this man out of his misery? I knew exactly where to aim. I knew the noise the skull would make as it broke. I knew what he'd look like afterwards. I knew how I'd feel – by God, did I not know that.

I said, 'I don't have a pistol.'

He hauled himself up onto both elbows and surveyed the

length of his body. His head came up – dark shaggy hair, white-stubbled face, blue pained eyes looking straight into mine. In a slow, hoarse voice he said, 'Then fuck you to hell.'

Pink frothy blood spouted from his mouth – the knife had pierced his lungs. A gurgling belch, and he fell back, dead.

I pulled down his eyelids. His old moth-eaten shapka was lying on the grass. I propped his white feet against each other, making a tent of them, and hung his hat on his toes. It'd keep the crows away for a bit. Then I went to meet Kobi, walking at first but soon trotting and then running as my anger returned. What devil had been in that man that made him ask me to shoot him? He and the quiet man on the train, both of them pounding at my memory. Was it my fate never to be allowed to forget her?

But it was for her good that I did it. She begged me to. Dishonoured, humiliated, and then tortured. Lying there in an agony you or I would have found unbearable.

'I had to, it was the only course left to me, none of you would have had a clue,' – there were other things I had to get off my chest and I shouted them wildly so that people in the street stared at me. Even those I'd passed looked back over their shoulders as they continued to walk.

A church came up, all pomp and golden baubles. I stopped and shook my fist at it. 'Why take it out on me? You up there, I'm talking to You.'

This last was overheard by some filthy priest who understood only too well whom I was addressing. He caught hold of me and swung me round by the coat. 'Let God alone. Keep Him out of it. Whoever you're speaking about, the quarrel's of your own making.'

I looked at him in amazement. He started to say it all again so I put my hand flat on his chest and pushed. He staggered back. I said, 'You wouldn't speak like that if you knew.' I gave him another push, and, tripping on a water hydrant, he tumbled to the ground. His smock burst down the buttons and his legs waved like those of an insect when it's flipped on its back. He was wearing long johns, dingy and discoloured, and a pair of natty black ankle-length bootees fashioned from first-class leather. They could only have been stolen from some aristocrat, perhaps one he'd visited and prayed over as he lay dying. 'Bless you, my son, bless you,' and then walking out with them stuffed into his bag of oils and nonsense. Bold as brass from doing something like it every single day. It enraged me that the man of God should first take me to task for something he could know nothing whatsoever about and then prove to be a common venal dog. My anger redoubled. I kicked him twice as he lay there, hard, in the ribs. Some bystanders set up a hue and cry, grabbed me by both arms and held me fast. Instantly I saw I'd gone too far. They swore at me for being a godless Bolshevik and tried to haul me off to the police station. I back-pedalled, talked about the journeys in Central Asia I'd undertaken for the Academy of Sciences, said I was the man who'd killed Glebov and topped it off with an edited version of Lizochka's death. I helped the priest to his feet, I dusted him down, I apologised with many bows.

He had a long verminous black beard, which waggled as he quoted the Bible at me: 'Wrath killeth the foolish man.'

'Yes, sir,' I said to him in English, 'yes sir, no sir, three bags full sir, you cheating cunt,' and then, my anger soothed, I went and found Kobi.

I guessed from the grin on his face that he and his fellow countryman had found some girls the night before and had a good time with them. He rose and walked smugly towards me as if he'd just stepped down from the communion rail, which got me mad again. Saying nothing, I pinched his arm just above the elbow joint and led him outside. A horse cab was idling past. I told the driver to get us across the river to the station and make it snappy.

Some Jap officers, three or four of them, were hanging round on the concourse looking lost. Their baggage was with them on a four-wheeler trolley: they'd obviously just stepped off a train from Vladivostok.

Smart-looking beggars, polished riding boots, everything pukka and according to the military dress manual.

Wishing for one thing only, which was to be gone from Irkutsk, and seeing in them a possible means towards this, I walked up to them and asked if I could be of assistance. One of them could speak a little Russian. He said they wanted to know where

51

the White generalissimo was – Admiral Kolchak. There were matters to be discussed with him that related to the war against the Bolsheviks. It was the reason for their mission. I said they weren't alone: from what I'd heard, some of Kolchak's own men hadn't seen him for a bit. Their best plan was to find a hotel that'd take them in and keep their ear to the ground.

They were wonderfully grateful – I suppose just because a Russian had spoken to them – bowed, hissed, clicked their heels.

I said, 'And who is your own generalissimo, here in Russia? You're going to need Russian speakers, people who know the country, who can fight. People like me and my man here. If we were looking to get employed by your military in Siberia, what name should we ask for?'

It was an improvement on my original idea that had suddenly come to me. If we were going to be among the Japs for a bit, why not make the most of the opportunity? Become a hired gun, kill some Reds, get paid for it?

This put them in a spin, for they were collegiate decision-takers. They got into a huddle and started jabbering at each other, their clipped black moustaches fluttering like pieces of charred paper.

'Ah so, General Sato, very fine man,' said the one I'd spoken to first, giving me his card. 'He is our top fellow here. But like your Admiral Kolchak, we cannot say where he is. We regret this deeply.'

'Sato, that's good, it's nice to have a name to throw around. So, which train did you arrive on?'

They pointed out a locomotive waiting with steam up.

Thus it turned out that while the Japs didn't actually own the Trans-Sib, they certainly were in control of it. Within five minutes we were on that train at no cost to ourselves and in an hour were on our way east, to the ocean.

Eleven

THEY WERE desperate. No women or children were on the train, just a thousand or so men heading off to try their luck in the world. Some already had family in America and were going to join them, maybe to open a boarding house if there was enough money in the kitty. Others were heading for the South Seas to work as stokers on the little coastal steamers. Those with a bit of polish about them were aiming for the fleshpots of Harbin or Shanghai. It was every man for himself. No one dared sleep without paying someone to keep watch for him. The exchange didn't have to be financial. It could turn on food, drink, tobacco, sexual favours, the loan of a blanket, anything.

Sugar was the most common item of barter. One tiny grey fragment, no bigger than a mouse turd, cost a minimum of a rouble. You can't imagine how debased a human can become when he has an unsatisfied craving for sugar. It's as bad as craving a woman. What am I saying, it's worse, far, far worse. Even if you masturbate, you still want sugar.

And it was cold, oh boy, was it cold if your place was out there in the corridor. The journey to Irkutsk had been a picnic by the lake compared to this.

It was fear that had brought us all together in that train, an inkling that whatever lay ahead for Russia was so horrible that even death in a foreign land, death among strangers, a tired, lonely, miserable death would be better than staying put. That was the bargain all of us had made in one form or another. It was why we tolerated being pissed on by the occupants of the overhead luggage racks who couldn't hold their bladders and had no friends to keep watch if they went to the squat. We smelt so awful anyway it just didn't matter – there were soldiers among us who hadn't seen hot water since they fought the Germans in Europe, months before – and the urine was always more weak tea than anything else. Eventually they were done in, those pissers. Single men, those without chums to stand watch for them, were invariably losers. Their pissing might in the end annoy the others too much or they might be heard fumbling through their belongings in the middle of the night so that people thought they had concealed wealth on them. Then they got the chop and were chucked out onto the track.

Kobi and I took it in turns to sleep. I'm sure he saved my life again. Any night prowler would have seen Kobi's eyes glinting and backed off. By myself I'd have been knifed, six foot two or not, because it was known I had a Luger Kriegsmarine and where a man possessed one thing that was desirable, he was certain to have more. That was how their minds worked on that train. You had to be tough to have made it that far.

About four or five days out of Irkutsk, the brakes engaged on a level run and we slowly came to a halt. There was something definitive about the way the wheels ceased to turn. The general forecast was a tree across the line, felled on the orders of Ataman Semyonov. Up and down the train, rifles were loaded.

When nothing happened, we all got out to see what was what.

It wasn't a tree. It was a whole section of the single-track line that had been lifted and chucked over the edge of the embankment.

A bunch of men started to argue about how to repair the track. More piled in. The talk turned to the necessity of electing a leader and thus to the method by which he was to be elected, this being an old Russian obsession. Kobi and I drifted away.

I looked out over Siberia, hands behind my back, flexing my toes over the end of a sleeper to keep them warm. The ground was undulating, with broken cover – the natural territory of bears, wolves and reindeer. There were spindly white-stemmed birches, red-budded alders and huge flagpole spruce trees with branches swept down almost to the ground by the weight of the snow. Streams and marshes were out there for sure, beavers probably. A land of roots, berries and mushrooms, of vast skies and intense cold.

We each had our rifles. Kobi had the pack. Below us a mossy glade stretched into the forest like a green road.

I said, 'Unless I'm mistaken, this is that long slow bend we saw on the map.' I could see it quite clearly, the map anchored on the table and Kobi's stubby forefinger pointing out the places at which he'd heard from his Mongolian pal that Semyonov was operating.

'Yes,' Kobi said, 'and down there' – pointing at the glade – 'that must be a *korotky put*, a short cut, between the last station and the next one. We could do it, Doig. We could walk there through the forest,' which he said with dancing eyes.

'Hold it,' I said, thinking it sounded too easy, to hop off the train, walk eighty miles to the next station and get on a new train that'd be waiting for us.

He said, 'It'll take them a week to get this track fixed up. Semyonov'll be at them all the time. Why risk our lives here when we can walk to Yerovef in peace?'

There was no stopping him, even though eighty miles was further than he'd ever walked in his entire life. He'd got the pack comfortable on his shoulders, had his rifle slung at a jaunty angle, was looking around to see if there was something he could use as a staff.

And he had logic on his side. We had food, we had firearms, we had ammo, we had time. Plus the fact that anything to do with the train spelt danger. 'OK,' I said, 'maybe that's not so stupid after all. Life's done what it wanted with us ever since we sank the gold. Let's go and bite it in the leg. Grrr!' and I playfully snapped my teeth at him.

But he paid no attention, and I noticed that his face had taken on the same peculiar sheen as it had had at Pychas, when he'd been speaking about the voices in the forest. It had to be something to do with his ancestors and woodland sprites. A god was kicking around in there somewhere, some queer old thing unknown to anyone except anthropologists.

I said to him, 'You lead, you know the way. We'll call this one your expedition.'

Twelve

DEEPER AND deeper we went. As soon as we got to the
bottom of one glade, another opened out before us. Good
firm going, the ground solid beneath our boots and scarcely a
speck of snow even though it lay in white rafts on every bough.
We came to a stream but by some quirk of topography never
had to wade across it: whenever we thought we might need to,
it would turn and glide along beside us. Its waters were smooth,
black and unhurried. They were thinking waters, and gleamed
in the bleak afternoon sun with a quiet mystery.

We saw no animals, nor any of their traces, whether footmarks
or spraints. We saw no birds nor heard any. We saw no humans,
no dogs, no farms, no cattle.

It was eerie, but we made good time.

I'd say it wasn't until the first faint tinge of purple crept
across the sky that Kobi fell silent. Until then he'd put on the
most extraordinary performance, not letting a minute go by
without commenting on something. The continued absence of
boggy ground, our luck in having hit off the glade, the clusters
of pretty pink dog violets – how they hung their heads, how
their nectar must be food for some special Siberian butterfly
– how great it was to have left the train, how ruthless all those
men had been – 'You never saw half the things that went on at
night, Doig' – how he'd stolen an axe, couldn't I see it hanging
in the loop on the pack, was I that blind? When we halted, he'd
cook me a meal in one of those skillets soldiers use. He'd stolen
a couple of them as well.

The commentary had continued in his deep voice for the
whole afternoon.

Then he said it was my turn to lead. I was to keep the evening star on my left. In about half an hour we'd find a nice place to spend the night. He stood aside and waited for me to pass him.

I said over my shoulder, 'How do you know there'll be a nice place?'

He said he just knew, that's all there was to it – and he sort of poked me with his staff.

I did as he said, and when the half-hour was up, I found the same stream was still with us, now with some exquisite moss as much like a sponge as moss, its honeycomb floating above the water and made wonderfully delicate and silvery by the profound cold. But the stream itself wasn't frozen over, not even in its little bays and backwaters. It was moving, observing everything, living at our side.

Above us were crags with scattered fir trees. On the skyline was a ragged row of them, the blackness of their trunks and the whiteness of their snowy branches striking against the purple sky. Around us was a low, creeping form of juniper. Where this wasn't doing, because of some change in the soil type, there were clumps of whortleberries, each one of their small stiff leaves containing a cupful of snow so that every plant glimmered in that fading light like a collection of tiny white eggs.

I halted, wondering if there was any sight its equal in the whole world.

The cold was reaching up for us from the ground like dead men's fingers. I muttered, 'At least we won't be troubled by fleas.' They'd been hell on the train.

Kobi, whose hide was flea-proof, was uninterested. He grunted – it was beside the mossy stream we were to make camp.

I said, 'Up here is more beautiful. It's healthier. We can watch the stars.' But Kobi was fierce that we camp down below, in the glade. It was his 'nice place'.

When I'd told him that this was his expedition, I'd meant, why don't you try taking the lead for an hour or two, then I'll go back to being boss. I certainly hadn't intended anything serious. But now I realised he wasn't taking it that way. Cocking his head imperiously, he ordered me to walk down to the glade, which was by now almost in darkness. He waited till I'd started and then followed me, snorting down his nose.

At the glade, I unloaded my rifle and leaned it in the lowest fork of an alder tree. He handed me the axe. I felled a couple of small birches, stripped their bark and got a fire going. I boiled up in the skillet and made porridge. I halved a piece of *vobla*, our Russian dried fish. We ate, we drank from the mossy stream, and I boiled up another lot of water for our tea. I swung the skillet handle towards him saying, 'OK, I'll have the expedition back again. You do the cleaning up.'

To my surprise, he consented to this without argument.

Then we dozed beside the fire, as close to it as we could get without burning our clothes, the collars of our greatcoats up around our ears.

I said to him, 'How many miles do you think we've done?'

He looked at me across the fire. The flames made his eyeballs look red. He said, 'Don't speak so loudly or they'll hear us.'

I knew immediately what he was on about. I said, 'How many of them are there?'

'I don't know. They're all around us. Can't you hear them? They're Tungus. A remnant of the tribe, the lost ones. We call ourselves the Lesser Tungus.'

'Your people, huh?'

'My people. I can feel their presence. They're moving into good positions to watch us as we sleep. My mother and my father are with them. They came from this tribe. I wouldn't be feeling them if they hadn't.'

'Your missionaries told you about the Tungus?'

'There are people up there on the crags watching us, from among the rocks. Those are the top people. That's why I said we had to come down here. Only the spirit of the Old Man and his wife are allowed up there.'

His voice had faded almost to a whisper. He kept on glancing around. He changed his position to sitting cross-legged. I threw on more wood. Sparks flurried up and illumined his face. He was in a funk, no doubt about it.

I said, 'You'd better sort out all that spirit stuff before morning. We need to get a move on in case the weather turns nasty.' Then I got out of the pack an army groundsheet, another of the things Kobi had stolen on the train. I spread it out beside the fire. I said, 'Same as before OK with you?'

He nodded.

I said, 'See you around midnight, then,' and rolled myself tight in the groundsheet. I was almost asleep when he began to speak, in a voice that reached me from a long way off. It was as if I'd been drugged.

'Listen to me, Doig. Spirits are behind all the most important events in your life. It's the spirit Bayanay who directs animals to migrate, to feed, to breed, to wish to live or to wish to die. Bayanay directs birds to fly. All animals are his children. He also *is* all animals. Bayanay is our lord. Therefore you should strive to be aware of your moods when we're in these forests and to make your behaviour suitable. Do not act wantonly. Treat the spirits with respect for they are more numerous than us and can surround us at any moment they choose. Do not let me down. This is the land of my forefathers, which I deserted. If I'm associated with poor behaviour, I'll be sent out to die, because the spirits will have fled from me. Höuki was the shaman who created the world. Let that be the last word you hear tonight. Höuki' – and strangely enough, the moment he finished speaking, I fell asleep.

I'd got into the habit on the train of waking every four hours in order to do my trick on watch. Now I did so again, at midnight. The fire was bright but Kobi was nowhere. At four o'clock it was the same. At dawn there was the smell of fresh smoke. I looked around and saw Kobi squatting by the stream washing some meat, stroking the pale flesh beneath the water, a most curious motion.

I sat up and shook my head, which felt thick. I said to him accusingly, 'That's an animal.'

He said, 'The hare offered itself. It was Bayanay who arranged that the hare and I should meet, who decreed that we needed it for our food. See, there is its skull upside down to stop the blood flowing out the wrong way and to stop it seeing me and being angry with me. Everything is in order. Its soul will be born to a new body. It will be as if the hare had never died.'

He was in earnest. I wanted to warn him not to be too dogmatic in case he found out later he'd been talking crap. On the other hand he could be going through a period of sensitiveness, having just discovered where he came from. I didn't want

59

to fight with him. I wanted to get to America, find a nice woman and live happily ever after. Maybe fix up with my kids to retrieve the gold, maybe have one last crusade against the Reds.

I stretched and said to him, 'You know, Kobi, that *vobla* we had last night was second-rate, let's only eat fresh while we're in the forest, stuff that's been OK'd by Bayanay.'

He put the dismembered hare in the skillet and brought it back to the fire, which I'd sparked up afresh with birch bark. He said, 'I'm glad you're paying attention to me.'

What was particularly queer was that he looked so fit, as though he'd slept like a dormouse for a straight eight hours.

Thirteen

I DON'T want to sound sniffy. Everyone should be free to believe in whatever he wants to believe in. But Kobi had gone in so deep and so suddenly, and this from a man who'd previously only once shown any interest in gods and spirits, indeed in anything invisible, that I was suspicious. I needed proof, some evidence of the sincerity of his conversion. All that stuff about Bayanay – you didn't need an introduction from a spirit to kill a hare. What you needed was to keep the wind in your face, one eye shut and to squeeze the trigger, not pull it.

I said, 'We could go hungry if we have to wait every day for Bayanay to match us with the right animal.'

He said, 'The Old Man will feed us if Bayanay forgets.'

'Who's the Old Man?'

'I don't know yet. Doig, I know how you think. You trust only what you can see or touch. With us it's different. Look, we're walking past a place where my people are buried. All our graves are near a path so that the dead can enjoy visits from the living.'

He stopped. Looking up into the trees – not spruces, but deciduous trees, I didn't know their names – I saw three or four bodies wrapped in birch bark and tied to platforms. Bones were sticking out, feet and hands mostly, some shoulder-blade angles.

I said, 'Don't the birds pull them around?'

'Why would they do that? They could have been humans themselves. These are our holiest places. In the dead are concentrated all the experiences and memories of a lifetime. This is where we come to speak to them and ask their advice. It may be that one of the paths to our summer lands in the north has

61

fallen into disuse so that not even our reindeer can remember it. Then we come here. The dead give us the answer.'

I thought, Christ, those saplings I cut down for the fire last night, did they have someone's tiny bones up them, dead kids for heaven's sake? Stuck up there out of harm's way by the grieving parents and now desecrated? Would Höuki pursue me and hurl me down into their kingdom of flame?

Kobi knew what I was thinking, for he turned and said, 'Don't worry, a voice would have called to you if they'd held graves.'

I began to understand why he should feel that the glades had led him unerringly to this spot, why the streams had run silently, why we hadn't had to ford them.

I said, 'That's why I thought I'd been drugged last night?'

'Yes, it was Höuki proving his power over your mind. Only important people like our doctors are buried in the trees. For the rest of us there are graves on the ground. Here are some. No wolf or fox will harm them. Bayanay won't let them. They know this and so walk straight past. We must leave a present for the dead on the pile over there.'

He laid down the pack and his rifle and inspected the trove. There were empty bullet cases, coins, cigarette papers, brass buttons, bottle tops, all sorts of stuff a ghost might need as it waited for rebirth.

I said, 'You know, this gives me the creeps. Rubbish, that's what you're talking.'

His face flushed – his eyes became thin and hard. He said, 'I didn't insult the customs of your country. I thought better of you.'

I said, 'Come off it, you were down and out when I picked you up. Remember? In the marketplace in Samarkand? You were anybody's then. You didn't insult anything because you weren't in a position to. You wanted my money, it was as straightforward as that. So let your hackles down.'

When he still looked at me sourly, I said, 'You want to stay here and get friendly with Höuki, that's your choice. I'm pushing on.'

Now he looked right through me, from one side to the other. He was a short man and to have him scorch me with a look from down there made me feel like the village idiot. I thought,

62

Are all these guys such hard going when they get in a pet? In a mollifying but dignified tone, I said, 'I could have phrased that better. I'd really appreciate it if you stayed with me. I'm serious about that, one hundred per cent. We go well as a team. But if you feel you need to stay here and catch up with a few things, don't think you have to oblige me. I know how it is to have these deep feelings spring from the heart.'

I thought of saying something about paying him more but the look on his face put me off. This was about Bayanay and animal spirits, not about money.

He considered it – made an effort and nodded, neither yes nor no, just a quick dip of the head. He bowed, first to the graves in the trees, then to those on the ground. He fished a toothpick out of his pocket and threw it on the pile. I added a twenty-rouble *kerenka*, which I weighted down with a stone.

Kobi glanced disdainfully at it. I said, 'It's four times more valuable than the five-rouble one.' He picked up the pack and rifle and set off down the path.

After a few yards I stopped and looked back, thinking, maybe I should have left one of Lenin's banknotes. They were surely the future for any wandering spirits, not the bits of Kerensky's trash.

Kobi whirled round on me. 'Never look back when walking away from a grave. You've made bad trouble for us now, Doig, really bad trouble.'

That and the tone of his voice stirred me up all over again. How the hell had he got so intimate with the customs of the Lesser Tungus? Weren't they the lost bunch, the tiddlers in the jam jar? Was I going to get one lecture after another until somehow we got to a train?

I said, 'You listen to me, you little crapper' – yes, I was on the point of shouting at him, of really getting stuck into a quarrel, when I heard it.

You have to understand that the air was absolutely still, frozen into place as if it were specimen air in a museum. The stream might have been the Styx for all the noise it was making, the trees were motionless, there were no pillows of snow thumping onto the ground. There was no machinery blasting away, no gunfire, no trains, klaxons, screeching streetcars, no mechanical noise of any sort. We were deep in a Siberian forest with only spirits for company. Miles from anywhere. A hundred, five hundred miles, pick any large number you want. And from the heart of the silence had come two liquid, haunting chimes of birdsong, dark in colour, dark as the mossy stream, dark as old blood.

Kobi gripped my arm. 'Bayanay!'

But I knew better, and I wasn't going to tell Kobi what it was I knew, at least not for a bit, because what we'd just heard was the Tungus' sacred bird, had to be, and I didn't want him flying into a paddy about how it could never be tampered with or the world would come to an end.

I stood ramrod still, waiting for it to repeat its call. That snatch of song, it'd been exactly as the texts described it. Unbelievable! The bird that travellers had heard but no Westerner had yet seen. Every museum in the world would want it, would give up Sunday to get its hands on the skin. Just the two of us, birdie and me. Nobody to try and steal my thunder. Another first for Charlie Doig –

That no Westerner had yet seen!

Colossal! It was the only word for my luck.

But Kobi would go crazy if I plunged into the killing without preparing him. All the Tungus stuff in his head had turned him into a fanatic. So I'd have to humour him and introduce him to the possibility of a fatality with tact – a little grease here, a little smudge there.

Fourteen

P RJEVALSKI WAS the first authority. In the journal he kept of his Mongolian expedition, he includes as an appendix the report of a scouting party that tangled with the Lesser Tungus:

> Our prisoner, who gave us the name of Daik and was clearly a man of consequence in the tribe, said the bird with that call was their sacred bird. Anyone who harmed it would suffer terrible illness in his family for three generations. This is what the interpreter told us that Daik had said. This bird was heard on five separate occasions but never seen by any of the party. The month was April. The call was clearly its mating call.

Goetz had of course heard tell of it. By rights the bird should have fallen to him. But this was a part of the world to which he was never tempted. He preferred warmer climes, where the vegetation was thicker and insect life more plentiful. He once said to me, 'Siberia, Spitzbergen and Sakhalin I leave to you. I leave to you anywhere I cannot wear shorts when I go out with my collecting net. But the rest is mine, and all the creatures on it.'

Douglas Carruthers, who was a frequent visitor to the Darwin Club in London at the time when I was starting my career, had, like Prjevalski, heard its call during his travels but hadn't seen it. It was he who'd christened it the Lala bird. 'Tralala, tralala – and then nothing, not even the sound of its wings,' was how he'd explained it to Goetz.

Suddenly I had coals glowing in my skull. I'd be a hero again! The Lala bird, sacred to the Lesser Tungus! I saw it on its plinth, I saw its label, I saw its glass eye staring coolly out at the crowds. I saw Amy Carson bent over her typewriter, teeth shaking with excitement as she hammered out the publicity leaflet for the Field Museum – I saw my photograph all over the newspapers (I was in skins, riding a sledge, my breath a cloud of frosty vapour as I yelled at the dogs), saw acclaim swirling around me like snowflakes –

I had Kobi halt. Fingers trembling, I started to untie my blowpipe – it was corded into the gap between the pack and its frame.

He said, 'What's that for?'

'Food, Kobi. In case I suddenly get the nod from Bayanay. I've got to be ready.'

'It's that bird, isn't it?'

'That's a nice plump birdie,' I said.

'Is it a rare bird?'

'Nothing special.'

'I can tell you're lying from your voice. You think it's their holy bird, don't you? I once heard you telling Xenia about it and how that sort of prize would be a naturalist's crowning achievement. It was when you said 'Tungus' that I started to listen. I remember things like that, when my tribe gets mentioned.'

I was looking towards the mossy stream to see what the soil was like, if there was any clay down there. My heart was doing a hop, skip and thud routine, the same as when I captured the jewel beetle. I didn't take in a word of Kobi's because of that and because of thinking about the colour of the clay and how hard a ball it'd shape into. I said, 'That bird's no more sacred than my arsehole. Just because it has a strange call doesn't make it sacred.'

He stood there, absolutely rigid, glaring at me.

Now the cat was out of the bag, no mistake about it. Battering on, I said, 'I'm going to have this bird one way or another and the only question left is this: are you with me or aren't you? Cos if you aren't, I'll have my pack and rifle back. That's for starters.'

He said jeeringly, 'You wouldn't get far by yourself.'

'Go wherever you want, I don't mind. Go and complain to Höuki if you feel like it. Only think twice how you speak.

These Tungus relatives of yours aren't going to know you from Adam. They're going to say, Who're your parents, what's the family moniker, why do you only speak Russian, things like that. Or do you think someone's going to jump up and say, I know him, that's the kid the Russkis pinched from his cradle? You consider it, pal. These people may not think the same way about you as you do about them.'

He gave me a long look, then turned his back. Stood still, a little hunched, thinking.

Meanwhile I had a pop down the blowpipe in case the wood had swollen since I last used it. It made a good clean noise. The cylinder has to be as smooth as a girl's bottom or the ball gets out of shape on its way through. Then it deviates in flight. A tiny bulge at one end can make a big difference at the other. You want to kill something like a goldcrest at twenty yards, a bird that's only three inches long, you can't afford any sort of difference.

I said, 'What's the answer then?'

He sighed, not looking repentant or reformed or any of those – but he bowed his head. I said firmly, 'Nip down to the stream then and find me some clay.'

Which he did, taking his time about it – but he went.

It was strong blue stuff streaked with whaleback grey that he returned with. If you'd stood in it, you'd have left your boots behind. I sat down and rolled balls for the blowpipe between my palms, twenty of them.

Standing over me, he said, 'You should be able to hit something with one of those,' which was more like his old self. I thought to myself, That takes care of him and the Tungus, that deals with Höuki and Bayanay and the Old Man, and took a practice shot at a leaf browned and tattered by winter. It'd surprise you the force that a ball carries so long as you blow the right way. A novice only thinks of blowing directly from his cheeks and is astonished when the ball hardly makes it to the end of the cylinder. Craftsmen blow their cheeks and lungs simultaneously, using their stomach muscles. When they've got the air just so, on tiptoe, they *spit* it into the blowpipe. *Spit* it, not like a tomato seed but as if it were a bunch of phlegm, with full lips.

I retrieved the ball and stowed it with the others in a leather pouch that I slid along my belt until it was over my right hip. The flap had a poppit fastener which I left loose. If I missed the bird I wanted to be able to get into the pouch quickly without thinking.

A tiny brown spider, its body little bigger than a pinhead, ventured out of the grass and started to climb up my trouser leg. 'You watch out,' I said. 'You and yours are a banquet to a bird at this time of year. You're solid protein, you're the goods for a Lala bird.'

Kobi said, 'You'll never find it. Think how big the forest is.'

I said we would so, and pointed out the general direction we'd take.

I led the way. I was carrying the blowpipe loaded, with the muzzle facing upwards and my thumb over the bottom to stop the ball rolling out.

At the first halt I said, 'Goetz would have had the answers by now. The bird's order, family, species – its length, wingspan and weight, even the shape of its wings in flight, all would have become apparent to him from hearing it call once. Without question he was the greatest naturalist of his era. If he hadn't remembered he was German and gone off to the war, I'd still be with him. Then there'd have been no place for you.' I said it like that to remind him who was the boss in all this.

'Would he have killed a sacred bird?' Kobi asked.

'Heavens, yes.'

'Why?'

'Science doesn't know what sacred means. You know that. You've been with me long enough.'

'You're the same as him,' he said accusingly.

'Didn't I just say that? A museum'll buy the skin from me and enter it in the book of history. The Lala bird never even made it onto the Ark. It's going to be as if I'd brought in the skin of a dragon.'

'You'll kill the bird, take away its magic and receive money for what's left,' he said, and spat.

I sighed. 'OK, let's start again. Here we have an extremely rare bird—'

'The last bird you had like that was the white swift I captured for you in Samarkand. It was so rare and important that you exchanged it for a Luger pistol. Why should you do the same to the sacred bird of the Tungus?'

I burst out, 'For Christ's sake, another first like my beetle and I'll be a made man. Everyone'll want to employ me, and if they want me, they'll want you as well. Doig and Kobi. Sounds good, eh? I'm made, you're made. Don't you want success? Sure you do, everyone does. Let's get on with it.'

Before he could reply, I thought of something else. 'And consider this while you're at it. This sacred bird isn't the only one of its sort. These woods are most likely crammed with sacred birds. That one we heard, how did it get here? Bayanay made it? Nonsense. It had a mother and a father and in the nest it had brothers and sisters, all of them shitting and squawking. Could be dozens of sacred birds around here, what do you say to that?' which I said glaring at him, the answer was so obvious.

He said, 'Sacred is in the mind, not the flesh.'

'OK, so are a lot of good ideas but you can't live off them. Try this one, and it's my last offer. In these woods are twenty sacred birds – don't argue, it's just a figure. And right now, there's not much food for them. Look around, am I right or not? OK, I kill one of them. What happens? The remaining nineteen have more to eat and become stronger and more fertile. Thus we get more sacred eggs and so on. Now I'm going to set out and find it. If you want to leave me, put down the pack and rifle and start walking.'

After a while, he shouldered the pack. I said, 'We'll mark our territory so we know where we've been. Here, take the axe and put a blaze on that tree.'

Fifteen

FOUR DAYS passed. I sat, I listened, I chewed a lot of grass stems. The interminable clouds of Siberia paraded above my head with snow stuffing their bellies. Sometimes they were plain black and at others a gross and sinister purple that seemed to presage thunder. But we got nothing except flitters of snow, small gritty stuff that didn't lie.

There was no sign of the bird, nor could we find the heaps of shit that would have told us where it roosted.

I extended our territory by a furlong on each side, then by another furlong, then by half a mile. I had Kobi mark the trees with the axe as we went, for in places the forest was so thick that the ground was impossible to read. A man could have gone round and round in circles for days on end. In fact, the only certain landmark was our mossy stream.

Kobi was in a sour mood throughout. On the fourth day we were back at the stream. It was late afternoon, night not far off. He said, 'The bird also has eyes. It sees our marks and keeps clear.'

Exasperated, I raised my head to the snowy skies and cried out, 'You win, Bayanay. Tell that bird if one of the family would like a quick clean death instead of lingering on in this unpleasant weather, to hang around our camp. Would you kindly take that message, sir? Kobi, join with me on this prayer, you know the ropes.'

But he wasn't going to agree to that until I'd agreed to acknowledge the divinity of Bayanay, Höuki and the Old Man. 'Just give me my orders,' I said on account of my extreme desire to nail the bird.

He made me face the east and kneel down with my forehead touching the ground. I had to close my eyes – hell, it felt vulnerable bent over like that, him moving around behind me in the dead grass, chanting and moaning, the strangest noises you could imagine, not real words at all.

Speaking into the soil, I said in a muffled way, 'You never had any of this lingo before.'

He said, 'Say, "I believe in Höuki, who is the Lord of all, I believe in Bayanay," – you can say it in Russian, they'll make allowances. I'll say a sentence and then you repeat it.'

Like my marriage vows, I thought. What would Lizochka say to me now? 'What you're doing is the absolute limit of human stupidity, Charlenka. You have no idea how ridiculous you look with your bottom in the air like that, all for a silly bird?' That's what she'd say, plus some more.

I said, '"I believe in Höuki"' – and as the words came out so that damned bird began calling, not a hundred yards away, *plink*, *plink*. It turned its head in the other direction – a fainter *plink* was followed by a number of short dry rattles, *chrrt chrrt chrrt*. Then it turned back again to us – *plink plink plink* like a dripping tap. I shot to my feet and grabbed the blowpipe. I saw a dark flash through the trees, heard a single wingbeat – it was gone. From a safe distance, it *plinked* again, mockingly.

Thrusting my face at him, I said to Kobi, 'You're a bloody rascal – I'd have got it if you hadn't had me kneeling on the ground mouthing all that tosh. You were trying to hogwash me, that's what you were doing.'

He said, 'You spoke the words and Bayanay heard you. Therefore he sent the bird. That is the truth. Truth has power.'

Quietening down, I said, 'OK, I'd forgotten about him . . . anyway, that's twice we've heard the bird here. You know what that tells us? That since it eats and shits like any other bird, it likes to come here to do it. The mossy stream, that's the key to this.'

'How do you know it was eating and shitting? All it did was fly past us.'

'Don't get picky. Maybe it was its mating call we've been hearing. It's that time of year. Either way, for love or something

71

else, it comes here. Base camp, that's what the stream means to it. Give it another hour or so and it'll be back for the night.'

It didn't have to roost up a tree, it could jug down in the mosses, that was my way of thinking. Bayanay would have done a deal with the foxes and wolves to make them skirt round it as it slept.

My next thought: If I make myself a little scrape between two of those graves up there, I'll be in cover and just close enough to the stream to get a shot. I eyed it up and down. Fifteen yards. Light poor but the range by no means difficult.

Not wanting Kobi to see bits of his family flying out of their graves as I dug myself in, I sent him off for a walk. Then I excavated my lair, spread out the groundsheet and settled in, looking down at the mosses. I lined up five clay balls on the lip of my burrow. That's the great thing about a blowpipe. If a steady hand and a vigorous, decisive expulsion of the breath don't do the trick first time, you can have another go.

Phht. Why ever would a bird want to pay attention to such a tiny noise?

I looked up – would there be a moon tonight? Could the bird be a night feeder, something with a long beak, long toes and huge lustrous eyes that would prowl through the mosses guddling for tiny freshwater snails? That would make for tricky work, having to shoot when the moon was bright yet at the same time judging the shadows correctly. But I didn't see it as that sort. I saw it as one of the thrush family, a day bird, with a steady trusting flight. It would come in fast, as all birds do when making for their beds, chuckle a bit as it made itself comfortable – then silence. Then *phht.*

'Don't jump up and rattle your bones at the wrong moment,' I whispered to the graves. 'I don't know any Tungus names so I can't be truly friendly. The most I can say is that I mean you no ill, be assured of that. I'm Charlie Doig, a respectful gent. But I just have to shoot your bird.'

I began to think about skinning it. This is the most delicate task in our profession. A badly prepared skin can make it worthless to science. One must take real pains to come out with a skin that looks as if the bird once soared, stooped, cracked seeds, shattered snails' shells and buried acorns. Failure here is total failure.

Thirty minutes, that's what I'd need for the skin to cool. Maybe I'd spit the carcass and roast it over the fire. Then a sacred mouthful or two, and if the moon was bright enough, we'd light out. Move quickly. Get well clear of the Tungus before they found out.

I took the right-hand ball and placed it on the left.

Too early for mosquitoes, thank God.

Where was Kobi? I didn't want him blundering into my killing area. But he never would. No one could walk as noiselessly as Kobi. If he wanted to creep up behind and surprise me, the first I'd know about it would be his foot touching mine. Not a twig would crack—

It flew low out of the trees on my right, a swift, certain flight – landed on the mosses beside the stream, shook its feathers out, preened itself briefly, looked up, looked around, preened again, shat. Slowly I raised my blowpipe and put it to my lips. As if to give me the go-ahead, Bayanay had the bird *plink* and turn to look in my direction.

A straight-on shot. A hit anywhere would kill or stun it – no broken wings or legs, no hopping about, no chasing through the mosses.

OK, a small, narrow target. But up-and-down is the easiest shot in the book. Traversing is where mistakes occur. And there was no wind to allow for.

Doigii, my second one.

I'd get into the encyclopedias. Same volume as Darwin.

Phht – the ball nailed it between the eyes. It shivered – all down its breast the plumage trembled, which I'd never before seen happen to the birds I shot. Then its little legs crumpled and it toppled over on its side, stunned.

I leapt out and ran down to the stream. It lay motionless on the silvery mosses. I slid my palm down its breast and squeezed it gently. Thin, far too thin to have got through the rest of the winter. I inserted the point of my knife into its skull from below. It knew no pain.

I stood there, a smile splitting my face. Blowpipe in one hand, sacred bird of the Tungus in the other. The bird of legend, unseen by any other Westerner. My destiny, my fortune! I fairly waltzed back to our camp.

Kobi was waiting for me, leaning against a tree with his arms folded.

Sixteen

A THRUSH, just as I'd thought. Livery dull, as is always the case with our good singers. The exception was its super-cilium or eyebrow, which was a strong, dark purple, similar to the colour of the thunder clouds. It could be properly seen only when I held the torch at the right angle.

Kobi handed me my paintbox and I made a record of the colours at the moment of death, which is vital. Then I spat on my whetstone, put a fresh edge on my knife and began to skin it, saying to Kobi, 'Don't move that light an inch, even if Bayanay calls out to you. It was he who decreed it should die.'

He squatted there holding the light. After a bit he said, 'If it was a bear they'd killed, the Tungus would sew up its eyes and tell the bear it had been killed by Russians.'

'This is a bird,' I said, getting on with the last and trickiest part of the job, i.e. getting the skull out of the skin without having it fouled by any of the internal grease or juices. 'Keep the light steady,' I growled.

He said, 'Cover up its eyes so it can't see us.'

I said, 'In a moment they'll be yours to do what you like with,' and I flicked out the brain and then the eyes, neither of which are of consequence to museums, and offered him the latter on the tip of my knife.

'You deal with them,' I said, 'while I do the labelling,' which I did, perforce omitting its scientific name but readily seeing the word *doigii* in the cramped, diligent black ink that taxono-mists use when writing labels. I filled in the details of its eyelids and naked skin, how and where I'd killed it, all the usual – there's no room for sentimentalism or inaccuracy when dealing with museums. I finished off by giving the bird a good dusting with Taxidermine No. 1, first on the bare skin to sterilise it and then, after turning it outside in, on the plumage to kill off its mites.

Kobi said, 'It's still sacred, even in death.'

When I didn't reply, he said, 'They're watching us from up on the crag. I can see them.'

'You mean the Old Man?'

'Yes, the Old Man and his wife. They'll be guiding the Tungus towards us.'

The skin was firm by now. I shone the light on it and checked inside that I'd scraped off every trace of fat. I compared the plumage colours against those on the label. I checked that the label was accurate in its description of the bird's most striking features: the bill, eyelid, ear and, of course, its purple eyebrow. ('Don't omit and don't defer,' Goetz's never-to-be-broken rule floated through my mind.)

I wiped my instruments, boiled them and packed them away. I squatted down beside Kobi. The firelight was flickering between us, the moon constant above. I said, 'Tell me, pal, how do you know these are your people?'

'I know.'

'How?'

'I just know, I know from my heart.'

'OK, so do you think you're making a family visit or coming home for good?'

He couldn't answer that, just dropped his head. I said, 'You need to get a grip on yourself before you meet them. Get things clear in your mind, make a plan.'

He whispered, 'I must ask my gods.'

'Höuki and his gang?'

'Yes.'

I rose, poured water over my hands from the skillet, then walked around kicking the log ends into the fire. Standing over him, I said, 'Are you sure about all this? You sure you're not expecting too much from a new religion? It's what usually happens with converts.'

He couldn't answer that either.

I went off out of his sight and corded the bird skin under

76

my shirt and vest so that it was against my stomach. If I had to leave Kobi behind, I'd pack it into the bottom compartment of my collecting box. In the meantime I was going to keep it handy in case I got separated from the pack.

I had a piss looking down at the mossy stream, at the moonlight playing on its dark and oily glide. A whale would look like that if it came up beside your boat at night to see who you were, that's what I thought. I spoke into its depths: 'Well, Bayanay, so long,' in case that was where he lived. Maybe my bird had been Bayanay himself.

Kobi was curled up beneath his greatcoat when I got back. He looked at me and said, 'Let me sleep. I wish to be alone with myself tonight.' I said, 'OK, but we leave when I say and that's soon.' Then I too lay down and so was fast asleep when the Old Man came.

Seventeen

M Y DREAM contained enormous multicoloured creatures
that were floating through a tropical glade, their wings
stirring the heavy air with the indolence of punkahs. I was seated
at a table in a canvas-backed chair with a glass of Austrian beer
at my side. The table legs rested in tin pannikins filled with
water to defend them against assault by ants. Every time I shifted
there was a squeak of protest from the tins. All around me were
the noises of the jungle – creaks, groans, the chatterings of
monkeys and the beautiful treetop melodies of small proud
birds.

In front of me was a memorandum on the Lala bird that I
was writing for the Field Museum. My pen was slippery with
sweat.

A toad of truly monstrous size waddled out of the jungle
and sat on my foot. Awakening, I discovered Kobi's boot pressing
against mine.

I was up on my elbows in a trice – saw the Old Man standing
there with his arms folded across his chest, saw his bodyguard
behind him, slant-eyed men in skins with bows at the ready and
quivers of arrows slung over their shoulders. I said to Kobi,
'You dirty fucking snitch.'

He said, 'They wouldn't accept me. I told them nothing about
the bird.'

Then the Old Man was in the picture, wanting to know what
we were saying. Not a big man, Kobi's size, but compact and
full of presence. He was wearing a long robe of tanned reindeer
hide. Around his waist was a leather belt from which hung
braided tassels of reindeer fur. On one side of his chest was a

brass sun with golden spikes and on the other were crude iron images of animals and birds. Over his nose was strapped the huge brass beak of an eagle. His headdress was made of fur divided into four by crossed strips of bleached cloth. His boots looked like leather sacks bound with strips of bark.

The bronze beak had me nailed. I said, 'We should speak together, you and I. We are rulers, both of us – big men.'

The Old Man again turned questioningly to Kobi – said something I didn't understand. Nor did Kobi, who began to consult one of the archers, using exactly the same Russian words that I had but trying to shape them into what he fancied was Tungus language, thickening the consonants and adding a grunt or two. 'That's what my master said,' he finished with, in Russian, giving the air a straight-up stab with the fingers of both hands.

I said, 'Listen to me, Mr Snitch, you may have had your mother's Tungus milk but you certainly didn't get her talk.'

I think he realised then that he was in danger of getting the worst of both worlds – rejected by the Tungus and sacked by me. He said in a low voice, 'They know nothing about it, you have my word.'

More talk followed between Kobi and the archer, how we'd entered the woods, why we were camping so near the graves – the words went back and forth with supplementary explanations since the archer's Russian was itself rusty. In the end agreement was reached and Kobi said deadpan, 'They are the guardians of this bit of the country for the Tsar—'

That made me sit up. Could that really be how the land lay? That they'd heard nothing about the Revolution? True, they had no newspapers, no wirelesses, and spent half the year with their reindeer a thousand miles away in the Arctic. Even so – but it was no business of mine to do their thinking for them.

I said to Kobi in hurried Russian, 'How did he refer to the Tsar? Favourably? Royal Majesty, what?'

'Like Höuki. Top man, another god, only a little smaller.'

'Nothing about Lenin or the rest of them?'

'Nothing.'

'You sure of that?'

'This man's Russian is slow but good, so yes, I am sure. His name is Eyk.'

'OK, here's what, you tell Eyk that I'm the nephew of the Tsar and he's to treat me like I was another small Höuki. Grand Duke, those are the key words in this. He'll say, "How do I know?" You reply, "You will when His Majesty stands up. The only tall men in Russia are the Romanovs."'

I'd never thought it would come to this, that I could be glad I looked like a Romanov. All that ducking and crouching when the Bolsheviks were around – but now – beating Kobi to it, I jumped up, threw back my greatcoat and stood erect, sticking my chin out to make me six foot three. I bowed to the Old Man, I bowed to Eyk, I bowed to the archers in the trees. Not as a junior, but impassively, head-and-shoulders only, the bow of a man accepting the allegiance of his people.

The Old Man spoke to Eyk, who threw half a dozen birch logs onto the fire, making it flare up. His beak glinting red, the Old Man stalked around me. The only way they could have known of the death of their sacred bird was if Kobi had told them. But I knew he was speaking the truth, the atmosphere was too calm. So they'd have to strip me to find the skin.

The Old Man completed the circuit on his soft-soled boots and halted. His black eyes stared into mine with real power. The way they held me, you'd have thought they were screwed into his head. He spoke. Eyk said, 'First you must prove you're a Grand Duke.'

I'd been expecting this. I fiddled through the pack and got out the commission from the Academy of Sciences for my expedition to Samarkand, a really impressive document made of woven parchment. I made a good play – took my time unbundling it – explained the majesty that had been delegated to me – recited line by line the honours of the men who'd signed it – all the while watching him like a hawk to see if he could read. Deciding that he couldn't, I said, 'Here, have a squint for yourself.' He took it gingerly, glanced at Eyk and was obviously on the point of having him vet it, so I quickly grabbed it back. 'Only princes and kings are allowed to read documents of that level. And priests, of course' – and I gave him a big grin to show that we were equals.

The Old Man said to Eyk who said to Kobi, 'Ask him his name.'

'The Grand Duke Boris Vladimirovich,' I said. 'His Majesty's representative on the Academy of Sciences, for whom I travel with my man. You are to give us every assistance we may request.'

'Boris Vladimirovich,' murmured the Old Man, getting his mind round it. Then he embraced me, his brass sun and animal symbols digging into my chest. He smelt of woodsmoke and pine needles and stale milk.

He spoke at length to Eyk, who did a lot of nodding and bowing. Then Eyk said to me, 'Tonight will be the Feast of Höuki's Birth. On this occasion he will descend from the twelfth level of the sky. It will be an honour to have a royal guest. There will be dancing, drinking and worship. The Old Man will be travelling into another hemisphere to meet Höuki. He will be unable to look after you personally. I am to do that.'

The Old Man said something further. 'Our women are all away. It is only men who are allowed to be present. The women might be unclean. That is the reason for that.'

They drew water from the mossy stream and damped the fire. Kobi got everything into the pack. We showed them our rifles were unloaded and at about eleven o'clock we marched off. The Old Man and I were in the middle, archers front and back of us with their bows at the ready.

Eighteen

To one side of the clearing was a village of about thirty of their *chums*, as they called them: conical tepees of reindeer hide. In the centre of the clearing, where the torches were thickest, a wooden platform had been erected three feet off the ground. At each corner was a pole and on top of each pole was a crude iron animal – reindeer, elk, bear and dog. Men were hanging around, obviously waiting for the Old Man's return.

Eyk bade me take one of the seats of honour at the edge of the platform. I made sure Kobi was standing immediately behind me.

Leaning back on my chair, speaking out of the corner of my mouth, I said to him, 'What happens now? You're on the inside track.'

'You forget, they don't want me.'

'There'll be more to it than drink and games,' I said.

'We can be sure of it,' he said.

At that moment a drum with bells attached to it started up. A man in skins and a round fur hat was at it with a paddle stick. The beat was like a dead man's march – boom boom boom, nothing in between except the tinkle of the bells, which made me think of goats grazing across an arid mountain.

'Mind you keep the pack close to you,' I said to Kobi. 'Sitting on it would be best.'

The place began to fill up. A fire was lit, birch bark being tossed on in armfuls so that soon the flames were leaping. Pine chips and some sort of dried herb were thrown in – a sweet, high-minded smell.

Leaning back again, I said to Kobi, 'They're like monks who're suddenly let out of the cloister and know they've got to make the most of it by dawn. But no women, I don't understand that part.'

'They'd smell,' Kobi said. 'They rub themselves in fat to keep the cold out.'

'What about summer? They wouldn't want to do that when the flies are around.'

Eyk joining us, heard that last bit. He said, 'In summer our women wear frocks. They look very beautiful. Babies are made at that time.'

'Frocks?' I said, having instantly in my mind a picture of Lizochka chasing a peacock butterfly with my net, of her long brown tomboy legs and girlish yelps. 'Frocks?' I repeated. '*Sarafan* up here in all this cold?'

'Maybe wrong word,' Eyk said in an untroubled way. 'Majesty, I was sent to a priest to learn your language, to bring us good luck. I did only one month, then I ran away. You like a drink now, Majesty? Special vodka? Tungus vodka?'

He came back with a brass pitcher and three horn cups, which he jiggled on the ends of his fingers as if he were a railway sharper. 'Royal vodka,' he murmured, pouring.

I said, 'My man doesn't.'

'But Majesty does,' said Eyk soothingly.

The drummer upped his tempo. A boy in an apron with some special, maybe ritualistic, design on it, came strutting out of a *chum* with a couple of small regular drums on his hip. Sitting on a stool next to the older man, he started on them with long fingers and undulating wrists, moving swiftly from one to the other.

'Soon they two do it together,' Eyk said. 'Go quicker and quicker, like men making babies. Boy is man's son. One spunk between them, drummer's spunk. Boy has top quality, father gets jealous sometimes, beats him. You like our vodka, Majesty? This is our special vodka, which we drink only at Höuki's festival. For one year it has lain with the root of a ginseng plant. Big one, this size, Majesty,' and he outlined a large sausage for me with his hands

The drink was working, everything was hotting up. Some of the Tungus had started to play a vicious sort of leapfrog, others were battling each other with wooden staves like quarter-sticks. In the thick of it were the youths, men of sixteen or so. They were wearing short robes tied at the waist. Thick sturdy legs, weightlifters' knees. Some had their cheeks painted with yellow stripes, some with a dull red.

I asked Eyk why that was so. He said that those with red paint had killed a wolf, that was the only difference. 'Wolves have no souls,' he added. 'That's why Höuki doesn't allow them into his festival. Look at the Old Man when he appears. You'll see he wears a badge for every one of Höuki's animals except the wolf. We won't even wear their skins.'

The drums were fairly chattering now. Eyk said, 'Drink, Majesty. For one night of the year, every man is allowed to get drunk . . . some food, Majesty? The women have left it all prepared. Special foods.'

The vodka had had a bitter and unpleasant taste to it at first. But now it was getting to me. I said, 'Kobi, you'll have to carry me to bed if this goes on all night.'

There was no reply. Twisting round in my chair, I saw him deep into a piece of meat.

'Pad from a bear's paw,' Eyk said. 'The Old Man's orders: our royal friends to be given first choice of the special food. Your man selected the paw. It will fill him with desire. He will be able to release himself at the wall.' He pointed to a smooth wooden screen about eight feet high at the edge of the arena. 'The boys use it until they get married. Tonight, of course, everyone uses it. Everyone who can.'

I said cautiously, 'What do I get to eat?'

'The greatest medicinal power lies in the bear's gall bladder and its kidneys. The Old Man has commanded that these be baked in clay for Your Majesty's solitary pleasure. No one in the memory of our entire tribe has before been given the honour of them both. But you are our royal guest. When you return to your home, you will tell Our Lord, His Most Noble Excellency the Tsar of All the Russias, that we, his servants, are in the first order of men.'

I said I would, by God I would, and then a platter of polished pinewood was set on my knees, on it two small footballs of roasted clay that were the colour of brick.

84

I've knocked about the world. I've drunk hot goat's blood and I can get a brace of sheep's eyeballs down in a single gulp. But the gall bladder, a bear's *bile*, all its dirty thoughts and bad language – it was too much. 'Very sorry,' I said to Eyk and told him how gall bladders had been banned from the royal table ever since Dmitri, heir to the throne, had been poisoned via this organ and the false Pyotr set up in his place.

Eyk said eagerly, 'I'll eat it then, you have the kidneys, Majesty. They're the bigger one.'

I cracked the clay with a swift chop of the hand. The two kidneys, hot, plump, greasy, bark-coloured, lay curled like fossils in the debris. I ate them with my fingers as the Tungus crowded round watching.

I belched, I picked bits of gristle from between my teeth, I drained my vodka and held out my horn cup for more. 'Let's start, boys!' I shouted and clapped my hands.

By then everyone was drunk except Kobi. They'd finished their roughhousing and were onto the next stage, laughing, crying, hugging each other, plucking at each other's whiskers with ribald shouts – nipping out the clumps of long black hair and counting them, some virility ritual.

There was a signal I didn't see: the drums hushed to a patter, the gong rang out twice and the crowd took their seats around me, cross-legged on their skins.

Here's the picture: flat open ground, fir trees jutting all round as black as sin, a ring of thirty or forty tepees, the crisp, merciless moonlight, the Lesser Tungus, the lost tribe, maybe a hundred men in all gathered round the platform – and suddenly there was the Old Man up there, the flame from the resin torches dancing on his eagle's beak and on his brass sun.

He raised his arms above his head – a tin bowl in his hands, the chalice. He lowered it to his mouth and drained it.

The drums started. The chanting started. I looked at Eyk for guidance. He seemed to nod at me. Bending forward I saw that he was actually far removed, his eyes showing nothing but white.

I whispered to Kobi, 'I'm not comfortable sitting around with their sacred bird in my pocket.'

He said, 'They'd make our death horrible.'

Nineteen

The fire was damped with a barrel of woodchips; fresh smoke billowed out and up and drifted over us in wonderful shapes – I saw gods and djinns and Eastern nymphs which were spinning blue-veiled down the vaulted alleys of a bazaar. That's vodka ginseng acting on a clean brain, I said to myself. Get smart, get sober.

And get out – I peered over my shoulder to check that Kobi was still guarding my back. 'Stand by to run for it,' I muttered.

But now the drums were building up to a climax. The Old Man was swaying on his feet, eyes half open, in another state of consciousness. Around me the men were shouting and weeping, pulling their robes off and lacerating their chests with sharp forks of pinewood shaped like catapults.

The Old Man's head was right back on his shoulders, his arms outstretched, his fingers clawing at the smoky clouds drifting past him as if he wished to divide them and thus be able to gaze directly upon Höuki, whom I envisaged sitting upon a throne not far above us, a meagre person with sharp, rat-like features. He was shambling around his platform, shouting up to Höuki, pleading, begging, cursing. Watch out, Old Man! There's a three-foot drop if you don't look where you're going – I wasn't that drunk that I couldn't think it. But no one would have heard me. The whole lot of them were migrating to a full trance, were rising to speak with tongues of drunkenness to the Old Man – were sobbing and yelling, maybe asking him questions about their dead relatives, I really haven't a clue.

I don't think the Old Man was smoking anything, I don't

think any of them were. It was the moonlight, the forest, the home brew, the absence of women, it was the greatest festival of their year – it was extraordinary, a scene from the birth of God. I shivered, feeling myself gripped. I didn't want to. I wanted to get the hell out of that place with the sacred bird intact. But I was held. Something was going on between the Old Man and someone up there in the sky and I was part of it. Don't ask me how I came to feel like that. It was the way it was under that stark moon in the woodland clearing.

Suddenly the drums went quiet. Five seconds passed. Then whack! – a gong struck a single booming note that went up to the stars. My blood began to tingle as if it was itching. Everyone rose to their feet. The Old Man acquired an extra force. His body stiffened, grew taller and began to shake – his soul was taking off to receive its blessing from Höuki. He started to spin. His fur tassels swirled, the iron animals and brass sun clanked on his breast. Faster and faster he went, crying out the same undistinguishable words as the smoke enveloped him in a blue whirl.

I had stood up as well. I was sweating, it was pouring off me in bucketfuls. A headache was knocking at my left temple, at exactly the same place with every blow.

The Old Man was at the edge of his platform. Then he was in front of me, his glinting beak thrusting into my face. I was swaying, having difficulty holding myself erect – until he put out his hand and touched mine. It was like sandpaper, and a moment later I felt electricity crackle up my wrist and into my shoulder, my neck and my head. He did the same with the other arm. I shook my head and the headache, which up to that moment had gripped me like a snare wire, snapped. He put both hands to my face and drew his fingertips down my cheeks – down my ribs, past the sacred bird and on down my legs. He tapped me on the ankle and I lifted my foot. He drew one boot off and then the other so that I was standing only in foot wrappings on the bitterly cold ground. But I felt no discomfort.

He unwound the wrappings. For half a minute or so he studied my feet. He ran his thumb up the groove between my second and third toes – did it hard, finding a nerve of which I'd known nothing and, in so doing, scoring my skin with his thumbnail.

87

The pain was intolerable. I cried out – I howled. Then he did the same for the other foot.

Smoothing and stroking my feet, bowing over them repeatedly, maybe six or seven times, he spoke some of his own words.

Then he sat back on his haunches. He spoke to Eyk. Eyk said to me softly, 'Now you are free, Majesty. That which was causing you ill has departed.'

The sweat was pouring out from beneath the Old Man's cheek plates and his beak was all askew. This was no time to be sacrilegious, cheap, anything less than royal. I said to Eyk, 'Please thank the Old Man. Please ask him the nature of the spirit he has released from my body.'

'He says, "An old sorrow."'

'A woman?'

'Yes.'

'Does she have a name?'

'He says, "There is no writing in our customs."'

'Does she have a face?' I said.

'It had gone. Only the spirit was there, inhabiting your eighth level and therefore close to your soul. It was dangerous to Your Majesty. He asks, 'Can you feel lightness at your core?' Eyk dug the points of his fingers into his own solar plexus. 'Right there. Light, air, freedom?'

It could only have been Lizochka the Old Man had glimpsed.

He rose unsteadily to his feet, clearly exhausted. Eyk said, 'He is weary from his meeting with Höuki and from working with you. Now he will leave us so that his soul can return without being alarmed by the people watching. In this respect it is like our sacred bird, which is also a creature of quietness.'

'Sacred bird, eh,' I said.

'Yes. It is the mother of Höuki.'

'Mother, eh . . . Is that something you wish to be kept secret?'

'It is, Majesty.'

'Then I shall omit it from my report. We must respect each other's traditions.'

'Your Majesty is most gracious . . . You have been cleansed in spirit. Now you must be cleansed in body.' He pointed to the wooden screen. 'A bad spirit carries with it bad seed. To get rid of one only is insufficient. Both must be expulsed.'

I demurred, saying royalty had no need of such a practice. When we felt the need, we sent for a woman. He was insistent, pointing at my trousers and then at the screen. 'To get rid of the bad seed, Majesty. It is our custom.'

I looked round to see where Kobi was.

'Here,' said his soft voice. 'Ready.'

Fighting had broken out behind us. The drink was getting to them. The noise was terrific, the drumming, the gong, the shouting – Eyk said something in my ear, which I had him repeat, bellowing this time. It was simple: he was thirsty and wanted to be with his friends. Yes, I said, oh yes, my friend, off you go, and he scampered away doing a cartwheel down the slope.

In the same soft voice Kobi said to me, 'Doig, behind the screen is an old man. He got lost in the forest as a boy and had to kill one of the sacred birds to stay alive. Once he'd eaten it, he fell asleep and that's how he was caught, with the feathers all round him. This is his punishment. Once a year, to draw the seed from the bucks with his mouth.'

'Sweet Jesus, sweet fucking Jesus.' It was all I could say.

'In five minutes the moon will drop below the trees. I can find the way out.'

The moon dipped, shadows fell and we scooted, by God we did.

Twenty

GASPING, CURSING, we stumbled through the moon-flecked
forest. *Zhivo, zhivo!* – they were the only words we knew
– quickly, quickly! The old fellow killing a sacred bird, him
kneeling behind the wooden screen, the connection was too
repulsive to contemplate.

Dawn came slowly, squeezing out of the east like grey paste
and foretelling snow.

Mid-morning we halted. Kobi had pocketed some bear meat
from the feast. We speared it on the ends of our knives and ate
standing up. He sucked his teeth and said, 'I don't want to do
what the old man had to do.'

'Nor I. They think a lot of their bird,' I said.

'Yes.' He picked at his teeth with his knife. Looking at a piece
of gristle, 'Imagine it, a hundred young bucks at you. Even
though it's only once a year, you'd be thinking about it all the
rest of the time.'

I said, 'Lay off it, Kobi. Count yourself lucky they're not
your folk. Let's concentrate on keeping in front. Horses won't
go for them, not in the snow we're going to get.'

He said, 'It's reindeer they use for their journeys. But for us
they'll come on foot, same as they hunt animals. The first we'll
know will be an arrow quivering in a tree.'

'In the back would be a mercy,' I said. '*Shhlug* – the light
goes out, *finita la musica*. One day it'll happen to us. We can't
go on being lucky.'

Kobi was remorseless. 'If they caught us, they'd jack our front
teeth out to give the bucks more pleasure.'

I said again for him to pipe down, that I wasn't interested in the subject. In any case, they weren't going to catch us as they were drunk And by the time they were sober, the remains of the bird I'd killed would be under a foot of snow.

Kobi said, 'If there's anything to be found, they're the people to do it.'

I said, 'We'll be well away before they find anything,' and he gave me a queer look as if to say, all right then, let's pretend the danger doesn't exist.

I had a sudden panic. 'Where did you put the blowpipe?'

He showed it to me, tied to the frame as usual. 'Don't drink so much, Doig,' he said, tapping his temple. 'Here, you carry the pack, it'll sweat you clean.'

We kept enough bear meat for a meal at night and resumed our trek. A compass would've been handy, but the last I'd seen of mine had been before Kazan, six months ago. However, it wasn't difficult to figure the business out. The railway at this point described a long slow semicircular bend, like a crescent, to get the best route through the forest. Our line of march was across that bend, from one tip to the other. We couldn't fail to hit the railway again as long as we kept going east, to the rising sun.

Maybe by using the word 'forest', I've got you picturing trees planted in rows, and foresters' wooden huts with a sprig of smoke arising from a chimney with a bend in it to keep the snow out. That's not how it is in Siberia. The fir trees have been there since the Creation. They've been blown over by tempests, felled by bears sharpening their claws, burnt by the sun and split by lightning. Some are young, some are withered, some are bent and others would make a mainmast for the grandest schooner on the seas. When one falls over, the limbs of the survivors creep close, shut out the storms and give support to each other. They sing in the wind, melancholy tunes in the minor keys. They bow, they nod, they sway, and together with their lifelong chum, the water – as in streams, rivers, ponds, lakes, kettle bogs, in fact every conceivable type of watery obstacle – are adept at making life utter hell for anyone trying to take the shortest route between two fixed points.

In the afternoon we left the forest. Open ground lay before us. There was no path. It was wet, tussocky land, difficult to anyone in a hurry. Exposed too, making my shoulder blades twitch. As the weather closed in, the wind gathered strength, brisking the snow along to form small white ridges. To begin with the stems of grass stood out and told us where the footing was secure. When they disappeared we had to make the best guesses we could and were often left floundering – sinking up to our knees, staggering and lurching like drunken old men trying to dance. The cold in that wind was intense. My mouth went numb. A blade of steel drove through my scarf, my shapka, my earflaps, through the bones of my skull until it reached the centre of my head where it froze everything. After an hour it felt as though my brain had been shrunk to the size of a raisin.

The snow came slatting and swirling, plastering us all the way down the front and freezing on us so that our greatcoats crackled as we moved. To make matters worse, my testicles broke through the fabric of my underpants. I didn't feel it happening, only the consequence: the action, painful in a most ominous way, as they rubbed against the wet, coarse, hairy worsted of my trousers. Because I was carrying the pack, I couldn't put my hands in my pockets to coddle my balls. I just had to keep my head down and hope for better times.

It seemed like an eternity that we were out there in the open. There was sheltered ground where we could have stopped until the storm blew itself out – but we kept going, driven by nothing more complicated than fear, fear that a posse of Tungus warriors was on our trail.

At last we reached the main body of the forest again. I said to Kobi, 'That's enough.' I unshouldered the pack and sat on it. 'We've got rifles, we can defend ourselves. If it comes to that.'

Kobi said, 'Watch how you sit down. You could break the blowpipe.'

I said, 'My balls have burst through and are rubbing against my trousers. It's torture.'

'Ah,' he said, and going down on his knees at my side he opened one of the pack's sidepockets and came up with a leather pouch tied with a leather cord. He placed it in my hand saying, 'Bear's grease. Now I'm going to gather fuel for our fire.'

I said, 'We'd best go without food tonight. This storm could last a week.'

He said, 'You can watch me, then. I'm not starving myself for you.'

He returned with twigs and bark and fir cones. I said for him to build his fire in a hollow so that the Tungus wouldn't spot us. He said he wasn't born yesterday.

It didn't matter that we were well armed or that the snow had covered our tracks or that the Tungus were probably still drunk or that they couldn't possibly have found the carcass of their sacred bird. The fact was that I'd been as nervous as a cat throughout the day. In retrospect I think it may have been a reaction to the Old Man ridding me of Lizochka's spirit. No other reason seems plausible.

Of course the moment Kobi'd got his bear steak sizzling, I was as hungry as a hyena. I should have made myself busy so I didn't think about eating but I couldn't help watching him. I stood over him, my juices boiling. After a couple of bites he became aware of me – cut the meat in two and pushed the larger bit towards me. Said nothing, just did it. And this from a man who hated walking and who'd just put in eighteen hours of slog, in the vilest possible conditions, since we slipped away from the Old Man's party. That was Kobi, in a nutshell.

There are always sheltered places in the forest, in all but the very deepest of snows. We made our bivouac between the roots of a wind-blown tree. No sooner had we done this than the snow relented and after an hour ceased altogether. The wind fell away and the temperature dropped even lower, as if over the edge of a precipice. From all around the night breathed its monstrous cold upon us. We crept together and lay like spoons, neither of us sleeping for very long periods.

I awoke for the last time at four or so. The sky above was as bright as a pincushion. Kobi said into my ear, 'How many stars can we see?'

That was the sort of information I'd learned at Goetz's tit. 'Four thousand, five hundred. On the other side of the Earth's curve is another four thousand, five hundred. Mind you, that's what we can see. It's not how many there are.'

'How many's that?'

'The largest number you could write down multiplied by a thousand.'

'I'm sure that in my country we have names for most of them. How can a nation of horsemen not have names for their stars?'

I said, 'Kobi, I have to piss. I've got to move.'

'You never want to hear me talk about my own country.'

'One day your country's Mongolia, the next day Siberia, that's my problem. Shall we go to Mongolia one day, speak to people, find someone who knew those missionaries of yours?'

He sighed. 'That would be good, Doig.'

Then he too rose. He kicked the fire into life and began to melt snow. We drank our tea and set out, two pinpricks beneath the starry dome.

It was past dawn when we got out of the forest. We found ourselves standing on a rocky outcrop with a view to the east that stretched for miles. Far out the fresh snow had a whiteness that must have surpassed anything God had thought possible, even in His wildest dreams. Nearer to hand, it was bluey-white, exactly the colour of junket, and over the top of it the tiniest of breezes was puffing snow crystals that glittered like a million sparklers.

I said, 'Count all those and you'll know how many stars there are.'

He said, 'One day I'll have a wife. To begin with I'll be the strong one, ramming her like a bull.' Every detail of his face was exposed by the glitter from the snow. The bunch of long frosted hairs on his chin sprouted like a spray of milk. His eyes were the soft brown of moles' fur. 'She'll be happy. I could make a woman happy, I know I could.'

'What makes you say that?'

'Looking out over the snow and seeing nothing but beauty and peace, that's why I said it. But then' – he shrugged – 'after a few years, she'll get the upper hand. She'll turn out to be the strong one and that's how it'll be until one of us dies.'

It moved me to hear him talk like this. He'd never said anything so personal to me before. I was going to tell him something of what I knew about women when he grabbed my arm and said, 'Look, there's Yerovef out there on our right, we've overshot it. But there's no train. You'd be able to see where they'd charged the snowdrifts.'

'But that's new snow we're looking at. We can't tell.'

'Look how deep the snow is in those cuttings. No train has passed this way for a long time.'

I said, '*Korotky put*, eh? Funny sort of short cut you've brought us on.'

He said, 'The next station is Zhigalovo. We'll have better luck there.'

'If the Tungus don't get us.'

'They won't.'

'They're certain to have snowshoes. The going'll be hard after that frost.'

'They'll still be drunk. Here, Doig, I slept longer than you, my turn with the pack.'

Twenty-one

BUT THEN things went downhill. As I split wood, the shaft of the axe popped out of the head, and, while knocking it back in, I hit my thumb. A blood blister formed beneath the nail, causing both nail and thumb to heat up. Within a couple of days it had become too tender to touch.

Kobi took out a sewing needle and drove it through my thumbnail, leaning with his whole weight on my wrist so that I couldn't jerk away. A weak solution of blood and pus oozed out, the colour of streaky bacon. Drawing it off with a pipette would have been the answer, like blowing a bird's egg, for it was impossible to get in behind the nail and force the pus out by hand. He stabbed two more holes, right at the base of the nail, which helped. The pain eased for an hour or so but by nightfall I was in agony, my thumb having swollen to the size of a spoon head. The poison started up my wrist. My forearm began to throb. I had little sleep.

The next day I felt lumpy, fevered, drained – not merely exhausted but emptied of everything positive, all strength and willpower. Following Kobi was all I was good for. He was carrying both rifles and the pack. I can see him now, this small, tough man, bent beneath his burden, plodding rhythmically across those snowfields as if he was capable of doing it for a hundred miles without stopping.

Several times he had to halt and wait for me to catch up. Leaning on my staff, I said on one of these occasions, 'But you've never walked more than a hundred yards in your life, and when you did, it was only to jump onto a horse. Thank God you've taken to it.'

He ignored that and said, 'Give me the bird skin. The sweat will run down inside your clothes and rot the skin. Then we'd have done all this for nothing.'

When I resisted, he said 'Come on, Doig,' and started to unfasten my clothes so as to get at the pouch at my waist.

I tried to brush his hands off but hadn't the strength – stood there helpless and shivering. The landscape was so desolate around us – firs, birch, some stunted alder, vast stretches of snow concealing all sorts of pitfalls and treachery. It was the same for miles, for maybe five hundred miles in any direction, and there we were in the middle of it, piddlingly tiny. *Men Arguing with their Destiny*, that would be the caption to the picture.

'We could die here,' I said.

He made no reply; pulled out my shirt and unstrapped the canvas belt. The pouch had two poppit fasteners. He snapped them open, took out the Lala skin and felt it as a doctor would feel his patient's forehead. Nodding, he stowed it in the pack.

'Can you dress yourself?'

I said pointlessly, 'The station will be somewhere.'

'Yes,' he said. 'Whether or not the Tungus catch us, the station will be somewhere.'

'Their territory won't stretch this far,' I said.

'I expect you're right,' he said.

I straightened out my front shirt tail and began to stuff it back into trousers. 'Wait,' he said, and bending he poked around in the fold of skin across my stomach – flicked out half a dozen lice. He said, 'We've been on the road for too long. Think of the last time.'

He meant when I'd caught typhus on the troop train out of Samarkand. I'd come within an inch of death that time.

I said, 'Never look back, you know what we agreed.'

He said, 'But you do, all the time,' and shouldering the pack and the rifles, he set off again. Making me get a move on, nagging at my self-pity.

The next day could have been the fifth, maybe the sixth, since we left Eyk and the Tungus. Kobi stood up from blowing on the embers of our fire and said, 'Those animals, they may still be drunk, even now. I hope so.' He turned full on to me. 'That

97

was a dangerous thing you did, killing the bird. It could've cost us our lives.'

I hadn't the strength to defend myself. The pain was shooting up my arm in surges and from there into the glands in my neck and thus into my lower jaw where it set off a dull and wearisome throb. I begged him to give me a little longer before we broke camp. He agreed – slid the bolt from his rifle and cleaned it on a corner of his shirt tails, then got the stone and our little tin of oil out of the pack and whetted his knife. I said, 'There'll be no blade left soon.' He pressed his thumb against it – snapped his knife shut – told me to shift myself.

As I stumbled along, I compiled a list of the things I'd be unable to do when my arm had been amputated. The law of compensation, was it infallible? Would I be able to run much faster? Would my remaining arm develop superhuman strength – would I be able to make money weightlifting with one arm in a circus booth? Would I find that my good hand had a talent for painting?

What about women? Would they shun me? Would they take me into their beds only out of curiosity?

I began to think about amputation, about Kobi straining a leather strap between my jaws so that I wouldn't cry out. The scene filled my mind. I wondered which would be greater, the pain or the relief as the rotten limb dropped into the snow. I tried to imagine the pain, was so engrossed in the exercise that I didn't hear Kobi when he began to point out the stumps of recently felled trees. I only woke up when he remarked on the fresh hoof marks where two horses had been hauling butts out that very morning. Then all I could think was that he yearned to be riding one of them and was about to desert me. How would I survive without him? If my arm had to come off, he shouldn't be allowed to escape.

Escape! This time the word galvanised me. I stuck to his heels, even though every step cost me a fortune in energy. As he lifted one of his feet, so my own boot slid into its place.

Then all of a sudden the noise of a kennel of dogs being trenchered broke out – a terrific rancorous brawl, as if the meat they were being thrown was the last in the world. Kobi stopped dead. I bumped into him and stayed there, clinging to the pack.

He said, 'Smell that.' Wearily, I lifted my head, and it came to me as sweetly as a woman's perfume – woodsmoke, from a stove or a cooking fire, I didn't care which. I saw in my mind a bed with cotton sheets neatly turned down, all toasty inside, right down to my toes. I saw the pillow, which was picked out in the soft yellow light of a wax candle. I saw Nanny Agafya waiting for me to finish my prayers.

Taking a step sideways to get a better view, Kobi knocked the pack against my bad arm. The pain skewered me like a bolt of lightning. I clamped down on a scream, staggered, and was in the act of collapsing when he swiftly stooped and with his left hand grabbed me at the waist by a bundle of coat.

The way we ended up, which was a complete accident resulting from the angle at which I was falling, he was, for a moment, a foot beneath me and I was looking right down into his face. It was how it happened, an above man and a below man, and I was the above one, as if I were superior to him, in fact as if he were my slave whose only duty was to save me from the consequences of my own actions. As if I owned him. That was the phrase that came to me in that instant, *as if I owned him.* It was utterly wrong. I tried to pull him up and make him taller than me, which was stupidity itself considering he was six inches shorter to begin with. In any case he wasn't letting go until he knew I could stand properly. That was what he said in a clucking mother-hen voice and that was what he did, propping me upright with one hand while he shuffled round holding me steady until he could stand behind me with his arms tight across my chest. After a minute or so he slackened his grip, as a test. When I didn't fall down, he released me altogether and had me walk five steps. I managed them, totteringly, but I managed them.

He said, 'You could die without a doctor.'

I sat down on one of the newly cut stumps and watched my legs tremble.

Let me not talk about the pure love that can exist between men of intellect, for that falls under a more profound heading than what existed between Kobi and myself. However, a man can reserve a section of his love for another man on account of some aspect of his character. I'd always been aware of Kobi's mulishness and had considered it something to be put up with, as one tolerates a friend's outbursts of temper. But now, after these days of increasing helplessness, I saw that this stubbornness was a tree within him which had a number of branches, every one of them with a virtue for its fruit – patience, endurance, determination and, above all else, loyalty. He could have abandoned me with ease and at no danger to himself at almost any point since my hand got poisoned. He must have known what I carried in my boots. He could have murdered me and pulled them off as the robbers had done in the cemetery at Irkutsk; he could have walked away a wealthy man and no one in that great wilderness would have been any the wiser. At innumerable times he could have taken advantage of me, and hadn't.

Yet for that brief moment, I'd found myself with the idea that I was his superior.

It was a disgrace. Sitting there, I told him what had happened. My head raised, looking him straight in the eye, in a firm, clear, bold voice so that he should not be mistaken about my humbleness.

He said, 'Your fever's getting worse, Doig.'

I said, 'I love you for that,' at which his eyes widened. But he said nothing, maybe out of suspicion as to what I might want, maybe out of embarrassment, and after a few seconds his face closed right up, back into its usual obstinate shape.

He was such a decent man at heart, I can't say this often enough. And from a practical point of view, he was utterly invincible. Whenever I saw the look that he now had on his face, it didn't matter how bad the position was, I knew that victory was certain and that he'd share it with me.

I smiled, I sighed – the moment was over. I said, 'Pray God these aren't Semyonov's men who've been cutting the trees.'

He handed me my rifle. 'Stay here while I look.'

In front of us was a boulder the size of a house, quite unlike anything else we'd passed during this so-called short cut. On its right was a smaller version, the child of its mother. Between them was a narrow defile. Kobi cocked his rifle and fiddled sideways through this passage so as not to bring their sheaths of snow crashing down on him.

A little weak sun appeared. I lifted my face to it and closed my eyes.

Scherze-terze, scherze-terze – it was the unmistakable sound of a big two-man cross-cut saw in operation. *Whumf*, the tree fell.

From a different direction I heard a hammer striking home a nail – Semyonov was crucifying a prisoner. The hammering ceased: Semyonov's soldiers were pushing the cross upright, maybe with a horse helping from the other side. My turn was next . . .

Then Kobi was pulling me to my feet. The forest thinned and we came to a half-built stockade. The ground was too hard for the uprights to be dug in. They'd been laid out side by side and left there, the yellow of the sawn timber made soft by the harsh reflection from the snow.

Behind the stockade, the trees had been cleared. It was park-land in the Siberian style we were looking at, and in the centre of it was a large wooden mansion built on two floors, its rawness so glaring that it hurt my eyes. A road had been constructed to it, winding down a slight incline between fir trees. At the top of this incline were the houses of a village and the golden dome of its church. It had to be Zhigalovo. Somehow we'd managed to hit it off at our first shot.

'Not Semyonov,' grunted Kobi. 'Too good a house for a peasant like him. Whoever has it must be important. He'll have medicine or a doctor, one or the other.'

My arm was burning, was really hurting like the Devil. Kobi began to support me across the parkland. Halfway over, he said, 'I can hear someone coming down the hill. It'll be a general at least, for a house like this.'

The builders downed tools and stood watching us, maybe wondering what the world was coming to. We reached the road. Kobi put down the pack for me to sit on. He laid our rifles on the ground.

He said, 'It's a young horse in the shafts to be going so quickly. Look at the ice on the road. An older animal would be more careful. I wouldn't employ that coachman.'

'You're guessing,' I said.

'Then watch, see for yourself if I'm right.'

Twenty-two

IT WASN'T a horse but a reindeer, a young one with antlers like spikes, which it must have been about ready to cast. A tiny Japanese flag had been tied with wire to one antler.

The Russian coachman had a bearskin across his knees. He was so swaddled around with scarves that amid the foam of his whiskers all that could readily be made out were a squashed purple nose and two eyes that stared out at us like bright blue sofa buttons.

Kobi said, 'Am I right or what am I?'

I nodded, but less at him than at the carriage, which as it came bowling out of the fir trees smacked me in the eye. It was for two people only, a box on wheels more or less, but so neat, and its black paintwork so fresh and the gold ornamentation and dib-dabs in the corners of its door panels so utterly *ancien régime* that I clutched at Kobi. 'It can't be his, there aren't enough aristocrats left in Russia to fit on a pony. He can't have got here, not old Stupichkin!' I was thinking of the prison governor in Strabinsk. He'd had such a carriage in exactly those colours. On the strength of having known my father (a 'scamp' he'd called him), he'd given me a horse, two machine guns and the crucial information about Trotsky's battle plan. Could he somehow have evaded the Reds and got here with his carriage?

On it came down the hill, bouncing on the rutted ice and making the chains on its wheels jangle. They'd been painted gold – like the bracelets on Salome's ankles, that's what I thought.

Gold was everywhere, shimmering black and gold. My eyes crinkled in disbelief. An hour before I'd been dragging myself through the forest. And now – I slapped myself on the cheek and when the carriage continued to come rattling towards us like something out of a fairy story, I said to Kobi, 'You do it, you hit me, you wake me up.'

He said, 'You need a doctor, Doig.'

Made giddy by fever bred to elation, I cried out, 'But why no trumpeter standing on the back?'

He gave me a strange look. 'Like this!' I said, and I made a trumpet from my fist and sent forth a squeak that left me bent and coughing.

As if in response, the coachman braced his boots against the splashboard and hauled back. The reindeer slowed to a walk and halted, tossing its head. The golden bracelets ceased to spin. I waddled up to the door, suddenly nervous at the prospect of re-entering society – conscious at the last moment of the bear grease spread thickly round my balls.

Stupichkin? Surely not. Then who?

The door flew open. She came hurtling out as if she'd taken a twenty-yard run at it, and slammed into my arms like a cannonball rolled up in fur. In that stupendous moment I glimpsed her hat – small, round, a sort of Mexican shapka – a flash of Neapolitan pink round her neck, rich red lips, brown eyes already crying.

She laced her arms round my neck – 'Charlie!'

Twenty-three

THIS WAS the woman whom I'd known, whom all St Petersburg society had known, as Countess Cynthia Zipf, Countess Cynthia von Zipf or even Countess Cynthia von erst und zu Zipf, according to her need for money and thus the need to impress. This was her story:

She'd been born in the Lower East Side, Manhattan, 'within the wires', and at the age of five had been packed off by her itinerant and discontented parents to an aunt in New Jersey. With her went nothing more than the clothes she wore and a suitcase of favourite toys and hand-me-downs tied round with three-ply cord and carrying on its label the words CYNTHIA RUTH COHEN, MUST BE SIGNED FOR. For a further five years she'd stayed with the aunt, whose company she greatly enjoyed. Then guilt had encircled her parents and forced them to relent. Against her will she returned to live with them. For the rest of her childhood she did everything she could to equip an ambition that began to devour her – to get free, famous and living in Russia.

We were in St Petersburg when she told me all this, sitting side by side on a Récamier style of sofa that had been upholstered in the Romanov colours, while our host, an old friend of my parents, played a Chopin mazurka to his guests after dinner. It was less of a conversation that took place between us than a declaration, which tumbled out of her almost in one go in her quick, twangy voice.

She whispered into my ear, 'I mean more than devoured, Charlie, I mean absolutely *munched*. By a wolf whose breath was a blast of sheer white crystals. Snow, wolves, palaces, footmen, that's all I ever dreamed of. Russia was my bride-groom from the moment I could read, which was about the age of four.'

She'd known she was attractive: too many boys had told her this to be mistaken. But how attractive?

One night at about two she went, as she put it, 'over the wall'. Lowered her suitcase (a new one by now) out of the window on her tied-up sheets and tiptoed down the stairs wearing three pairs of socks. Her father's snores were rocking the house. She thought, no wonder my parents quarrel so much – then she was out of the door, had freed her suitcase (folding up the sheets and leaving them in the porch, for she was always tidy) and by breakfast had been taken on as a maid on a transatlantic liner.

In Paris she'd discovered, at the age of seventeen, the answer to the most pressing of a girl's questions. Then she'd had an upset, had decided to try her luck in Berlin and there, having first purchased an entire wardrobe on tick – except for some French knickers she'd had to pay cash for – had set her cap at the wealthy old merchant Zipf. By one means and another she became his bride.

He'd been good to her. He'd pumped up her self-confidence and eventually admitted her to his counting house, where she discovered that she had an aptitude for commerce.

But when he suddenly died, what should happen ('Goodness gracious me!' she exclaimed at this point, as if describing not a disaster but some domestic event, like an old hen suddenly starting to lay again) but creditor after creditor came storming into the counting house and, with icy blue eyes such as only the Germans have, made clear that her throat would be slit if such-and-such a sum wasn't paid by tomorrow's close of busi-ness. Zipf had been as heavy with debt as if he'd been put up against a wall and peppered with lead IOUs.

So there she was, down in the gutter again. It was to avenge herself on fate that she'd taken for herself the rank of countess, of which there were anyway thousands in Germany so who was going to worry about one more, even if the lady in question was actually a Cohen from the Lower East Side. Then she said to herself, but the real dough's across the frontier in Russia.

Also, more or less in the same breath, that's where countesses really come into their own. She purchased an atlas to remind herself of the geography, said 'Oh my' a lot as she considered Russia's seven time zones, and again counted what remained of her money. 'Well,' she continued – we were still on the sofa, her fan from time to time rapping me on the kneecap – 'I wasn't such an idiot as to waste my time on boors and ruminants in the provinces. St Petersburg was obviously the place to be and here I am. My timing could have been better, though.'

So that was how she landed up in Russia, at the age of twenty-five, with a first-rate wardrobe, a body glowing with fearlessness and femininity, and a mind furnished with the strongest set of nerves since the heyday of Solomon Loeb, banker.

The day after this conversation we'd bumped into each other on Nevsky, just outside the Rykov palace. She prevailed on me to take her to Filippov's, on the corner of Nevsky and the Troitzkaya, for a cream and raspberry jam pastry, into which she sank her teeth so voraciously that a blob of cream attached to the tip of her nose.

I took it off with my finger. She murmured, 'Zipf would have licked it off, he was like that, the old dear . . . But those debts of his, Charlie, I was speechless. How could he have done that to me?'

So I told her about my own father, who'd suffered from exactly the same disease.

Thus did one thing lead to another – but to a friendship only, for this was the period when I was mad for Lizochka.

And now here she was, back in my life – from out of the Siberian forest, from out of this relic of the aristocracy that was still rocking on its springs from the force with which she'd thrown herself into my arms.

She hugged me, we hugged each other, kissing and crying. I held her off, marvelled at her plump, humorous face, her dancing brown eyes, her straight, firm nose – leaned forward and whipped off the little Mexican sombrero. Her hair was longer than in St Petersburg but exactly the same chestnut colour. I don't mean that now it fell like knitting, just that before the Revolution she'd favoured a spiky, stubborn, hard-hitting style. I tugged at it, I tugged at her ears, I waggled the tip of her

nose, exactly where that blob of cream and raspberry jam had
been. Then I kissed her on the lips, which were tipped upwards
and offering a delicious welcome, like an Easter bun at Filippov's,
warm and moist and tasty.

I said, 'And me with all my talk about renunciation!'

She said, 'What have you been and renounced?'

'Women,' I said.

'That's bad. How come I got the chop?'

'You remember the name Prokhor Fedorovich Glebov?'

She shuddered, said, 'Oh you poor lamb, what a tragedy that
was. I hope you caught him and strangled him, very slowly.'

'I went after him. To help me I took a girl along—'

She cried out, 'Have you done it again, have you slain another
lover?'

I said fiercely, 'She betrayed me, Xenia was her name—'

'Xenia? Charlie Doig with a common little thing called Xenia?
She was up to no good, I can tell that from her name. What
was she really called, or didn't you bother?'

'You've no idea—'

'Oh yes I have,' she laughed. 'Look at me, at my furs, my
carriage, my coachman, my palace – think it all came from
Santa?'

The reindeer gave a jangling shake and started to paw at the
snow. Still laughing, she said, 'So let it eat moss . . . God, it's
great to be looking at you again.'

What a history there was between us, not quite there yet in
the fullest sense, but on the brink. I could feel the electricity
in my fingertips. This was the woman who tried to seduce my
old homosexual Great-Uncle Igor. This was the woman who
had me buy the common stock of the Archangel Timber
Company first at forty-five roubles and then at twenty – in 1917,
I ask you, when the monster was already greasing the tumbril's
axle. This was the woman – oh, I'm telling you, Cynthia von
Zipf was the hottest, the wittiest, the snazziest woman in the
whole of wartime St Petersburg.

'I was going to ask what happened to you when the Reds
took over, but now I don't need to. You've been making your
way here, taking advantage of your advantages,' I said, trying
to smile but feeling my legs beginning to wobble.

'Like you,' she said, everything about her shining. 'Oh, Carlos, the way things turn out, isn't it remarkable? What's behind it? God moving us around like chess pieces? No, I don't buy that. It's something else, it's the wind blowing dust, that sort of thing, nothing ordained. The last I heard of you was some act of daring the night Lenin took over. Or Ulianov, whatever he calls himself. I've had enough of all these modern Russian names. They give me the creeps.'

'Put it there,' I said. 'You want to know what I'm doing, in a word? Moving on.'

'Me too. I got as far as Irkutsk under my own steam, a few setbacks on the way but I did it. Found a hotel, made a friend and then – well, then I got here. Moving on, that's a good description of it.'

I said, 'Just one thing I *have* to know: what on earth possessed you to try your luck with Uncle Igor? He must have been eighty by then.'

'I'll tell you. I was down to my last kopek – no, don't get me wrong, I had roubles, a whole lot of them, but they just weren't available to me at the time, you know what I mean, and I thought, here's Uncle Igor with two palaces plus all his dough, I mean absolute *stacks* of the stuff, and here's Cynthia, still a pretty girl despite everything, and she only needs a *loan*, and he needs company, he doesn't have to bed me, he doesn't even have to think about me naked – well, I thought I'd try it.'

'Joseph, his butler, told me all about your visit.'

'Joseph did? Then he shouldn't have. Cost me two hundred roubles to hire the carriage to go visit with your uncle. Bet Joseph didn't tell you *that*. But this carriage I've got now, nifty, isn't it? – Hey, you don't look too crisp, you ill?' She laid her hand across my forehead. 'Ouch! You're coming with me, Charlie Doig, and no arguing.'

She yelled at the coachman and got back into the carriage, turning in the doorway and hauling me in behind her, Kobi helping with his shoulder under my arse.

Suddenly I'd had enough. The excitement – the jubilation – the feeling of triumph at having made it through – they vanished as quickly as they'd come. I could take no more. I toppled onto her, wanting only warmth and softness and for the day to be completed. She took my shapka off and tossed it into the corner – kissed my temple – tidied my hair back. 'There was no grey in it eighteen months ago. You've grown up, Charlie. Not old but up. Can you hear me? Nod if you can. OK, that's good. I've seen too many dead men in the last year. There's a Jap doctor here, Hijo. He's a bit weird but he's good. He'll get you right in a jiffy.'

In a haze, in agony as the carriage bounced around in the ice ruts, I heard her slide back the panel and shout, 'Move your fucking ass, Ivan, this man's my best old friend.' Then everything went blank.

Twenty-four

THAT DOCTOR could have told you exactly how long I was out for. I know only that the day I came round all the Japs in that little hospital were as happy as grasshoppers and the reason for this was that it was Buddha's birthday. So it had to be 8 April. And unless I'd been in a deep coma, the year was still 1919.

Here's our Dr Hijo, exactly as he was when I opened my eyes. One: a head that was absolutely circular. It was a shock, finding such an object orbiting about a foot above me. I must have stared at him as a baby does at a stranger, for he smiled at me in an experimental way, and when I smiled back, screwed his face up into a grin. Cyn asked me later what my first impression was. 'Hideous, he should never smile,' I said, and here's why. Two: an upper jaw that was so overshot I don't know how he managed to chew his food. Three: teeth so stained from smoking that while the small ones at the bottom were rather black, those on the top row faced me like a fan of yellow playing cards.

It was an awful face, goggling at me through his wire-framed spectacles.

But he'd cured me. I was grateful for that and I told him so as soon as I had my wits about me.

At some stage during our first proper conversation, I remarked that it had taken me seven months to get halfway across Siberia.

He always spluttered a bit when he spoke, which he did in poor Russian. I watched his jaw, I couldn't help myself. 'There are many who don't even get to Irkutsk,' he said. 'There's cholera, typhus, dysentery, poverty plus all the other diseases that affect the body when it receives insufficient food and heat. This country of yours is no tea party, sir.'

'You missed the bullet off your list,' I said.

'Yes, that especially. The Bolsheviks are animals. All Japanese people will tell you the same thing, that if Bolshevism came to our country, they'd rather die on their feet than live on their knees.'

'They were responsible for the death of my wife.'

'I know. The Countess has been speaking about you. That was most unfortunate, sir.'

'Strange business, life,' I said. 'Had you told me five years ago all that was going to happen to me between then and now, I'd have said you should be locked up. A pack of lies like that is a criminal offence, that's what I'd have said to you.'

'It has been identical for me, sir, but in a different sense. The opportunities that this war has brought me have been beyond my wildest dreams. Good sir, it is from nothing that I come, from the poorest family in my town. Now the means are within my grasp to become Japan's foremost modern doctor. *Nota bene*, dear sir, modern doctor! Modern! Modern!' Tucking his pencil into the top pocket of his white coat, he rose from the edge of my bed. He shuffled his hand through his cropped black hair. 'One cannot be too careful working with lice. It is essential to be modern.'

'It's interesting you say that, doc. I've never understood how they get onto one's scalp. Why doesn't one feel them crawling up one's neck?'

He sat down again and took off his spectacles. For the first time I saw his face complete. It was that of a man who's got his teeth sunk into a lifelong cause. Unshaven for a day or two, eyeballs slightly bulging and with a sheen on them like black chinaware, making me want to tap them. Dr Earnest Hijo, MD.

He said, 'This is the explanation, dear sir. In Siberia, both men and women grow their hair to a great length in order to keep their heads warm. The louse is a good climber, slow and skilful. He has to be, so as not to alert his host. He creeps up through the body hair and he climbs up the seams of our clothes, leaving babies on the way to carry the good work forward. At night, when we are recumbent, he doesn't even need to climb.

He can stroll at his leisure and, what is more, do so in company. The louse is a sociable creature. I'm sure it would surprise you to know that on some of the corpses I examine, there can be as many as six thousand lice. A man carrying that number will never stop itching. Even asleep he'll be itching his bites. The skin gets broken. Along comes a troop of lice. They say to themselves, Huuh! here is a decent *benjo* at last. They excrete into the wound. That is the start of the trouble. All the diseases that lice cause start in this selfsame manner, which is to say, as a consequence of their excrement. They are my specialty, dear sir. I have devoted my life to *Pediculus humanus*.'

'The little brutes nearly did for me. Would've if it hadn't been for Kobi – you know, the Mongolian who comes to see me. Heart of gold. I'd be dead without him.'

'Yes, I am aware you've had typhus. The lesions on your body cannot be mistaken.'

'What sort of corpses do you get in here, doc?' I said, raising myself onto one elbow. 'I mean, do things vary between one nation and another? Are the Russians more particular about their health than you lot? That'd make an interesting study for you.'

'Anyone who dies comes to me,' he said. Then, 'Please excuse my poor Russian. What I meant is that I don't only get soldiers' bodies, I get the bodies of everyone. They are always brought to me, it is my command. You understand me now, Mr Doig, sir? This is the work which will make me famous throughout the world. Siberia in the present epoch offers opportunities that are available nowhere else. There are so many people here who are cold and starving – and also without hope, that is another important factor in the transmission of disease. And there are the Bolshevik prisoners. They all get sent to me. The General permits me to use them as I wish in my work.'

I said, 'Does it make me interesting that I've survived typhus?'

'Indeed. It also makes you immune to a further attack—'

'Is that all?'

'You should have allowed me to finish. I was going to say, and for that reason it makes you valuable.' He got up, jabbing his spectacles back up his nose. 'I have a use for people like you, Mr Doig, sir.'

Twenty-five

Toshi became my friend among the orderlies, all of whom were Japanese. From him I learned that Cynthia's protector and Hijo's superior was none other than the General Sato I'd been told about in Irkutsk. This man was in sole command of the Japanese military effort. A huge army had been assembled for him. The force presently at Zhigalovo was just an advance party. Soon thousands more men would be landed to fight the Reds. They'd push up the railway line from Vladivostok and take control of the whole of Siberia as far as Irkutsk. Sato was the man of the moment, Cynthia was his mistress, and between them –

'There'll soon be big money leaving this country, Doig-san, and where'll it be going? Into certain very large pockets, and they'll need to be very large, as you'll understand when I tell you where the General is now. I say nothing against the Countess. But she is an American, and the Americans have a great attachment to money, the world knows that. Therefore—'

Another orderly came into my room to do the cleaning – Toshi fell silent and began to change the dressing on my hand. As soon as the coast was clear, he continued.

The reason Sato hadn't been to visit me was that he'd gone down to Vladivostok to negotiate a gold-mining concession. He'd left in a furious temper because the bureaucrats were completely out of touch with conditions in the wilderness and the royalty they were demanding was wildly excessive. 'Six per cent,' Toshi said with authority—

'Five,' said Cynthia, wafting in with her furs swirling, cheeks pinkened by the sudden warmth in the hospital. 'I'll thank you to get the facts right, Toshi, and I'll thank you not to gossip behind my back. Now scram.'

She tossed her sombrero onto a chair. 'Royalties my ass. Donations, that's the real word for it. Five per cent's what they're asking for dredging gold, twelve for pickaxe work. Which is easier, dredging or hacking at rock? Right. So which should pay the larger royalty? Right again. They're idiots, like all politicians.' She glanced at my chart then plonked herself down in the chair with the hat on her lap. 'Assholes, typical desk assholes.'

I said, 'You've got to get me out of here. Hijo'll drive me crazy. He's so dedicated – you've only got to say 'good morning' to get a half-hour lecture on lice.'

She said, 'Why do you think I'm here?'

At that moment Hijo came in. Cyn said she was removing me, said it like that, no space for quibbling. He made as if he was considering a protest – hemmed and spluttered, fiddled with the four pens he always kept in the top outside pocket of his white coat. He said how much he'd miss our conversations – how rare it was to find anyone interested in insects – that he'd like to show me round his laboratory. He'd perfected a system for manufacturing typhus vaccine. It was a long way superior to Dr Weigl's –

'Not now you don't,' I said, throwing back the covers. 'I'm for off.'

Cyn put on her sombrero – made a face at Hijo for my benefit when his back was turned. Toshi laid out my shirt and trousers, bowed to me and stood to attention. Cyn, sitting there like a queen, said to him, 'Now show me every single seam and show me there are no lice anywhere. If just one of them gets into my house, the General'll have you whipped.'

Toshi went down every seam slowly with his thumbnail, inside and out.

She said to me, 'Carlos, you could use a visit to a decent haberdasher. Hey, Hijo-san, the man doesn't have any underpants. You expect him to keep ahead of the Reds without any underpants?' Saying nothing, the doctor left.

Swinging my legs out of bed, I said, 'The General on his way home, is he, hmm?'

She said, 'This isn't Manhattan. Communications are scanty.'

'Big fellow, is he?'

'Doing a spot of reconnaissance, are we?'

'You could say that.'

'OK, here's the picture. Not big but bulky. I'm not saying fat, not our General Sato. Solid, well fleshed, needs a decent horse under him, that's what I'm saying.' She grinned. Hers wasn't the pudding-bowl face you can get on Russian women. It was a quick, sharp Cohen face that split into all sorts of angular geometrical patterns when she grinned. 'I wouldn't want to be beaten by him. He's strong. Has a temper too. A two-minute job but when it blows, oh boy.'

'What do you do, jump clear?'

'I used to. Then I worked him out. He's a persecution guy at heart. Only has to see a street corner and he's sure there's a thrashing waiting for him around it. Like all the Japs. Comes from having an emperor they still think of as god. Yeah, really and truly! Most other nations had that crap beaten out of them centuries ago – pardon me, except for the Russkis who've only just got round to it. Anyway, when Sato flares up, I go down on all fours and start growling. Grrrr! I'm a guard dog, I'll look after you! Grrrr – zipf zipf! That always calms him, knowing there's someone going to protect him. Oh, he's a pet, really is, we get on fine together.'

I did a few steps, my first out of bed for a while. Cyn's lip curled as she eyed my hospital shift, which was a rough sort of calico.

Hijo came back in. Cyn said for him to drop round for sake as soon as Sato was back. Nodding at me, he said, 'I have to check him before he leaves.'

I said, 'You've done a great job. I'm fine.' Holding up my bandaged thumb, 'That's what we do when things are going well: stick our thumbs up.'

Hijo stared at me blankly. Cyn did the translating.

I said to her, 'I had no idea. Is there any limit to the lady's talents?'

'Four languages so far, all in American. Tell you about it later.'

Hijo was reluctant to let me go without an inspection. 'Of me or the lab?' I said.

'Of my patient, of course,' he said primly. 'A good doctor always errs on the safe side and I am a good modern doctor. I cannot let you out of the hospital without checking.'

Cynthia sighed and sat down again while Hijo listened to my chest, peered behind my eyes, tapped my kneecaps, enquired of Toshi about my stools and generally acted the busybody. I could see he'd had a surge of self-importance and was going to drag matters out in order to impress Cyn. 'Let's get on with it, for Christ's sake,' I cried, and whipping the calico shift over my head, stood to attention in front of him, naked as the day I was born. 'Tap my cock, doctor. That's what really counts.'

Toshi snickered with glee but not so the other orderly, who began hissing and pawing at me, trying to push me back into bed, all the while apologising to Hijo. Cyn stifled her giggles and stumbled from the room holding a handkerchief over her face.

I put my arm round Hijo's shoulders and gave him a good squeeze. 'I'll join you and Sato over that sake bottle, I'd like that. You've done me proud. Without you I'd have been a goner. You created life where there was no life, you – hell, how does that piece from the Bible go? Anyway, miracle worker. Thanks, Hijo-san,' and I squeezed him again and went on squeezing him until he started to purr.

Then I shook Toshi and his mate by the hand. The last one had got over his shock at my nakedness and was holding out new underpants. 'Drawers too,' I exclaimed, 'that's real service, that's stupendous, that's the first new clothing I've had in two years.'

Hijo said, 'Please observe, Doig-san, that the material is silk. It is not our best silk but it is silk and that is important. Silk is too slippery for lice to climb, it is a fact. You have only to inspect your lower limbs regularly and you'll stay healthy and living.'

I said, 'As a matter of interest, how long can a louse feed off a corpse, doc?'

He said, 'Fourteen days from the date of death and no more. Now please, get into the clothes before the Countess returns.'

Toshi, acting as my valet, had grabbed the pants from the other orderly and now held them ready for me to step into,

116

the right leg lower than the other. My hand on the top of his head to balance myself, I got the pants above my knees – slowly, with one or two small convalescent wobbles. A bit tight in places, but then the Japs are built differently. The slickness of that silk, the gloss, the perfume! 'Ecstasy,' I murmured to Hijo. Toshi, standing behind me, drew them up over my thighs, stretched the waist elastic to completely capture my backside, pinged it tight and with a cry of laughter slapped me on both buttocks simultaneously.

I swatted at him behind my back, saying, 'Watch out, everyone, there's a wasp in here,' which raised a laugh. Then I did a slow knees-bend. I trailed my hands up those wonderful pants. Words were exchanged between the orderlies followed by more laughter. I knew they were saying something like, 'He may think he's a ladykiller but he'd better watch out for Sato.' I said to Hijo, 'Tell them, "Sure, I wasn't born yesterday."'

I looked down at my svelte and shining advertisement thighs. I thought, Christ, you fellows really know about laundering, smart is good, smart is success, no wonder Togo wapped the Russian fleet at Tsushima if all his sailors were turned out like this.

Hijo said, 'A parcel with two more pairs is waiting for you at the main door. A gift from the people of Japan.'

I thanked him, I thanked them all, bowed left and right – collected the parcel of drawers and went out into the cold evening with a goodly feeling towards humanity.

The same fat coachman opened the carriage door. I stepped up, had to have him shove me the last little bit, being still somewhat groggy on my pins, and flopped down beside La Zipfa.

She'd had the great idea of bringing along a couple of foot warmers – stoneware bottles with hot water inside. She said, 'I told you I wasn't leaving the place by myself.'

We rattled across the cobbles of Zhigalovo's central square in silence. As we turned down the hill by the barracks, she said, 'You remember the Archangel Timber Company? That I said you should have a flutter on it? Just when Lenin was getting into his stride?'

'Do I not! A dog, if ever there was one.'

'You remember me saying I'd make up for it?' which she said in a voice that was suddenly as soft as summer.

'Yeah, I remember that too.'

'I keep my word. I always keep my word,' and she rubbed her foot against mine.

Then her voice toughened up and she said, 'But first I have to make something clear.'

I liked her for this. Firing from the hip. No false coyness. 'About the General . . .' I said, wanting to get more of a feel for the man.

'Exactly, Sato-san. He's been a real blessing to me. I don't know where I'd be without him, in one of Semyonov's cages maybe. I'm not someone who acts grateful and then kicks her man in the teeth. That just gives a girl a bad name. So this is the deal, OK? I told you to invest, you lost money, now I'm repaying you. Squaring up a debt, that's what I'll be doing. We'll have a good time then that's it, nothing clinging, OK? Look at me and say OK.'

'OK.'

'Great. That's good clean air flowing between us, I can feel it already. You know, Carlos, I really am a straight up-and-down sort of girl—'

'Please, Countess!'

'OK, maybe that was a bit strong. What I meant was that I always intend to be a good traditional Jewish girl. I see a man first time and I think, Yep, he's a hound all right and as I go to sleep I'm thinking, hound hound hound, one thing only on his mind, but you know what, come the morning I begin to think, whoa, perhaps that was too quick a judgement and maybe he's not a hound at all but a fellow who just happens to be kind and intelligent and it's not his fault he's darned handsome as well and what's wrong with having just one Martini with him, no gin in it to speak of. I mean, come on, Cyn, you've only got one life, that's what I end up by thinking. It's a healthy philosophy to have. Keeps one from mouldering away. However, no one could have started out with finer intentions.'

'But . . .'

'You've got it. But circumstances have gone against me.'

She slipped her hands out of her fur muff and enclosed mine. Her hands were warm and pink and fleshy, short strong hands.

We said nothing more. Tap tap tap went the reindeer's hooves, crimple crimple went the golden bracelets round the wheels – the freezing air of Siberia rushed past the window as the snow-laden branches of the fir trees braced themselves for another hard night.

Twenty-six

$\mathbf{T}$HE FRONT door swung open. A grizzled servitor in a long grey robe bowed to us – positioned the indoor slippers for our greatest convenience – helped us off with our boots – set down a ewer of hot water on the low table between us – stood waiting with a crisp white napkin over her forearm – and when dismissed shuffled backwards into the main body of the house, abasing herself to Cynthia.

'Mushi,' said Cyn economically.

We followed her into a large open room – still retreating, still bowing. She halted and gestured with a dipping motion of her arm to a table laden with food. Cyn thanked her: she bowed herself out.

I said, 'There's got to be a better word for this than just food. Cornucopia's too small. Like my stomach, which is shrivelled. I haven't seen a table like this since my wedding feast.'

'Bet you can eat it if you try,' she said.

What had been prepared for us: cold meats sliced as thin as paper, eels done in about seven different ways, fillets of young winter pike, a brilliant scarlet-and-black lacquer rice cask from which the grains of rice – which were far larger than any I'd seen before – gleamed like the best sort of pearls, curds and pickled cucumbers and pickled radishes and unknown pickled things in graceful round bowls, and things being kept hot over small spirit lamps, and on one huge silver dish a boar's head complete with its tusks and snarling teeth and on another a juicy rump of reindeer, as I supposed it. There were fragrances and wisps of steam and invisible among it all were intimations of lust that were on the one hand denied by a set of brand-new candles, which gave the whole thing a decorous temple atmosphere, and on the other hand affirmed by the cushions that were lying around all soft and cosseted and waiting for our bodies.

'Tiberius has been here. He's been giving you lessons,' I said in awe.

'Whatever did happen to that statue of him, the one that used to face you as you drove up to Uncle Igor's palace?'

'I stuck it on the front of my train to infuriate the Reds. They shot at it first, and us second – invariably. Then it fell to bits and I discovered it was made not of ancient marble but of modern concrete. Uncle Igor had been sold a pup.'

'Rich men are easily tricked. Sake or vodka, Nip or Russki, which is it to be?'

'Vodka,' I said, not being ready to go over to Japanese ways. Standing over the banquet, we clinked glasses. '*Kanpai*!' she said, which I repeated.

I said, 'How come you got this lot together?'

'Easy. I wasn't leaving the hospital without you, that was my starting point. Charlie, just reverting for a moment to our previous conversation, if I know I'm leaving smooth water behind me, I can deal better with the storms out there ahead. I don't want nasty stuff popping up out of the past. Always shift the backlog, that's my motto. That's what this is all about.'

'I'm nasty stuff?'

'Nope, but you're a debt. In a while we'll go upstairs and get all square.'

'Then?'

'Then I'll look at you differently.'

Just glancing at the food had made my juices race like a cougar. I picked out an eel tail and dropped it into my mouth, my head right back.

She was standing with her hands resting on her hips. She watched me swallow the eel, watched me considering in turn the vodka bottle peeping out of the shimmering tumble of ice blocks, the mats and cushions on the floor, the paper lanterns, the big blue-tiled stove up against the wall – she was watching me as I turned my head to the staircase of bright new wood that circled the stovepipe and glided upwards with easy, inviting steps to the bedroom.

Soft, downy candlelight spilled out above us.

She put her head on one side. 'Which comes first?'

I looked at her, I looked at the laden table, I looked at the staircase.

She said, 'Upstairs there are two dishes of *zapiski* to keep you going.' Then her eyes grew playful and her face crinkled and I knew she wasn't thinking any longer about the Archangel Timber Company.

We approached the bottom of the staircase from our different angles. I ended up on her right. With her left hand she took a pinch of the hem of her dress, which was made of a soft green velvety material – a good match for her dark chestnut hair and creamy complexion. It was buttoned down the front. The buttons, which were shiny black, were partially concealed by a strip, no wider than a mouse, of some rare Arctic fur that ran from the bottom of her dress right up to the base of her throat and there turned into a collar.

That green material, it was a close fit. She had deep, generous breasts. Swaying breasts, stately breasts, my first breasts for seven months. The fur trim running between them gave me the idea of a cleft, which grew more vivid with every step.

Halfway up I just had to stop. Her right hand was in my left. Pointing downwards, I said, 'Look what you've done to me.'

'Like a schoolboy,' she laughed, eyes flashing, tossing her hair back. 'My first boyfriend was the same. Arnie Feldstein, the guy on the boat to Europe who taught me poker. His bunk in a gale was an experience by itself.' Looking down again, 'That's pure Arnie, showing off like that.'

'Seven months' worth,' I cried, 'what do you expect?'

'From you, Charlie, the best. Now, are we going to do it on the stairs or what?'

Saying this, she placed her foot on the next tread – it was her answer.

She was wearing silk stockings, I could see the loose folds above the heel of her slipper. Hmm, I thought, go carefully there, that's real money she's wearing, even if it's Sato's.

I said, 'I bought a lot of shares in Archangel Timber.'

She said, 'History'll remember Russia and 1917. You can't

run a world without money . . . Oh, I see what you mean. Don't worry, you'll get full value.'

The staircase had completed its curl round the stovepipe. I could see right into her room, could see the futon, already unrolled, the rack of towels, her bedside book, the soft yellow buds of the candles.

Cocky began to yell at me, Sod the shares and crack on, Charlie, drag her up there, push her up there, for God's sake get her clothes off and tuck me in.

I said, 'As to the whereabouts of the General—'

'Nothing to concern you there. That's the great thing about Russia. Whenever a man has to jump from a bedroom window, there's always a snowdrift beneath it.'

I said, 'I'd make it, but it wouldn't go well for you. Not if he's like you say.'

She said, 'Honey, would I be leading you up the staircase just to get you into trouble? Here's the truth of it. When he's leaving Vladi, he cables me. The guy at the station who operates the telegraph collars one of the Nip soldiers who trots down to me with the cable. I get myself ready. Two or three days later he's here. Comes riding a white horse down from the station. The horse is called Inazuma, which means lightning. He thinks it makes him look like Lochinvar.'

'So no cable, no Sato?'

'That's it.'

'How it'd be if bandits had cut down all the telegraph poles for firewood?' I said, wishing I didn't have in my mind such a perfectly formed image of General Sato with his heftiness and his thunder-and-lightning charger and his million-acre gold concession.

'You want me or you don't want me?' she cried.

I said, 'I sure as hell hope that cable of his gets here before he does,' and gripping her right buttock I propelled her up the last three steps at the trot and into the bedroom.

'I'll show you what I want,' I muttered as I started to strip, and before anyone could have said rikitikitavi I was down to my silk underpants.

She said something like, 'It's so easy for men,' and then she had her dress unbuttoned down the furry cleft and was smiling

123

at me, was laughing, was stepping out of it as the green velvet crumpled to the floor and her thick, warm, earthy odour, which could have belonged to no other woman, came wafting across the room and made my nostrils swell. We measured each other off, both of us laughing. I knew I was rough, I knew I wasn't going to win any prizes as boudoir man, but that's how it was for me after seven months, with Cyn standing right there flaunting what every woman should flaunt and as proud of it as Eve.

Her thighs glowed between the top of her stockings and the bottom of her garter belt. They glowed, they dimpled, Oh God, great God, the flesh of angels, that's what I was seeing, unprotected by anything except the flimsy thongs of her garter belt, which I could snap between my fingers—

And now she was smiling at me in a different way, with the funny cracked smile of experience – such a smile! All the giving spirit of womanhood was there, all the generosity, the tender-ness, the understanding – she undid her bodice, tumbled out her breasts and sort of shoogled them at me, as if I needed the excitement—

'Even as a schoolgirl I'd get glances,' she said, pouting play-fully. 'Girls love glances.'

'Don't do that,' I whispered, 'it'll finish me off.'

My fingers were jumping like tiddlywinks, couldn't have opened a door to let the cat out.

She came gliding up to me, everything swaying, not a rib in sight, a miracle.

Hopping about as if I had a scorpion in my underpants, I scrabbled them down past my knees, then had to caper around with one foot stuck.

She bent down to help, a little sideways, knees together, beautiful smooth creamy haunches. 'We don't want to split those nice new pants, do we, Carlos? Here, let me – first we extricate the foot – and then – oh my, that's quite something, Mr Doig, just a little lick as we pass – will he hold for a lick? – there, he held, and on we go, onwards and upwards,' which she did, trailing her fantastic breasts up my chest as she straightened.

She stepped back. My cock was out there quivering like a compass needle. She took it between both hands.

'Take care of my stockings. They really cost. The General won't—'

I could stand no more. I grabbed her, shoved both hands under the belt and all the eyes and hooks and poppits flew away pinging. I swung her up into my arms.

'Caveman, *primitivo*,' she purred, still somehow holding on to my cock.

I got her down on the futon.

She murmured, 'The stockings may be the only silk ones in all of Siberia.' A moment later, closing her eyes, 'They'd better be.'

I said nothing to that, went on rolling them down as fast as I could, thinking of the pink and marbled flesh of angels and their popping cheeks and swept-back wings as they hurtled down for a close-up. I scuttered the stockings round her heels, which were a little calloused.

'They can split at the toes, be careful,' she whispered. 'Be careful – but be quick, Oh, Charlie, for God's sake be quick.'

Twenty-seven

SHE – PERKY, curious about my story, sitting up in bed with a brown woollen shawl around her shoulders. I – spent, slovenly, stretched out, one hand limp on her thigh, the other ferrying *zapiski* into my mouth from the bowl on the floor, thinking about the vodka downstairs and whether the pike had been boned.

She said, 'You know, Charlie, not once since I left New York have I thought, gee, I wish I'd stayed at home. I was a tough kid on a tough street. The Lower East Side was good training for the Revolution.'

I said, 'Was that kid tougher in New York than this kid was in Moscow?'

'Oh sure. If I recall it rightly, the Moscow kid was a rich one.'

'It was all gone by the time my parents married.'

'Father? Wasn't he a bit touch-and-go? Tell me if I overstep the mark.'

'He took chances, made promises he couldn't keep and stacked up a mountain of debts. It all came out when he died. He didn't even make forty so heaven knows what he might have done if he'd been spared. It was bubonic plague that got him. I thought Hijo would have been more interested when I told him.'

'Too concerned with his typhus business. Not enough people get plague to make it worthwhile, that's what he'd say. But he's Sato's affair. Hijo belongs to him. Two humanitarians hard at work, I don't think. Go on.'

'My mother was knocked out by his death. The money we

lived off came from Uncle Igor. The rest of our Russian relatives all thought Father was a rascal who'd got what he deserved. I was fourteen.' I took a grip of her thigh. 'My dad and your Mr Zipf, what a mess they could have made of the world if they'd gone into business together.'

'OK,' she said, 'so I was wrong about the money. It was all those posh Rykov connections, plus the way you walked down Nevsky – chest out, look at me, here's Charles the Great.'

'All a pose. Acting broke never won a woman.'

'Uncle Igor left you nothing?'

I said, 'Lenin got there first,' and with a jolt remembered I'd left my boots and therefore my wealth in the vestibule. I said warily, 'Mushi still hanging around, is she?'

'Her name means "insect". The General makes her live in a shed at the end of the house. That's where she'll be.' She went straight on, 'My attitude to money was born on the boat over to Paris: Arnie taught me at the poker table. I've learned how to look after myself, that's what I mean. I'm not after billions, not stupid money. A low figure of millions will do me fine. Same for you?'

She spoke with confidence, as if icebergs, earthquakes and war existed for everyone but her. It seemed to me that the thigh I was holding was throbbing like the skin of one of those big African war drums – I said 'Zipfa, do you have a dynamo factory inside you?' and then I rolled over, got under the shawl with her, and, since we were talking about proper money, launched straight away into my gold barge story.

'Mmm, sounds *un peu* interesting. Of course you took some bearings as the boat went down,' she said, picturing the great grey sweep of the Volga in a winter flood, a mile in width, and thinking to herself, where the hell's the treasure in all that? She spoke lazily, but her eyeballs were twitching.

I said I hadn't written down a single thing in case it fell into the wrong hands. But I knew exactly where it was.

'A couple of days below Kazan, huh?' she said next, quite sharply. Then, 'That gold you gave away, a ton of the Tsar's red gold – that cuts at a woman's heart. She can see so clearly the things she could've had made out of it, the bangles and bracelets and sauce boats and curtain rings and statuary for the dinner

table, all of it with that nice flush that'd pick up her skin tones
– frankly, Charlie, that was dumb of you . . . What purity, huh?'

'Top grade,' I said.

She rolled up her fingers and stuck her fist under my nose.
'Tell me it's a hundred per cent, make me suffer, make the welts
bleed like fresh, I mean, I don't just mean goddamn, I mean
jesuschristgoddamn, what made you do a thing like that? A whole
ton given away like sweeties? How many ounces does that make
at how many bucks an ounce, Christ' – voice rising – 'good
Yankee bucks as well, not the junk you get here, Christ almighty'
– she fell back onto the pillows and threw out her arms sideways, an elbow catching me in the eye – 'it gives me a migraine
just to think about it. At least that guy Boltikov got nothing. I
disliked him from the very start. Creep, if you ask me.'

Cynthia riled up was a performance. Other women get lemon-
lipped and keep a bundle of gripes in reserve for a later date.
But Cyn didn't hold back, and nor did I. We went at it hammer
and tongs until she cornered me in my last defensive position
and forced me to admit that I'd only ever inspected a few of
the ingots.

She was speechless. I repeated myself. The ingots had been
wrapped in sacking. On the sacking had been the red seal of
the Imperial Bank of Russia and the serial number of the ingot.
Why would a rational man have wanted to see more than half
a dozen?

The moment I said it, I twigged what she was driving at. You
meet a woman with a good hard mind like Cyn's and you've
got to admire her. I gawped, all the puff vanishing from my
argument in a flash. What if someone had pulled a fast one on
the Tsar? What if there hadn't been gold under the top layer
but something worthless, like slabs of granite?

I began to laugh. 'One hundred per cent pure stone!'

'You've got it, Charlie. Royal crap.'

Tears of laughter started. To think that maybe I'd risked my
life for rubbish! It got so that I could scarcely form my words.
'But the Davidova woman will have defended her ingots with
her life, I know it. The Reds'll have caught her she's so weighed
down and just as the firing squad's lining her up at the regulation
eight paces, someone'll say, "Madama, actually it's only granite

but we're going to shoot you anyway." Oh my God, wouldn't that be hilarious?'

I know why I found that idea so funny, because she'd been a pest from the moment I rescued her and I was thinking about her sounding off at the firing squad. But of course Cyn had never experienced her awfulness. She said, 'Oh yeah, completely hilarious, the poor girl. Now let's get serious again. I'll give you the benefit of the doubt and we'll call it gold. There are twenty-seven tons of it at the bottom of the Volga but here you are going in the opposite direction. Tell me about that.'

I said, 'I'd never have got it to Odessa and onto a ship, it's as simple as that. But for a couple of days I was the richest man in Russia.'

She sighed. 'Yeah, you're probably right, the Reds would've caught you somewhere on the steppe. You'd never have gone fast enough, not carrying as much gold as that. You should've got it onto a train, hired some men with guns and then gone like a bat out of hell for the high seas. First stop Lake Michigan. Chicago dockside on a foggy morning. Armoured car, bodyguard, hoods plus shooters on the running board, all that business. You'd've found buyers in Chicago . . . but what I want to know is how come you're moving on when you've got treasure stashed in the Volga? Too tricky to go back? Too impossible?'

'Call it a long-term interest.'

She wrinkled her nose: 'Do I smell *un peu de merde* in that reply? Long-term interest – whose? No, don't say anything, we'll let it pass for now. So where are you aiming? The truth, Charlie. We're survivors, we have to share stuff.'

I said cautiously, 'I had a bit of luck on my way here.'

'Oh that! You and your big-pal luck. Destiny's another one of those feeble ideas. Whenever I hear someone say, it wasn't my fault, it was written in the stars, i.e. *it was destiny*, I want to throw up. So what did the old lady bring you, a brand-new beetle with your name on it or what?'

I grinned, flickered my eyebrows, tantalised her a bit – and went down the curving stairs and got us each a vodka, big ones, so cold it frosted up the glasses. Then we snuggled up and I told her about the sacred bird. I had a collector ready to buy it, a man living in Nagasaki who'd been outbid for the jewel beetle by the Field Museum. I'd be set up for life. 'Two *doigii* to my name and only just turning thirty. That can't be bad.'

Twenty-eight

HER HEAD was in the crook between my shoulder and my ear. She eased her way out, stared up at me with narrowed eyes. 'The bird of legend pouched by Charlie Doig? Actually in the bag? Not still hopping around somewhere?'

'Yes.'

'Wow. The only one and Charlie has it? That's classy.' Then, spilling out of her, full of scepticism, 'How d'ya manage not to shoot it to shreds, you tell me that, buster?'

'With a blowpipe.' I put an imaginary one to my lips. '*Phht, phht.* Watch my cheeks. I do it exactly as if I were an opera singer.'

'A *blowpipe?*'

'Yes.'

'No kidding . . . a goddamn blowpipe . . . well, I guess I'm just not a country girl. You know, you're quite a fellow, Carlos. You survive, you kill the baddie, you even manage to lean out of the cab and grab the gold as you flee. You should have a word with my old man, he's looking for guys who can come across as Russians – the likely sort, men like you, not halfwits. But – hey, you sure none of these Tungus tribesmen are after you? Killing their sacred bird, well, that must be like killing their god. I mean, pardon my *français*, but who killed fucking cock robin, that's what I'd be asking if I was one of them and I found the corpse. Sato wouldn't thank us if a thousand Tungus came out of the woods whooping and hollering. Them first, then us.' She drew her finger across her throat. 'He's capable of it, believe you me.'

I kept quiet while she ruminated, sipping her vodka. Then

she put the glass down and said, 'So what's the little birdie worth?'

I wasn't telling her that any more than I was telling her about the diamonds in my boots. So I just repeated myself, about a buyer who lived in Nagasaki. She said, 'Well done, lots of dough in Japan right now. You may think of them as fuddy-duddies but you're wrong – I shouldn't be telling you this, Charlie, but we've got a good thing in the offing, that's what my old man's doing now—'

'You and Sato together?'

'Sure. He's a solid customer, has lots of contacts in government and the military. And I—'

'And you're Cynthia Cohen from the Lower East Side.'

'Put it like this, when it comes to business, there are things I think of before he does, enough said? Boy, are there opportunities out here! That guy Lenin doesn't know the half of what he's let out of the bag. But I have to point them out to my fellow . . . that Lala bird – hell, that's such a fabulous thing to have done, to have shot a bird-god no one's ever seen before – hey, how about we make copies of it? Shouldn't be difficult – big feathers, medium feathers, some nice downy stuff, then a couple of itsy-bitsy feet and a beak – I'd say there must be lots of those items lying around if one knew where to look.'

I told her there were other things a scientist would consider and listed a dozen, snapping them off on my fingers as I went. She listened carefully, nibbling away at her lower lip, then said, 'Correct me if you need to, but I reckon that if the Lala breed has figured out the body parts that suit it best, we humans can do it as well. Aren't we cleverer than birds, didn't Plato or one of those guys prove that? So if some collector says our copy's missing something, hey, we just hire someone to make it for us. We should think about this.'

She continued bright as a spark, knocking her vodka back and thumping the glass down. 'Once one museum has it they'll all want a Lala skin. Take away their white coats and you'll find these scientists are snobs and charlatans like anyone else. You're in with them, you should know.'

I said it was a fundamentally dishonest thing to do – scientists

132

were meant to be above lies – that my reputation would be dirt when the trick was uncovered.

That made her laugh, me bringing my reputation into it. 'There's a fortune waiting for us out there, too bad you're so choosy . . . I'm getting up, I've had enough of this lounging around. Want to see how Cynthia von Zipf looks in a kimono?'

But she'd only got into her garter belt and clipped on the silk stockings when she had a fresh idea. Throwing her arms wide—

'For all averred, I had killed the Bird
That made the breeze to blow.
Instead of the cross, the Albatross
About my neck was hung.

'Tant piss for cock robin, it's the albatross I'm now seeing in the frame. You want to watch out it doesn't do for you what it did for the wedding guest. He had a bad time after he shot it and his chums had worse. Don't you look at me like that. I'm not some ill-educated booby, I'm a Jew and Jews pass their exams. Great illustrations in my copy, would keep me awake half the night. So you watch it, you make sure that Lala bird of yours doesn't turn into an albatross.'

She got into an under-kimono and had me tie the tapes from behind. 'I simply *adore* all this bogey-bogey business. Like the poker school on the liner, like Zipf and his debts, like the night Lenin took over, like being the special friend of a Jap general, like you walking in from the wilderness, like this gold-mine concession – that's all pure Cynthia. I'm not a retail lady, definitely not, bogey-bogey's the name of the game for me . . . You sure you want to see me in my full Jap outfit? Why not look at it in the chest? By the way, that's big money in Japan, a kimono stash. I'm getting to be like a geisha.'

There she was, not a tall woman but a woman who filled every corner of her skin, packed it out with brains and gelignite – standing there in her under-kimono, her face full of zest, I being the first non-hostile white person she could have seen for months – and there was I, lazy after love, relishing her chatter and thinking about the sweetmeats below. The two of us were behaving as if we had the year to ourselves and snow was falling

133

outside making it all nice and cosy and we had someone to chop wood and stoke the stove and Lenin had never been born – when crash! the front door went rocking back and Mushi's voice flew screeching up the staircase.

I knew instantly what it was and so did Cyn.

No one can ever have moved faster than we did. 'And for Christ's sake wipe my fingerprints off your fanny,' I yelled up the stairs as I pulled on my diamond boots and sprinted towards the kitchen and the back door.

Twenty-nine

'Sorry about this, babushka –' I ran past Mushi, naked except for my boots, all my stuff bundled in my arms.

'The store shed,' Cyn shouted after me and within seconds I was there, shoving my clothes on, back to front, top to bottom, it didn't matter how as long as they went on, it was so bloody cold in that shed. It'd been knocked together to house the building materials for the mansion. Bits and pieces everywhere – rats too, scurryings and rustlings and small chittering sounds like I used to hear all night long in the Burmese jungle.

The door had a spyhole, presumably having once been hung on an outside shithouse, the hole so positioned that an employer could check his fellow wasn't reading the newspaper. I peered out, still getting my breath back.

First came Mushi to light the resin flambeaux above the front door. Having done so, she stepped away and stood with her back to the wall of the house. She was in her serving dress, a white towel folded over her hands. I said to myself, hope you're wearing leggings and they're really good woollen ones and go all the way up.

Cyn stuck her nose out to see where the carriage had got to – its two oil lamps were jinking through the trees about a hundred yards away. From the sound of it, a horse was tied on behind the carriage, which I supposed to be Inazuma, Sato's charger. The man would have come up the line in a private carriage with heating and waiters and maroon plush seats and an overhead green-shaded reading light beneath which he'd have studied the details of his gold concession, making pencil notes in the margin to impress Cynthia – glancing out at the tiny

135

snow-mantled fields of the peasant farmers and the palisades of fir trees massed against the pale sky – staring at the snow, always snow wherever he went. Bloody snow, he'd have thought, day after day of it – and would've settled back in his seat to dream of the first wave of summer heat in his home town.

Which would probably be Kyoto, somewhere smart like that.

Then the reindeer was bringing the black-box carriage round in a circle in front of the mansion with Inazuma slithering along behind.

Showing off, just like any man with his woman – and there she was, framed beneath the flambeaux in the doorway, in full Japanese regalia, God knows how she'd managed it so quickly – kimono and butterfly-shaped obi, slippers, hair in a bun with a stick through it. Bowing too, the lady from the Lower East Side bowing to a son of Nippon, that told me how much power he had.

The carriage halted. Cyn and Mushi remained bowed. For a moment nothing happened.

From the station came the sound of a locomotive shunting, maybe preparing a troop train for the morning.

The moon, round and yellow, watched from about three-quarters of the way down the line of firs – was resting on the topmost boughs, as if the cosmos god had bowled it down them.

Everything stood still, time suspended.

The Emperor cometh, hail the Emperor, and hail to you, General Sato, I just nipped out in time. Your girl's a wonder, don't you go mistreating her.

But why the devil didn't he get out and show himself?

Then suddenly the coachman had thrown off his rugs and jumped down from his box with remarkable speed for such a fat fellow. He unfolded the steps, retired a couple of paces and stood with his head bowed. The stooping figure of General Sato, lover and protector of Countess Cynthia von Zipf, placed a shining black boot on the top step, slapped aside the coachman's proffered paw and descended, his long dress sword bouncing behind him on the steps.

Getting himself dolled up for his Countess, that's what he'd been doing.

He raised his cap stiffly, his skull gleaming from a recent shave. He bowed to Cyn, as well he might, she being the brains in their arrangement. She returned the bow with a faint smile, which was obviously legitimate for their degree of familiarity. As she raised her head she gave it a little toss, in the Western style. She'd put them on specially for him – earrings like chandeliers, a hundred diamonds in each flashing like fireflies in the light of the flambeaux. She'd have a chest crammed with jewels and necklaces, bulging with the stuff, putting real pressure on the hasp, I'd bet on it.

Sato flipped his sword off the last rung of the steps, got himself properly squared away, then looked up, not at Cyn but straight at my hut – at me. Forty yards away or less, the moon like a million candlewatts above us. Maybe catching the glint of my eyeball viewing him through the shithouse peephole, could that be why?

I drew back, making everything smaller, so that I had him and him alone in the aperture – Sato and his sword and the carriage door which the coachman couldn't close because his master was standing in the way looking at me.

Automatically I began to breathe through my mouth; one makes far less noise like that.

He was exactly as Cyn had said, short and bulky with a trim black moustache. Polished black knee boots, puffed-out twill breeches, uniform with ribbons on his breast, military cap. Nothing showy. But strong: a vigorous man who understood that the power he had was to be shared on his terms alone.

He continued to stare at me. Then he snapped his fingers and spoke harshly to the coachman – raised his fist at him. I understood immediately. Sato hadn't been looking at me, he'd been waiting for something to be fetched from the carriage and didn't expect to have to ask for it. Sure enough, in two seconds the coachman was holding it out with much bowing and scraping – a long grey wolfskin cloak. Sato swept it round his shoulders, buckled it at the neck, and only then did he go to the house.

Mushi bowed to him. He took the towel and wiped his face and his hands. He held out his cap. Bowing, she took it.

Then he advanced on Cynthia – Mushi came between us and obscured my view so that I never saw how they greeted each other. I heard the front door close. I heard a gong sound from within the house, presumably to give thanks for Sato's safe return. In a moment or two, Mushi would be displaying that magnificent banquet to him. Mushi and Cyn together, allies conniving to keep him sweet. Lucky I hadn't got stuck into the food myself. How'd she ever have accounted for the scarlet-and-black lacquered rice cask being half empty or the plates robbed of meat or the things I'd chewed at a bit and said how disgusting and spat onto the floor?

Which comes first? she'd said, giving me the eye, and without ado we'd made for upstairs. Not for the food and drink, which the body can do without for long periods, but to satisfy our lust, which is the greater imperative by far. So it was all still present and correct except for one small eel. Thank God!

And now he'd be changing out of his uniform into a belted robe that'd stop halfway up his hairy calves. He might have gone with a whore in Vladivostok or had one on his train and so would be too spent to have Cyn. But I didn't think so. That look as he waited for his wolfskin cloak – the cloak itself – everything that I'd glimpsed proclaimed his virility. The sword'd be part of that whole idea.

He'd jump the Countess as soon as Mushi closed the door. She'd be wanting to get her hands on the small print of the gold concession and see if he'd conceded too much. The royalty rate, that'd come first. Then the method by which the output tonnage was to be verified, she'd home in on that like a terrier. Was she a cheat? No, but she was a Cohen from the Lower East Side. You say the word percentage to her and she'd say, honey, a percentage of what, exactly? – no no, I mean *exactly*, that was how she'd say it.

But he was the boss, he'd get what he wanted.

And Cynthia would go down on the futon with him and really put her back into it, because she belonged to him, and for the moment there was no alternative. Maybe she wasn't even thinking about an alternative. Maybe she'd said to herself, I've had enough traipsing around, I'm gonna stick with this guy with his bald head and wolfskin cloak. He needs me, I can be true and tender if I try. She could have. She always kept her word, that's what she'd told me.

Thirty

THE COACHMAN was fishing around in his pocket for titbits for the reindeer and Inazuma. This done, he climbed up onto his box, got under all his rugs and drove back up the hill. The moon had dipped below the trees, leaving the mansion in a sort of twilight. The white charger was like a ghost trotting through the woods.

Now silence lay everywhere, cold and empty. I turned away from the peephole and, putting my hands in front of me, began to feel my way round.

The sensation – I can't easily describe it. If you were diving for abalone, thinking solely about their shape beneath the sand, and an octopus grabbed you – uncoiled a tentacle and whipped it out of its grotto, unerringly, like a Cossack with his lash – that might be about the same. Kobi had often come to see me in the field hospital. But on this, the day of my release, he'd been totally expelled from my mind by the pleasures of Cynthia. And now his hand shot out just as I've said and pincered my ankle with fingers of steel. Of course I knew whose hand it was, but there were two or three seconds of uncharted territory – it's the same when you switch on electric light, there's a pause before the bulb shines. I thought, Christ, it's one of those Tungus, it's Eyk or someone sent to kill me. The albatross could still have been in my mind, or maybe I felt plain guilty. Anyway, Tungus was what I thought, and I kicked out, which of course got me nowhere with Kobi.

He said, 'I've got a woman with me. There are more sacks in the corner, you can have those.'

Sleep didn't come easily, it never does when it's as cold as that. And something was bothering me about the manner of Sato's homecoming.

I lay huddled while the rats pattered around. Moonlight was streaming in again and I could see them very clearly – watched them as I turned Sato over in my mind. Diligent, capable, fussy animals are rats, and excellent to eat. One big bastard got a bit too interested in me so the next time he came within reach I snuck out my hand and broke his neck. You can do that with rats if you're quick because their bones are so brittle. Get them where a dog does, just above the shoulders, and flick them. The weight of the body acting against the vertebrae in the neck does the rest.

I got up and threw it out of the door. I reckoned if they were that hungry, they'd all leave the hut and go and eat it – which is what happened.

I got myself comfortable again – and it was then that I realised, almost out of the blue, what had been giving me the itch. That stopped my brain racing and I had a good bit of sleep until dawn when Kobi set about his woman again.

The heap of old sacks and dust sheets and bits of tarpaulin quivered, then broke into a trot and finally a gallop. The dust started to fly. She broke into a fit of sneezing. Kobi must have clamped his hand over her mouth and she must have bitten it for there was a sudden uproar in their corner.

As soon as they'd finished, I went over and rolled Kobi's buttocks to and fro with my foot until he raised himself from her. Looking up at me, he said sulkily, 'I didn't do that to you.'

I said, 'I didn't make as much noise.' And then, 'Tell the girl to go home. We're getting out of here.'

He knuckled his eyes, began to pay attention.

'I don't trust our friend the Countess, that's why. We're being set up for something. Bogey-bogey business is what gets her excited and last night was part of it. There were just too many coincidences – my getting out of the hospital, a banquet on the table, drink, the bed all handy – and then suddenly Sato turns up, straight out of the night. Every time before he's given her two or three days' notice. But this time, by chance when I'm there in his bed, he arrives without any sort of warning. Is that the work of pure chance or is it her playing bogey-bogey games? We don't need to take the risk.'

Kobi stood up. Turning his back on me, he buttoned himself. The girl, a large, fat girl in the Russian build, very red in the face and with straw twined through her hair, yelped about the cold and grabbed at her clothes.

Kobi said to me, 'I don't understand. Wasn't she good enough?'

I said, 'You really don't? A woman who loves play-acting and dressing up, who loves complications just for the sake of them, you can't see the dangers for us there? How far'd you trust her – you tell me that.'

'Isn't everything complicated?'

'OK, it's the cold that's making you a bit slow this morning. So here's how I see it in nice small words. The Countess is a woman who gets her thrills from watching people jump through hoops which she herself is holding. Suddenly she whips a hoop away and you fall into a pit of deadly snakes, which makes her laugh like hell. Bogey-bogey business, that's what that is. Hang around and we could become part of her game, that's what I'm saying.'

He stretched and said, 'We leave right now?'

'Yep. Move the girl along, chop-chop.'

Best was going to be for him to take the girl home and while he was passing the station to ask about trains going east. 'I heard shunting going on last night, and Sato arrived on one. So they can't say they've got neither the locomotives nor the rolling stock. Lay it on thick about being a pal of the General. Might help.'

However, this was easier said than done, for the girl had qualms about being seen walking through the village at dawn with an unmarried man.

Let me rephrase that: first she had a piss in the straw, full on to us, farting as she went, and when she saw Kobi avert his face, *then* she came out with the qualms. When they did her no good, she had herself pregnant by him. Hadn't he done her every night – and sometimes twice a night – since I went into hospital? Here she had an advantage over me, for I had no idea how long I'd been grounded. She spotted it in an instant, came close to me and, tipping up her red puffy face, started in on a story about her nine impoverished siblings and the earthen floor of their hut – until Kobi said, 'Pay her some money, Doig, they're all like this,' and while she slipped away into the woods, he shouldered our pack, I took the rifles and we went over to the front of the mansion to say our adieux.

Thirty-one

T HE COACHMAN had arrived while we were arguing with the girl. Same as before, the young reindeer between the shafts, Inazuma tied on behind all tacked up and ready to go.

It was a bitter morning, an east wind, a real nipple-stiffener. The coachman looked like a bear sitting up there on his box. The only part of his skin that was visible was his eyelids.

Kobi set down the pack. I propped my rifle against it. No man should say farewell to a lover while carrying arms.

The coachman, yawning mightily, clambered down, led the horse to the mounting block, gave it a muffled order to fucking well stand there until it was told not to and jagged the bridle a couple of times, hard.

Sato came out of the house for his early-morning ride. He latched the throat buckle of his wolfskin cloak. He glanced at the sky. He regarded us briefly and made a sort of nod, no curiosity in his face at all.

He went to the mounting block and climbed on, ponderously considering that he started three-quarters of the way up the animal. He fiddled with his cloak to get it lying smartly on the horse's rump. He settled himself better in the saddle. The horse did some business.

Kobi was watching – not Sato but the horse. Feeling lighter in the gut, it made a few trial plunges, which Sato checked in a rather rustic way. I saw Kobi wince, and knew he was wincing for the horse. It was at that moment that I formed the idea that the Japanese were not natural horse riders, despite their general slightness of stature and bandy legs.

Sato was snagging the horse's mouth just as the coachman

had done, and when it objected, spoke to it in a throaty, ugly voice. The horse, full of oats and morning strength, went on thrashing its head around – executed a few petulant caracoles, getting its own back on mankind no doubt, but doing so dangerously, for there was ice underfoot.

I murmured to Kobi, 'That animal should watch out,' and as I spoke, it slipped, its rear legs buckled and it went down onto its hindquarters – sank like a ship with its bows in the air. Sato bellowed like fury – clung to its neck, his arms right round it, his head buried in its mane and his military cap toppling absurdly down his cheek. Terrified, the horse went skeetering across the ice and slid into the reindeer which calmly watched it coming, lowered its left spike and jabbed it upwards into the horse's belly.

Blood didn't spurt. No great injury was inflicted upon the horse. But it had smelt more of the reindeer than it liked and the sense of its own dignity had been impaired. It rolled back its lips, bared its long teeth and began to whinny, an extraordinary high-pitched noise combining anger, fright and outrage.

At last it found a footing. The muscles in its hindquarters bunched exactly like the sculpture which Uncle Igor had had in front of his palace next to the bust of Tiberius – a horse struggling after being jumped by a mountain lion. Within seconds, it was on all four feet and upright again, breathing hard, eyes rolling, flecks of foam round its mouth.

What should have happened next was for Sato, who by this time was pretty pallid round the chops, to have dismounted and given the coachman the mother and father of a bollocking for not having sprinkled gravel on the ice. What did happen was that the reindeer, which we should remember was only a young animal, seeing the horse (which may have bullied it mercilessly in the stable, one has no hope of understanding these matters) still standing there, almost within reach, decided to attack it again and did so, jerking the little black carriage behind it. Two bounds – three – then down went its head and up went the spikes, this time with a twisting, rending movement that clearly meant business. The horse screamed and bucked at the reindeer, really lashing out, going for its head. Sato rose vertically, a foot above his saddle – I saw the daylight between his crotch and the leather.

'Help me, help me, you fools,' he yelled, and started thrashing around with his whip – at the horse, the reindeer, everything within reach.

The horse laid back its ears and with eyes as white as dinner plates and a great rough snickering of fear sprang forward. We could all see that it had no destination in mind, that it was panicked, that its sole wish in life was to escape, it didn't matter where.

Sato was bobbling around on its back like potatoes on the boil, was shouting and flailing – a lost cause if ever I saw one. His cap had fallen off and one foot had come out of its stirrup. He was certain to fall, no ifs or buts about it. Then his huge shaven skull would strike the ice and he'd be dead.

There was Kobi, the coachman and myself – we all knew about horses, we could all see what was going to happen in less than a minute. We were going to watch the General die. There was no way out for him.

The next thing I knew was Kobi airborne in front of me. I mean that literally. His hands were out there as if he was swimming and his body was flying, upwards, on the diagonal, like a javelin. He seized the horse's reins and swung there for a moment, dragging the animal's head down. But it had the greater strength and, more terrified than ever, whisked him along, bouncing him on the ice.

The scene is imprinted on my memory: Sato gripping the horn and cantle of the saddle, one hand between his legs, the other behind him; the horse determined to make its exit; Kobi determined that it should not, refusing to release the reins, being dragged bumping and rattling over that horrible ice.

The way we were all placed, there was only one way the horse could go, which was round the back of the carriage. Spotting this, the coachman darted behind it and as the horse came past jumped out and like an idiot started flapping his arms and shouting at it. Maddened by fear, its gaping nostrils crimson with blood, the horse redoubled its efforts to escape and swerved sharply to one side. The quick change of direction, the increase in speed, an unlucky jolt on the ice, who can say how one of the reins got itself looped round Kobi's little finger on his right hand – who can swear to the truth of anything that happens in seconds?

It didn't pop up in the air or anything, but we all heard Kobi scream and we all saw the red lance of blood.

I shouted and ran towards him. In its confusion the horse had described a complete circle and was heading back for the reindeer and the carriage, pulling Kobi behind it, he still hanging onto the reins with his good hand. I could see only too easily what would happen. Unless Kobi released the reins, he'd get his head smashed against the carriage wheel as the horse dragged him round.

'Let go,' I screamed – then tripped and smashed my face into the ice ruts. Raising my head, 'Let go, you idiot, let go.'

The ice was beneath my hands, I was gripping it, snatching at it, pulling pieces off it in my desperation. Blood was pouring from my nose, I could it feel it all over my chin. 'Don't be so stupid, let go,' I yelled – and then, as if in the most wonderful dream in existence, the coachman jumped out from behind the carriage and in one vast bear-like motion threw his greatcoat over the horse's head and hugged it tight. Instantly, as if the god of horses had commanded it, the creature slithered to a halt and stood quietly, its flanks heaving.

The coachman wiped its head and its nose with his coat and began muttering to it. Sato just sat there, still gripping the saddle fore and aft.

Kobi picked himself up, tossed the reins to the coachman with one hand and regarded the other with curiosity. He laid his thumb and surviving fingers flat against his palm. One, two, three, four. I could see his lips moving. The pain must have been dulled by the shock and intense cold. The blood was no longer spouting, just pumping sullenly out and running in a slow stream off his hand and onto the ice.

He walked around searching for his finger; picked it up, a funny stump of a thing with curling red whiskers at one end – the broken tendons. It was hard to connect it with the human body.

He held it in front of his face, twiddled it round, looked down at his hand.

No one spoke, no one moved. Some of the biblical miracles must have been like that, people motionless as they waited to see what was going to happen next, unconscious of any part of their bodies.

He compared it to his good pinkie and offered it to the hole it had come from.

I shouted, 'Quick, wrap it up in something, Hijo can sew it back on.'

He stared at me, his face very pale. He said, 'You don't look too good. I'd say you've broken your nose.'

He gazed once more at the finger – staggered a bit – then came to a decision. He walked slowly over to the coachman, his head lowered, full of menace. He held the finger out on the flat of his palm, he flipped it into the air, he caught it. The coachman backed away. Like a snake after a bird, Kobi darted forward, grabbed the fellow by his beard, coiled his hand round it and heaved on it as if he were a bell-ringer.

His mouth opened. I glimpsed pink slippery lips. 'For you,' Kobi said, and stuffed his finger inside. 'See what you've done to me, you hairy swine.' Then he slammed the man's jaw shut with the heel of his hand.

Despite all his beard and whiskers, I could see Kobi's finger pushing out the coachman's cheek like a hot carrot. He picked it out, glanced at it and then tossed it away over his shoulder.

The spell broke: I ran to Kobi. As I did so, he started to waver and then diminish, getting smaller and smaller as his legs folded until he toppled over. When I got there he was lying unconscious on his back.

Maybe Sato was rubbish on the back of a runaway horse, but now I could understand why he was a general. By the time we got to the hospital, which can't have been more than three or four minutes, Toshi and the other orderlies were waiting for us at the door and Hijo was tying the tapes of his green surgeon's apron. Sato insisted on inspecting everything for himself before Hijo could start. Kobi was still unconscious but I was only groggy, sitting on the edge of the bed and dripping blood into a metal basin. Every time Sato passed me, he bowed.

Eventually he was satisfied with the arrangements. He went and stood in the doorway. He bowed again, bowed deeply and stayed down. Raising his head at last, he said, 'You have saved my life. Thank you, Doig-san. You will be rewarded.'

Thirty-two

I SAID TO Cyn, 'You were wrong, luck is everything. If the reindeer hadn't butted the horse, none of this would have happened. I'd have my old nose and Kobi his pinkie. We'd be miles away by now.'

'Yeah, well, it just goes to show . . . By the way, that new schnozz of yours is a beaut. The old one, it got sort of hunch-backed halfway down, made you look like a bruiser. But now – you could go into the movies, you know that?' She fluttered her hands, twirled her jewelled fingers, made everything flashing and magical. Cupping her hands around her mouth: 'Ladies and gentlemen, I give you tonight the one and only Charlie Doig as Romeo – as General Sherman – as the last Tsar of Russia . . . You'd wow them, I know it. When you grabbed Lizochka, people said, oh, he's a real brute of a fellow, don't know what she sees in him. But I was always on Lizochka's side. For me you were a big beautiful brute who could look after a girl. You'd be fabulous on the screen, Carlos.'

'But I failed her, didn't I?'

'You did what she asked, you acted for the best in *those* circumstances on *that* night. Don't ever forget that. You weren't in the bridal suite at the Metropole with the house doctor a telephone call away.'

'That Tungus witch doctor took her away from me, did I tell you? She'd always been there, clinging to me and he – well, he pulled her off. Reached down inside me and lifted out the brass vessel in which her spirit lived, that's how it seemed to me, maybe because he had brass suns and moons all over him. I had a terrific headache at the time and the moment he did his stuff, it vanished. My head became as clear as a bell, even though I was halfways drunk. It was extraordinary. Already I'm forgetting the worst of it. I'll get there in the end.'

'Don't! Be her friend, wave to her, say nice things. But forget about forgetting. You've got to be dead before you can manage that. If I'd been in love like you loved Lizochka, I'd say to myself, OK, Cyn, you've had the best that the world has to offer, you can die any time you want, no regrets. Think of her like that. Remember her with joy. Women don't want soggy old bums for lovers who despair about everything.'

I said, 'I sometimes think the worst mistake I ever made in my life was falling in love.'

She said, 'That's the way a loser talks and you're no loser. Remember what I've just said and believe me. I've learned things in my life you've never even dreamed of.'

She'd been speaking to the Jap officer who was in charge of the building works at the mansion and had only just come back in. Her cheeks were still pink and her eyebrows sprayed with frost. Her kimono outfit was only for evening wear, I'd discovered. Now she was in a long skirt of a soft green material and a double-breasted jacket of the same colour with large mauve buttons. She sat on the low couch opposite me, her legs elegantly crossed. She looked sensational. How could I have ever thought she'd set me up just so she could have some fun?

I said, 'Sometimes her name catches me on the elbow, that's all. Anyway, thanks for the advice. You never were a girl to keep silent.'

'Oh, now wait, that's not fair, no one is more *discreet* than Cynthia Zipf. But silent is different. After all I've been through? You're crazy. At least I don't babble. In fact, now we're going to quit the small talk and get down to business. OK, the thing is this. The General, who's a very traditional sort of Japanese man in case you hadn't noticed, says you and Kobi saved his life – honoured guests – for ever and ever – sacred duty, la-di-da-di-da. I say back to him, *shacho*, my love, let's not get too carried away here, let's go behind the scenes a little. This young man's brave and resourceful and after he's flogged some bird skin to your cousin in Nagasaki—'

'Yamaguchi is Sato's cousin? How do you know about Yamaguchi anyway? I haven't mentioned his name even to Kobi.'

'Natural history collector – lives in Nagasaki – wealthy, by definition – what do two and two make? The cousin thing's a bonus, small world and all that. May I continue? So I'm saying to Sato that you're just the sort of man we could use to transact a little business we have in mind and I say this and I say that, all in a caressing manner, stroking and patting his ego, and after a while he's saying humph like only a Jap can and looking at me in a certain way – what I'm saying here is that maybe the General has employment for you.'

'It'll have to be good. We were on our way to the train station when the reindeer and the horse fell out.'

'It's up to him to make the pitch, not me. He's not a man to be rushed into anything, so don't start counting your chickens, but there's a chance . . . You think about that while I get Mushi to bring us some tea. Russian, proper chai with raspberry jam, that suit you?'

A little later, Sato himself came in for his mid-morning tiffin. I heard Mushi having the devil of a tussle pulling off his heavy riding boots in the vestibule. The fact that he'd bothered to do so told me we were in for a session.

Cyn and I were in that same large downstairs room that the banquet had been laid in. Sato entered, nodded to Cyn and bowed to me as if his life depended on it.

Here let me remark on the whole question of bowing, which, with the onset of Bolshevist theories about equality will soon have to be replaced by other means of signalling inferiority. It was my mother who taught me to bow – when I was a youth, which is to say in about 1900 – because in the world as it was then, everyone bowed to everyone else in Russia: peasants to their masters, the masters to the lords, the lords to the Tsar, and the Tsar to God. From her I learned the four main bows – to convey insolence, respect, gratitude or ambition. 'The further forward the left foot is, the greater the sincerity' – I can hear it now, the anxious voice of this woman who through no fault of her own had a husband whose every dream portended a new scheme and whose every scheme brought home a fresh disaster. It showed in her soft, disappointed face.

She wore only beige or grey dresses, mostly ill-fitting, and possessed no jewellery that I can remember. Her shoes were always scuffed.

Teaching me to bow was part of a private campaign she was waging to restore the family fortunes. I was to be its spearhead. When I'd triumphed, as of course I would, I'd be decorated by the Tsar. This was the reasoning that underlay my lessons. 'Bend at the waist, Charlenka darling, at the waist I tell you! The neck has no part in a proper gentleman's bow.' And so my poor mother would continue and so of course I became an absolute master of the bow insolent. It was only towards the end of my apprenticeship that she let the penny drop: 'Think what you want to get out of the man you're bowing to, can't you even do that?'

I'd never say I was an expert in anything much but when it came to bowing I'd at least had a thorough education.

Sato rose, he went down, he rose again, placed his hand across his heart and made a final bob – a speedy little dab of a thing to inform me that that concluded the bowing, that I didn't have to respond. He brushed up his tash – in one sweep, not one side and then another, as an old-fashioned Russian officer would do – mounted the two slight steps to the sitting area and as a further concession to me sat on a chair, awkwardly, overflowing it in places.

He cleared his throat terrifically and said in Russian, ploughing through his sentences without caring how many mistakes he made, 'Countess tells me you arrive out of the blue, that you were friends in olden Russia of St Petersburg, that you have had unhappy life because of the Bolsheviks. Please tell the details to me.'

I did so, in short sentences. He kept his eyes fixed on me throughout. The light on his spectacles made his eyes appear as brilliant black, as though they were operated by an electric current. Nothing moved in his face while I was speaking. All that happened was that he picked up a silver paper knife and repositioned it on the low table between us. At the end he said, 'Russia is a bad neighbour for Japanese people. They have killed their Emperor. They want our land, our fish, our navy, our silk, our factories – everything that we have, they want for themselves.

They have no culture, no moral character of any sort – they are barbarians. We have defeated them once, through Admiral Togo. We shall defeat them again.' He tapped the paper knife against a vase of wild Siberian snowdrops. 'We shall shatter them like a brick shatters glass.'

I glanced over at Cyn. Her eyes were fixed on Sato and stayed there, which I took as a signal to let him do all the talking.

'A wise man takes steps to prevent the undesirable happening. Japanese people would never be able to feel safe if these Bolshevik savages were close to us. It is why our Emperor is sending the Japanese Army into Siberia. When the dispositions are complete, the total of our forces will be more than seventy thousand men.' He looked across at me. 'Seventy thousand is many.'

'Who will take their orders from you,' I said.

'Correct,' he said.

I mumbled something about them being lucky to have General Sato at their head.

Cyn shot me a warning look and said in a sickeningly oily voice, 'Charlie, I should have told you, there's no longer a General Sato, only a Governor Sato. As of a week ago. He got the appointment when he was down in Vladi.'

I rose and bowed. It wasn't just a soldier who was giving me an audience, but a man of political consequence. It was a most handsome bow that I made him.

He said, 'My territory is the same, from the Pacific Ocean to Irkutsk, which as you know is a very great distance. It is my duties that have changed. My headquarters can no longer be here in Zhigalovo. Another soldier will come here in my place. The Countess and I will move to Vladivostok, which is where the Siberian railway commences. From the point of view of warfare in this desolate country, there is the railway and nothing else. Whoever has the railway wears the crown.'

I bowed again.

He continued, 'We are looking for men who speak good Russian, who are resolute in character and who hate the Bolsheviks as much as Japanese people do.'

'Wait a moment, Excellency, who's "we" in all this?'

'Countess and I,' he said impatiently. 'Countess she says that you are such a person. What is further, Countess says, is that you have personally slain the man Glebov. If you could also slay the man who calls himself Lenin and the man who calls himself Trotsky, all Japan would be in your debt. Great wealth would be awarded you, lands, riches, women, philosophers, possibly a portion of the salt tax.' He upended the paper knife and tapped its butt on the table twice. 'Can you kill those two men?'

'No.'

'Thank you. Honest men are rare. Men who are also intelligent and decisive are even rarer. Countess she says that you hate the Bolsheviks because the man Glebov killed your wife. She says you have no home and no family, that you are washing upon the sea of life.'

He eyed me. The chair was small and he was wide. I said to myself, Don't lean too much to one side, Excellency.

Suddenly he said, 'Stand up, I want to be reminded. Stand straight, please . . . Ah so, you are exactly as I thought, a man who is tall, quick and strong. Also honest. I have a purpose for you.'

Cynthia said, 'OK, you toss it around between yourselves now. Call me when you're ready.' She rose and stepped down into the eating area, a lovely lilt to her buttocks, which Sato missed through having his back to her. I said to myself, If this isn't more bogey-bogey business, I'll eat my hat. Has it become a habit with her, a sort of drug?

Thirty-three

THINKING THIS, and wondering how much I wanted to get ravelled in yet more complications, and even going to the extent of thinking, and maybe, Charlie, it was a serious error getting into bed with her, and for Christ's sake, will you ever remember that a man always has to pay for a woman's body in one way or another, I looked across at Sato and said, 'Since you're sizing me up for something, let me tell you right here and now that I'm not a man looking for succour. There've been times when I've lived off bark and leather and stuff like that. But no longer. I'm in good shape. What's more, I've got something no one else in the world has. The moment I find a buyer, I won't need help from anyone. Just telling you this, Excellency, 'cos I saw the look in your eye back there.'

'You misunderstand me, Doig-san. I am seeking to reward you for having saved my life. You are a suspicious man.'

'Then let me hear about the reward, Excellency.'

He leaned forward and, resting his forearms along his thighs, tapped at the top knee-button of his breeches with the tip of his spectacles. 'The reward for saving the life of the future Governor of Siberia, what do you think that should be?'

'A lot.'

'A lot of what?'

'What are you offering?'

He straightened. 'My present life is worth nothing when it ceases. Every Buddhist knows that. But that may not happen for twenty years. If those years are happy ones, your reward should be very great. If those years are spent in poverty and

154

disgrace, you should have no reward, for I would wish that I were dead – that you had not saved me.'

'Excuse me, Excellency, but if that's going to be your line, I'm as well to get on the next train east. Twenty years is a long time to keep me waiting.'

Now polishing his spectacles, he said quite casually, 'My information is that you kill men. Is that correct?'

'I have done so.'

'It is possible that I may ask you to kill someone. Would that cause you any trouble with your morality, or your religion? I do not ask for details of your beliefs. What I need to know is whether you would do it or whether you would not do it. I am a military man. I wish to have things clear.'

I said, 'I will kill any Bolshevik you ask me to. I will not kill a single woman or a child. As for the others, my decision would rest on the usual balance of rewards and penalties.'

He said, 'The rewards will be inconceivable. The penalties would be the normal ones that attach to murder. So of course you'd get your servant to do it.'

That was hurtful to me and I cried out, 'You want the man who lost a finger saving you – goddamnit, you want Kobi to carry the can for a killing?'

'Every servant should be prepared to die for his master. Every Japanese soldier who dies does so for his Emperor.'

'You've got the wrong man, Excellency. I'm getting out.' I jumped to my feet. I was angry, believe me.

'Why do you say that?'

'I couldn't ask Kobi to hang so that I prosper. What sort of man do you take me for?'

He said calmly, 'This is a question of honour for you?'

'There's no question anywhere. It's honour pure and simple.'

He stood up. 'Two words have been used in our conversation that are of the greatest interest to me. Honesty and honour. We shall leave it there for the moment.'

Maybe Cyn had been at the keyhole. At any rate she now came bustling in and seemed to know without having to ask what stage we'd reached.

She said to Sato, 'Don't forget you've got the medal ceremony with Hijo at the lab this afternoon.' She turned on me her best hostess smile. 'And how much he deserves it, he does such noble work!'

Sato said to me, 'Yes, the work he has undertaken will benefit all mankind. The Emperor has given me a medal which I am to confer upon him in front of his assistants, his prisoners, the soldiers – everyone. Afterwards I shall invite him to show us round his laboratory.'

'Kobi too?'

He misheard or misunderstood me, for he said, 'It wouldn't have to be the man you call Kobi who did it. You could always hire someone in Nagasaki, some ruffian from down near the docks.'

Cyn ignored him, saying, 'If Kobi's going to come with us, he'll need strong nerves, same as you will. The first room was enough for me.'

Thirty-four

M EN ENJOY risk, women prefer danger, that's my experience of the world, and the example of Cynthia von Zipf bore out the truth of it.

This whole thing with Sato was perfect for her. On every side there were dangers, principally that one day a raiding party of Semyonov's mercenaries would come slinking out of the forest and abduct her before the Japs could pull themselves together. Would Sato risk losing men by going in pursuit? Would he pay the ransom demand outright? Quibble about her age and value? Write her off? Would she end up in that notorious railway carriage where Semyonov kept all his beautiful women?

There was a danger Sato would get bored with her.

There was a danger she'd be cold-shouldered by his Japanese entourage when she set up in Vladivostok as the Governor's mistress.

There was a danger this great financial enterprise they were planning would come crashing down.

There was a danger he'd get her with child. Then what? My God, then what – the long stony road of female servitude in Japan, surely.

There were dangers everywhere. In civilised parts of the world they'd be called hazards. But out here they were much more than that. In the badlands most things are a danger for an attractive woman.

So I ruminated as I pulled on my boots. She had to be tough to have got this far, supertough. But in what part could it reside when the rest of her was so womanly? Had it reached its limits? Or was it still on the spread, was it reaching out to conquer all the juicy bits so that in ten years' time a man might no longer consider her worth the trouble?

Cynthia von Zipf, here in Siberia! How strange life was!

I began the walk up the hill to the laboratory, which butted onto the hospital. The weather had suddenly turned mild. Spring couldn't be far away. The bursting smell of the soil, the headiness of the air, the buds, the colours, the encouraging sky – and any day now the arrival, using God knows what senses, of our migrant birds. The warblers first, and foremost among them the unobtrusive chiffchaff with its piping optimism.

I paused, my ears spread like fronds to catch their music. But instead it was another voice I heard—

Yes indeed, Charlie, all praise and honour to La Zipfa and the little birdies but wake up there, wake up, it's the money that counts! It preserves your health and buys you pleasures that might otherwise never become available. It brings you power and fame, which is what makes a man. Why'd you go to the trouble of capturing the gold barge if you didn't know all that? The risks you ran! It can only have been for the money.

Of course you know. So why are you doing nothing about getting hold of some? Do you consider yourself to be effete and above-it-all? I have to say that's quite contrary to your record.

Don't turn your head away like that, pretending to be someone who's either frightened of money or overcome by modesty. Look me in the eye and repeat after me, Yes, I understand the importance of money.

Oh, I see, you think the Lala bird's going to make your fortune? You disappoint me, you really do. Ask yourself this: what money did Charles Darwin make in his entire life? Not inherit or marry, but make. Spot on. Very little is the right answer. And you think you can do better? I call that bad judgement. I thought better of you, Charles. Good luck with your life.

The nagging voice was correct, I knew it was. I should concentrate more on building up my wealth while I was young and strong. Should cultivate ambition of the basest sort, welcome sleepless nights and wear down my fingernails. I should really worry about the future, get inside its head and work out where the money was stored.

Therefore I should go to Nagasaki asap and flog the skin to

Yamaguchi on condition that he let me take it to the Field Museum to have it authenticated. When the news spread through Chicago that I'd done it again, I'd be the toast of the town. The money would come rolling in. Next thing I knew a beautiful woman would be tripping my way on her barley-sugar ankles having smelt success and the loose diamonds and the two Gorevsky necklaces and maybe also the sunken gold. A woman who was any good would expect me to have money. So she could feel safe. So she could bear my children and have herself photographed with them all smiling and rosy beside the swing, not like here where the garden would be full of Bolsheviks or Tungus creeping around hoping to butcher them.

I considered it as I walked. Chicago was the place for me, everyone had always told me that. Hard yet fair, they said, rough enough for a man like you to feel comfy in. But would I take to mowing the lawn? How'd I feel about drinking cocktails? What'd it be like to go round whistling for day after day, boring or what? And of course there were other things that'd take some getting used to, Christ were there not, things like no fleas, no lice—

Clop, clop, Inazuma's hooves were almost scraping my heels it'd got that close without my hearing it.

The two of us halted, he still not a horseman, his long Japanese sword tapping the horse's ribs as it fidgeted, I just standing there, my greatcoat open from top to bottom, my thumbs sticking out of its pockets, my head heavy with thoughts about money and safety and the Russian exiles already in Chicago who mightn't be too loving towards me.

Sato said, 'It feeds the soul to be alone.'

I looked at him with surprise.

He said, 'All Japanese people know what melancholy is. It is at the heart of our culture. Would it surprise you to know that I hate this country and its people? The Russians had little civilisation before Mr Lenin appeared and soon they will have none. When the Tsar built this railway he had it laid on human bones. It is true. I myself have had knuckles pointed out to me. There are some in the ticket office up there, lying on the window-sill. If you make a reference to them, the stationmaster laughs. Russians are savages.'

'You're telling me' – and at that very instant I heard it, my first warbler of the spring, my first of 1919 – *penochka*, the chiffchaff – *zilp-zalp*, *zilp-zalp*, from the centre of a dense clump of snowberry. I said to him, 'Your cure, my cure, a tiny bird with a voice like a bugle.'

He said, 'In Japan we have a similar bird, which you would call a bush-warbler. With us it is *uguisu*, which signifies good luck and rejoicing, or *harudori*, which is "spring bird", or *hatsune*, which is "first song". We have other names for it too. Its song is bewitching.'

Then he said, 'I shall be happy to live in Vladivostok because by exercising my imagination, I shall be able to visualise my own country on the other side of the sea, not far at all – the peaks of Hokkaido, its volcanoes, its mud, its bears, the people in the pigsties, the pigs in the houses. In my mind I shall see everything and be once again eating our thick mountain yam soup, which we call *tororo-jiru*. I shall have my Countess with me. Except for her accent, she is now a Japanese woman almost through and through. She is a miracle. My American woman is a very clever miracle.'

Because it was still on my mind and I wasn't much interested in what Sato might imagine when he reached Vladivostok, I said, 'What sort of money's in that job you were talking about?' – and I thought with a start, If I don't look out I'll become like Cyn and get money in place of eyes, great golden crowns glinting from the sockets.

Thirty-five

I WALKED beside his stirrup. Head angled down to me, he said, 'Let me first tell you the problem that has arisen in our country. It is this: last year our people increased in number by more than one million. Yes, one million more people were born than died. But our island is already too crowded, everyone agrees on that. Therefore measures must be taken in a number of directions . . . But here they are waiting for us. Now I must deal with our Dr Hijo. Afterwards we shall speak more.'

One of the soldiers guarding the laboratory held Sato's horse while he dismounted. A second threw open the door of a long wooden shed with metal grilles on the windows.

Hijo had been waiting inside. He was in his element. The overshot jaw, the yellow shelf of teeth, the thick spectacles, the creased white coat down to the knees – it was a man besotted by the possibilities of medical discovery who stood before us.

Sato spoke. Hijo and his five assistants, all of whom were Japanese, trooped out of the building. They lined up, giggling – nerves: it was their big moment. The soldiers snapped to attention. A couple of village women who were passing stopped. They set their pails on the wall behind them and eased the yokes off their shoulders. One of them said to the other, 'Small, ain't they?' The other said, '*Na morskoy trave vyrosli*' – 'That's what comes from eating seaweed.' When I smiled at them, they tittered into their hands. Sato whirled round and told them to shut up.

They shouldered their yokes and waddled off, water slopping out of the pails in silvery splashing gouts as they broke into laughter.

Sato walked up to Hijo and pinned a gold medal on his white coat, just below his array of pens. They bowed to each other. Everyone clapped. The chiffchaff sang in the distance.

He did the same to the assistants, some lesser award. More bowing and scraping.

Sato gave a command and the soldiers stood easy. He turned to me and said, 'Now we will show you the use to which we put our Bolshevik prisoners.'

First was an anteroom. We had to pass between two desks. At the left-hand one sat two clerks. One had the job of entering in a ledger the details of those taking part in the experiments – age, sex and state of health. Everyone got recorded, whether they were local volunteers or Sato's prisoners.

It was the job of the second clerk to clock in the volunteers and pay them on exit.

At the desk opposite the clerks sat two soldiers. Their job was to check everyone who came into the building for weapons.

They all leapt to attention as we walked through, Hijo leading the way.

The next room, which was painted a brilliant white and lit by powerful overhead lighting run off a generator, was where Hijo and his assistants confected the typhus vaccine. Everything was pristine: the glass tanks into which the lice were placed, the metal tables on which they were processed – then a complicated procedure I didn't understand – and finally a system of slender steel vats with glass jars at the bottom into which, like the optics behind a bar, the vaccine, which was the colour of weak tea, dripped. All along one wall of this room was a glass storage chamber in which was shelf upon shelf of phials of vaccine.

'Explain it properly,' Sato said to Hijo. 'Show Doig-san how you get to this point.' And to me, 'There will be a magnificent future for anything that improves our health. You will of course know our saying: The Health of the People is the Highest Law.'

The little fellow drew himself up. I could see he was going to love this. 'Following the method of the celebrated Dr Rudolf Weigl, I take lice that are ten days old and inject into the anus of each one a tiny dose of typhus-affected cerebral matter. Each of my men can inject two thousand lice a day. Because

162

the anus is so small, it is necessary for the louse to be positioned in a gallows structure, that is what slows us down. My number-one assistant will demonstrate the process to you later. Within a few days the typhus microbes are swarming in the louse's intestines. We dissect the creature and remove the guts, which are pounded into a mash. From this comes the liquid vaccine. It takes only an infinitesimal dose to save a man's life.'

'Where do you get the actual bug, then?' I asked, having some interest in the subject as a result of my own experience.

'You will see.'

'No one here ever gets the disease accidentally? Nothing ever rubs off on anyone, gets on their clothing?'

'We take the necessary precautions,' Hijo said briskly. 'Are we complete? Shall we pass through to the room where we breed the lice? You will find this most interesting, I guarantee it, Mr Doig.'

He knocked on the door to the next room. A soldier's face appeared at a small glass window. A signal passed between them and we entered.

In the centre of the room was a stove, its chimney going through the roof. Around the stove was a metal cage in which sat four armed soldiers. Two other soldiers were on guard at the door by which we'd entered. At the far end was a line of cells. Each of them had a wooden shelf, which served as bed and table.

I think Hijo had Sato's men round up the most suspicious-looking fellows in the neighbourhood whenever he needed fresh blood for his experiments. Both men always referred to them sweepingly as Bolsheviks, on what grounds it was impossible to say. Anyway prisoners is what they were, of all ages: hungry, ragged, bearded and indescribably wretched.

Their trousers had been cut off above the knee. Around their emaciated calves were clamped little boxes with netting on one side, the other side open against the skin.

'Stand up!' shouted Hijo at the nearest prisoner. 'Come here. Show the gentlemen.'

You know what a louse looks like? It's a dingy wingless grub such as you might find in rotten wood, and has six legs, each of which has a claw for gripping. It's born with the knowledge that the human blood supply is most plentiful where the skin is warm. It is therefore at its happiest in our glens and wooded glades. Having got into position, it transfers blood from the human body into its own via a rostrum or nozzle. It is this action that causes the irritation that ultimately leads to typhus. Wherever you have poor living conditions you have *Pediculus humanus*.

(We have an excellent and expressive word in Russian for this form of louse. In the plural, which is how it's usually spoken, it's *vshi*. But whenever he could, Hijo referred to it by its full Latin name, which is a good measure of the fellow.)

The man slowly pirouetted before us, not speaking.

I had to bend right down to get an idea of the number of lice in each of the boxes.

Hijo yelled at him, 'Raise your leg. Put your foot on the bench. No, no, that's no good for us. Orderly, have this man's legs shaved immediately. Here, you, take his place.'

Hijo was going round with a pointer like a schoolmaster. He jabbed it at a second man and had him get into position.

This one must have had five hundred lice grazing on each leg. When I looked closely, I could see his skin flickering as the lice clambered over each other and fought to get on top of a vein.

Hijo said, 'On the outside of the box is a rag. On this I place a batch of eggs at the start of each treatment. It is important to have broods of lice of exactly the same age. Their management becomes too difficult otherwise. Imagine it, Mr Doig, if you have some a week old and others a month old, imagine all the problems I would face. As it is, the eggs hatch simultaneously and these people feed them with their blood for ten days. On the eleventh day the lice are collected and taken next door to be infected and processed.'

Turning, he pointed to the benches on the other side of the room where sat the volunteers, both men and women. 'They enjoy it in the warmth here. Our conditions are so much better than in their own houses. They enjoy the money also.'

One of the women had her skirt rolled almost to the waist. On both her calves and her massive pink thighs she was feeding lice, many boxes of them. She grinned across at us. 'Must be five roubles' worth altogether, eh, doctor!' which she said flapping her skirt. 'If you want me to feed them any higher, you'll have to pay me double. That's valuable blood up there, so it is . . . Hey, when are you going to let us smoke in here?'

He said, 'These are people who have already had typhus and have survived. It is possible to be reinfected but it is rare in my experience.' Eyeing me coldly, 'A man of your height and weight could feed four thousand lice, Mr Doig.'

Sato said, 'Russian people are so simple. They think it's the sensation of the century to be paid for something that they've previously done for free – to harbour lice. It doesn't disturb them at all that they might catch typhus again and die. Doctor, you say the louse bites itch very much. So when these people leave they can't stop itching?'

'We give them a cream, Excellency.'

'Very commendable. How much do we pay them?'

'One rouble for ten hours, Excellency.'

'Old money?'

'Lenin's money, Excellency. It is easily printed.'

'Very well. Carry on.'

'Do you want me to show him everything, Excellency?'

'Of course.'

'Now we shall go to the holiest of my rooms, Mr Doig. Follow me this way, please.'

Thirty-six

WE RETURNED to the lab. There was a door beside the storage cabinet I hadn't previously noticed. Hijo unlocked it and relocked it behind us. In front was a short corridor without windows. Two more doors, both locked and relocked by Hijo, and then we were somewhere at the back of the hospital. I knew by the smell.

He unlocked a third door. Facing us and so barring us from entering, he said, 'This is where my best work is done.' He stepped aside.

Ducking my head I walked into a small bare white window-less room. The first thing I saw was a row of cages, each with a guinea pig. The next—

Hijo said, 'A Bolshevik spy. He had typhus anyway.'

He was a young man with a thin blond beard, eyes closed, moving restlessly within the leather straps that bound him to an iron-framed cot.

I looked sharply at Hijo. His teeth seemed huger than ever, and his eyes swirling. He said to me, 'To make the vaccine live, we must infect our lice with typhus. This is where that process begins. This is the point at which my work advances and overtakes that of Dr Weigl. It is for this that I received my medal.'

I couldn't believe what I was seeing. I said, 'OK, the guinea pigs I understand, but the spy?'

'Human brains are larger and more intricate than those of animals. Therefore the human rickettsiae is very much more valuable in a vaccine than the rickettsiae we might draw from guinea pigs. A little human typhus goes a long way. Also it is more plentiful on account of the size of the human brain. I call it the home-bred variety, ha ha, Mr Doig!'

Hissing at his joke, he turned from me to Sato and back again for applause.

'This was my advance, a very simple one. In fact, I have often thought it unjust that Dr Weigl, who twice contracted the disease himself, should not have been honoured at the highest level.' His voice grew shriller: he began to speak rapidly in his awful Russian, his whole grotesque jaw yammering up and down. 'But I dared to think what he didn't! That the brain of a man will produce more vaccine than the brain of a guinea pig! Yes, Mr Doig sir, that was my daring! Let me now be precise. From the brain of one man I can distil sufficient vaccine to save the lives of seven thousand, eight hundred other men. Wa! One very good equation!'

Sato coughed and said, 'It's not that we kill the man, though we could. It's the typhus that kills him.'

'Yes, it's nicer to wait for him to die if you're going to have his brains out,' I said.

They both stared at me. I said, 'I've had typhus and lived. This man might survive as well. That's what I'm saying.'

The man in the bed murmured, '*Christos voskresse, Christos voskresse,*' and thumped his head against the pillow.

It was the chant for the Easter celebrations – 'Christ is risen.' Maybe he wasn't a Bolshevik at all.

Sato glanced at Hijo. The doctor leaned over the man and pressed with his finger on one of the splodges of rash on the man's chest. 'See how quickly it goes white. Two days, no longer. Then kaput.'

Sato said, 'There's no danger to anyone else in the hospital?'

'None, Excellency. After I've extracted his brain, it's carried in a covered glass bowl from here to the processing room by an orderly. This man then comes back and takes the corpse away to be incinerated. By using the same man for both purposes, I minimise the risk of infection to the other workers.'

Turning to me, Hijo said, 'It will doubtless have occurred to you that the most efficient method of producing vaccine and at the same time of eliminating the vile disease that is called communism, would be to infect our Bolshevik prisoners with typhus so that their cerebral matter, once processed, at least gives some benefit to the world. That will be the next step, on my return.'

Sato said to me, 'The doctor is returning to Japan to present his report to the Emperor's committee.'

Smirking, Hijo bowed to me, his medal dangling.

The whole idea was more horrible than anything I'd met in my life. From that moment on I hated Hijo.

Thirty-seven

JUST AS we were leaving the lab, a soldier came trotting down from the station with a cable for Sato. He slit the envelope with his thumbnail, glanced at it – and disappeared to consult his cipher books.

I didn't see him again until the evening. Kobi and I had been promoted from the outside shed to a room next to Mushi's. There was still light in the sky when Sato sent her to fetch me.

Having changed into robes, he looked quite different, like an authentic Japanese man. He led me into the sitting area where we'd talked before. Cyn's perfume lay lightly in the air. I got the impression they'd been having a powwow.

We sat round a low table, he on his hunkers, I sprawled as usual. He came straight to the point: held his hand upright and bent down four fingers in turn. 'To resume our earlier conversation – out of the twenty-five materials that are essential to prosperity, we Japanese people possess only four.' He repeated the business with his fingers. 'Only four. What is the solution?'

'You must make conquests, Excellency. Start with Siberia and work your way west. When you reach Moscow, splatter the brutes all over the Kremlin wall, that's what I'd do.'

'That is also the opinion of our Emperor. The opportunity to invade Russia cannot be ignored. When the kettle boils, you make tea, everyone knows that. It's why I'm here, to set up the procedures by which we shall govern the Kingdom of Eastern Siberia. Yes, Mr Doig, that is to be its name, the Kingdom of Eastern Siberia,' which he said with great emphasis, dashing the palm of his hand against his thigh. 'It will act as a barrier against the Bolsheviks and provide the resources by which Japanese people can live. The figure of one million more people per annum on our islands frightens everybody.'

'The Reds'll just lie down with their paws in the air?'

'They are headless. And we are capable of everything. We have become a modern people – modern thought, modern equipment, modern objectives.'

He replaced his spectacles – pushed them up his nose with a forefinger, blinked a couple of times. 'You are a notorious man. You have shot your wife, you have captured a ship full of gold and you have killed the criminal Glebov.'

I waited, but he waited longer – just sat there cross-legged looking at me. I said, 'You can come right out with the proposition, Excellency, if you feel like it. Just so long as you remember about me and Kobi and the killing you spoke of.'

Had Sato been Russian, I'd have known within a notch of the compass which way the wind was blowing. But with this man, there was a space behind those wire-framed spectacles I couldn't enter. And I very much wanted to hear his proposal. Chicago could wait and so could the glamorous wife and the kids and the limousine with its deep crushed leather seats. This could be my big chance. The hidden ace. The one-and-only in a man's life.

Thinking that maybe he'd got into a sudden funk because of my Russian mother and some question mark over my loyalty, I said, 'You should know this before you say anything definite: I'm like you, I'm through with the Russians. Had enough of them for twenty lifetimes. Bastards.'

'Good. So now I shall come to the point. You will have noted that I spoke of the Kingdom of Eastern Siberia in the future tense. There is a reason for that. The Emperor will never sign the decree to bring it into existence while my cousin Yamaguchi-san is connected with it. I will tell you why. Yamaguchi-san, who is also my business partner in the exploitation of the Kingdom, took over a small concern started by his father and has made it enormous. He is the most successful man in Nagasaki, maybe in all the island of Kyushu. He builds ships, he repairs them, he has engineering works, he does every-thing. In the course of building a new factory, he destroyed an ancient temple. It had a graveyard, and a shrine to which pilgrims came from all over Japan. He told no one, gave no warnings – sent his men in and had the site level within two days. Unfortunately, this temple had been built by the family of the Empress and was still maintained by her. It is even said that her grandmother is buried there. You cannot imagine how serious that is for us. Yamaguchi-san could not have done anything worse.'

'So the Emperor is saying no dice to the new Kingdom as long as Yamaguchi has anything to do with it?'

'Correct.'

'What does he himself have to say about it?'

'He says the Empress's temple hasn't been touched, nor has her grandmother's grave. The temple that he knocked down is a quite different one, that's what he says, that his enemies in Nagasaki are just making trouble for him.'

'Why doesn't the Emperor send someone to inspect the temple?'

'We expect that this will happen. Meanwhile the problem is of time. We have many competitors. The cable I had this afternoon was from our ally at the court saying there are dark forces at work against us and we must hurry.'

'Are you saying that you want me to go to Nagasaki and persuade Yamaguchi to drop out of this Kingdom scheme?'

'Correct.'

'But – Excellency, what can I possibly say to change the mind of a man who's so successful?'

'That problem is yours.'

I made some motion of doubt with my hands. 'OK, let's suppose I can bring it off.' Cocking an eye at him, 'No guarantees, mind you, just supposing. So he backs down and the Emperor says to you, Fine, I'll sign the decree now. Would that mean you're personally going to be the ruler of this new Kingdom? Top fellow, wearing the crown? Orb and sceptre? Spats? Is that what all this is about?'

'I shall only be the Governor.'

'Be that as it may, Excellency, I smell great wealth in the offing.'

'Correct. I shall become richer than Yamaguchi-san ever was.

I'm not ashamed to say that. But none of this will happen while he lives.'

'A moment ago you said only that I was to persuade him. There was nothing about killing him.'

'Being a soldier, I am used to taking quick decisions. As I spoke I decided that killing was best. My cousin is made of rubber. Unless he is killed, he will bounce back. Even if he were thrown down a volcano, he'd still climb out alive. He must be killed.'

I said nothing to that through wanting to hear about the reward.

'One thing more. There must be no rings in the water. Perhaps the body could be eaten a little by sharks.'

'OK, but what do I get out of it?'

He had a go at his tash, squeezing and crumpling his upper lip. I said, 'I can keep a secret, Excellency.'

He stiffened his back. 'It's the highest position any *gaijin* will ever have held in Japan.'

I shook my head. 'Not for me then. I don't have that sort of ambition.'

He said, 'You are wrong. Ambition is like a beautiful woman. Before you see her, you don't give her a single thought. The moment you see how beautiful she is, you think about her every minute of the day. Are you prepared?'

'OK then, try me.'

He braced his hands on his knees and leaned forward, staring intently into my face from about a foot away. 'You would become the Prince of Siberia. Yes! The Prince of Siberia!'

He swayed back, satisfied. 'A throne, costumes, personal herald, an escort of mounted Cossacks, things like that. Whatever gave you pleasure would be yours. Whatsoever you wanted.' He began to beam at me. 'Whatever pleased you would be yours to command, every little thing at every minute of every hour of the day. Now you know what I meant about being the top *gaijin* in Japanese history books.'

'Well,' I said, 'that would be unusual,' wanting to spread the conversation out so that I could come to grips with my thoughts. Then, 'The Countess told you I'd enjoy a throne – was that how that got into your head?'

There was a shuffle of slippers at the head of the winding staircase. Cyn was leaning on the rail looking down at us. I said, 'Charlie Doig seated on a throne? What did you mean by that? An insult or what?'

'Carlos, there's something of the peacock in you that'd go very well on a throne. Who wants a little mouse of a man in a dark suit up there? You speak Russian, you speak English, we'll soon get you going in Jap, and you'd polish up well. You remember me saying what a great film star you'd make? Prince of Siberia, it's the same idea.'

Sato said, 'You have the natural air of a ruler. Only a little while ago I heard of your success as the Grand Duke Boris.'

Speaking in English now, Cyn said, 'The Romanov bit comes naturally to you. And let's face it, Charlie, you haven't got a heap of other work.'

'Except to have Yamaguchi rubbed out,' I said.

'Don't pay any attention to what he said about that. Yamaguchi'll back down if *you* tell him how things stand. Of course he never listens to my old man, that's family for you. But you're the famous Charlie Doig. He tried to buy your beetle. He respects you.'

Sato said softly, 'We haven't yet talked about the commissions that would be yours. On all transactions there'd be a percentage for the Prince.'

Going back to Russian, Cyn said, 'The Archangel Timber Company'll look like a pot of boiled tripe by comparison.'

I said, 'OK, OK, I hear you both. But what about the power, eh, the gallows, the firing squad, the whatever you want to call it? That's what it comes down to in the end. Power. "Do it or you're dead" – who'd get to make that kind of speech? For instance, could I boot you out, Excellency?'

Sato said, 'Whoever controls the army has the power.'

I could have told them I wasn't an idiot but I held my tongue. The only reason I'd asked the question was to see how shameless the pair of them were.

I said, 'And where does honesty and honour come into this? As I recollect, there was some talk of them earlier. You singled them out among my virtues, Excellency.'

'You would be the Prince. Your subjects would expect the

highest standards from you. Honesty and honour are at the top of the list. Justice for all, that would be our motto.'

'Hang All Reds, that'd be mine,' I said.

Cyn was wearing a loose gown, lots of froth and glimpses. She leaned over the banister to expose a little more and said, 'I can just see you in uniform, Charlie. Trotting along the main drag at the head of your Cossacks, bouquets raining down from the balconies.'

'How many years would I get as Prince? Could my sons come after me?'

Sato said, 'Everything of that nature would depend on the Emperor.'

I closed one eye as if taking aim at something. Five years, I said to myself, that'd do me nicely.

'Women'll throw themselves at your feet,' Cyn said, sort of squirming as she spoke. 'You'll have to kick them out the way.'

I said I'd have to think about it. Someone who was sophisti-cated with money would have come up with all manner of objections on the spot, and followed through with an absolute necessity for clarification on the percentages and then, 'Just one last tiny point, Excellency,' as Sato was preparing to shake on it, and somehow the rewards would have been doubled in five minutes. But it wasn't my style.

Her chin in her hands, her elbows on the banister rail, Cyn said, 'You want to do it, Charlie, I can tell from your expression.'

How could I know what my face was showing or what she reckoned she'd seen? How could I know if she'd seen anything at all? But I wasn't going to argue. The moment the offer popped out I knew I'd accept it. Could any man with a full quota of blood have turned it down? Prince of Siberia! How Papa would have roared!

Thirty-eight

A SQUAD of soldiers was formed up on the platform to perform the honours of departure. Sato had me inspect them, which I did with my hands clasped behind my back, looking closely into each face to see if I could discern any interest in Siberia. Except for the case of one man, who had a wound on his cheek sewn up with Hijo's special blue thread and who scowled at me with spectacular ferocity, I saw nothing except apathy. Their Emperor had sent them; one day he'd order them home; it was as far as their thinking went.

The train came puffing in from a siding. The soldiers manning the machine guns looked surly, as would anyone facing a night in an open wagon.

Cyn was standing next to me all bundled up in furs. Sato had gone off down the platform, slapping his riding crop against his boot.

She said, 'Whenever I see a train, I get a bad feeling. Second wives are fine and dandy when a Nip's out in the bush but once he gets close to home, it'll be goodbye, number two, sure as eggs are eggs. He says he'll never treat me like that. I say I believe him. And you know what else? It's difficult to set up a store of value in a place like this. See any banks around?'

'You know how to make money for him. That'll keep him attached.'

'Yeah, well, there's that to it. And I get jewellery from him, he's good at that line. But when push turns to shove, you can't beat cash – and I don't mean this Russian crap. I mean a currency that's good wherever I land up, which means sterling, dollars or gold and nothing in between. Anyway,' she sniffed, 'here's

175

where I am in my life, here and nowhere else. Better than being in a Moscow prison, better than being dead . . . Hey, I was almost feeling sorry for myself back then and that'll never do. So moving right ahead now – this Kingdom business, let's get down to it, let's you and I have ourselves a ball. Five years max, and then out, what do you say? You and I. Exclusive.'

'Five's perfect. A little less and you haven't got your eye in, a little more and you get too trustful.'

'No getting greedy,' she said.

'No swollen heads,' I said. 'What's the target?'

'Ten million bucks apiece and then we're on the boat together – American crew, American flag, American food – OK, Charlie, OK?'

'It was five million a little while back.'

'I've done some thinking since then.'

I grinned at her, a big, whole, genuine grin. She was an extraordinary woman. 'Cyn, don't you go worrying about him. You're as safe as houses. Take the gold concession, never mind anything else. He's never going to be able to manage it by himself. You'll get to ten million in a year.'

She grunted. 'What does a girl from the Lower East Side know about gold mining?' Suddenly her perkiness faded. Chewing her lip, 'The fact of the matter is that Siberia's one hell of a place for a girl to be alone. He's not white and that counts for me. Like I'm not yellow and that counts for him. In times like these it doesn't matter too much. Everyone hangs on to whatever floats past. But one day things'll settle and people'll look at each other and say, What in Hades am I doing with you? Then all hell'll be let loose. Another thing: I'm not getting younger, Charlie. I'm beginning to think about babies and corny things like that. Before it's too late. By the way, you never said OK.'

It was the first mention of children I'd heard from her. 'What about the bogey-bogey stuff? Nappies and a pram don't come into that category.'

'You're right, I need to sort myself out. Get some time alone, and space, and the sun on my back. Yeah, maybe start a garden as well as a family. Somewhere to stroll around in the evening with a Martini. No digging, though, that's not what Cynthia von Zipf does.'

Thinking to get into my mind how many years she and I might have left in which to meet again and fall in love in comfort, I said, 'How old are you, Cyn?'

But of course that wasn't what she read into it. She raked me up and down with a look of total disbelief that any man could speak to her like that. Before I could explain myself, she said, 'Old enough, asshole,' fairly spitting it out, and stalked down the platform to join Sato – the Mexican sombrero, a grey fur pelisse down to the back of her knees, slim, slick-heeled boots crackling on the skin of ice.

She halted – pondered – turned – came walking back, slowly.

Getting close but not too close, she said, 'You know what really riles me? That you don't need me. That's what it boils down to. For me, at any rate.'

She started off down the platform again – then turned back a second time. 'You're up and away and I – I'm a woman and I'm alone in a repulsive little town in Siberia having to share my bed with a Jap.' Her big brown eyes grew moist. 'I'd much rather it was you. Good luck, Charlie Doig,' she whispered – and then Sato was striding towards us, still slapping his riding whip against his boot.

I bowed to him. I bowed to Cyn. Her look pierced me to the quick.

Hijo and Kobi stepped forward. I hadn't bargained on Hijo being with us but here he was, so I said nothing. We ascended the steps of our carriage, at the top of which a smart Japanese attendant was waiting. The other two went into the carriage. I remained outside on the metal platform.

Sato bowed again to me and I bowed back. I couldn't bring myself even to glance at Cyn.

The stationmaster blew his whistle, smoke volleyed out of the chimney, the stay rods tightened, the pistons sucked, and thus I left Zhigalovo, Cyn waving to me at the last minute, sad tick-tocks of one hand in its white Japanese glove.

Thirty-nine

EVEN THOUGH it was April, there was still ice in the harbour, slabs of it rucked up around the shore so that the bay appeared like a grinning madman with froth all round his mouth. The sea was as grey as gunmetal. The sky was grey, the fog hanging among the doleful trees was grey. The warships were grey. People's faces were grey. Solid grey, broken grey, grey and white, grey verging into black, suicide grey, such was Vladivostok, and the stench was vile.

I thought, Cyn will kill herself if Sato brings her to live here.

I thought, Do I really want to be Prince of a Siberia like this?

The tired sea heaved and fell against the quay. A little further on was a stretch of mud on which lay the clothed body of a man. Small crabs were tugging at him. As I watched I realised that in fact the body was moving with crabs, especially his face.

I thought, That's what Yamaguchi'll look like when they fish him out. Will he have deserved it? When I'm sitting on that poncey throne, will I see the crabs coming out of his eye sockets – will there be a second great burden for my mind to carry?

Then Hijo was beside me. He'd gone to sort out our tickets with the Nippon Yusen Kaisha line. They'd been waiting at the desk, Sato having cabled through for the reservations. For me, first class with stateroom.

Our ship, the *Taiyou Maru*, was docked in front of us, pale green up to the line and white thereafter. Two funnels. Frayed hawsers, streaks of rust everywhere. Nothing smart about it. A refugee ship, that's what we were to sail on.

On our left, bulging out of the customs sheds, were the crowds hoping to board. Between them and the ship was a cordon of soldiers with bayonets.

Kobi said, 'So this is the sea.'

'Yes,' I said.

'Mongolia has no sea,' he said. 'This is the first time I've seen it.' He surveyed the vessel warily. 'If it sinks, we must drown. No one drowns in Mongolia.'

'Even though none of you can swim?'

'That's what I mean. We don't have to.'

'You have rivers,' I said.

'Rivers are not the sea,' he said. 'You can see the other side. So can your horse, and the horse can swim. Therefore you have a chance. But the sea . . . What happens when a man drowns, can you tell me that, Doig?'

'I cannot,' I said.

'I would rather own a horse than a boat,' he said simply.

Our vessel gave a great blast on its hooter. A pair of double gangways were trundled out and lowered to the quay. The soldiers moved forward to get people into lines. Embarkation was about to commence.

I said to Kobi, 'Getting that lot aboard'll take for ever. Let's go and have a meal.' What I meant was a drink. The sea, the crabs, the corpse, the snaking queues of exiles with their corded suitcases, Vladivostok itself, it was all getting to me. The past was a nightmare and the future invisible. Only the present was available, and I wanted to blot it out.

Hijo didn't wish to come, which suited me. I nobbled a couple of American sailors who were passing and got from them the address in the Syvetlanskaya of the Zolotoi Rog, or Solitary Dog as they called it.

It had three long bare tables, so shoulder-to-shoulder eating. On a chair by the stove an old man played the balalaika and sang songs of the sea in a fluttering voice. A party of Americans made room for us to squeeze onto the end of a table. I ordered a pitcher of vodka and some bread. For the first time since I'd known him, Kobi touched drink. We both did. We touched it good and proper. He was soon lost – fell sideways against me as he was relating all the scrapes he'd got me out of since we met in Samarkand. By then his face had gone red and puffy.

He started to cry, because he was leaving the only country he'd ever known.

The restaurant was full of Yanks, Tommies, Frogs, every nationality under the sun it seemed, all of them on the way to being as drunk as we were because everything outside was grey and no one cared a brass farthing about Russia, not even the officers. All anyone wanted was to be warm and drunk. The air was thick with pipe smoke and cigarette smoke and the smoke from the burning fat in the kitchen. Above us was a brothel. Thumpa-thumpa-thump went the headboard against the wall, making me think of Cyn.

There was no gaiety about the drunkenness, only the sullen air of people oppressed by events they cannot possibly influence. We all of us wished to be somewhere else, indeed wished it very much. When the old man sang a song about a baby whale lost upon the ocean after its mother had been killed by a harpooner, Kobi laid his head against my shoulder and burst into tears all over again.

Pushing him upright, I said, 'Before this, when did you last weep?'

But he was too far gone to speak and slumped onto my lap.

An American officer sitting opposite leaned forward and said, 'I think I understood your lingo. I'll tell you when I last wept. When I waved goodbye to my wife and kids to come here. They saw me to the station. I said they shouldn't but they said they should. The train pulled out, they got smaller and smaller and disappeared. I fell into my seat and wept. I wasn't alone either. This is my first overseas tour . . . Hope some of that got through to you.'

Drink had loosened me up. Each and every time I'd wept was laid out before me in full colour: when my father died, on my wedding night, when I buried Lizochka, when Kobi saved me from myself after the death of Xenia. The American was looking across at me expectantly. But I couldn't bring myself to tell him these stories because his face was too decent. It would ruin him to think that someone such as myself existed or that people could behave as I'd done. Smiling vaguely, I said to him, 'Russians cry at the drop of a hat, it's something you'll just have to get used to.'

It made him jump to hear me speak in English. 'Death to all

Bolsheviks,' I said. Then I took Kobi by his collar and hauled him out into the fresh air.

My guts were wrenching at me, saying it was my last meal in Russia, my last whiff of our filthy yellow cigarettes, of our mouldy furs, our cloaks, our foot wrappings, soup, bread, vodka, women – my last experience of the *smell* of Russia, which is as no other, which is close to the very soul of the country, which in fact ranks in importance second only to our Russian God – the smell which had been gathering in my nostrils since the day my mother gave birth to me.

A horse cab pulled up. I said to the man, 'Don't expect any sense from me, I'm drunk.'

He said politely, 'Do you know which quay you're leaving from, *barin?*'

I said, 'How do you know I'm leaving?'

He said, 'I've taken many like you to the docks from this place. You all have wet cheeks and empty eyes. It's a special sort of drunkenness. You don't smash things up, you just want to die, that's what one gentleman said to me. Which quay, for Nagasaki or Shanghai?'

I told him Nagasaki, I was sober enough for that. On the way to the docks we stopped at a pump and I threw water into Kobi's face. I didn't want him being turned away from the ship.

The crowds on the quay had been sorted out. A frieze of heads was watching proceedings from the upper deck. I got Kobi by the elbow and coaxed him up the gangplank. One of the first-class stewards took him off my hands. I found a quiet spot on a lower deck. At about 5 p.m. the hawsers were cast off and we slipped past the foreign warships and out of the Golden Horn. We made a course that took us to the east of Russian Island and then turned south into Peter the Great Bay.

I bundled my greatcoat collar round my ears. Darkness fell. The lighthouse on Russian Island started up astern, a feeble glimmering effort. Feeble, like everything to do with my country.

The propellers thrashed and below me the ship's wake stretched out as white as bier linen. On the lowest deck of all, mesh had been erected round the taffrail to stop people throwing themselves over the side. By leaning over the edge, I could see them doing as I was, lingering over the last sight they'd have of home. The last sight in their entire lives, I'd bet on it. Children were on their parents' shoulders, hanging onto the mesh. There was little noise from them, none of the usual hurly-burly you get when you have a crowd of Russians. Just a mass of shapkas and scarves and gabardine and dark heads, hats and shoulders, wedged against each other, the pallid light from two swaying bulbs emphasising their despair.

Our God, our brilliance, our hissing sleighs, our arguments, the interminable land mass we call Russia – going, going . . .

A vessel, perhaps a warship from yet another country, crossed between us and the lighthouse and deprived us of the sight of that last island . . .

Gone.

Somehow, in my febrile condition, I expected the captain to stop his ship and order that something be done to console his cargo of refugees. A religious service perhaps, or an hour of mourning. We Russians are not as others are. We'd been forced from our land. Times would be hard. Many of us would die in misery. Could not the captain understand this? Did he have a heart of stone?

Then from the deck below rose a sound that will haunt me for evermore. The men were singing, deep Russian voices that spoke not of our puny affairs but of that which pertains to the heart – of God, love and suffering. They were the voices I'd listened to uncomprehendingly, once a week, when my mother and father took me to the Cathedral of the Assumption. Only now did I understand what they were trying to express. They were the voices of glory, of hope and of every single element in our lives that can never be seen.

The throng took it up. From all around the ship rose the voices of my countrymen. It was the old song beginning,

> Chto my poteryaly, togo ne vernut,
> Uzh netu otechestva, netu uzh very . . .

> What is lost cannot be returned,
> Our Motherland is gone, our Faith is gone,
> And our route is marked with blood . . .

I fled to my cabin to weep.

Forty

THERE'D been bad blood between the Japanese and the Mongolians ever since Kublai Khan had tried to conquer the country and had his navy sunk by a typhoon. Hijo had no intention of letting the matter rest at that. There was definitely malice as well as cruelty in the man.

Remember, please, that Kobi had lost a little pinkie while saving General Sato. When a right-handed man is missing the pinkie on his right hand, it shows. The sense of balance is askew when holding a cup, for instance. It tips; the tea spills; people think you're drunk or have a palsy. Going to grip something is the same: the span of the hand is narrower than it was; an adjustment is needed, which can often look clumsy.

Throughout the voyage across the Sea of Japan, Hijo made a point of sitting next to Kobi at mealtimes and making fun of him when he dropped his chopsticks or miscued with them. When he went to the squat it was the same. Hijo would twirl his little finger in the air and splutter things like 'Good shooting' or 'Don't fall over' – words that were utterly stupid and could only have been said to show superiority. He even went so far as to suggest that he cut open and re-stitch Kobi's wound so as to make it more attractive. '*Attractive*,' I exclaimed in disbelief. 'More beautiful,' Hijo said. 'Our friend needs to have some beauty about him.'

He wore his surgeon's white coat most days – more than just wore it, he paraded in it, with the Emperor's medal still swinging where Sato had pinned it, below his array of pens. He spoke to everyone who would listen about the work he'd done at Zhigalovo and the international honours that were coming his way.

The more I shrank from him, the closer he stuck to me. What fascinated him was my size. Several times he came back to my experience of typhus. He said he was working on a theory that in tall, well-built men, the microbes responsible for the disease were dissipated through the system in lower concentrations than in small men. Height and weight were among the details the clerks in the laboratory at Zhigalovo had been collecting. He was studying the ledgers in his cabin. He put his forefinger to his eye and measured me as an undertaker would. 'Six foot two, a most interesting specimen, Mr Doig.'

We were going through the Straits of Tsushima, when Kobi came up to me at the rail. He said, 'Doig, when we get there I want money.'

I fed him, I clothed him, I horsed him and when he asked for money, I usually gave it him, that's how it worked between us. There'd been times when he demanded a monthly wage, which he set at an impossibly high rate, sometimes as much as Lenin was paid, and invariably with a huge additional figure for arrears. When this occurred, I knew he was hankering after a change of employment and wanted to impress someone by turning up with two horses or with a new rifle. But I couldn't see that happening this time, not in Japan.

I said, 'What it's to be, one of those short Japanese stabbing swords?'

He shook his head and wouldn't tell me.

I said, 'There's no revolution here. You can't go around slicing people up in Japan.'

He grunted. 'Him,' he said, pointing to Hijo who was holding forth on the deck below to a group of Russians. The words 'Bolshevik prisoners' floated up: without doubt he was telling them about his experiments. It still made me sick to think of that young man whose head he'd been going to cut open.

I said to Kobi, 'He'll do anything to get to the top. If he were in a fishbowl, he'd want to be top fish.'

'But not floating,' Kobi said.

'Look at the woman fingering his medal. He's loving every minute of it.'

'We don't have men like him in Mongolia,' Kobi said. 'His

184

parents would have been embarrassed by his behaviour and sold him to a Chinese merchant as a slave.'

I said, 'Do you think you were sold by your parents as a slave?'

'How many yen will you get for your roubles?' he said.

'One of the gold biscuits would attract more demand,' I said, admiring his sleight of hand in turning the conversation.

Kobi said, 'But you won't need the roubles any more. You should sell those first. We're not going back there.'

'Damn right we're not,' I said, and went to count them.

On the upper deck, a Jew from Minsk had set up a stall as a money-changer. The rates were displayed on a blackboard behind his chair. There was always a group of onlookers who came solely to watch the bargaining, which was wonderfully theatrical. I never actually saw money change hands. I think the whole see-saw of bid and offer, of grimace and counter-grimace, of ejaculation, cursing and flattery was just a way of passing the time during the voyage. When I approached the Jew, he offered me a rate for my roubles that only a man brought to his knees by starvation would have accepted.

It was a lovely pearly dawn when we steamed into Nagasaki. There was no other ship waiting for a pilot so we were soon threading our way through the outlying islands, through the small boats of the inshore fishing fleet with their different coloured flags, down the alley of navigation buoys on which cormorants were standing, like witches, with their coal-black wings spread out to dry, and thus into the mouth of the long deep inlet that the Portuguese and Dutch traders would have prayed for during their epic voyages on the high seas.

I stood as far forward as I could get. To left and right were stiff, jagged mountains sticking up through the mist. On their slopes were trees that were narrow, feathery and graceful, not a bit like our cumbersome Russian firs. Everything around me shone and shimmered, was tranquil and well ordered. Nothing was grey any longer, even the sea. Had the colour been abolished? I clapped my hands in delight at the notion, like a child.

As if in response, the captain pulled the lanyard and sent a great booming bellow round the harbour. I turned and looked up at him on the bridge – white-suited, with a blue gold-braided cap and sporting a neat, tight beard, just like Chekhov on his way to the spa. He removed his cap, held it over his heart and bowed to me. I bowed back, deeply. I was safe at last, I could feel it spreading through my limbs like the warmth that comes from alcohol. Here was where I'd start again, in a land where there was no ice, no snow, no hunger.

'Good morning, you splendid day,' I shouted, but no one could have heard since at that moment the captain threw the engines into reverse and with a great shudder and clanking the ship sidled into its berth at Quay No. 4.

Forty-one

'OH NO,' said Hijo, 'that is not the Japanese way at all. Yamaguchi-san is not a road sweeper. You cannot walk up to his house and say, Hello, would you like to buy something from me? His guards would beat you and throw you back into the street. The word would spread through the city that there was a tall *gaijin* around with very low manners. Then you might never get to see him.'

'Well?'

'For now we go to hotel which General Sato has ordered and then I will make the enquiry in Japanese way. I will discover where this man lives and arrange the introduction. That is the path to success and no other.'

He gestured to some porters to pick up our bags. He had a steamer trunk for the papers relating to his researches and a small yellow suitcase of plaited rice straw for his personal organisation. We followed the men to the rickshaw line.

On our left, on a flat piece of marshland, was the Russian refugee camp. A flag with the faded imperial colours stirred in the breeze. Beneath it was all the filth and squalor that a nation as undisciplined as ours is capable of. Barricades had been set up to prevent people breaking out and getting into the city. Armed soldiers were patrolling them. A gunboat was lying about a hundred yards offshore.

Hijo said, 'This is the worst class of Russian. Every month our government sends down a boat to take them to Hokkaido in the north. They are closer to their own sort there. They can wave across the sea to them. Also, our own people up there are completely primitive. A most suitable arrangement for both sides.'

'Adding to that extra million people, are they?' I said to annoy him.

'It's Hokkaido, what does it matter?' he said, and we piled into the rickshaws and had them take us to the France Hotel, a severe three-storey building next to a wonderfully gaudy Confucian temple with massive wooden gates guarded by winged griffins. Patrolling the walls of the compound were red-tongued dragons and other well-omened myths. A gong from deep within the temple sounded the hour, which was midday.

The hotel manager, a stocky fellow in a high collar and wearing a black swallow-tail coat, glanced at me and said sharply to Hijo in a strange mixture of Russian and Japanese, 'From Russia? This morning's boat?'

The doctor didn't like the tone of voice at all. He swung his straw suitcase up onto the desk, knocking over the curved stand of miniature flags as he did so. He grasped his gold medal and thrust it at the manager. 'What does that tell you, *baka*?'

The man said calmly, 'Refugees have no money. They have their own place to go to at the harbour. As for that thing, you could have got it anywhere. It's no good waving it at me like that. I can tell from here it's rubbish.'

That fairly got Hijo going. He swept aside the register and the bell push with his forearm and shoved his suitcase off in the opposite direction. Then damn me if he didn't whip out his money pouch, lick his thumb and with a flourish fan out brand-new Tsarist notes on his left and brand-new yen on his right, the light blue five-yen notes that carry a picture of some legendary white-bearded old man. I never thought I'd admire Hijo but on that occasion I did. He was like a gambler plonking down a winning hand. Shoving his teeth out at the manager, he said, 'Which do you prefer – or do you only take Bolshevik muck?'

Of course the manager didn't know which he wanted. The yen was his currency but the Tsarist five-hundreds were huge and pink, the sort of money a man knew by instinct would buy him the best whore in town for a week. His long fingernails hovered over the yen. The electric light made them shine like mother-of-pearl. They moved to the roubles – Hijo knocked his hand away and scooped up the cash. 'You need to have quicker reactions – I suggest you visit your doctor. Now you know we are top men. You remember that and treat us like top men.'

The manager placed his finger pads on the blotter in front of him, made wigwams from them and leaned forward aggressively, which I thought was a foolish attitude to take. 'No top men have got off the Vladivostok boat in the last two years. They've all been scum, refugee scum with forged money and women who steal everything. My losses—'

'Governor Sato forges money, is that what you're saying?'

The effect was instantaneous. The manager bowed to his waist and the bellhops to their knees, little rolls with plum paste inside turned up and then sweet rice cakes called *o-manjuh* and then delicate cups of tea and when we'd finished the process of registration, a flask of sake. Hijo spittled happily at me, 'News will get to Yamaguchi that Sato has some men in town. That'll smooth our way.'

Two days later he took me aside at breakfast and told me he'd seen Yamaguchi and had arranged a time later that morning when we could visit him. I asked if he'd discovered whether Yamaguchi was still interested in forming a cabinet of natural history specimens. But he neither knew nor cared. All that mattered to him was getting back into his ledgers and ascertaining whether small people succumbed to disease more quickly than big people. Japanese versus Europeans, there was a touch of that in it, I felt, something that was personal.

Forty-two

Kobi was nowhere to be found. I'd given him money. He'd gone off into the Chinese quarter and hadn't returned. His absence concerned me, for I'd drifted into the position almost of being his guardian. But I reckoned that if he could look after me, he should be able to look after himself twice as well.

The hotel rickshaw was waiting: cracked tarpaulin roof, yellow wheels with brown hubs and a yellow body with the words FRANCE HOTEL painted erratically in black below the freeboard. The *kurumaya* or puller was leaning against the shafts smoking. He was wearing a dirty cotton lungi and a singlet. He asked Hijo if he wanted the window grilles put up. Hijo said he wasn't a geisha. The puller pinched out his cigarette and put the shreds of tobacco in a pouch at his waist. He went barefooted, his extraordinarily leathery feet splayed out on the road like a pair of dusty brown gauntlets.

He turned round and readied himself, pressing down on the shafts so that the rickshaw didn't tip up when we climbed in. He had a number cloth on his back like a jockey – 3719, in English and Japanese characters. Hijo said he'd woken up with a stiff neck and wanted to draw the flimsy muslin curtains across the back window. But I wouldn't let him. It was April, which in Nagasaki is well into spring. I wanted to make the most of it, to feel the sweet breezes blowing around me.

The puller trotted us down to the Oura Bund, where we turned south along the edge of the harbour. There was none of the rotting odour and despondency of Vladivostok. The nets were spread out neatly, the fishy smells were freshly fishy, the bobbing boats were gaily painted and the calls of the men swaying their catches onto barrows like huge sacks of silver tinkled in the clean, vigorous air.

Splendid! I lay back, placed my ankle on top of my knee and gripped it. The clouds weren't ponderous and Russian but light and fleecy, with fairy-tale pinnacles and banners and battlements and rosy bottoms like cherubs. The men didn't hulk, not a beard was in sight, the women were lithe. Splendid! I dug Hijo in the ribs and beamed on him. 'Splendid! No lice for you here, doc!'

We crossed the Benten Bridge with its row of tea houses and fancy eating places looking out over the river. We passed the Club, the British Consulate with its flag of empire and the Customs House for Quay No. 4. A hundred yards on we came to the Hongkong & Shanghai Bank. It looked modern, imposing, secure. 'Splendid!' I said again and had the puller stop.

A couple of Europeans were lounging at the vast mahogany counter, spread all over it, chatting – cotton trousers, big-buckled belts, panama hats. I was still in my Russian gear, which I'd been wearing since we pulled out of Uncle Igor's palace eighteen months ago. Cyn and Mushi had had a go at sprucing me up. But I'd got shabby, and my hair was too long. I looked like what I was, a refugee, and there was no escaping the fact.

They pushed back their panamas and examined me with disdain, had me labelled in a tick as White rubbish. One man spoke, the other glanced at me and spoke back, a quip at my expense that pulled the corners of his mouth down in mirth. Then they continued their chat. Maybe they were American, maybe English. Every Western nation did business through Nagasaki.

A notice on the desk said that Mr N. J. Stabb was Chief Manager. I asked loudly in English for his company in a private room. That made everyone look up. It was not only the clerks who'd been expecting a babble of Russian.

'Well then, how can I help you today, Mr Bog,' said Stabb, preceding me into the room and tossing the words back over his substantial shoulder.

The room had a table and two chairs, one very hard and one very comfortable – a planter's chair. I took the latter and spread myself at length. A clerk darted in with paper and pencil for us. 'A cup of tea'd be more like it,' I said and patted the arm of my chair. Having been made for some thirsty planter it was nice and wide, well suited to glass or cup.

'A big day for you, Mr Bog,' said Stabb. 'At last you've reached a civilised country. This'll be your first bank account, I suppose. You'll remember the occasion for the rest of your life.'

My tea arrived quickly and while I drank it I lay back and made Stabb listen to some of my adventures with money, starting with the last occasion I had recourse to a bank, which was the Imperial, in Chernaevski Prospekt, Samarkand, five years ago. 'A Greek from Odessa called Simeonidis ran it. It was from him that I heard the Tsar had ceased to pay me. As he explained it all, his wife began to play the piano in the room above us. Isn't that a curiosity? Simeonidis later absconded, maybe with that lady, maybe with another. For certain he took the bank's money. From that day to this, I've lived by my wits, never had any need of a bank. In fact, where I come from, Lenin has said we can live very easily without banks.'

'Blowing his own miserable trumpet, that's what he's doing. Living without banks, ha ha ha!'

'He called your lot vultures, lined up all he could find and had them shot. Outside their own banks. Just like that, while people went in and out as normal. "Taking money out today, are we, sir?" "A thousand, if you please." Bang bang. "Pay no attention, sir. New management, that's all. Here's your cash. Ten, twenty, thirty . . ."'

Stabb shifted his buttocks. He glanced out of the window and then at me, sideways on, like a nervous cow, showing a lot of eye white. I could see the matter of references rising like dough in his mind. But I wasn't going to cut him any width. I said, 'You want a character for me and you'll have to apply to the Cheka in Moscow. That's Lenin's dossier department. In case they don't reply, all you need know is that I own twenty-eight tons of the Tsar's gold and if that doesn't satisfy you, I'm leaving. What's it to be, eh, Mr Stub?'

'Mr Bog,' he said—

I slipped my boots off, got out my knife and slit open the linings. Onto the table I shook all that remained of my diamonds, still neatly wrapped in Shansky's tissues, my three gold biscuits, the Gorevsky necklaces and my last thousand-rouble note. I made them into orderly piles, shaped up the diamonds nicely and patted them. I smiled upon Stabb. 'These boots of mine, best bank I ever had.'

He looked from the diamonds to me and back again. 'Who exactly are you? Do you have a passport?'

'Do I look to you like a passport fellow? All that concerns you is that my name is not Bog but Doig, and that you're going to open a bank account for me with the cash. The jewels and biscuits are going into one of your safes.'

'No passport – well, I suppose times are unsettled – but might you have an address in the city – something – some paperwork – credentials of some sort – Mr, er, Doig?'

'Nigel,' I said, having a guess at what the N. stood for, 'I don't care for your manner. It's no business of yours what your customers look like or where they live. Are you going to do my work or aren't you?'

He didn't care for the first-name business, looked at me very huffily, only changing and that very speedily when I said I was on my way to see Yamaguchi. Taking advantage of his change of tune I had him bring me six decent-sized cigar boxes, which I knew they'd have somewhere for pencils and suchlike. I filled three of them with the diamonds and the biscuits and two with the necklaces. While Stabb looked on, I used the last of my Taxidermine to dust the Lala bird skin and placed it very carefully in the remaining box, breast down, head turned sideways, utterly nondescript except for its purple eyebrow.

'A bird,' said Stabb, leaning over the box. 'I don't know—'

'A sacred bird,' I said. 'You and I are the only Westerners ever to have seen it. That's right, the only white men since history began. Tell your children about it when you go home tonight.'

Once I'd seen Stabb clamp the bar of the Milner's Patent Safe and had the numbers of the dial in my wallet, I went upstairs. The banking parlour was a large, handsome, open room, pale green in colour, with elegant appointments and a finely coffered ceiling. I strolled round taking everything in. It was good to be reminded of the form of beauty.

The two white men were still chatting away at the counter.

Their conversation drifted off as I walked round, taking my time about it.

Stabb was lingering at the door to see I didn't go off with anything. I said, 'Who are those men?'

'Those are the Walker brothers. R. N. Walker & Co., Stevedores, Shipping Agents and Customs Brokers.'

'Do they stare like that at everyone?'

'You are a conspicuous figure, Mr Doig. And if I may say so, sir, your English is uncommonly good.'

I thanked him and walked out to the rickshaw.

When starting off in a foreign country, it can never be said too often: take nothing for granted. Observe and beware – one step at a time – gradualness the key word at all points.

The fresh shoots on the plum trees, some of which still had tatters of red and white blossom, were startling by contrast with the trunks, which were as black and withered as if they'd been charred by fire. The peach trees were coming into bud, the young rice had just started to poke out, the blue dingle-dangles of wistaria were everywhere, as rampant as ivy, and on the hillsides were vast pink clumps of wild weigela. There were camellias, there were magnolias, even goddamn bougainvillea was about to burst – there was stuff there I hadn't clapped eyes on since Goetz and I were tramping through the tropics.

And bamboos! Christ were there bamboos!

'By heavens this is not Russia!' I exclaimed to Hijo – and then, 'Oh, but look at that rice, I swear it grew an inch while I blinked! Let me tell you something, only an idiot would think of dying today.'

The peasants were bent over hoeing, their backs like hoops, their conical straw hats tied beneath the chin. I went on, 'Look at that for industry. At home our peasants spend half the day gazing into the sky and scratching their tits.'

He grunted, not looking up from his notes, said something about the Russian porters at the hospital having had huge heads in which not a single thought ever moved.

I said, 'I don't know about your porters but actually the Russian peasant thinks a lot. About God, about sunspots, which he's convinced affect the yields of his crops, about money, women and drink, and when his children'll be old enough to

194

work in the fields. As long as he's got the Russian sky above him, he's content. It's where all our national mysteries are. He spends his life turning the whole thing over in his head.'

'Such peasants will not do well under your Mr Lenin,' Hijo said.

'Japanese people think about nothing but work?'

Jerking his head up, 'They think most of all about their health. When they see other people living longer, they'll stop thinking they'll be dead by nightfall. That is the day I live for.'

'Coming sometime soon?' I said, meaning to be sarcastic but speaking with too sweet a tone on account of the glorious day.

He said, 'When I complete my work, everyone in the world will live longer. It is my intention to abolish disease. Yes, Mr Doig, that is my aim.'

We'd passed the fine hillside houses where the English traders lived and turned off up the next valley. Hijo slipped a marker into his ledger and closed it carefully. 'We are here. This' – with a sweep of his arm out of the side of the rickshaw – 'is the property of Yamaguchi-san. Its name in Japanese means Little Paradise.'

In front was a turning off the road with a short length of stone wall on either side, a gate and a sentry box beside it. The puller spat and said something to Hijo. Hijo said to me, 'He asked, does he need to take us all the way to the top of the hill? I said, were you born *baka* or did it come to you from your work?'

Yamaguchi's set-up looked as if he'd enclosed an entire section of the slope and turned it into private parkland. From where we were his driveway curled quite steeply upwards through an avenue of cherries, bursting with flower, into which had been planted magnolias, maples and *sugi*, which is a sort of Japanese redwood with flaking red bark. Perhaps the *sugi* had been there at the beginning, for they were strong, graceful trees and held the landscape together.

The house was about a hundred feet above us, a long, low, wooden structure beneath a roof of bronze tiles that had a lot of fussy little angles. I couldn't make out any more detail because of the trees and shrubs around it.

I said to Hijo, 'He did all this himself?'

'His father started their business, I told you that,' Hijo said, and we turned off the road.

A soldier came out of the box and barred our way by holding his rifle across the puller's chest. Hijo spoke to him. He went back to his sentry box and cranked up his field telephone. A brief discussion and we were through.

I said reflectively, 'Yamaguchi's a big shot in town.'

'*Shacho* is our Japanese word,' he said.

'*Nachalnik* in Russian. Yours is the better word.'

Our puller glanced at the hill in front of us and spat. Hijo told him to get on with it. He spat again, this time in earnest, clapped a hand against one ear as if to swat a fly, shook his head and started the climb.

His calves were the shape of skittles. Grunting and spitting, teeth bared and head bowed, he slowly hauled us up the hill. At halfway he stopped, wiped his face on a corner of his singlet and said to me via Hijo that the 'buffalo *gaijin*' should eat less. On hearing this, I enquired if I should get out to make it easier for such a feeble fellow – and did so. I thought Hijo would be obliged to do likewise so as not to lose face, but he stayed put, clearly not going to be separated from his ledger, which he clutched against his chest.

The puller squatted down beside the rickshaw and relit his old cigarette.

I left the two of them and, jumping over a little rill bordered by wild blue irises, entered Yamaguchi's pleasure grounds.

Forty-three

Some of the redwoods still had last year's cones, which hung from the branches in tight clusters, like old friends. Between the trees were banks of clipped azaleas, mostly pink or pinkish, their small sharp leaves glittering in the sun. They funnelled me into a sort of defile, through which I passed.

Someone else had been there that morning, I could tell from the crushed grass. Male or female, I couldn't say which, they all have such small feet.

I found myself in a new compartment, ringed by waxy camellias. In the centre was a wooden bench. On the arm lay the reed for a clarinet or flute or one of those. I tried it but it was split and could only squawk for me. I put it in my pocket.

On my left a glade led out of the camellias between winding hedges of evergreen aucuba. In the centre of the glade, flowing between banks of irises and bubbling over small, artfully arranged falls, was another stream, about four feet wide with clear spring-fed water and a nice gravel bottom for crayfish. I wandered along beside it for about fifty yards until I reached a lily pool, after which the stream turned sharply downhill and went under the driveway via a bridge with bamboo latticework balustrades. I hadn't noticed it when in the rickshaw: too busy taking everything else in. Below it the stream meandered through a series of pools in which frogs were croaking about love, even at that time of the day, and various cultivars of lotus spread their enormous veined leaves like mats of greeny-blue rubber.

The scale of the undertaking was astonishing. I shook my head and set out back up the path, which soon wandered off to the left. I guessed it was going to hook back through the trees and end up at Yamaguchi's house.

The time was now 11 a.m.

I say this so that you can picture for yourselves the angle at which the sun was coming through the trees and how it picked out the cherry blossom, which without the slightest breeze to send the petals flying, hung in balls of startling whiteness, as if small clouds had come down for a rest. I strolled along the path in total wonderment. It was one of those days when everything in the heavens is at a standstill and man can believe in luck without having to cross his fingers.

Put it another way: on a day such as this, I could think only that to be alive was a miracle and death an impossibility.

Of course the moment I describe how it was without a wind, I see again a most handsome eucalyptus with grasshopper-green leaves that were trembling *furiously*, as if wishing to passionately denounce my untruth. But it was the only one doing it! As I passed by I admonished it, saying, Don't wring your hands like that, you won't see many days as fine as this one.

I walked on, still following the same set of footprints, now growing fainter as the trodden grass unfurled its stems. The planting grew denser. I passed through thickets of bamboo thirty or forty feet high that were so silent and impenetrable as to be intimidating. Were wild boar lying up in them? Had a murder taken place and the corpse been dragged into the tangle of stems and there dismembered? The contrast was so great that it invited conjecture. Then I was out of them and into the laughing sunshine again and almost immediately I found myself passing what was virtually a wall of early honeysuckle with long, slender, curling, yellow and white flowers on which two hummingbird hawkmoths were feasting. Had they overwintered in some cosy cranny or were the winters in Nagasaki extraordinarily benign? Their tongues, did they carry them in a coil? I couldn't see how they could possibly retract and store such an organ. The moths were hovering an inch off the flower. The nectar must have been two inches down the flower – which made three inches of tongue to be carried by an insect only two inches in length.

'You little beauties!' That was what I said and with the scent from the flowers dancing in my nostrils, I moved towards a grove of *akamatsu*, which is a tree very similar to a Scots pine.

A bold outcrop of rock was before me, a stand of delicate ferns springing from a crack in its face. On top of the rock was growing a single stunted *akamatsu*.

I skirted the base, setting my feet down carefully. Whenever I'm walking upon pine needles, that's what I do. Softness invites softness in return, always, whatever the circumstances.

A tiny movement caught my eye, and I froze. After a moment I picked her up – a doe, on the edge of a dappled glade, her coat having exactly the same texture of colour as the sunlight filtering through the pine trees. She'd seen me – her head was rock steady. Her large brown eyes regarded me unblinking and without fear. She stood there, stock-still.

She shifted her gaze from me to something round the corner of the buttress of rock.

I leaned against the cool face of the rock, and waited.

Then a strong, hoarse voice entered the glade and said in exactly the same bad Russian as Hijo spoke, 'Hana, meet Doig-san. He's a brave man. He saved the life of my cousin.'

Forty-four

H E STOOD in front of the pavilion with his arms folded across his chest, a man of medium height dressed in a dark blue robe with a lining of lighter blue. The sash, which he wore casually around his waist, was a soft raspberry red. His hair, black with grey among it, was pulled back from his forehead and tied in a ponytail with a white band. He was clean-shaven.

His eyes – upward slanting, devilish, pupils like black tabs. His nose – so narrow you could have sliced onions with it. His cheeks – hollow; his figure – whipcord.

I put his age at about fifty-five.

'Welcome to my pavilion! Hana will accept you immediately. She knows that the only people I allow this far have honourable intentions. Her name means "flower".'

'I'd have been turned back?'

'Had you been a stranger, my guards would have stopped you before you'd gone twenty yards.'

'And if Dr Hijo had been with me?'

'I gave orders that only the *gaijin* was to be admitted. The pleasure grounds are for me, my family and my guests. All other people are forbidden.'

I stepped further into the glade and bowed. 'Then I count myself fortunate.'

'It is I who am fortunate. You are the famous Charlie Doig.'

Hana lifted her damp nose and took a couple of paces towards me. Lovely slender legs, black shining hooves like chips of coal. Yamaguchi said, 'She hopes you've got a cake for her. She's very partial to sweet red-bean paste. I'm afraid I spoil her terribly.'

His pavilion was open to the winds on three sides, with honey-coloured timbers supporting the roof. At the other end, behind the usual glazed paper screens, was a room for cooking and eating.

The roof, which was made of old clay tiles weathered to a light shade of turquoise, had the swooping elevations of a temple. Instead of the usual gutter stops were dragons, four of them, one at each corner, to keep devils away. The external timbers were all scarlet.

I took my boots off, pointing them outwards for when I left. I mounted the three steps onto the decking. I felt no apprehension or worry. The man standing above me in the blue robe was an ally. I knew it unquestioningly.

We bowed simultaneously. He looked me in the eye. Such a face! A Red Indian's! Rugged, cracked, lined, rough as an oyster shell, with dark ledges beneath his eyes. It was a face that was full of power and decision. He said, 'At last, Mr Charlie Doig, the man who discovered a beetle.'

'Chicago was determined to have it. The Field has the most extensive collection of Lepidoptera of any museum in the world.'

He said, 'I know. I could have gone on bidding against them. Your jewel would have been a sensational addition to my collection. And I like to get my own way. But something happened to dissuade me. Let us make ourselves comfortable.'

He sat cross-legged on the tatami mat. I did my best to copy him.

He started: 'One morning, at a dawn very like today, I came down here. There was a business decision I had to make, more important even than the decision about your beetle. It had been preying on my mind all night long. The morning was chilly. I lit the brazier. I was sitting where you are' – he laughed – 'where you are sitting so awkwardly, if I may say so, and Hana's mother came pacing through the trees towards me looking for a titbit. At the sight of her, the business matter that had so engrossed me fled from my mind and I thought, Why should I spend my money on a dead creature when the living one is so much more interesting – do I really want this beetle, even though it's a first? My next thought was this, that for a man such as myself, who's not trained as a scientist, there's no point in filling a house with what's dead. Don't misunderstand me. I was very fond of my collection, especially my moths. It wasn't the frivolous whim of a rich man. For example, all those Lucanidae are extraordinary examples of the lengths to which nature will go to get its own way. Whenever I looked at them I would reflect how impoverished we humans are. But on that cold morning I preferred to see a living stag beetle to a dead jewel – to watch it clambering through all the bits and pieces on the forest floor that so interest it. Maybe it's a transition that happens at a certain point in a man's life: we stop being ruthless and become weak and sentimental instead. You're still young, only just thirty. You're nowhere near it. But I . . . I'm old enough to be your father.'

Seeing my expression, he smiled and said, 'Governor Sato and his American lady have a file on you. Your age is the least interesting fact in it. Anyway, you can imagine the rest. Within a year my collection had gone, most of it to two museums here in Japan. Their directors were kind enough to say I'd done a service to mankind.'

I said, 'I had no knowledge of the extent of your collection, only that you were competing with the Field for my jewel beetle. I was just going on a hunch when I decided to bring you my bird skin.'

He frowned slightly. 'The Lala bird, am I correct?'

'Yes. I've no idea what its Linnaean name will be. I'd hope it would be a second *doigii*. That'd stand me in good stead with the museums.'

'But you find me an uninterested party and you must accept that. I'd have liked to help you. You've survived many ordeals. A lesser man would have died several times getting from Moscow to Nagasaki with things as bad as they are.'

I nodded at the compliment.

'To have to flee one's country of birth cannot be pleasant. Governor Sato says you have lost all your family, that you are one hundred per cent alone in the world. Is that so?'

'Yes. I once had a wife and cousins. Now I have no one.'

'A man needs the solidarity of a family to bring out the best in him. A family, a home, children. These fix the shape to his life. But it's up to him to provide the purpose. What drives you on, Doig-san?'

I had to reflect on that. Yamaguchi noted my indecision and turned his head to watch me think. That was disconcerting. A fumbled answer and my stock would sink. I knew it from his silence and from the sharp, unwavering angle of his nose, which I could see from the corner of my eye.

I said, 'Since the death of my wife, everything has been negative for me. At every corner I've turned, I've faced the likelihood of disaster, often of death. Only by escaping from Russia have I managed to get free of my past. I can't yet tell you what I'm looking for.'

He said nothing. Gently smoothing at his kneecaps with his hands, he looked straight in front.

I thought, I could never kill this man, I could never arrange for his death, I could never even go against him. That I'd met him only ten minutes before was irrelevant. He and I were moving in the same orbit. The strength of his character, of his intellect and of his internal powers had enveloped me as if he were emitting a field of some special brand of electricity that only I could feel.

I'd met no one like him in my life.

Should I tell him about Sato's instructions? I made my mind up instantly. The first words were on the tip of my tongue when suddenly a ripple of music came stealing through the wood from somewhere above us. Yamaguchi didn't budge an inch. I felt in my pocket and showed him the broken reed. 'Your wife? A daughter?'

A look of joy came into his face. 'My younger daughter. The older one, whose name is Yumi, enjoys money: she heads the treasury department of my business. It is Mimosa who is my favourite. She looks like me and thinks like me. The only point at which we differ is this, her musical talent. To me, it is all noise.'

'Mimosa,' I said contemplatively.

'Yes, Mimosa.'

Here he looked at me intently, waiting for a reaction.

'*Mimosa pudica*, the sensitive plant,' I said.

'Go on.'

'Which is also called touch-me-not.'

'Go on.'

I described *pudica* for him, in the forms in which I'd seen it. 'It originates in Central America. Maybe it's mutated on its way here? I don't know. I haven't been a week in your country. It's a great curiosity wherever it grows.'

He said, 'I've tried it here but without much success. Our climate is suitable so the fault, if I can use that word, must lie with our soil. Would it interest you to know why my daughter is called Mimosa?'

'Of course.'

'Because her birth, which was premature, was a most perilous and agonising process for her mother. In fact, I think it was the principal reason for her death two years later. Mimosa was so tiny and shrivelled that everyone was afraid even to pick her up. Our large hands and this small fragile package, only four pounds or something like that – everything seemed so dangerous, even the act of touching her, in case she'd fall to pieces. My wife, lying there so white and exhausted, whispered, "What shall we call her?" I'd hoped for a boy, of course I had. But right then, I was just glad they were both alive. I said, "*Mimosa pudica*, because if you touch one single flower of it, the whole plant may collapse." So Mimosa she is. She likes the name. She sings as well as playing the flute.'

The music, that haunting, plaintive, drug-like music, returned to us again, much louder – she must have been facing the other way when she first played.

Yamaguchi said, 'She keeps the music pinned to a camellia. She says the flower gives her inspiration.'

I said, 'My family wasn't musical at all.'

He smiled and said, 'Like me. The composer of this piece was a Frenchman called Debussy who died very recently, I believe. My daughter is playing her favourite. It is called *Prelude à l'après-midi d'un faune*. The faun is of course our pet Hana, who is also listening to the music. It is nothing like our Japanese music. My friends cannot understand why she is so fond of this piece – of the entirety of your Western music. To tell the truth, I do not understand why myself. All I can say is what she herself tells me, that it strikes the region of her heart.'

I said, 'And if the deer wasn't here, what do you think she'd be playing?'

'But the deer is here. It may have been something else in a previous life but now it's a deer, like its mother, whose name was Haru, which means "spring" in our language. Your question is not relevant.'

A silence fell upon us, into which that flute-playing (which she accomplished without a single pause or falter) descended like some ghost visiting from the heavens, maybe a current of air, maybe a myth. The doe, the glade, the pine trees above us splintering the sun, Yamaguchi straight-backed with his hands cupping his knees, the girl Mimosa and her flute – it was what I'd never had, the tranquillity of soul that every human yearns for. For the first time since the death of my footling, lovely father, I felt secure. No longer was every minute a matter of life or death. I'd found a place of refuge.

I stood up. Yamaguchi did the same. I wiped my face on my sleeve – dashed my arm across. We bowed to each other, without embarrassment.

He said, 'You bow like one of us, not like a *gaijin* at all.'

I said, 'My mother taught me. She came from the Russian aristocracy. In her world everyone learned how to bow properly. That was my life until the age of fourteen – my home and my world.'

'Which has now vanished and will never return,' he said.

'Yes.'

'What happened when you were fourteen?'

'My father died.'

'Ah-so, your father . . . Doig-san, it would give me pleasure if you would come to my house and take food with me.'

We stepped down from the pavilion. He put on his sandals and I my boots. He took a *manjuh* cake from his pocket and held it out to Hana. Without hesitation she came up to him and stood only a yard away, her damp nostrils wrinkling, her eyes bright.

He said to me, 'I never touch her. That would be one degree of familiarity too many.' He placed the cake on a round stone stool. 'Unless I leave her something, she follows me. She'll come right up to the house. She is fearless, that one.'

The path was of such a width that we could walk and converse in comfort. When we were about halfway there, the flute-playing stopped. Yamaguchi said, 'I know what she's doing now,' and he vigorously shook the spittle from an imaginary flute. 'An angel, that's how I think of her, even though there are no angels in our Buddhist religion.'

Forty-five

WE REACHED the terrace through a walkway of clipped box bushes. Brushing his hand over their tops, he said, 'When the summer rains come, the smell from the leaves rises like a perfume.' Then we were outside the house, which was long, low and single-storeyed. In front of it was a dragon rearing up on its hind legs, with bluey-gold scales, glaring red eyes and a back serrated like a crocodile's tail. It was carrying something in its claws, a round stone dressed up to resemble a jewel. Yamaguchi said with a wave, 'By means of that globe, the dragon controls the winds and the rains and the movements of the planets themselves. He also keeps out any devils that may be tempted to come looking for us in the house.'

I said, 'And yet you still have bodyguards?'

'Of course. There is a life here and a life that is not here. A sensible man must protect himself from the bad elements in each. You will call it superstition. I call it realism. Four claws to a paw is an ordinary dragon. Mine has five, which makes it imperial. I like to excel.'

Giving the dragon's head a good rub in order to acquire some of its juju, I said, 'Is the doctor still waiting on the hill? Has the *kurumaya* just left him there?'

'Hey!' – Yamaguchi shouted for the guard at the end of the terrace. The man ran towards us, rifle in his hand, the flap on the back of his kepi bouncing on his neck. There was some talk then Yamaguchi said to me, 'He told me that the doctor is being fed with the servants. That is how it should be. I do not care for our doctor. I am suspicious of him. Why is he here? – that's what I ask myself.'

We passed through a sort of lychgate where there were two more guards. Then we were in a large sunny courtyard, of pale round pebbles laid in a swirl like the human eye. Around it was a gravel path. In the centre was a single-jet fountain from which issued a cloud of fine spray, twinkling as if a man was throwing diamond dust at it. Butting onto the house was a wooden veranda with a bench running along the back wall. To one side of it was a pair of heavy bronze doors with leaping carp for handles. To open them you gripped the fish round the slender shank immediately above the tail.

'Why is the doctor here, Doig-san? You tell me.'

'I had no idea that he was coming until he hopped onto the train. His own explanation is that he's on his way to Tokyo to hand in his research.'

'Since when has Nagasaki been on the way from Vladivostok to Tokyo? If that was his intention he should have got on a ship to Tsuruga. There are two a week. The crossing takes less than forty-eight hours. He will have another purpose in coming here.'

The doors were opened from the inside by an elderly servitor. The old man took my boots away to clean them. We entered the house.

The wooden floor, which was made of wide planks that ran with the flow of the house, gave off a thin, cool scent. Yamaguchi glanced at my shabby socks and handed me a pair of house slippers, saying something about servants over-waxing the floor and turning it into an ice rink. Then we set off down the long dark room, which was virtually devoid of furniture.

He said, 'None of my servants speak Russian. We can talk about whatever we wish.'

I said, 'I want to learn your language. Your customs and your writing also.'

He gave a terse laugh and said something in Japanese. I said to him in Russian, 'Play the game, *barin*.' He said, also in Russian, 'What I said was, You need to get a woman.'

'It sounded a much longer sentence to me.'

'That is well observed. I said also, and long nights, a firm futon, and love.'

'That's a tall order for a *gaijin* who's only been in Japan for a couple of days.'

'But not an impossible one. In Japan, our women believe that their life's work is to help their men and their family.'

'What do men have to give in return?'

'That you will have to discover for yourself . . . If you would permit me to show you my house, afterwards we can eat. My father called it Kogane-Yakata, which means Gold Mansion. The name I have given it is Little Paradise.'

He stopped suddenly, his face like stone. 'You didn't take the chances I offered you.'

I looked blankly at him.

'When I asked you why the doctor was here, that was your first chance. You ignored me. When I asked you a second time, you asked me to believe some nonsense about doing research. Now I'm giving you a third chance. After that there will be no more. You have something to tell me. So tell it.'

The moment he mentioned Hijo again, I saw his drift. Because he was suspicious of Hijo, he was suspicious of me also. We'd arrived together and we came from Sato. By the same token that Sato knew about Yamaguchi's affairs, he might know about Sato's – might know every single thing. The quiet, almost invisible figure of Mushi flipped into my mind as the go-between. But how the hell did they manage to communicate?

Bowing my head, I said, 'I'm ashamed to tell you.'

'Tell it,' he roared.

'I agreed with Governor Sato that I would come to Nagasaki and arrange to have you killed if you didn't withdraw from the partnership with him. He explained to me about the Kingdom of Eastern Siberia. He said the project was too important to be allowed to fail.'

'His reasoning concerned the Empress and a temple I had razed?'

'Yes.'

'That was the only reason he gave you?'

'Yes.'

'Will you swear on the memory of your father that this was so?'

'Yes.'

'Then the matter is straightforward and I can relax. He's been trying to have me killed for many years. I'll tell you about it

209

later. Come, let us continue walking. Here is a subject that is more agreeable.'

We crossed to the other side of the room, where one section of the wall was devoted to a number of scrolls, some vertical, others horizontal, decorated with beautiful calligraphy. 'The brushes for this sort of work are made from the whiskers of rats. Every animal has a use,' he said when I paused to admire one. (Great sooty sweeping letters meaning God knows what. Goetz would have adored this country, would probably never have left it – it wasn't the first time I'd thought about him in Japan.)

A little further down the same wall was a large wooden case with its doors closed. Yamaguchi halted. Looking at me with a twisted smile, he said, 'My judgement is that you are a man who relishes the company of women.' He took a pace backwards to see the effect of his words.

I said, 'Love has brought me nothing but hurt.'

'Ah yes,' he said, 'but it wasn't love that I was talking about. It was women.'

I said, 'In that case you are right.'

He said abruptly, 'What was your price? What am I worth as a corpse?'

I didn't hesitate. 'In return for causing your death or your retirement from the partnership, I was to become the Prince of Siberia.'

He studied me. I could have no secrets. I knew my face was completely immature compared to his, which at that moment had the harsh, suspicious features of a medieval monarch. He said, 'My cousin honestly believed that you, a young man whom I'd never met before, could persuade me to withdraw?'

'It may have been his Countess's idea?'

He said, 'I will tell you presently how that whole matter has arisen, and why he wants me dead. Let us move the conversation forward.'

Pointing at the wooden wall-case, 'My mother, who is ninety-one, insists that the doors be kept closed. I say to her, "How can you still be shocked at your age, Mama?" She mutters, "They are lewd, that is enough," and saying no more crabs her way down the room with her maid, who is even older than she is, both of them bent over like peasant women. She was my father's number-one wife. So I obey her – and generally keep the cabinet closed.'

He unlatched the doors, folded them right out and stood back.

Within the case were six antique fans made of cypress wood, each one opened to its fullest extent.

'Oh yes,' I said, 'oh yes, I see your mother's point.'

Yamaguchi was at my shoulder, breathing softly. 'They were the property of a geisha who was a special friend of my father. When she died unexpectedly, he found she'd left them to him in her will. My father was like you, he greatly enjoyed having women around him. Like me, also.

'Don't touch them,' he called out, 'the moisture on your fingers would ruin the paint. Just enjoy the story.'

This was the order in which they were arranged:

Act One: a man is borne to a geisha's house in a curtained palanquin. One can't actually see him, only the hand draped along the side of the palanquin. The hand is very cleverly realised: it's impossible to say for certain whether it belongs to a man or a woman. But one knows it's going to turn out to be a man or the story has no point.

Act Two: the geisha, naked, is being oiled by her maid. Behind a screen one can see her dresser waiting to start working up her kimono.

Act Three: here she is, fully attired, sailing into the trysting room like a flagship carrying a royal bride to her king. In a close-up of her face we read hauteur, intelligence and worldliness. Also confidence. There's no question of nerves. She's the girl of the moment and she knows it.

On a table in the background is sake and food. Propped in the corner is an instrument like a balalaika.

Act Four: the man (his back to the painter) yawns, it can't be anything else with his arm bent like that; the geisha looks coy.

Act Five: geisha in the crab position, everything pink and juicy amid her furious black bush. She holds out her long, white, exquisite hands to grasp him.

The man rears above her naked with his cock (which by the

way is as long as his foot, a comparison that the eye demands just by the position of his body) at the ready. The look in his pronouncedly slanting eyes is completely diabolical. One could feel sorry for the girl were she not a seasoned practitioner.

In the passage behind the *shoji*, or paper screen, there is the suggestion of a figure crouching in the candlelit gloom – which may be that of the geisha's madam checking that the patron of her house is still aroused by the girl.

Act Six – 'A pity the paint's so faded,' I murmured, making him smile.

He said, 'I sometimes think I should engage a craftsman to repaint it in the most lurid fashion possible, then herd my mother up to it like the wilful old goose that she is and force her to look at it. I really don't understand why she objects. The geisha whom my father was so fond of wasn't even his wife number two.'

The old servant appeared from behind a screen and handed Yamaguchi a woven silk lead, lemon-coloured, at the end of which scampered in harness two diminutive black-and-white shiba, a sort of Japanese spaniel. They jumped up on him, made their huge black eyes yet more lustrous and pleaded for his attention.

He said, 'My servant always brings them to me when I walk through the house, in case I meet Yumi. She likes to play with them. Yumi is altogether very playful.'

We continued. His bare feet were leaving prints on the floor, as if he were walking through dew. The dogs began to paw at each other like cats sparring until Yamaguchi ordered them to behave. Then they walked daintily in front of him, frisking their plumed tails.

He said, 'Prince of Siberia! I call that an insult to us both. You know it means nothing. A few trifles here and there – you'd be like one of those tribesmen to whom the Russians give beads or vodka . . . So you'd really have arranged my killing for such a miserable reward?'

I said that I hadn't known him then – that I'd decided to have nothing to do with Sato's offer the moment I got to Vladivostok and saw how drab the place was. I couldn't possibly have lived there. Nor could the Countess if I'd judged her correctly. Had he, Yamaguchi-san, taken the Lala bird off my hands, I'd have already been down to Kunst & Albers and bought boat tickets for the States.

I said this tentatively, with little pauses here and there to see how he was taking it. But he didn't really listen. Shaking his head and talking as if to himself, he said when I'd finished, 'Hijo will have been sent by my cousin as his spy. When you show no sign of arranging my death, he'll cable Sato and say so. He's Sato's man through and through. What happens then? Only the Devil knows. I must be on my guard even when I sleep. That man is my enemy, I know it.'

Forty-six

A CORRIDOR LED out of the room. The window screens on either side were half open. Little breezes pulsed against my cheek as we walked.

We passed by many rooms, which may have been the sleeping quarters, without seeing anyone and after a few turns and twists – always the same dark wood, the silence, the emanation of power – entered what I took to be an office.

Yamaguchi unclipped the lead from the dogs, which instantly went and lay down on a deep quilt and gazed worshipfully at him. He said to me, 'This is where I used to keep my collection.'

I knew immediately it must have been rubbish. Whatever had lain on their pillows of cotton wool within the mahogany cabinets would have had no chance against mites and the steamy summer climate. They'd still have had some of their original beauty. Their provenance could have shed light on the role of other species of the same family. There could have been shreds of interest clinging to the tattered wings of the butterflies or to the corroded elytra of his beetles, but as specimens of scientific interest they would have been without merit. The bugs would have eaten the best bits.

He saw what I was thinking and said, 'I should have had them built from pawlonia wood, which shrinks or expands according to the temperature. I was too quick to go into it. When I want to do something, I don't pause. It's a fault I have. I should be like the English and their famous saying, "Wait and see."' He let out a short high laugh that made his dogs raise their heads.

214

'Pay attention to the climate,' I said. 'That was the first thing I learned from Goetz.'

'Of course. Everything has to be learned once. Someone suffers in the process, usually the pupil. But I didn't bring you here to show you the wreckage of a love I once had. It was to try to understand why my cousin and his American lady should speak so favourably of the strong, handsome, unhappy man who sits opposite me. It is remarkable that they had such confidence in your power to change my mind. Matters will become clearer during our conversation . . . Some luncheon is being prepared as we sit here, be assured I shall look after you . . . Meanwhile I shall tell you two things. One is of the greatest importance financially. The other you shall judge for yourself.'

There was a packet of W.D. & H.O. Wills cigarettes on his desk. He thought about lighting one and decided against it. 'My father was sent one day to the blacksmith by my grandfather, who was just an ordinary peasant, to get iron hoops made for the wheels of their best cart. He'd decided that the wheels would last much longer that way. When my father was in the smithy, he picked up an iron bolt the blacksmith had just made. A little while later he read that the Emperor, as part of his programme of modernising Japan, was going to have iron battleships built. He never looked back. When my father died he owned engineering works, a dry dock, even some vessels themselves. The day I took over I appointed the best managers I could find because I didn't trust myself to make the correct decisions. I always knew I was too impetuous . . . Our main shipbuilding works are right here in Nagasaki, on the opposite side of the harbour. Where you left the shore road, there's my jetty, down below on your right. I keep three boats, one for myself and one each for my daughters. Yumi is over there every day counting the money. Japanese women enjoy doing that very much. Mimi goes over whenever the business concerns our Russian enterprises. She is my negotiator – my Mimi is my everything.'

His lean face lit up; its hard edges turned soft. 'These Russians step off the boat like bears, thinking to gobble us up. There to meet them is Mimi in her dark kimono, hands folded in front of her, already bowing. They rub their hands in glee – but they are lost! They are like flies in a room where all the windows are shut. Even though they are huge people, she doesn't flinch. Her power is within her. They cannot believe that so beautiful a woman can be so exacting with her arguments. But slowly the truth sinks in – and they give up. Men are afraid of her, that's my opinion.'

'How often do you go over to the works?'

He smiled. 'Once a day, for my breakfast. I rise at dawn, walk down to say good morning to Hana, then continue through the woods to the jetty, where my boatman is waiting. At breakfast I learn what is new and look at yesterday's figures. Then I return here, to think. I'm the one who has the ideas. My managers tell me when I'm talking nonsense. In that way we control my rash nature. Twice a week, in the middle of the afternoon, I take my motor car and visit a certain lady on the other side of town. We always play *shogi* first. That is Japanese chess. I let her have the black pieces so that she can start. I don't know why I give her that advantage for she always beats me, I think because she reads the *shogi* column in the newspaper every day and I never do. The board is always laid out when I arrive. She cannot wait to start the game. I – I find it desperately boring.' He flicked the subject away with a finger. 'After that we make love. In this game I become her shogun, the most important piece. Because of this she calls me Hojo, which is the name of a famous old shogun family. Both in *shogi* and in our love games, the shogun can move one square in any direction. But one square only. You should think about that.'

He gave in and lit a cigarette. 'Now I shall tell you the real reason my cousin wants me dead. Have you remarked how dissimilar we are in appearance? It is because my grandfather, believing my grandmother to be incapable of childbearing, sired Sato's mother with a serving woman. A few years later he discovered, by siring my father with his wife, that he'd been wrong. This has made my cousin insanely jealous even though he's my senior by six years. When I was four he rowed me out in a boat and threw me overboard. A fisherman saw it happen and came to my rescue. A few years later it was the knife. After that he hired a man to push me into the sea from the deck of one of my own ships. You asked about my bodyguards. Now you know.'

'Why have him as a partner?'

'Because he is head of an army, because he is family and because I know every inch of his mind, which by the way is not a complicated one. Until now, I thought he'd given up on my life. Maybe it's the American who's revived his jealousy. She wants more, she wants to have the entire business in their hands, who can say.'

'She's a survivor.'

'You've slept with her, I suppose?'

'Why do you say that?'

He shrugged. 'You are both soldiers of fortune. One thing follows the other.'

'You're right, I have.'

'Is she a typical Western woman with large breasts and backside, rather lazy?'

'Not at all. She's Jewish and extremely intelligent. Not the submissive type, not our Countess.'

He grunted, lit another cigarette and blew smoke into the air. 'Tomorrow morning a freighter with our first shipment of Siberian timber will dock here. It will be an occasion of national importance. There will be a ceremony to welcome the vessel. The Emperor has sent his representative. Afterwards he will visit the temple that I'm supposed to have knocked down and inspect it for himself. That will dispose of my enemies' lies. The Emperor will then sign the decree, and the Kingdom of Eastern Siberia will come into being.'

I was thinking, How will this Kingdom thing work, will they get a trading monopoly from the government, Jesus but there's money to be made here, when Yamaguchi said, 'The second thing I want to tell you is more interesting. It is that until 1870, which falls within the period which we Japanese know as the Meiji reformation, ordinary people were not allowed to have family names. Everything was arranged in a wholly feudal way.'

I looked at him in amazement. 'No Doig? Just Charlie?'

'No Doig. You'd have been, for example, Charlie Who Lives By The Big Oak Tree – and that would have been the name registered at the local temple. The purpose of this was to demonstrate that everyone except the lords was insignificant.'

I stared at him. Could such a thing be true? Even in Russia nothing had been so primitive. It was unbelievable.

He slowly expelled a mouthful of smoke. 'Yes, it is the absolute truth. No family names except for the lords. Then, under Meiji, the law changed. My father took the name Yamaguchi, which means a pass leading into the mountains, and made his money. I, a Yamaguchi, will make more money to honour his name and my daughters will do likewise to honour me.'

He rose and crushed his cigarette angrily. 'We are still straightening up the history between us, the Yamaguchis and the lords. Now you know the purpose for which I live.' He bowed to me. 'That was the second thing. Let us go for our luncheon.'

Forty-seven

H IS BLACK eyes speckled me up and down. 'So what are you
going to do with the skin of the Lala bird?'

'It's in a safe in the Hongkong & Shanghai. It'll keep.'

'The one on the Oura Bund?'

'Yes.'

'You're an honest man, Doig-san.'

'Your cousin also called me that.'

'You're too honest for your own good.'

'Courage, wisdom, humour, those are the major virtues.
Honesty is a long way down the list for me.'

He said, 'I agree. A little honesty goes a long way. But you
have too much of it. One, you should never have told me which
bank you've put the bird in. Two, you should never have put it
in a bank at all. I'm surprised at you. You must know that
Lenin's robbers have helped themselves to the contents of every
single bank deposit box in Russia. Jewels, silver, love letters,
even historical relics that can mean nothing to anyone except
the owner, all have been seized. I know about these matters.
My spies are everywhere in Russia.'

I bridled. Honest was like nice, a death sentence. An honest
man would never have got a hundred yards down the road to
Vladivostok. I told him so. Then, to get my own back a little,
I said, 'So if you know so much, tell me where I've left the gold.'

Of course I expected him to say, 'What gold?' But he just
gave me a knowing smile and said, 'Again, too honest. Just by
asking that question you yourself are being drawn into providing
an answer. Or hinting at one, at any rate giving me something
to work on. You stand to gain nothing from my answer, not

one yen, whereas from you I stand to gain – twenty-eight tons at 99 per cent purity, isn't that the figure?'

I said nothing – closed my face right up.

'There were other ways to see whether I was bragging about the reach of my spy system. Your knowledge of recent events is so great that you could have tested me with any number of questions about Lenin and the other leaders. Delicate, personal questions that couldn't possibly have been answered by someone on the street. The colour of the necktie that Lenin was wearing at Smolny on the night of the Revolution, you could have asked me that. After all, you were there. You spoke to him.'

I saw it before me: the monster's comfortable bourgeois belly, the curling tips to his waistcoat, his wig, his green hate-filled eyes. But I didn't see his tie. I said, 'What colour was it, then?'

He said, 'Give me a fortnight and I'll have the answer. Then you'll believe me. By the way it's not spies that I have but business correspondents. I used a wrong word a moment ago. To get back to your gold, somewhere south of Kazan is where you and your servant sank the barge.'

Had I told Cynthia where it was? I didn't think so. If it was his contacts who'd come through with the information, it was impressive. But did they have the details that mattered, the cross-references – the church, the ravine, the two rounded hills? That was knowledge that could only have come from Kobi.

I smiled at him and said, 'Somewhere could be a lot of places.'

He said, 'I wonder if the Prince of Siberia's rule would have extended as far west as Kazan.'

I said, 'We'll never find out now.'

He said, 'So Charlie Doig is the first Prince of Siberia as well as the last. Hah! Will the history books remember to put you in?'

'The Reds will always win, no matter how many troops your Emperor sends over. No one'll ever come up with an argument that can trump the idea of equality.'

'Maybe that's true at the lowest levels of mankind, but business is different. Sooner or later the Bolsheviks will understand that philosophy is not sufficient when ruling a country. A sound currency, ample bread and dredgers to keep the shipping on the move, that's what'll keep the comrades quiet. They'll realise that in the end, they'll have to. And when they do, that'll be the moment we'll propose to them a joint cooperation in the dredging business, starting with a trial somewhere south of Kazan. When I go to Moscow, I shall be exquisitely polite to Mr Lenin and will get my way. When I have his permission to proceed, I shall come and consult your memory. Maybe your man's also.'

Just then the old servant came in to ask what was to be done with Dr Hijo. He was starting to make a nuisance of himself.

'Give him a spin round the harbour. In an hour I shall be able to see him.' When the servant had left, he said, 'Here's another question you could have asked to test my information network in Russia.'

He looked at me quizzically, was deciding whether or not to continue.

'Well?'

'You could have asked me what I knew about the whereabouts of Comrade Glebov.'

I looked at him astonished. 'In hell of course, in the very deepest section, where I put him.'

'Maybe not.'

I went cold all over. Of a sudden my heart was like a tomb with someone knocking to get out, someone made of ice with a blood-streaked face.

I sprang at him, caught him by his robe, two good strong handfuls of it, and swung him off his feet. 'Enough of this bowing crap,' I said, 'you tell me what you know about Glebov or I'll tie your tongue round your neck and throttle you.'

He smiled. Hanging there on tiptoe, he just smiled his lopsided smile at me, which was like inserting a whisk into my bloodstream.

I yelled – I blasted the words into his tiny black peephole eyes – 'Unless he's the new Jesus, he's dead, d-e-a-d, dead. No one falls five hundred feet to the ground without being dead.'

His arms were hanging at his side. He was still smiling, making no effort to get away from me. I shook him like a bag of oats, Christ, he was so infuriating, so slick, so expert.

He said, 'You are everything that is said about you, Doig-san. Sato was right: you are a top man. Now please remove your hands. I know nothing about Glebov other than he's dead. I was deceiving you cruelly. It was to test your spirit, your fire – your good energy, as we call it. It was necessary, and to be effective it had to be done without feeling. Forgive me.'

I was shaking. Some palsy of the mind, a relic of that snow-filled afternoon when I shot her, had crept back in from its banishment. He said gently, 'I knew everything about you except this one thing, what you are like inside. I beg forgiveness, Doig-san—' I dropped him and turned away. Putting his hand on my shoulder, he guided me out onto the terrace overlooking the harbour.

He said, 'What you are in need of is a good woman and a home. Then you will be cured.'

The sun was brilliant after his house. He said, 'May I touch you?'

He placed his hand across the back of my neck and dug lightly into the muscle. He had me sit down. Standing behind me, he applied both hands – not hard digging but opening the muscles and spreading them out. His presence behind me was huge, as if he were my father dropping in to catch up with all my news since he'd died. His smell was warm and comfortable, like a box of dates. We said nothing. Slowly, my shaking ceased. I thanked him. He patted the top of my head.

We strolled between the box bushes. He said, 'My people tell me that the Bolsheviks have put a price on your head – fifty thousand Tsarist roubles.'

I said, 'I doubt it. I know my countrymen. They like to sit behind their desks and smoke and make up fairy tales and then wander home in their galoshes. They like talking, not doing. No Russian would pay money for my head.'

'They'd pay if you were the Prince of Siberia.'

'That again – look, I'm Charlie Doig, I'm not a tea ceremony guy, I don't speak the lingo, and I don't wear the clothes. You're making a mistake if you think I'm going to be drawn into a crackpot venture with you and Sato. See Vladivostok and die, that's how it'd be for me. I couldn't give a shit about proto-cols and precedence and ambassadors. I know how to bow and that's it.'

'Tsk tsk, you get inflamed very easily . . . it drains so much of one's energy. Don't forget you're famous now. Everyone between Kazan and Vladivostok knows the name Charlie Doig. Who else has killed one of Lenin's most trusted lieutenants, captured a barge full of gold and escaped? There's no one like you in the East.' He squeezed his shoulders up and dropped them. 'Maybe there's no one like you anywhere.'

'Forget it, sir, I'm expected in America. Busy, occupied, booked up.'

'In Japan we have a saying, "Think quickly, regret slowly." Now, look who's walking out to greet us! My daughter has finished counting banknotes for the day and has come to soften our male conversation.'

Yumi glided along the terrace in a dark kimono stitched on the breast with crescent moons and a sprinkling of stars. She was neither small nor large, neither fat nor thin, neither one thing or another. But her lips were as pink as cherry buds and her throat as slender as a lily. Smooth, pale, untainted – the colour of bridal satin, a supernatural colour, that was the nature of her throat. I said to myself, Yumi, it'd be like licking a saint.

Not knowing what etiquette demanded, I raised her hand and brushed my lips across it, dusting her skin, no more. I glanced up at her. Her eyes were unmoving, completely stagnant. On an impulse, I flipped over her tiny paw and kissed her palm, which was grimed and curling from the money habit. Again I searched her eyes, I don't quite know what for – humour, flirtiness, some point of contact. But they were uninterested. As smoothly as a pickpocket, she slid her hand out of mine – bowed, straightened – and then suddenly, as sly as a snake, an inch of tongue flickered through her lips, in and out, in and out, the deed done without any change in expression so that I stood staring at her, wondering if deprivation was making me lose my mind.

She turned away and spoke rapidly to her father in Japanese. Then she bowed to me with a completely blank face and went into the house.

'It was about tomorrow. There is nothing for me to do except to look gracious. My daughters and the managers will do everything. That is why Yumi was short with us. She cannot bear anything less than perfection and so is preoccupied. Now let us go and see what has happened to Hijo. One of my guards will be watching him. The idea that he was sent to be a spy makes me nervous. A paid assassin can be guarded against. It's the man whose thoughts lie deep in shadow who represents the real danger . . . Doig-san, would you be my guest at the ceremony tomorrow? I would sleep better tonight. Yes? Excellent! My rickshaw will come for you at the hotel. You'll be given a seat on the stand next to the doctor. Your job is to prevent him killing me.'

Forty-eight

I WAS LEANING against the door watching him stow my box of skinning knives in our pack. I said, 'Kobi, do you ever reflect on the fact that you and I have been together for over two years and that this pack contains the sum total of our worldly possessions?'

He stood upright, a streak of sun catching the curve of his chin, exactly where a mole with several long black hairs grew.

Five foot five, five six, that's what we're talking about with Kobi: his height, the only thing about him that could have belonged to a woman. As for age, there were times he acted like forty and times he was a kid. He didn't know how old he was and I couldn't guess. Until they put on a paunch, these Mongolians could be any age. Lithe and tough, that's what they are, and proud too, proud as peacocks.

He said, 'Don't lie to me, Doig. I know you keep money in your boots.'

'Wrong, did. It's in the bank now.' I felt neither surprise nor alarm. If he'd wanted to kill me for the diamonds, he could've done so many times over.

He said, 'But what about me? One day there'll be no fighting. You'll start to look for a woman again, maybe in a city. What would I do in a city? In a place like this, maybe bigger?' He put his hands on his hips. 'You and your woman, you wouldn't need me.'

'You could go home and breed horses? If things have gone well for us, I'd help you.'

'I have no home. The Tungus people wouldn't accept me.'

225

'Because you're not one of them, that's why. Look at you, man, Mongolia's where you come from, not Siberia.'

'One day I'll get too stiff to ride horses. When that happens, I'll have nothing. But you, you'll still have your diamonds, and a woman, and children to work for you. Also you'll have your gold. Is some of it mine? You've never said. In my country I would be regarded as a great man if I possessed only one bar of that gold.'

'At the moment we have no means of getting at it, you know that. As for the horses, I'll be generous when we split up. Count on it. You and I've been partners. That's how it is between partners, an open hand – fellowship, love, all that goes with it.'

Again he fixed me with a look that was completely unknowable. I thought, What is whitey missing here? With Yamaguchi too – he'd probably been giving me signals throughout our conversation yesterday that had whistled over my head. A whole stretch of their meaning was vanishing down the drain whenever they spoke to me. 'It's just their way, the language of the Orient, *aziatsky yazyk*,' my mother would say when the Chinese tea merchant she used would take her money and retreat into his den without saying a word – 'but at the very least he should say thank you.'

That was fine for her in 1910 when the Rykovs were still among the rulers. But now they were no more, along with the rest of the lords and ladies. Their attitudes had gone with them. If I wanted to avoid their fate, I had to open my eyes, ears and soul, get into the minds of all sorts of people and understand their processes.

I said to Kobi, 'Next time I see you guys having a palaver in the street I'm going to watch your expressions and see if I can learn something.'

He said, 'Learning will be good for you, Doig. Don't drink, learn.'

He lowered his gaze – took out the box of knives and repacked it. He said, 'There is another thing. Several times I've risked my life to save yours. What do you say to that?'

'I say, Hell, I'd do the same for you any day. That's all I can say.'

He flared up: 'Nothing more than words? No diamonds from

your famous boots? No offers of gold? By saving your life –
listen, between men, that is the most sacred bond that can ever
exist. What you say is too little.'

This wasn't something I needed to learn and I cried out,
'What's got into you? I go out on a visit, get us a nice billet
instead of this crummy hotel and when I get back I find you
thinking of nothing but old age and a world which suddenly
has no horses. Didn't you hear Governor Sato say I'm a man
of honour? When we part it'll be on the best terms. You have
my word. Here, shake on it.'

He brushed my hand, nothing more, sliding his fingers over
mine. He said, 'I won't be displeased?'

'You won't be displeased, I guarantee it.'

'How can you give such a guarantee? Is it to be written?'

'I'm giving you my word, that's my guarantee.'

He finished the packing in silence – baring his teeth as he
pulled the cord tight round the mouth of the pack.

I said, 'Of course it may never come to that. You could get
yourself killed and then I won't have to think any more about
giving you gold, diamonds, horses.'

He said, 'You're more likely to get killed, you're the leader.'

I said, 'And if I am, you take my advice and grab the diamonds.
I bequeath them to you here and now. Go and see a fat fellow
in the bank called Stabb and get into my safe. Here, I'll give
you the numbers. Then stick the diamonds down your boot
lining and leg it. Leg it like hell.'

I wrote the numbers out for him. He took the paper, shaking
his head. 'Bad things will happen to us here. My dreams tell
me this. They wake me up. I have to sleep with the lamp lit.
Dreams are like snakes, looking for a warm bed at night.'

I said, 'I bet that as a boy you and your family all lived in
a great jumble in the yurt. Coming to this hotel after all we've
been through, the hardships and short rations and injuries,
Christ, after the whole business of just staying alive, of course
it feels different. Quit all that rubbish about dreams and
snakes, we're in the modern world now. You'll soon get used
to it.'

But I'd misjudged him. He wagged his finger under my nose.
'This is an island we're on. We could get trapped.' His eyes

went wide. 'An island, Doig, with sea all round. If I said, show me the bridge, you couldn't. It's a prison we're in.'

I said, 'What's different about an island? Feels the same to me as anywhere else.'

He said, 'We're caught. Whenever we try to escape, the sea will stop us.'

'Anything wrong with a boat? Look, I know you want to have a horse between your legs, a rifle in your hand and a thousand miles of steppe in front of you, but you can't, not here. For the moment you've got to make do with an island. It's an improvement, you've got to admit that at least. The Japs have still got an emperor, they've got peace and it's OK to have money.'

He said, 'I want to be a cowboy.'

I said, 'That's new. Been looking at the magazines downstairs?'

'Yes. I love America. There are no seas there.'

'Bet you do. They've got lots of horses and lots of pretty girls. Just your type – juicy, well fed, good cooks. Where we're going tonight after the ceremony, Yamaguchi's house, there'll be girls there too. His daughters, so keep your hands off them. Not that you'd want Yumi. She's just a tough little businesswoman.'

A sly smile inched across his face. 'We like different sorts of girls, Doig.'

'What do you mean?'

'Lili, that's what.'

'Lili?'

'You didn't like her, but I did, he he he' – an extraordinary tittering laugh that took his age down about ten years.

I stared at him. He'd come sidling out of the darkness, and while the others were scrabbling around for the gold, had had her, just like that? Was that what he was saying? Oh my my. And now he was smiling at me, the sort of superior smile a man goes in for when he's pinched another man's girl. So it was true. I'd turned her down and Kobi had snuck in and had her.

I said, 'OK, but that was before you lost your pinkie. How's it going to be now, Genghis?'

'Where does my pinkie come into it?'

228

It riled me, I don't mind admitting it. That Lili, the busty little broad, should hanker to be laid was fine. That her seducer should be some soldier-adventurer was natural – the uniform, the moustaches, the smell of leather, the rattle of hooves, the pealing trumpets as she came for the very first time in her life, the whole kaleidoscope would be a splendid scene in her mind, even if the man was the completest scoundrel in the world.

But with Kobi – that was different.

He must have seen the look in my face, for he said, 'But she offered herself to you first. I was watching.'

Lili had been choice, by Christ she had, and Kobi had had her in some wretched corner of the barge, and that white shift of hers would've been sullied by sump oil as he flicked it up and he'd have left oily fingerprints plastered over her luscious white buttocks and her white breasts and white neck. Everything white would have been turned to filth, whereas I'd have treated her like swansdown, like precious young royalty.

Kobi, of all people—

I shook my head. Don't think like that, Charlie! Don't let women trouble you so much! Cynthia Zipf, for instance, you couldn't give a fig what she got up to. Think of women as you do of her, snap your fingers, learn to walk away.

'Well, well,' I said, but could think of nothing to follow it up with.

There was a knock on the door. Yamaguchi's rickshaw was waiting outside.

Forty-nine

IT HAD been decided that for such an auspicious event the old quay on Dejima should be used. A ship of moderate draught could still get in there if handled carefully.

A wooden stand had been erected. Yamaguchi and the swells were in the front row. I was at the top (in row five of five). Hijo was next to me with the outside berth. I hadn't seen him for one whole day, which was a blessing. There was something pitiless about him that really struck at me. Whenever I saw him, I remembered the Bolshevik prisoner whose brains he'd been going to pull out and mash into pulp. A man who could take his trepanning saw off its hook, open a man's head and spoon out the muck with all its wriggling germs – and could do it without vomiting – was seriously unbalanced. He was another Lenin, wanting to get to the top and save the world. Anyone like that was a danger to society. DANGER. Red for danger, like the Red Army and the Red flag. I'd creep up on him one night and paint his teeth red, that's what I'd do.

What would he do about my failure to have Yamaguchi dealt with? Had he explained to Sato that the Emperor's man would declare later today whether the disputed temple had or had not been destroyed? That as likely as not Yamaguchi would be given a clean sheet and the Kingdom of Eastern Siberia be signed into existence pronto?

How had Sato replied? What would the next step be? Where did I come into it?

I took my seat next to Hijo and said good morning, nice day for the job, had he slept well and so on – adding, as if in an

230

afterthought, had he heard from Governor Sato since we'd got to Nagasaki.

He was wearing a black Western suit, very pressed, a stiff collar and a black tie. In his display pocket were the four silver pens.

He looked at me goofily – God, it was so difficult to know what was going on behind those spectacles. Eventually he said, 'You too look very pleasant this morning, Mr Doig.'

I'd had my hair cut – it felt good not to see so much grey every time I looked in the mirror. The hotel had come up with a selection of smarter clothes for me. All of them were too small but they were a great deal happier than what I had of my own. In the matter of footwear they'd been unsuccessful. But this was to my advantage since by wearing my Russian boots I was able to mitigate the fact that my trousers ended above my ankles. Elsewhere the waistband was too tight, the coat too short and too narrow across the shoulders, and because I was wearing a necktie, I was sweating like a pig before the monsoon breaks. The last time I'd worn one had been in London when I took Goetz to be interviewed for a Russian visa. Five years ago. A revolution ago. When I was a child.

'Thanks,' I said, and we left it at that. I could see he wasn't carrying a pistol. A throwing knife maybe, but I didn't see him as that sort of a killer. If he was going to kill, it'd be with a syringe.

Yamaguchi and his daughters were the only people not in Western clothes. He was walking around erect and martial, looking good in his robes. The ponytail with its white band gave him an air of distinction. Japan's destiny would be safe in his hands, no one could be mistaken about that.

The daughters were sitting out in the front by themselves. Mimosa was the taller of the two, a solid-looking girl from behind.

It was the calmest of days, without even the occasional puff of wind to deflect the warmth of the four o'clock sun. The bunting hung like damp washing. The sea slopped against the quay in a bored way.

The city band, maybe thirty strong, were in white suits. The two trombonists had blackened armpits even before they started.

Under the eye of their conductor from his perch up a portable, semicircular pulpit, they experimented manfully with a selection from 'Cavalleria Rusticana' by Mascagni, 'The Gaby Glide' by Hirsch and some Strauss waltzes.

The Mayor wore a chain round his neck. The Emperor's representative arrived late. His car drove him onto the quay and let him out just beside the band, which made for a perilous moment as the conductor whisked his baton and only a foot away the big cheese adjusted his top hat. Furling his kidskin gloves on the knob of his malacca cane, he posed for a photograph. Then he strutted across to his seat on the right of the Mayor – co-incidentally to a booming passage on the big bass drum.

I fanned myself with the programme of music and watched the freighter approach.

The entrance to Nagasaki harbour is a narrow one, with steep green-forested hills on either side. Once inside, there are no creeks or subdivisions of the harbour into which a ship can disappear. As a result, as soon as a vessel is within the harbour it becomes like one of those ships in a bottle that are displayed on people's mantelshelves. Every detail of it is open to inspection: its trim, the rake of its masts, its paintwork, all aspects of its gear. Its cargo is mentally weighed and valued by a thousand pairs of eyes. Nothing can be other than what it is.

On it came, smoothly, innocently, strolling through the flat sea and making the sampans and fishing boats sway in its wake. I can see it now, squat, bulky, loaded down to its marks, brick red up to the line and thereafter the tan of a light leather. It was broader in the beam than any of the other vessels in the harbour in order to compensate for the high centre of gravity, which was caused by all the timber stacked on top. It had a pronounced sheer forward to stop rough seas sweeping the deck and ripping loose the deckload. I could only just make out the bearded figure of the captain on his bridge because of all the deck timber.

Suddenly the conductor turned to face the ship and at the same moment raised his baton decisively. The music stopped, the drummer damped his drums – and with perfect timing, the captain pulled the lanyard. A vast mooing noise spread over city and harbour and a string of flags shot up the vessel's stubby mast.

Everyone clapped.

The band played the Tsarist national anthem and then the Japanese one.

The Mayor spoke.

The Emperor's representative spoke.

Yamaguchi stepped forward. His daughters rose to their feet and stood on either side of him. An easy shot, ten yards away.

But no rings in the water, that's what Sato had said to me.

And Hijo wasn't armed.

I thought, maybe Yamaguchi is one hundred per cent wrong and Hijo was asked to accompany me as a favour – to put me in touch with Yamaguchi, to help with the language, to get me going. Maybe he knows nothing whatsoever about the politics behind the Kingdom of Eastern Siberia.

Testing him, I said from the corner of my mouth, 'Governor Sato will be most interested to hear that such an impressive cargo has been landed while the Emperor's representative watches.'

But he paid me no attention. He was staring at Yamaguchi and his daughters.

An innocent doctor of medicine, a proper little Jap philanthropist, maybe that's all he was, maybe I was right the first time.

Yamaguchi spoke in his rasping, guttural voice. Spoke with confidence, like a man who sees the future with total clarity. You could tell just from the way he held himself that when the Emperor's representative inspected the site of the Empress's family temple, everything would be found to be clean and orderly. Yamaguchi's enemies would be flung down. Sato would eat humble pie, and the Kingdom of Eastern Siberia would come into being. That was how it was going to happen.

Yamaguchi finished. He and his daughters bowed to the captain on his bridge. Turning, they bowed to the assembled guests. Then they took up a position to one side of the area left open to receive the timber.

The band struck up again, the freighter was nudged against the quay by a couple of small tugs that had come shooting out from the mass of shipping, a crane with bunting coiled all the way up its jib lowered its slings, and unloading of the inaugural shipment of timber began.

The slings tightened and a parcel of about a dozen long straight sticks rose in the air. This was a symbolic hoist, everyone knew that. After we'd left they'd get down to it in earnest.

I said to Hijo, because it was important and I thought it should be shown that someone there had a few brains, 'If I'd been in charge of the operation, I'd have had the bark stripped before I shipped the timber. Yamaguchi-san should have known. He understands very well the damage beetles can do. Peeled logs, a buyer should never deal in anything else.'

He blinked at me. 'Are we to remain here while the entire ship is unloaded? I have my work.'

I said, 'Only for this load, then you can go and count germs.'

He grunted, then, 'Look at this spectacle, Mr Doig. Russia is carried in chains to Japan. That is how it should always be and will always be.'

So he spoke, a spasm of hatred for Russia flitting across his face. From his parents? His school? An incident at Zhigalovo? Where could these feelings have originated? I looked back at the freighter – vaguely, being more interested in Hijo than the timber.

It was then that it happened, at that very moment.

Fifty

WITHOUT A sound, without any slow parting of cable strands to act as a warning, the right-hand sling snapped, flinging one of its loose ends high into the air like a carnival streamer. The logs swung round, crashed against the crane, swung back and fanned out as if in a game of spillikins. I saw in an instant where we were heading.

I shouted – Yamaguchi recognised my voice and looked round. 'Look up!' I bellowed. He grabbed one of the girls. But the other—

Hijo – I sent him flying, just lowered my shoulder and flattened him as I leapt off the stand. Everyone was on their feet, their henhouse twittering reaching me like raindrops on a tin roof as I ran. I could see the logs starting to slide out of the remaining sling, could see Mimosa standing beneath them mesmerised, could see the conductor staring at me with his baton raised – and I knew there was no time to escort her away like a gentleman, that it was going to have to be a snatch-and-grab and into the sea for us both. I was running, oh how I was running in those stupid borrowed clothes, running and thinking about one thing only – how to scoop her up on the go, one arm behind the knees and the other under her shoulders, and whip her off her feet and hope like hell there was room for us between the quay and the ship's side. Cabbage stalks, cigarette ends, baulks of wood, loose oil, God knows what, all Nagasaki's flotsam flashed through my mind as I charged at her with my arms and knees pumping and my mouth tight as a bull's arse against the little blue jellyfish waiting for us, and next I knew I had her clamped squawking against my ribs as if I were a thief running off with a goose and the timber was crashing all around us and then we were over the edge and in among all the harbour muck and suddenly she wasn't kicking at all and I thought, Oh shit, she's cracked her head against something and I'm going to have to lay a corpse before her father.

I brought her up, right under the freighter's counter, its barnacles rasping against my cheek. Spluttering, I flipped over onto my back taking her with me – no trouble, she just lolled weightless in my arms. Dead? Dying? I thought, What's your status, lassie? and poked my finger round her mouth in case she'd got a gobful of seaweed or a jellyfish.

That got her going – she shook her head vigorously, like a young calf, opened her eyes and screwed her neck round to check that I was whom she thought I was.

A lifebelt flopped into the water from the freighter, which I ignored.

A few strokes and I got her to the steps built sideways into the quay. I hauled her out by the pits and got her sitting upright. 'You OK?' I said, not noticing much about her except the black hair, a strong face like her father's and a small cut on her chin.

She leaned forward and spat into the harbour – smiled up at me as if it had been an adventure. Nice, everything nice and healthy about the expression – and forthright too, that sort of a girl. She'll give as good as she gets, I thought to myself, no wonder men are frightened of her.

I said, 'Put your arms round my neck,' which she did and no demurring. Then I lifted her dripping into my arms, which I have to tell you took some doing owing to her clothes being water-logged. The ship's captain shouted down to me – bawdy, typically Russian. I looked up. Heads everywhere peering down at me, Yamaguchi advancing down the steps looking as a man should who's seen the daughter he loves saved from a certain death.

I walked up the steps with her head against my chest. She was staring at the sky over my shoulder, smiling – yes, a big fat smile on her face all the time I was carrying her up.

Then Yamaguchi was fluttering in front of me, his features contorted with anguish, grey and cracked like pumice stone. He wanted to share her with me. I grunted that it'd be easier to carry on as I was. Lifting his robe, he retreated backwards up the steps.

236

When we got to the top, I asked Mimosa how she felt. 'Alive,' she said, no longer smiling, probably a bit of shock showing itself. I let her down. Instinctively she put out her hands to straighten her clothes and get fluffed up. But of course she was wet through and it wasn't going to work. For seconds she stood there and I, just as wet, stood opposite. Beneath the sleeked material of her dark water-heavy kimono were clear indications of a sturdy figure.

She raised her eyes. 'Thank you,' she said. More seconds passed. Her eyes were a soft brown, the colour of a nightingale's eggs. I can't tell you anything definite about the rest, it was just an idea.

Wet as I was I lowered my head and bowed to her, keeping my eyes on her face. (Mother applauded from aloft, I heard her clearly.) Mimosa did the same. At the bottom of what was possible, I tried a smile. She smiled back – I straightened.

'Blankets, hot water, a bath and bloody chop-chop,' I shouted up at the captain. '*Zhivo*, man, quicker than you've ever done anything before.'

Then Yamaguchi and Yumi had taken Mimosa from me and hustled her up the gangway. The captain's wife was waiting with a velvet cloak large enough to cover a billiard table. She swathed Mimosa in it. The three women stepped over a coaming (the tail of the brown cloak rippling over the obstacle like an otter over a rocky ledge) and disappeared.

Yamaguchi came slowly down. Everyone was watching to see how he thanked me. He placed both hands on my shoulders and said, 'She is my life. You have saved two lives this morning.'

Nothing more, no false modesty or heroics. Without me, she'd have been strawberry jam, we both knew it. I said to him, 'Come and look at the timber. The bark's flaking. I'll bet you it's beetled.'

Hijo appeared, limping, wanting his moment of glory. I apologised for having sent him flying. He assured me his injury was of no consequence. 'You move quickly for a large man,' he said, goggling up at me.

A deckhand ran down the gangway with a blanket. I took off my hotel jacket and slung the blanket round my shoulders. Yamaguchi asked me again if I was all right. Then he and I began to inspect the logs, which were lying crazily, all over the place. The clattering they'd got had knocked sections of bark off – tufts, chunks, whole rafts of the stuff. I picked up the nearest one and looked at the inside curve. As I thought, it had been galleried by spruce bark beetle, the galleries quite dusty and fresh. Tapping the bark against my wrist and watching the little buggers fall out, I said, 'This beetle, which we call *Ips typographus*, will spend its life eating its way through the bark of its host until it girdles and kills the tree. All the bark lying around us is infected. If it hadn't been, it'd still be on the log. Your entire cargo will be affected.'

'Every single stick?'

'Yes. You've been cheated. You should have specified it was to be shipped without bark – peeled logs, always buy 'em peeled so you can see what you're getting. How was it bought?'

'A Russian timber agent approached Sato-san.'

'Have the agent shot.'

He looked at me wryly. 'To a Japanese, that would be a wasted opportunity. Since he has sent us bad timber, he'll have to work twice as hard in future to make up for it. Twice as hard for half the pay.'

'Your loss here is total. There'll certainly be living beetles among these trees. The females will produce eggs, which will become larvae, which will hatch and fly off to infect other trees in the vicinity. The danger is extreme.'

'The solution?'

'We shall walk away looking extremely satisfied with the shipment so that no face is lost. Once your guests have departed, get the stevedores to load the timber back onto the ship and then pay the captain to take it somewhere and burn it. Send one of your top men with him to make sure it's done properly, not just tipped over the side.'

Yamaguchi said to Hijo, who was hovering nearby, 'You've heard nothing of this, do you understand?'

'Yes.'

I said to Yamaguchi, 'The best would be for me to speak to the captain myself. One Russian speaking to another Russian has a different flavour from a Japanese speaking to one. If you permit me, I'll go aboard now and order him to cease unloading.

I'll say the harbour authority is very concerned about the sling that broke. The Emperor's representative himself might have been killed. Tests will have to be done on the crane to ensure its safe working. When you've assigned a man to supervise the burning of the timber, I'll go aboard a second time and see that everything is correct.'

He bowed. 'I am again indebted to you, Doig-san. Now I shall go to Mimi. May I suggest that you will be more comfortable in your hotel tonight than in my house? This accident, which would assuredly have killed her without your presence of mind, will mean that my household will not be at ease tonight. I wish to welcome you into a home that is perfect. "Unpolished jewels do not shine." It is something one of our most famous writers said.'

Fifty-one

'MR DOIG, Mr Doig, wake up, it's important' – it was Hijo standing beside my bed, a frightful sight to open one's eyes to.

'Turd,' I muttered and snuggled down. I'd had a good scoop of the hotel sake the evening before and then gone onto the freighter with Yamaguchi's man to finish off the business with the beetled timber. It turned out that the captain had come originally from Smolensk and had started to learn his craft on the grain barges that ply the Dnieper. His name was Pavel something or other. Of course he'd known of the Rykovs – who in Smolensk hadn't. I said I'd married one. He said, 'Is she still alive?' Warily, I said not. He said, 'But you're so young!' I said, 'Is there a bottle of good Russian vodka anywhere on this ship?'

Unlocking a wall cupboard, he said, 'Describe her for me, Charlenka . . . Oh, but her eyes cannot have been as dark as those of the women here. By the way, never trust a Japanese woman. They're too thin to know about love. Money, that's all they want.'

A little later he said, 'Somewhere between the ape and mankind there is a stage of development of which scientists knew nothing. Now they know: it's called Bolshevism. Can any human be imagined that is as primitive as a Bolshevik? I thought not,' he said, replying on his own behalf. Then he said, 'Why not spend the night on my ship, Charlenka? There are plenty of bunks.'

He'd had a table set out on the deck. We'd taken the bottle up to it, plus another as a reserve. A storm lantern hanging beside the gangway gave us just enough light to see each other by. Above us were the stars and all around the harbour was the twinkle of oil lamps in the boats of the fishermen. The night was a beauty, soft air, lapping wavelets, the dark mountains guarding us.

Being with Pavel and his large cabbage-smelling wife was as good as being back in Russia. We were both far gone with drink, but I was the worse, way over the other side of the hill.

'Stay,' he said, 'it's rude not to.'

'Stay,' she said, 'the mattress is goose down.'

So powerfully were my emotions stirred – the language, the food, the memories of Smolensk and its inhabitants, the evocation of our indolent, capricious, lovable people – and so loopy was I with drink that I believe I would have stayed and maybe even sailed back to Russia with them had not Yamaguchi's man suddenly emerged from his cabin in his white vest and long johns and asked the captain angrily if he intended to continue with the racket the whole night long.

The man had on his feet a pair of fluffy blue *pantoufles* shaped like rabbits. Pavel took it into his head to laugh at them – pointing, and slapping his thigh. The Jap stiffened as though he was about to be executed. A muscle in his cheek started to twitch.

I had just enough wits left in my head to know where this would end up. I grabbed the vodka bottle and threw it into the harbour. I bowed to the Jap, for whom I was responsible in a manner of speaking. I said I was sorry his sleep had been disturbed, I assured him the party was breaking up, and then I left. Taking the last pace down the gangway I tripped and fell. To my surprise – to my completely incapacitated surprise – I was immediately helped to my feet. It was the puller of Yamaguchi's rickshaw. He'd been detailed to look after me through thick and thin.

Thereafter I knew nothing, and now it was morning, a cat had slept in my mouth, and Hijo had started whining again. 'Mr Doig, Mr Doig' – I pulled the covers over my head – 'I have an urgent message from Yamaguchi-san. There's another boat coming in. He wants to know, does it have the beetle?'

I said, 'Tell him, of course it does – now get out.'

The idea of sticking my head up and having to see Hijo at

241

close quarters again was horrendous. I curled up with my hands between my knees.

'Yamaguchi-san's manager said that if you, Doig-san, would give them a paper stating that on such-and-such a date you inspected the timber on board the ship and that you found it beetled, then Governor Sato would have more strength in his argument with the agent. This agent is a Russian,' he added spitefully.

'I'm ill,' I said.

'The boat trip will cure you, Mr Doig. Sea air is very good for your condition.'

'How far off is the vessel?'

'It will be in the roads by midday, that is what the manager said.'

'Is the sea calm?'

'Everything is calm except for Yamaguchi-san. He does not like to be cheated.'

I felt the movement in the mattress as his legs touched the side of the bed. He was bending over me. I pinched my nostrils. The idea of inhaling his breath made my head throb like a volcano. His voice came silkily from the other side of the sheet. 'There will be a big reward, I'm certain of it.'

As it happened, I'd been thinking the same. Plus the fact that I didn't want the connection with Yamaguchi to get frayed, not in any respect. I'd thrown my lot in with the Japanese – the drinking party with Pavel had been my last fling with the Russian bear. I might have a sore head but I was clear about that. Lenin had put a price on my life. The only thing that could get me back to Russia would be my gold. And maybe not even that.

Groaning I said to Hijo, 'I may be sick.'

He whispered, 'I am a doctor, Mr Doig.'

'You'll need to be. OK, I'll do it. Now scram.' When I heard the door close, I clambered up from the futon and went swaying down the corridor to take a piss and alert Kobi.

He was lying on his futon, naked, staring at the flies on the ceiling.

He didn't look like a man keen to receive orders, and when I explained what was afoot, protested vigorously. He'd been born in a stable. He'd been seasick the entire way from

Vladivostok. He was never going to walk up another gangway in his life – etc., etc. I said if that was the case, he was sacked and should return to me the money I'd given him when we landed in Nagasaki, and what sort of frippery had he spent it on anyway, some little fucky-fucky tart, I'd bet, who'd probably given him the pox. If he knew anything at all, he should have known never to pick up a girl in a seaport. 'Men reach land after weeks on the briny and don't care tuppence for anything apart from sticking it up. We both know that.'

He said, 'You don't look very healthy, you shouldn't drink so much,' and rising like a panther from his futon, went over to the window and fished out a sabre from behind the curtain. I groaned inwardly. That was what he'd got up to with the money. Kobi with a sabre meant Kobi awash with grandeur. The Great Khan of Mongolia, Lord of the Steppes, something like that. Once he got himself convinced on that point, he'd start thinking about bloodshed, always had, always would, it was his nature.

I said, 'Give over, we've been through all this before.'

He drew the sabre from its scabbard and made the blade glitter by angling it in the sunlight.

He kissed it. 'A cavalry officer's,' he said and kissed it a second time. 'These letters engraved on it mean, "Presented to Lieutenant Kido for his brave action against the Russians at 203 Metre Hill." The man who sold it translated them for me.'

He had a couple of swings. 'I must keep fit. One day I shall be called upon.'

'We must also remember you're high-born,' I said.

'Perhaps you shouldn't drink at all,' he said, 'then you'll grow fresh brains. This is exercise number one.'

Bending at the knees, he started to swing the sabre, two-fisted, round his head. The blue blade hissed through the air. His eyes narrowed, his hair flopped, his lean, tight body rippled and shone. Between swings he said, 'Put the water carafe on the table there. Balance the tumbler on top of it. No broken glass, that's my promise.'

When that one had come off, the tumbler merely hopping up from the carafe for a moment, he said, 'If I spent a day sharpening this, I could take your head off your shoulders so neatly it'd fall back in its slot and you wouldn't know it had been away. You'd carry on drinking just as usual.'

Faster and faster the sabre went until it began to hum, as if an angry hornet was trapped in the room. He was rolling his wrists to make it easier on himself. Every time he rolled them, the pitch of the blade changed, making the sun flash on it in an explosion of bluish-white light.

He took a pace towards me and changed the rhythm of his swing, slowing down when the sabre was behind him but when it came to my sector, really letting it fly through its arc. I watched the blade as if hypnotised. He took another pace towards me, barefooted, bare everythinged, muscles working like well-oiled machinery. The sweat was pouring down his face and neck, down the groove between his ribs and into his navel. His eyes were bulging, like a temple god's. I thought, Did he also get hold of some sort of Jap weed? – and took a quick step backwards, looking over my shoulder for the door. He followed, pursuing me and pressing on me until the blade was whistling past only six inches from the tip of my nose. 'Hey,' I shouted, 'hey hey, that's enough of that. Stop playing the fool,' and next I knew I'd stumbled over one of his boots and was heading for the floor.

'Ha!' he shouted, a huge thick-of-the-battle shout with his mouth wide open.

I didn't yell – it had got past that stage – but as I hit the floor I rolled away from him and grabbing one of his boots tossed it up – not at him but high into the air to his left. As I hoped, he accepted the challenge and even managed to get in an extra whirl – on tiptoe, making me dizzy – before crack! he caught the boot on its way down and split it like butter, even though it was good Russian leather.

He stuck the point of the sabre into the little bit of matting and leaned on the hilt, breathing hard. He was drenched with sweat, and his flanks and stomach were heaving as if he were a racehorse.

Lying there I said, 'What was that all about? Was that your way of saying you want a proper deal when we break?'

He wiped his forearm across his face. He looked down at his feet, solemnly, like an owl perched on a post. He mumbled, 'The spirits were within me.'

'The shaman business again?'

'I cannot tell. It may have been my ancestors from Mongolia. We are a fighting people.' He shivered. 'I think they made me a little mad. I apologise, Doig.'

I rose from the floor, said it was nothing, said I'd pay for a new pair of boots, got him dressed and downstairs. He was still charged with energy – tossed back two cups of scalding green tea and refused point-blank to leave his sabre with the rest of our stuff.

'This isn't Russia,' I said, 'we're not going to meet a bunch of Reds. This country's at peace. Yamaguchi's is an honourable household. Why not leave it with the management, huh?'

He said proudly, 'If a Japanese officer can wear it, so can I, who have royal blood in my veins.' He banged the tip of the scabbard against the stone floor of the hotel lobby. The porters looked at us with fascination. On the other side of the doors I could see Hijo waiting with the hotel's yellow rickshaw.

I said – I can't remember what I said. It just seemed to me absurd that we should go to inspect a cargo of timber armed with a sabre.

At this he approached me slinking and purposefully. He came so close I could smell the tea on his breath. Speaking in quick low Russian, he said, 'We've had no experience of islanders, they could do anything to us. Once we're on a boat, I won't be able to help you.'

I said, 'I have island blood in my veins, I know what goes on in their heads. Don't make more problems for me this morning, I'm not up to it.'

As we went, the porters seemed to award us exceptional bows, going down as if to touch their toes. Kobi said, 'That's what I mean. They know something. Bastards.' He gripped the sabre tighter and flourished it at the men, who smiled upon him haughtily.

Then we were out in the glorious April sunshine. A gong sounded from the depths of the Confucian temple. A troop of shaven-headed monks processed chanting through the huge wooden gates. From the top of a blue plume of wistaria, a bush warbler sang cheerily.

'Listen to that,' I said to Kobi. 'You know what its song stands

245

for? Rejoicing. Good fortune is on the way, seeking us through the alleys, calling out our names. "Hello there, Kobi! Hello there, Doig!" I feel better just for hearing it.'

He said, 'If that's what a small bird does for you, a big one would send you to heaven.'

I said, 'You're talking proper balls today,' and we climbed into the rickshaw with Hijo.

Fifty-two

YAMAGUCHI'S JETTY reminded me of Uncle Igor's set-up at his palace in the Crimea, especially when a uniformed boatman stepped smartly out of his hut to greet us. Pointing at him, Hijo made sure I understood that he was dressed in an identical naval costume to that worn in 1905, when Admiral Togo sank the Russian Navy at Tsushima.

'When the time comes, we shall sink the Bolsheviks too,' he spluttered, bowing me and Kobi aboard.

The cutter's hull was of sleek yellow pine, its deck the same. A white canvas awning covered the wheelhouse and the benches, which were bolted to the deck.

The boatman gave us the choice between going below and staying on deck. The sea had become choppy since Hijo had awoken me. The wind would clear my head – I said we'd stay topsides. Kobi took a seat immediately, his sabre across his knees. Hijo said he needed a table for his papers and went below.

All over the bay fishing boats, two men apiece, were bobbing around on the sea beneath their green, blue or grey flags.

I asked the boatman if he spoke Russian, thinking he could explain to me the significance of the flags. But he could only smile and shrug. I guessed his uniform was that of a naval rating – blue, with a blue-and-white neckcloth. On his head was a dark blue beret with a swallowtail. He was wearing white gloves, which were no doubt fine for trips across the harbour with Yamaguchi and his daughters but seemed to me unrealistic for the skipper of a boat heading for the high seas, which was what we were doing.

'Hope we don't have to depend on him for life-saving,' I said to Kobi. But he was already grey and suffering, before we'd even left port.

The boatman called over to me, pointing to a locker on the port side. Inside, folded neatly, were smart new tartan rugs – a bright and bloody red. I heard my father, 'Hunting Stewart, laddie' – and smiled freely for the first time that day. I removed Kobi's sabre, tucked a rug round him as I would a child, and replaced the sabre on his lap.

Running along the jetty, the boatman slipped the mooring ropes and cast off.

Soon we were in the outer straits where we met the true force of the wind, which was gusting from the south-west. Our bows slammed into the waves, the spray reared. Kobi threw off his rug and stumbled to the side.

Wanting to spare Kobi by getting into calmer water, I gesticulated to the boatman to take us into the shelter of one of the islands that shield the entrance to the harbour. Stabbing at his chest, he said cheerily, 'Me Kenji,' then he flipped the wheel a spoke or two to the right. It wasn't by more than a fraction that he changed course but it was enough to bring Hijo up from below.

He stuck his head above the coaming and would have had Kenji reverse the change if I hadn't jumped up and, getting behind Kenji, clamped his hands to the wheel. I growled to Hijo, 'I'm the one who knows about beetles, I'm in charge and this is what we're doing.'

He stared at me, wondering if he should dispute my word – and disappeared.

I shouted after him, 'Is the ship waiting for us, does it know we're on our way, how's it been arranged?'

But he didn't bother to answer. Releasing Kenji, I picked up his binoculars to study a vessel lying out in the roads. It was too narrow to be carrying timber, and its decks were clean. A couple more were further out to sea, too far to make out any details.

'Could be a wild goose chase,' I shouted to Kobi who was leaning over the rail. 'Soon have you home.'

I urged Kenji to get us close in to the island, where the water was calmest, but the tide was wrong and we had to make do with chugging along about a hundred yards offshore.

It was pleasant like that, not a bad day at all out of the wind. The engine throbbed in a deep comfortable way. Yamaguchi's house flag, which consisted of a snow-capped mountain on a light green field – to give resonance to his family name, I suppose – rippled gaily above my head. The pain behind my eyeballs lessened. Only Kobi was having a hard time of it.

After a short while, the lie of the land revealed itself. I put it to Kenji in sign language that if we followed the coast round, there was only a short gap of choppy water between this island and the next one. If we then got to a certain woody cape, we should be able to review all the shipping heading into Nagasaki that day. There might be a squall here and there that would obscure vessels for a while, but they were all putting up smoke and lots of it. In the end we'd see everything.

Ah yes, he said, but there's a third island beyond these two – first he drew with his finger a rough map in the spray on the chart case and then with a snort opened the case itself and got out the chart. Did I appreciate that we'd have to jink around a bit to see if there was a ship behind the last island? He traced the course we'd have to take with a pencil and raised his eyebrows to me in a question mark.

I said it was fine. Yamaguchi wanted a job done? I was the man. Any time, any weather, I was his man.

With a motion of his hand Kenji indicated the sea would get worse. He mimed an island with steep cliffs, said we'd have to give it a wide berth as we rounded it.

'Let's get it over with,' I said. '*Hayo! Hayo!*' – at which Kenji smiled, because the words as I pronounced them probably meant something other than quickly, quickly.

The time was then a little after midday.

Don't get me wrong, there wasn't a gale and the sea wasn't rough by a mariner's standard. But it was awkward and the motion of the boat was lively, from the fact of the wind being thrown back by the hills at the entrance to Nagasaki harbour and then flipped around between the islands so that it was never constant for more than five minutes at a time. Moreover the tide had started to flood. When it was at its peak and got squeezed between the islands, it came fairly racing in, Kenji said. He pointed to the stakes for the fishermen's nets that stretched out into the shallows. There it was safe, even when the tide was ripping. Where there were no stakes it was too dangerous. The spring tides pulled everything up and deposited the wreckage on the mainland. 'Here,' he said, 'feel this,' and had me hold the wheel. Already I could feel the tide trying us with little tugs and nudges at the keel.

We were able to get much closer in to the second island, only a few yards away. Wonderfully clear turquoise water was beneath us, going down to a good depth, with shells glimmering at the bottom. I told Kenji to cut the engine to a putter.

'*Hayo, hayo?*' he said with a grin.

'Just having a look-see,' I said.

We entered a small lagoon, overhung on three sides by trees. It was like going into a secret room – totally sheltered, everything tranquil and warm. Two butterflies, huge ones, much larger than anything we have in Russia, appeared out of nowhere and chased each other round the deck. For an instant they settled on Kenji's chart case – black and bluish-white panes on their wings and a warm brown fringe at the tail. Somewhat tattered at their extremities and the colours on the dull side, so obviously they'd overwintered on the island.

'*Cho-cho*,' said Kenji, admiringly.

Then they were gone, flittering off at a rate of knots.

Kenji put his hand on the lever to give us more revs but I stayed him. The call had come to me from the lush, semi-tropical vegetation – Hey, Charlie boy, this could be your Galapagos. My heart surged, my brain scrawled the word 'genius' over some pink clouds of optimism that it'd been keeping handy. Had I not been singled out for the highest scientific honours from the day I caught my jewel beetle? If it wasn't my karma, why had I then been given the Lala bird? And now – maybe no one had looked at this small island in the way that I was doing. Just didn't have the curiosity, the forensic talent, the right instincts. Could see the entrance to Nagasaki harbour only a mile off and scorned the poor little island in their way, probably wished it didn't exist so they could keep going in a straight line, so they could get to the fleshpots quicker—

Hijo stuck his head out again wanting to know why we'd slowed down. I said casually, 'Anyone live on this island?'

He transferred the question to Kenji. 'About a thousand people, not including children,' came back the answer.

People meant domestic animals which meant rats which meant a wipe-out of ground-nesting birds and all the gentle species. So much for the pink clouds. I gestured to Kenji he could turn the revs up again.

'Why did you ask?' Hijo said.

'Oh, a thought occurred to me,' I said, and at that moment another butterfly came for a visit, a fritillary of some sort, with more or less the same markings as our own. Maybe my Galapagos idea had come to nothing but it didn't change the fact that there were still new discoveries to be made. Always were and always would be until the day the world ended. Nature, you couldn't beat it. That was my true profession, as its interpreter. It was at Darwin's shoulder that I'd stand, not in the temple with the money-changers. My name would be on museum labels, in drawers, cabinets, indexes and classification lists – Charlie Doig, naturalist.

Prince of Siberia? Commission man? Smiling at the utter ridiculousness of Sato's proposal, I said to Hijo, 'I was just wondering whether there might be a new Lala bird over there. In my business, one has to keep on one's toes. You know how it is, doctor.'

He smirked at me – or something like that, it was so difficult to tell. I said to him, 'Don't act superior with me, just because you think medicine is more important to mankind than the natural sciences.'

'But it is, Mr Doig. Their health is the most important thing to every single person in the world. You ask your servant there.'

'Even sailors get seasick. It can't be prevented.'

'One day it will be. One day every disease will have its cure. That is my promise to you.' He signalled to Kenji.

'Christ, you're a maniac,' I muttered, but benevolently, as it didn't matter to me one way or another what Hijo might promise. Then we were out of the lagoon, out of the protection of the island and the sea had got rougher.

I said to him, 'Where's this freighter, then?' I put up the binoculars. Nothing was in sight that could conceivably have been a ship carrying timber.

'We'll find it,' he said. 'No manager would have dared speak untruthfully to Yamaguchi-san.'

I said, 'I'm giving it five minutes then I'm going home, Yamaguchi or no Yamaguchi. It's been delayed, developed engine trouble, cargo's shifted, something like that. Yamaguchi's men can signal the captain and tell him to wait in the roads and I'll come and inspect the timber tomorrow.'

'Only one more island,' Hijo said. 'When we've looked there, then we may go back.'

I said, 'It won't be there. Bet you my bottom dollar.'

He said, 'But it might be.'

I said, 'But it won't be.'

He said, 'We're almost there. We have ample fuel. The typhoon season is months away. There's no danger anywhere. We must look, so we can say with truth to Yamaguchi-san that we've carried out his orders.'

I supposed he was right. Acceding with bad grace, I turned up my greatcoat collar over my ears and sat on a bench with my hands deep in my pockets.

The island, the last of the three, was half a mile away and the wind was still rising. Towering black cliffs were facing us, waves rearing halfway up them, sheets of spume spouting into the sky. No place to be wrecked, that was for sure. A man might get lucky and be washed up onto one of those shelves of rough sand. He'd scramble to his knees and say prayers to his God for deliverance. Then he'd look at the sheer cliffs above him, examine them one way and the other, trace one route up and a second and a third, find each of them impossible – look back over his shoulder at the rising tide – start to panic – and, already knowing he was doomed, scrabble as high as he could till he either fell to his death or was licked off the cliff by the muscular sea.

Why couldn't Yamaguchi have waited till the ship got into the harbour? Having to burn the timber wouldn't matter to a man as rich as he was. Was he insisting I board it on the ocean just to save face? Pathetic, I said to myself. No Russian would behave like that. He wouldn't have bought beetled timber in the first place. He'd have used what God had put between his ears and drilled some test holes – flaked off some bark – said to the agent, 'You rotten fucking swine, cheat me, would you?' and had his men hang him from the lowest limb of an oak, saying to him as the noose was placed, 'Now you'll discover what a strong healthy tree is.'

I got up and said to Hijo, 'Let's get this clear. We take a peek round the corner and if the ship isn't in sight we head for home, no farting about, straight home as in straight as a die. Agreed?'

He gave me a horrid little nod. The boat thudded against the waves as we headed towards the cliffs.

Fifty-three

KOBI, GROANING: 'Anything?'

'Nix, no smoke between here and Shanghai.'

Moreover, it was obvious now we'd got this far out that the traffic between Vladivostok and Nagasaki would hug the mainland.

'That's it,' I said to Hijo. 'About turn. Home.'

He bowed to me – straddling his legs and having to hang onto the rail, the boat was pitching that much. 'Regretful apologies for the negative use of this day.' His head went up, his teeth glared at me – 'But there is something we could do to eliminate total waste.'

'OK, you've brought me after a ship that doesn't exist, what are you going to spring next?'

'Have you noticed how different this island is from the others? The strong cliffs! The rocks! The savagery! You'll have said to yourself, this place is not for me. But it has a tiny harbour of its own and there live some people who have never left this island. Never! Not once in their own lives, not once in the lives of their ancestors.'

'You suggesting we drop in on them for a chat?'

'Don't make fun of me, Mr Doig. These people have been thought worthy of study by the topmost class of our anthropologists. A man of your scientific acclaim should welcome the chance to inspect them. You see, many of them suffer from a hereditary deformity. That is why they won't leave the island.'

'Freaks? Let's go there, you'll really feel at home. What sort?'

'The skin on their chests becomes brown and deeply

254

corrugated, rough too, like the bark of a walnut tree. From the base of the neck down to the navel, that's the area affected.'

'Men and women?'

'Yes. I've seen a photograph. With their children it starts as a rash at about the age of five. The rash is very similar to that which afflicts those who have typhus. That was what caught my attention originally.'

'It's found nowhere else in the world?'

'Nowhere else.'

Kobi, gripping the rail, looked back at us and asked if it was contagious.

Hijo laughed. 'Would I put you in danger and myself too?'

I said, 'So what do you want to do?'

'They'll probably collect at the harbour when they see the boat turn in. I suggest we go ashore and walk among them. It would be an interesting experience for us both.'

'Thirty minutes max. Not a moment longer.'

'I agree, Mr Doig,' he said softly, and spoke to Kenji, who looked stonily ahead as he laid the boat on its new course.

It took an hour to work our way round the cliffs. Kobi was lying flat on his back by now. He'd complained of feeling cold so I'd put a couple of the tartan rugs over him. Eventually Kenji brought us round at a wide angle to be able to make the passage into the harbour, which lay between two fangs of black rock that shone like wet ebony amid the slapping sea.

The islanders' settlement was a group of small stone hovels on our left, set back from the harbour by a couple of hundred yards. Just as Hijo had said, a group of people gathered to watch us, both men and women, a few children too. Rudely dressed, some of them even in sealskins. Standing in a tight bunch, as if for safety.

One of them, a huge shambling fellow whom I knew at once couldn't be other than Russian, split off and trudged towards the jetty carrying a boathook.

I said to Hijo, 'How do they get their supplies?'

'A boat gets sent out from Nagasaki once a month. They have sympathisers all over Japan. New money is raised every time a study of them is published. There's very little they lack.'

'Some decent clothing,' I said – then Kenji cut the engine.

We glided smoothly in to the jetty and were grabbed with the boathook.

'Thirty minutes max,' I said again. 'Freaks don't interest me more than that.'

'We should thank our gods it isn't us,' Hijo said.

I had a good retort to that, but let it go unsaid. 'Come on, Kobi, it'll do you a power of good,' and with those words I stepped onto the jetty, which had chunks of kelp and seaweed strewn over it from a recent storm. Looking back, I checked that Kobi was on my heels. He was clutching a rug around his body.

Hijo called out, 'Watch your footing!'

'Spastic,' I growled, and stuck out a hand to help Kobi.

I got him onto terra firma, an arm round his shoulder since it looked as though he was about to retch. He leaned right over trying to gob something out. 'Easy, Genghis, easy, one last heave' – I was bent over with him, our heads right down. He had a couple of whooping spasms like a dog and then brought up a great slop of rubbish. He straightened, said, 'That's better' – and I heard the diesel engines flutter. I thought, the man's lost his grip with the boathook and here's Kenji the good and honest seaman bringing the boat back in to the jetty. I looked round – no, I just glanced, that's all I did, without an atom of suspicion, as if I were a boy on a farm and knew only about buttercups.

The boat was nosing out into the eel-grey sea, squaring off for the channel between the two black rocks. Kenji was at the wheel, the swallowtails on his beret flying. Face set like granite, giving nothing away. On my side of him was Hijo, his left hand on the rail. No question of the boat being brought to the jetty. It was leaving, that was what it was doing, as clear as a cowbell.

'Hey – HEY!' – but neither of them even looked at me.

'Hijo, you fucking bastard' – and I took off down the jetty, hurdling the lobster pots, nets, buoys – slipping, sliding, grabbing at the stacks of pots to keep my balance.

The boat completed its turn through the rocks, was broadside on, not twenty yards away. The end of the jetty was coming up, thick with seaweed.

'You little yellow fucker, what d'you think you're doing, what about us?' – and my heels went flying. Face down in the fish guts and seaweed and the rotting helmet crabs and bird-picked bones and the brine and iodine and stink, with the sound of the sea pawing at the jetty's foundations only inches away – right down there I was, scrabbling and slipping, mad with rage. Somehow I got to my knees.

'I'll see you in hell, I'll cunt you so badly—'

'Take the greatest care of your health, Mr Doig,' he shouted, doffing an imaginary hat. Then he signalled to Kenji. The chugging of the boat's engine turned to a roar. Foam billowed beneath the stern counter. Yamaguchi's flag unpeeled and became a taut green blade.

I hopped, I danced, I roared, I shook both fists at them. 'I'll, I'll—'

'You'll do nothing, because nothing is the only thing possible.' It was Kobi, standing a yard behind me.

'But what the fuck's he doing this for? What does he want?'

'We are not clever enough to know,' Kobi said. Then he added sarcastically, 'Such an honourable household, that of Mr Yamaguchi.'

Footsteps sounded a few yards away – the soles of rubber boots squeaking on a patch of seaweed.

We turned as one.

The wind moaning off the sea, the gulls screaming, the water thudding rhythmically into the jetty like a piledriver at work—

The terns scudding through the spume, the angry grey sea and the light green flag of the departing boat—

The hulking figure of the boatman—

Two hundred yards away, grouped in front of their low grey stone houses, the villagers, motionless, staring—

Children strapped to their mothers' backs, old men leaning on hoes, men arrested in the act of mending nets – villagers, that's what you'd say, just the same as villagers and fisherfolk on any impoverished island. But poorly dressed – OK, so they were poorly dressed villagers and fisherfolk because none of them dared leave their island for fear of being mocked. Hanging back from us for the same reason—

But many were in cowls, and the hoes weren't always

257

gardening hoes for some were sticks for leaning on, for the bents and cripples among them—

All this my mind saw and heard and registered as a backdrop to the boatman. He had rubber sea boots up to his chest, black ones, with rubber braces. A large man, glistening with spray. And in his dark, dead, shrivelled eyes was the remorseless look of a gaoler.

'Christ.' That's all I said, and Kobi and I edged closer to each other, as animals in danger will.

Fifty-four

'Don't be afraid,' he said, stretching out a rubber gauntlet. 'We're all brothers and sisters in this place.'

'Like hell we are,' I said, looking around for a way to get off the jetty without having him touch me. 'You keep your fucking spores to yourself.'

'Everyone on this island is a sufferer. You're in a safe place, both of you. No one will chase you away. No one will spit on you. No one will send you hungry from their door. You have found a refuge. Praise the Lord!'

He stepped towards us – lumbering, having to look where he put his feet. His sunken nose, his huge round face, his elephant's ears, all of them a mass of tubercles, reddish mahogany in colour and flowing into each other, came looming towards me. A wave broke against the jetty and drenched him. He put up a hand and slicked back his long wet hair. His eyelids were so weighted down by pustules, which were deep red in the centre and flaking on their slopes, that they covered more than half his eyeballs. It was his pupils that I'd noticed first, that anyone would have, for they'd been reduced by the disease to just slivers, like a couple of sliced black olives.

Kobi had the same idea as I, for he jumped one way and I jumped the other and the leper lost us – stood there crouched with his fumbling eyes.

'Boss?' – Kobi had the sabre half drawn.

I said, 'Old man, we're wondering whether to slice your head off.'

'You wouldn't get far. The others'd find you and kill you. I can't see well but I can hear everything. It's the younger ones who can still see. They're the ones who'd kill you.'

'What with, old man?' said Kobi, taunting the fellow by scraping his sabre in and out of the scabbard. I told him to go easy, told him to hold back until we could figure out where an advantage lay.

'With our disease,' he said. He'd had time to pinpoint my voice. Now he stretched out his rubber hands and came groping for me.

'Wrong way, over here, old man,' said Kobi.

He halted undecided, questing like a blind dog. 'They'd catch you in the end. One night you'd try to get down to the well. They'd be waiting, they'd have been waiting every night since you got here. There's no other fresh water on the island, see. Then they'd bind you and take you to the meeting room. Your clothes'd be removed and the women'd get down and rub themselves against you. All of you as naked as tapeworms, them as well as you. Then you'd be caught all right. It's a ritual with new arrivals . . . but come, brothers, that's no cause to be afraid, we're in this together.'

'Say the word, boss,' hissed Kobi. 'They're lepers, weaklings, we'd get the better of them.'

'But they are fifty and we are two. Be patient. We'll find a way . . . Old man, you just have to take our word that we're clean. You know what suffering is. Help us avoid it. Tell us where you keep your boat.'

'Suffering? I've been ill for so long that I've forgotten what the word means.' His throat was swollen and his voice rasping, as though it was being scraped against something on its way out. 'You'd be surprised how many say they're clean, the people who're sent here. Rich or poor, it makes no difference. They show me their wounds – that's what we call them, wounds – and sometimes they're only the size of a fifty-sen coin, tiny, and these people say to me, In a month they'll have disappeared, that's what the doctor told me, and then the boat'll come and take me off, won't it? Poor, poor people! But I never say to them, Wrong, you're here until you die. That would just make them unhappy and upset everyone else. I look at their wounds, tiny and white, like flicks of paint, and say, Oh, I don't know, about a month, maybe nearer six months. It helps, you see, to put a longer period in their minds. They say, Six months? What will my family say, the doctor told them a few weeks at the most . . . But the idea gets into their minds. One six months leads to another, and so it goes on, until they become like me.'

Then he said, 'Boys, let's not allow ourselves to get gloomy. Here's a right hearty welcome for you,' and raising his arm he signalled to where the villagers were standing. I hadn't noticed them before, a small band of violinists, all of them men, who were standing to one side. They sank their chins onto their instruments, cocked their wrists and advanced towards us, grinning in the most repulsive way. They were like the Hungarians on the Tran-Sib I'd seen begging for food. God knows what they were trying to play. Their reedy whine challenged the terns, which dived screaming at them. They finished their music and halted about twenty yards away, bowing and smiling and tapping on their instruments with their bows – applauding us.

He said, 'Doesn't that put you at your ease? We're one family here. Music is what binds us together. You've nothing further to be frightened of for the rest of your lives. Come, come.'

I said, 'Look at my finger, I was a jeweller once. That ring of mine has the largest emerald in Japan.'

I stuck my finger into the air. Was he looking at it? It was hard to say, his eyes were in that much of a mess. I moved it left, towards the centre of his face. 'You're not wearing a ring, you're a liar, mister.'

'Sorry, wrong finger,' I said, 'try this one,' and I moved my finger to the right.

'Oh, that's a beaut, we'll put it somewhere safe,' he said, and I knew that outside a narrow arc he was quite blind.

I slipped round his back and joined Kobi. Pace by pace we retreated, to get onto higher ground. The band, the villagers, everyone watched us. There was a strip of shingle before we could reach the greensward. I thought we were far enough away from him to talk, but he was right about his hearing. He had ears like a bat. The moment we started across the stones, he lurched round.

'That's not going to get you anywhere. Gentlemen, gentlemen, why not resign yourselves to your lot? It's pointless to resist. Tonight we'll give you a banquet. For a week you need do no work. There are girls here who are hungry for fit young men. You're free to make your own choice. You'll get a special room to yourselves. If a baby arrives, we'll welcome it. We have five at the moment. There's a little school for them. We pride ourselves on doing something useful, every one of us. We don't let ourselves become ashamed. We're like no other community in the world. Let us have no trouble. We don't like trouble, we are a peaceable society.'

We were on the grass by now, where the old man couldn't see or hear us. But the villagers were shouting to him, telling him what we were doing – dobbing us.

Kobi looked me plumb between the eyes and said, 'Don't think I'm going to forget this. Ever.'

I stared back at him. 'We've only got to find their boat. The rest's easy.'

'If they had one, it'd be here. See it, do you?'

'They're bound to keep one. Islanders without a boat? Not likely.'

'Old sick people don't do well in boats. How's that man going to row with those hands of his? Can you imagine a leper – look, Doig, a month ago I'd never even seen the sea but that doesn't mean I can't imagine a leper trying to tie knots or hoist a sail. They just don't have boats. They fish from the shore, they set their pots in the gullies between the rocks, that's how they exist.'

'I know. I was trying to give us hope.'

'There's good hope and there's bad.'

'Don't be so negative. Somehow we'll escape, you wait and see.'

'Escape? You told me never to use that word. Only the losing side needs to escape, that's what you said.'

It was getting us nowhere. I set out up a path that led to the top of the cliff to see what sort of a place we'd landed up on.

But no sooner had I taken a few steps than the villagers started baying like dogs. A boy ran out of their midst to lead the old man after us – tugged him across the shingle shouting to him everything we were doing.

I stopped and said quietly, 'Kobi, my friend, we're in a pickle and there's no getting away from it. I'm sorry, I'm truly sorry.'

We embraced, just as we had below the smoking monastery at Zilantov when between us we'd pulled off a victory no one had thought possible. He held me off and said, 'I'll jump off a cliff before they touch me.'

I said, 'The sabre is the last resort, do we agree?'

We thought about it together, saying nothing, visualising all the heads we could slice off, perhaps half a dozen before they rushed us. 'What'd it be like?' he said after a few seconds, not needing to say more. What'd it be like to be lynched by a mob of lepers, that's what he meant.

'But no sabre until it's hopeless, agreed?'

'Agreed,' he said, then the old man and the boy had stopped a couple of yards below us on the path and the old man had got his breath back and was saying, 'Listen, I run this island. I've been here since the age of six. My father was a Russian like you. He lived in Sakhalin and worked as a fisherman. But he got caught in a storm and his boat was carried to Hokkaido. There he met my mother. My parents ate nothing but fish. First my mother caught the disease, and then I did. The villagers threw stones at us and made us leave. We went into the forest. The government sent men to hunt us down. They put us on a boat. Halfway here, my mother jumped overboard, out of shame. There's nothing I don't know about faking good health and people feeling sorry for themselves. Why would someone go to all that trouble of bringing you here if you weren't lepers?'

I said, 'How often does the official leper boat call?'

'Whenever it needs to. A cargo of one is enough. They hate us over there. When they see the wounds starting to appear, they go mad with anger. That's what happened to my mother and me.'

'When was the boat last here?'

'That's not the point. I'm not here to give out sailing timetables, I'm here to keep order and make people behave suitably. That includes you.'

Kobi said, 'You want us to obey *you*?'

'Yes, I'm the ruler here.'

I said, 'What's your name, old man?'

263

'Daimyo, that's what they call me. It's a Japanese word for a sort of king.'

'So how do we get released from your kingdom, Daimyo?'

'Sometimes a doctor comes. You have to present yourselves to him to be inspected. The last one stayed on his boat and made us parade along the jetty in front of him. He never got closer than ten feet. After a few minutes he wrote something in his book, shouted to me, 'Carry on,' and was taken away by his boatman.'

He'd got himself properly focused on me by now – glanced down to see if there was anything between us he might trip over.

'The path's clear,' I called to him. 'But go slowly or you might slip. See, I'm not afraid of you.'

'Then you're a leper like the rest of us. Only people who've got it aren't afraid of me touching them. That's what I'm going to do, mister, I'm going to take your hands in mine and give them a good rub, as if we were warming ourselves in front of a fire. We had a wedding here once – there, that surprised you, I saw the look on your face, I'm not all blind, you know. That's what I did to their hands, to seal them in their holy bonds. You'll easily get a bride here, you're still a very handsome man. We have some nice girls. Just because they're lepers, it doesn't mean there's anything wrong with them down there. Everyone uses everyone, if you know what I mean. To begin with, the appetite is very strong in lepers. Only later does it affect a man's parts. Now let me touch you and make you one of us. Don't be afraid, I'll be gentle.'

He held his hands out to the boy, who pulled the rubber gauntlets off, finger by finger. I say 'finger by finger' but of course he had no fingers, just red scaly stumps.

Breathing hoarsely he waddled towards me, wringing his hands. The boy stayed where he was, his black eyes darting around like tadpoles.

I easily sidestepped the old man's advance and said to Kobi, 'He's our best hope. We'll go back with him to the village and see what's what. We may need them. What if we have to get them to build a boat for us?'

'With hands like his? How're they going to plane the wood

and joint it? Anyway, where's the wood to come from?' It was true. Nothing was to be seen on the island except windswept groves of bamboo.

But I too could be stubborn. I wanted to believe in the existence of a boat. There had to be one. How else were we to get free? I said, 'Getting them to lend us their boat is only the start of it. We'll need to know about the sea currents and tides. We'll need food and bedding for tonight. We'll need to know where the well is. These are people we have to be nice to. He'll love us for it. Bet you no one's been kind to him for the last fifty years.'

Kobi said in a low voice, 'If we touch him, will we get the disease?'

'We're not going to touch him.'

'He may stumble, he may suddenly reach out for one of us.' Kobi whipped out his hand and grabbed my arm. 'Ha! Like that!'

'Stop playing the fool.'

Very deliberately, his eyes on me all the time, he wiped his hand on my sleeve. 'That's the white shit you've got on your clothes.' He seized my hand and began to stroke it as a woman might. He whispered, 'Now it's on your skin, a sort of fungus. You could burn your clothes. You couldn't burn your hand.'

I snatched my hand back. I looked at it for traces, couldn't help myself.

The old man said, 'That's right, you and your friend talk it over while I get that nice rug you brought with you. Come down to the meeting place when you're ready.' He shuffled off with the boy.

Kobi said, 'Doig, will you look after me if I get it?'

'At home, you mean, instead of sending you here, is that what you're asking?'

'Yes.'

'What else would I do, pal?'

'Then say it properly, like a lawyer'd write it. "I, Doig . . ."'

I loved this man. I owed him a debt – probably several life-debts. I'd repay him, get someone to look after him, pay whatever had to be paid. But this was no place for sentimentalism. I said, 'Let's just concentrate on not getting it, shall we? It's not like the clap. It doesn't call for impossible strength of mind to keep clear. We'll stick together. One of us'll keep watch while the other's asleep. We'll hold out till the doctor comes.'

'You're speaking in riddles. One moment we're to become their friends, the next we have to keep clear.'

'We'll need their help for food. They can cook it and leave it somewhere. They'll understand. Then the boat'll be here.'

'You can be the one to be kind to the old man. Keep me out of it.'

'So you think we can live off the land till the boat comes, for a month, say?'

'You come up with a better idea, then. You got us into this.' He grabbed me by the wrist. 'There, it was the old man who did that, just imagine it. Caught you napping, didn't he? Gave you the pox good and proper, didn't he? You want to take the risk of going with him, you take it. I'm staying put.'

So I gave in, telling him his argument was better than mine, which it was, and said he should go down and retrieve his rug before the old man fouled it. 'If we're going to spend forty nights in the wilderness, we'll need it.'

But it was too late. The old man already had the Hunting Stewart in his hands, stroking and petting it. As we watched he cuddled it against his cheek and then against the boy's cheek. They spoke. The old man draped it round his shoulders like a plaid, looked up to us, waved ironically.

Kobi said, 'It'll be a cold night.'

'We've been through worse,' I said. 'Think of those nights in the taiga with the Tungus on our tail.'

'You're talking shit, Doig. This is the worst possible situation in the world.'

Fifty-five

I SAID, 'FOR heaven's sake, they've got to have goats. Meat, milk for the children, the hide for making slippers, the sinews for fish-hooks – there'll be goats somewhere on the island, you take my word. All islands have goats. We'll grab the kids and roast them. We won't starve.'

'Goats?' he said in astonishment. 'Goats? Hear them bleating? See their shit? They don't have goats here. They may have once but I'd say they caught the white shit and died. These people are Japs, they eat fish not meat.'

We'd had a couple of nests of gulls' eggs – whipped the top of the eggs off with Kobi's knife and tipped them back, slippery raw. We'd gone down among the nodding pink heads of the thrift, scrambled out onto the rocks and prised off some limpets. But that was like eating rubber sprinkled with grit. Then we'd climbed back up and as the sun was sinking into the sea, exactly like it does in the pictures of Japan, not that that was sod all use to us, we made our base under a rocky overhang close to the highest point on the island, which was a dumpy little cone, old volcanic stuff perhaps. There were dwarf bamboos all round. I made Kobi hack them down with his sabre so we had a clear field of view. I really did not want to be taken by surprise during the night. The old man had been happy enough when he went off with the rug but when he'd brooded over things a bit, he could get biled up that the two of us were still at large. Even as I was thinking about it, he could be herding the lepers into the meeting hall and getting them in a lather about the *gaijin*. If they took drink, there was no knowing where it'd end.

I said, 'Do you reckon they've got booze down there?'

'Give it up, I've told you that before. It'd improve you in every way.'

'It wasn't for me. I was thinking, here's the old man, and maybe he has a snort at night, who knows, and let's suppose that tonight he has a couple of snorts to celebrate grabbing the rug – let's then suppose the drink gets to him and he comes out with all guns blazing, has them scour the island for us. That mightn't end up too nicely.'

'Depends if they've got the stuff to make the booze. Rice any good to them?'

'Sake rice isn't the same as eating rice. It'll be eating rice they grow here, has to be. However, I suppose they could make a spirit from the husks. Grind them up and get a fermentation going.'

Kobi said, 'How should I know, I don't drink.'

'You did once, I was there. You got yourself legless.'

'That's not the point. The point is that you just asked if they made booze. I said I didn't know. That's not the end of it?'

'Yeah, I suppose so. The question wasn't much of a one to start with.'

'What were we to do about it in any case?'

'Nothing, except think of the booze going down their throats.'

'Wasted if they can't swallow properly.'

'Everything is wasted to a leper,' I said.

Night was falling. Gloom was riding in at us from all angles. Kobi was right, the situation couldn't be worse. But I wasn't going to admit it.

Some way out we could see where a couple of ships, decent-sized ones to judge by their lights, were riding at anchor, probably waiting to go in to Nagasaki at dawn when the pilots started work. Scattered across the sea was a sprinkling of absolutely tiny lights – pinpricks, the night shift of fisherfolk.

At our side were the bamboo fronds Kobi had cut. We'd spread them out to dry, thinking they'd be better to sleep on than on the ground.

I said, 'I wouldn't want to have to try and row to Nagasaki from here. That tide race was vicious. God knows where we'd end up.'

'So now we need not just a boat but a boat with an engine,' Kobi said. Sarcasm or obstinacy, I rarely had a conversation with him without meeting one of them.

'That's about it.'

'Did you see any fuel tanks near the jetty? Did you smell any oil?'

I said not.

He went on: 'What makes you think they'd give the lepers a way to escape from the island? Why did they send them here? So they can never escape, there's the answer for you. As for the leper boat, the doctor won't let us aboard. He'll be as afraid of us as he is of the real lepers.'

I stayed silent, head sunk in my hands.

Kobi said, 'Wounds, that's what the bastard called their sores. The first wound that appears on me, I'll kill myself. You've fucked me this time, Doig.'

I said, 'I'll tell you how it is we're here. How I *think* it is.' I wanted to get it off my chest. You could say I wanted to torture myself with blame for the disaster. And maybe it was worse than a disaster, maybe it was our own death, of the two of us, that I'd brought about.

He said, 'No lying, not between us.'

'Sure . . . When we were in Zhigalovo, I made a bargain with Sato: I would go to Nagasaki, meet up with Yamaguchi on the pretext of selling him the bird skin and arrange for him to be killed if he didn't cooperate.'

Kobi's head, dark against the starry sky, swivelled.

'I know your question, and the answer is yes. You were to be the assassin. By his death, Sato would have got rid of his partner in the trading side of the new Kingdom. He and the Countess would have gained access to immense wealth.'

He grunted. 'How big is that?'

'I don't know. Wealth on a scale we cannot understand.'

'Why do they want such riches? A horse, a woman, food and fire, that'd satisfy me.' He spat. 'But I'm only a Mongolian, not a modern man. What would you have got out of it, Doig? Tell it me all, without deception.'

'I would have become the Prince of Siberia.' I went quickly on. 'But I found I couldn't have Yamaguchi killed—'

'This Prince man, this you, would he also have got some of the wealth you just mentioned?'

'I would have received commissions, I believe. I would have shared them with you, of course—'

'And if I didn't want them?'

'Pal, don't play the simpleton with me, I know you too well. Who begged me for five thousand roubles and a horse and a rifle so he could go and enlist with some White cavalry general? Huh? We're men – we're vain, we're selfish, we're crap, both of us. So don't let's pretend we're saints. OK, maybe you wouldn't have taken money but you'd have taken a thousand horses if I'd offered them to you, and if that isn't the same as money, I'm the man in the moon. So just listen to the story and stop baiting me. The reason I couldn't ask you to kill Yamaguchi was simple: I liked him too much and I liked you too much.'

'Thank you,' he said, looking away, grunting it out.

'Sato sent Hijo with us to make sure I didn't flinch, I understand that now. When he saw I'd changed sides, he reported back to Sato, must have. Sato'll have cabled him saying, Get rid of Doig and the Mongolian. Doesn't matter how, just don't do it so they bob up in the harbour in a week. That's why we're on an island reserved for lepers. End of story.'

Kobi looked fixedly at me, his head butting forward a bit. Some moments passed while he chewed on his lip and looked for the words. Then, bursting out of him as if he hadn't spoken to anyone for months, 'What's your title of Prince compared to me dying from leprosy? What's all the wealth you talk about compared to me rotting away limb by limb? My toes. My cock. My nose' – he jabbed angrily at it with his forefinger – 'what'll I do when it disappears? When I can't smell anything, when I look as if I had syphilis, shall I say to myself, so long as the Prince my master is happy, it's worth it? Is that what I'm worth? Is that all I'm worth, Doig?'

I sat in silence now. There was no argument here, could never be, the way things had turned out for us. I'd done for him. Had I been content with capturing the Lala bird, we'd be on a steamer to America right now. Had I done this, had I not done that, had I – I felt like jumping up and shouting to God, Had I not fallen in love, wasn't that where this all started—

270

Kobi was still staring at me. 'You remember what Boltikov called you when you told him to take some gold and get out of your life? A capital shit, those were his words. Now it's my turn to say it. Into your face, before it gets eaten away by the disease. You are one capital shit, Doig.'

'We'll get away from here, we shall, I promise you.'

'How?' Then, 'There's only one way I can make the score equal.'

I raised my head and looked at him.

'I shall kill you. Not from behind, but where you can see the blow coming – in a way that will give you time to think.'

I said, 'What shall I think that I'm not already thinking?'

'An eye for an eye and a tooth for a tooth. That's what my missionary parents taught me and that's what you'll be thinking. The very last thing.'

He rose. He gathered up an armful of the bamboo that he'd cut earlier. He said, 'Fuck you, Doig,' and took it to the furthest corner from me. He threw it down, kicked it into shape. He came back to me. I hadn't moved. I'd said all that could be said. He curled the sabre upwards into my face, just a twist of moonlight on the blade. He said, 'That's the last thing you'll see in your life.'

Then he lay down on his bed of bamboo with his knees drawn up and his back turned against me.

Fifty-six

I REFLECTED ON my life. Circumstances had gone against me. The death of my father had whipped me down to the bone. I'd been angry, had hurled myself at everything in order to get even. Maybe I'd got in my own way, maybe a meek and provident attitude would have served me better. I can't say. A man who smells glory once, as I'd done with my beetle, is a man forever lost to providence. Then had come my love for Lizochka, out of nowhere, with a swooshing and thrashing of wings and a gnawing at my liver. Love, the greatest scourge of man. And as if it were not enough by itself, with it had arrived the apostle of Bolshevism: Comrade Prokhor Fedorovich Glebov. You know how that worked out.

With her death a portcullis had dropped in front of me, barring me from progress. On the far side I'd seen a pleasant, intricate existence, involving people with different appearances and heights and noses, wearing spectacles or not, young and old, rich and the not so rich and the very poor. But I'd been powerless to join them because of my past and my anger. Therefore I'd carried on as before and concerned myself with petty issues such as the whore Xenia and killing Glebov.

But I'd always had hope that the day would come, when I'd passed the test, whatever it was, that I'd have the confidence to present myself once more at the portcullis. I'd be able to see through the grille the same golden sunlight, people strolling arm in arm or playing chess with soft smiles and murmurs. I'd yank the bell pull and say in my strong voice, Charlie Doig back again, open up. A covert eye would examine me. The mechanism would click and I'd pass through.

Would it be to the death Kobi had just promised me, to the peace that comes to all men eventually?

Who could say? Meanwhile this was where I was, this was where my angry existence had led me, to a leper colony off the coast of Japan with no means of escape.

I said to myself, List your achievements, Charlie, make a declaration as to whether you've justified the efforts your father and mother put into you.

Chin cupped in my hand, elbow on my knee, I gazed out to sea. The whole panorama of Kyushu and the islands was spread out before me beneath the quilt of night. Men and women were busy fucking, creating children who might one day very well ask this selfsame question of themselves: *What good have you ever done?*

Maybe they'd be giants, born with genius and glory, all the godlike qualities and none of the measures of doubt, and have no cause to reply – the answer would be obvious to everyone.

But I, Charlie Doig, had lied and murdered and fornicated and acted without charity to my fellow human beings and in general had sinned like hell. All that could be scored to my credit by the tribunal would be:

Survival: for without it everything founders.

Discovery: I'd had a beetle named after me and had brought the skin of a Lala bird out of the forests of Siberia for the first time since the age of slime.

Mercy: shooting my wife.

Generosity: I'd given pleasure to a few women – I'd buried my cousin Nicholas and my godfather, which the Bolsheviks never would have. And I'd rescued Kobi from a rootless life in Samarkand – perhaps I'd saved him from slavery.

Otherwise, nix. In particular, I found my parents nowhere on the list, no gifts bestowed on them, no blessings, no gratitude, no help to my mother when she was in need, no bedside presence as she died. I'd loved them in my way, but I'd done nothing for them. It was no good excusing myself by saying that the love of a child is all that parents expect. Solid fare is a bonus to everyone.

Was my hour yet to come? Had the gods preserved me specifically so that I might benefit the world by future good deeds? Had they spotted me and said, Charlie's the man to atone for our mistakes, he's the man to go into battle for us – hey, you down there! Keep that fellow safe, keep him fresh and vigorous and lusty!

It didn't look like it.

Because of greed, which had never once tempted me before, I was going to die as a leper and have my corpse tossed into the sea for the waves to batter and the octopuses to rend.

Maybe fifty years of life remained to me on this island. I'd know every stone, bush and cliff by the end.

I'd jump before Kobi came for me. I'd say, 'My friend, grant me this, that I may die in the manner of my own choosing.'

Maybe we'd jump together, holding hands.

I got up and went over to his bed. His eyes were wide open with little pricks of starlight on them. He'd been crying. I said, 'I'm sorry, even though it makes no difference.'

Then I returned to my side and lay down.

Curiously enough, I wasn't a bit morbid. I didn't bemoan what hadn't been or could never be. All that I saw were the tubercles that would appear on my body. Like the old man's, reddish mahogany in the centre, paler at the extremities. Then the thickening skin and its furrows, the greasy cheeks, the widened nose and then the only thing that men knew for certain about leprosy – atrophy of the testicles.

Quite calmly, I reviewed all the symptoms.

As I began to doze off, I made a picture of my last moments. I'd climb up the path to the top of the cliff – seabirds screaming, beating at my head with their wings in case I trod on a nest. I'd select a drop without rocks at the bottom: I'd go straight into the sea without making a mess of myself. Could I really be that vain?

At which point I fell asleep, I must have, for when I opened my eyes I could see no starlight, only a crouching wheezing bulk of darkness from which a hand was reaching towards me.

God, that hand, it wakes me yet.

Fifty-seven

THE OLD man was kneeling above me, black against the sky, and as his hands came forward to touch my face, the starlight caught them – the trembling stumps, no more than a foot away and aiming straight for my eyes.

Had I been sleeping under the tartan rug, I'd have been lost – fumbling, tangled up in everything. He'd have had time to get at me and smear the white shit over my face. But I was untrammelled, thank God – I jacked my knee back and let fly, my boot catching him right in the belly. Terror was in that kick of mine, sheer terror, unqualified by any other consideration. He staggered away in retreat. I followed him still on my back, screaming for Kobi, kicking at him, at his balls, his guts, ankles, knees, whatever was in reach. He could easily have sidestepped me but he was a fat old leper and back he went until he tripped. Arms flailing, he fell, landing on his arse with his feet in the air.

To hurl myself at him, to get my hands round his throat and strangle him, that was my immediate reaction. It was a miracle I held back, an effort of superhuman determination. I stuffed my hands deep into my pockets, wodged them in and clenched my fists. Then Kobi was beside me with the sabre, had it raised aloft, both hands on the hilt. 'Swipe him, boss?'

The old man's horrid face stared up at us. I said, 'Do you want to live?'

It was a thick, hoarse whisper, his tongue boiling with ulcers: 'Yes, please God, yes.'

'Why? You're as good as dead the way you are.'

'They're going to find a cure, that's what the doctor told me.'

'But you still want us to become lepers? That's not healthy.

275

That doesn't give you a reason for living as far as I'm concerned. Do it, Kobi.'

He put his foot on the old man's shoulder and rolled him over until he was lying on his stomach. He fiddled round with his boot, pushing at one part of the old man and then another, trying to get him right for the stroke. He said, 'I can't get a clean strike the way he is. There's rock below his neck. It'll damage the blade.'

The old man just lay there, wheezing.

I said to him, 'Crawl forward a couple of yards and put your head over the edge.'

Whimpering, he began to move, dragging himself on his stumps. We stood over him, the blade of the sabre the faintest blue in the starlight, like a petrol stain.

He stopped, too knackered to go any further and turned his mutilated face towards me. He said something I couldn't decipher. I bent down. 'Say it again, old man.'

His mouth opened, he raised his head off the ground – and it was then that I saw it, glinting far more brightly than any gold ingot ever did. Only then, at the eleventh hour and fifty-ninth minute.

Nudging Kobi, I pointed at it. He lowered his sabre and delicately worked the blade beneath the crucifix. Grinning, I said to him, 'Didn't I say so?'

He didn't get me at first, just stood there woodenly.

I said to the old man, 'How often does the priest come?'

He refused to answer. I said to Kobi, 'They're still hung up on the times when Christians were burnt at the stake,' and to the old man I said, 'It's OK, Ivan, no harm's going to come to any of you who're believers. The days of persecution are long gone.'

But still he would say nothing – buried his mouth in the soil. I told Kobi what he had to do. Standing upright, he slowly drew the tip of the blade across the back of the man's neck. A long welt of blood appeared, like a black worm crawling out of his spine. Kobi gathered a lick of it on the flat of the blade and smeared it over the old man's cheek.

I said to the old man, 'Next time it'll be an inch deeper.'

So he told us all that we needed to know, and the gods were

276

in our favour. I explained to him what would happen if he squealed on us between now and then. Kobi proposed we keep him with us until dawn so that he could see our faces in daylight and understand how completely serious we were.

We found a comfortable seat in the rocks looking to the east and made the old man sit a couple of yards in front of us. We didn't bind him or anything.

It was a sunrise to make your heart ache, rising out of seas swathed in a pinkish white mist that tinged the ocean and magnified everything. Islets and solitary rocks poked out of it like nails through cotton wool. This was what all the pictures in the France Hotel had been about, life and death in the Japanese imagination.

Even the seabirds were quietened – stood gawping on their ledges.

I said to the old man, 'Here, have my boots. One of them touched you.' I tossed them in front of him.

He said, 'May I go now, *barin*?' The moment he used that fine Tsarist word, I knew he wouldn't give us any trouble. Nevertheless I had him stand in front of us while Kobi told him precisely which parts of his body he'd lose if he squealed. When he'd finished, I said, 'And remember, there's a cure on the way. Think of the living you'd miss out on, think of the drink and the women waiting for you.'

He bowed to us. I cannot describe the horror of that face. Its hideousness combined with the act of bowing, which one may loosely describe as the act of trying to please, was a travesty of all that mankind should stand for. He shambled away down the hill, placing his damaged feet with care.

I said to Kobi, 'Which is the more important, that the man of God lives or that we get off the island?'

He looked scornfully at me – hand on the hilt of the sabre, chin up, the pose of a true khan. The question wasn't worth answering.

Then we went to gather our breakfast, birds' eggs again and some berries we found on a creeping plant.

Fifty-eight

We WATCHED from our hilltop, glad to see that nothing was happening very quickly. Certainly the alarm hadn't been raised, that much was clear.

After breakfast the male lepers dispersed in twos and threes to visit their fishing grounds. To avoid getting brine in their wounds, they wore rubber gloves. But this made it difficult to bait the hooks and kill the fish. Twice, someone dropped a fish. Of course he was too slow and ungainly to prevent it slapping back into the sea. When they returned with their meagre catches in mid-morning, they handed them to the women to be cleaned. This done they went down to the jetty to stand around the nets and think about which of them might need mending.

After a midday meal, the women hoed the one small rice field. The well (the only one on the island according to Daimyo) was obviously somewhere on the hill above the field: I saw the women winding up a small sluice gate in order to divert the irrigation water from one channel to another.

Otherwise the lepers kept close to the houses and did nothing too strenuous.

'Lassitude, that's another part of it,' I said.

'Maybe. But I'd like some of that water,' Kobi said. The dawn mist had blanketed our island and made us shiver. But now it had cleared and the afternoon was getting hot.

The instant Kobi talked about feeling thirsty, I too became thirsty. I saw the glitter of water, I smelt it, I felt it rushing down my throat and I savoured the taste, which for some reason had a bit of lemon in it. From that moment on, I didn't want any more raw eggs, just water. Everything became parched and wrinkled, all the way round the inside of my mouth and down the tube. I sucked on a stone to give myself relief.

Later in the day the lepers began to assemble outside their hall. Smoke was coming from the chimney – from driftwood presumably. They went in, led by the old man.

Kobi said, 'Maybe they're having a council of war. Maybe he's split on us.'

But I was confident he wouldn't. He knew what a Mongolian with a sabre could do to his lumps. We'd made contact, as one Russian to another. He wasn't going to squeal. I said, 'I'm parched. Let's go and find that spring while the coast's clear.'

We came down off our hill and made our way through thick bamboo groves to the back of the gully where we reckoned the well was. We'd nothing to carry the water away in so would have to drink what we wanted on the spot.

I stayed in the bamboos and sent Kobi forward to spy out the land. The flies were bad, even though it was only April. Not stingers but a swarm of small inquisitive insects that attacked my face like a hail of buckshot. I tied my handkerchief round my head to keep them out of my mouth.

In five minutes Kobi was back. He'd found the well, very handily placed, just down the bank from us. It even had a scoop, tied by a string to a post.

He wiped the back of his hand across his mouth. 'I'm not that big a fool, I'm not going to risk it.'

I said, 'The lepers'll all drink from the same place on the scoop. You want to split hairs about left-handers?'

'It doesn't matter, there'll be germs,' he said.

'Then drink from the middle of the scoop without touching the sides. You can do that.'

'They may have spat in it,' he said.

I said, 'OK, then don't drink from the well, drink from the irrigation channel. Stop behaving like an old woman.'

He said, 'You go first.'

But I suddenly had something else on my mind. From where I was lying I had a good view of the harbour below, and as Kobi was speaking my eye had alighted on a metal buoy on the shore side of the two fangs of rock. It told me what I'd been wondering about – whether the priest came with a boatman and what happened to the boat while he was administering to his flock. He wouldn't want to run the risk of having it stolen by the lepers. So the priest had to have a boatman and when he went off to say the holy words, this fellow would tie up at the buoy and have a smoke. Probably not opium but bhang, which they called *taima* – anyway, one of the magic-makers. He'd spread himself out in the stern and for a couple of hours enjoy himself chasing the dragon. That was how it'd work.

I went and got myself a drink of water while I thought about it.

Kobi said on my return, 'What's that little white mark on your hand?'

I said he shouldn't joke about that subject, by God he should not. Then I pointed out the buoy to him and explained my line of thought. He said, 'I can't swim, I've told you that before.'

I said, had I asked him to? I said, hadn't I told him I'd get him off the island in one piece? Then I urged him to go to the well before the lepers came out of their powwow. That gave rise to the usual discussions – but in the end his thirst got the better of him. When he returned, he shook his head, swilled his last mouthful around and spat it out – said, 'The priest arrives after dark?'

'About ten, the old man said.'

Kobi said, 'I was thinking, don't let the phosphorescence give you away.'

'How do you know about that? You'd never seen the sea until the other day.'

'I've watched the harbour in the night when I couldn't sleep. The foam that boats make is as white as a black man's teeth. Does that satisfy you?' He paused. 'And, Doig?'

I waited for the next bit without answering. But he wanted my full attention – forced me to look up and engage with him. 'It's this, Doig. You're going to have to swim out and kill him: if you lose my knife, I'll leave you. Just for that, nothing to do with leprosy. It's the only thing I have from my childhood in Mongolia – from when the missionaries kept me.'

He passed it to me in its sheath. I rasped my thumb against the blade. 'It'll do,' I said.

'Don't lose it, you just remember that.' Then, flapping at the flies, 'You haven't killed a man with a knife yet,' which he said without any thought of contradiction.

'No.'

'For the throat, across. For the body, up. There are no downward strokes that kill cleanly.'

I said, 'It's going to be difficult if there's a strong moon.'

He said, 'Best will be if the fog returns and there's a slight ripple to cover your noise in the water.'

I said, 'If the fog's too bad, he won't come.'

We debated these things for a while. It became clear that I'd have to be in the water by the time the priest arrived, probably in the shadow of one of the guardian rocks. Daimyo would come down to the jetty to welcome the priest. He'd see the lights on the boat as it approached and would probably time his arrival to give himself a wait of a couple of minutes at most. If he played up at all, Kobi'd show him the sabre as a reminder of the damage it could do.

One question remained: how was I to get silently from the shelter of the rock to the boat? I eyed the distance, tried to compute how many strokes it would take, asked Kobi what he thought about the currents close in.

But of course he couldn't help me because his mind was hemmed in on all sides by prairies and such, and herds of horses, camels and goats. He said, 'Why should the sea have currents? Is there something down there that causes them, some great animal?'

'Boils on your arse,' I said and moved our conversation on, to all the eventualities that could go wrong, everything, down to the way the boatman would light up as he prepared for dreamland. I said, 'So, the priest comes at ten and stays for a couple of hours. But there's something else. According to the old man, he sometimes has an underling with him.'

'Another holy man or are you talking about a second boatman?'

'Someone to help the priest with the communion, that's what I understood.'

Kobi thought about it. 'With two priests there is no problem. With two boatmen there is a problem: I have only one knife.'

Fifty-nine

THE SEA flirted sullenly with the rocks, the boatman's pipe glowed rhythmically, the cloying smell of bhang drifted through the moonless night. The moment he'd landed the priest and seen him depart with Daimyo, he'd clipped onto the buoy, spread cushions on the stern counter and made himself at home. He'd put some sort of cap on his head, something from the priest's wardrobe. He was imagining himself preaching to a multitude, dishing out wafers to the penitent, at any rate undertaking something stupendous – bhanged up and dreaming, in a better place altogether.

A bell tolled as the old man and the priest walked from the jetty to the village. Candlelight showed as the door into the hall was opened. The light was snuffed – the bell fell silent – I took a deep breath, pulling it down into my lungs, right down into their very toes, and allowed myself to sink beneath the sea. I was naked, Kobi's knife between my teeth.

Fifteen strokes, that's what I'd reckoned, looking down from the hillside. Fifteen good strokes, which was the most I thought I could do without surfacing.

I tried to swim in a smooth, controlled manner, hoarding my breath. It was so crucial that I got the next bit right. It couldn't be almost right, it was all or nothing. Dead men can't shout, can't howl, can't raise the alarm. Dead was the word and nothing else.

But I got flustered. I misspent my energy by swimming too powerfully and then lost my place counting the strokes.

When I completed what I believed to be my fifteenth stroke, I reached up, expecting to feel some part of the boat's hull.

I flipped to the right – to the left – straight on. I could see nothing, could feel nothing – and my breath was getting low. I began flailing around for the buoy cable, getting desperate, choked, ready to explode. Then suddenly there it was, slantwise under my chin. God knows how I missed it, I thought, and somehow this got me in a state and I grabbed wildly at it, not thinking about the knife in my mouth. The blade snagged the cable and fell glittering away.

It was that which saved me, which forced me to get a grip on myself and think clearly.

Hands flat against my side, I kicked up swiftly and sleekly. I was like a seal. Kobi said he never saw me break water. In one motion I slid my head out, took a breath and went back down the cable hand over hand. There was no problem with the knife: it was lying on the sand just where I expected. Suddenly full of confidence, I scooped it up and with half a dozen strong kicks I shot out of the water as though I were Poseidon and had my elbows on the boat's counter and my forearm crooked beneath Johnny's chin before he could even get the hash pipe out of his mouth. A sort of wheezing gasp came out as I wrenched his head back towards me and twisted it to expose the artery – he choked and let fly a cloud of smoke. Then the blade entered his neck and the blood spurted out with such force that its first charge went clean over the side of the boat into the sea.

No thrashing about, no prolonged agony, not even any drumming from his heels as he took off. A perfect death for us both.

I pulled the knife out, wiped it on his jerkin and stabbed it into the boat's counter. I unclipped the buoy. The wind started to push the boat towards the jetty. I had only to guide it. Kobi was waiting there, crouching, a dark bundle of fishing nets that suddenly arose and gripped the side of the boat. He swung himself aboard in one easy movement – glanced at the corpse – chucked my clothes at me – pulled his knife out of the wood.

While I dickered with the engine, he poled us out of the harbour towards the two sentinel rocks. When the pole got out of its depth, I said a prayer and tried the engine. It started second time, nice and quiet, too low for the priest to hear.

We slid between the rocks and went straight for a while as Hijo had done when he dumped us. Then Kobi picked up his landmark and raised a hand. I gave the wheel a couple of spokes to the starboard and the bow bit into the swell. But I still kept her going quietly. As I've said, there was no moon so I had to reckon our course by the thunder of the waves against the cliffs and the dull tints of phosphorescence. Only when I knew we were well clear of the island did I turn the lever to full throttle.

Kobi came up to hug me, arms outspread. Dancing back, I said, 'You keep your distance, I don't want any of your fucking microbes, pal' – then we embraced, leaving the boat to look after itself. There was no need to say anything.

I said he should take the helm for a bit, that there was nothing to it. Then I went below to see if there was a bottle of anything on board. I was prepared to wager that a priest would carry something to sustain his faith when his flock was ungrateful. But there wasn't even the sniff of a cork.

I went back on deck. I said, 'I should feel bad about dumping the priest with the lepers – but I don't.'

'He probably had signs of leprosy himself,' Kobi said, 'that's why he was willing to make the trip. Wounds,' he added as an afterthought.

I wasn't so sure about that. 'These sons of God, they undertake all sorts of risks so long as they think they're bettering our lot.'

He said, 'Have we done anything good, Doig? Anything we'll be remembered for?' There was a sweetness in his voice I'd never heard before.

I said I'd spent a good part of the previous night asking myself the same question.

Quietly, as if debating with himself, he said, 'What does it feel like to do good? How do you know when you've done good?'

I said it probably depended on whether one had set out to do good or whether it was the casual result of one's actions.

He snorted, hoicking a great bulb of stuff back up his nose. He said, 'Can ordinary people be good? Could I be good?'

'Why not?'

'I thought, maybe one had to be special, like my missionary parents.' He spat into the sea. 'So what did you come up with?'

'Nothing great.'

'Nothing at all?'

'Surviving, not much more than that.'

'That's something,' he said.

I said, 'When you feel like it, pitch that fellow's body over and clean up, make it appear as though he's never been on the boat,' and went back to thinking. The way Kobi had phrased the question was different from the way I had. I called over to him, 'You've saved my life, I've saved you from leprosy. There're two good things to be remembered for. We killed Glebov, which is number three. Hell, man, we're still young. We'll do our good deeds yet – save them up and do them when we're old enough to have a proper understanding of what we've done. Something'll come our way.'

'Watch out!'

I wrenched the wheel over and we skidded past a fishing boat not showing any lights, a man and his wife in it who jabbered like loonies at our backs. I thought of hoisting lights – the priest would have. But murder is murder under any system of law and I didn't want to draw attention to our boat. In fact I took us out to sea a bit more. The tide rip wasn't nearly as bad as Kenji had described it. We bounced a bit, found ourselves swooping down into a gulch at one point with the screw out of the water, but nothing too bad. And Kobi never even spluttered. It must have been the adrenaline that was keeping his seasickness at bay.

A wispy moon appeared and I saw the start of the navigation buoys that'd take us into the bay. Ships weren't allowed to anchor there, so it was a clear run home. I turned the engine to Slow, told Kobi to dawdle and went below for an hour's shut-eye. It was then a little after one in the morning.

I'd no intention of using Yamaguchi's jetty. The unknown quantities were too numerous. Hijo, believing us to be on the leper island for the duration, could've been told by Sato to hire another assassin for Yamaguchi. Maybe the deed had already been done, the knife, the noose, some Japanese refinement with poisonous fish, God knows what. Maybe this, maybe that – there were too many of them. I wanted to be like a fly on an orange – prowl around, make no noise, see what was over the curve.

Kobi shook me awake. The cloud cover had cleared. The moon, he said, was shining on us like a spotlight. He didn't like it. People could be watching, could be asking themselves why the priest was returning so soon. We should put into shore as soon as possible.

I went on deck with him. 'Too much potential for bogey-bogey by moonlight, is that it, pal?'

'I never liked that side of her.'

'Oh, you didn't? How you surprise me . . . Now is that a landing place over there beside those bamboo huts or isn't it?'

Kobi was non-committal. Huts on beaches usually meant fishing communities. But I knew that when they were built with that tight funnel-like shape, they could only be for drying sardines, and no one in their right minds would want to sleep near sardines.

I turned the lever to Dead Slow and we puttered in to the little wooden landing stage.

I hopped out and stretched – fingers knotted behind my neck, bones crackling. My sleep had done me the world of good. All I needed now was a decent meal. Borscht, piroshki and a flask of vodka came immediately to mind. No more fucking gulls' eggs and things out of the sea.

I pissed on the sand, a hot glittering magnificent arc – wrote out my name and still had enough left at the end for a little worm cast of a full stop.

Then I stretched my tendons.

I touched my toes ten times.

Kobi patted everything to make sure he was in full marching order. Standing to attention, he raised the sabre to his lips and kissed it. Together we faced out over the bay. I said, 'God bless you, Nagasaki. It's good to see you again.'

He said, 'What would your father have said if he'd heard you?'

'He'd have said, "Nagasaki, watch out, laddie!" Everyone east of Vladivostok was a Chinaman to him.'

Kobi said, 'I wonder how many wives my father had. He was a chieftain, you know.'

I said, 'Kobi, I should never have given my boots to that old man, just because I kicked him. I should have washed them in the sea, that'd have been good enough. Your knife is your past. Those boots were mine.'

'No, my father was my real past, whoever he was.'

'Sure, I miss my father as well. But that was a while ago. As we stand here, it's my boots I miss most. They carried the diamonds, the necklaces, the cash, the gold – they were my bank from St Petersburg to Nagasaki. Through a revolution as well. That's not bad for a pair of boots.'

He said, 'I sometimes think I must be older than I think I am. There are things I remember that must have happened long ago.'

I said, 'We'll go to Mongolia one day and ask around, find people who can put a date on the things you can remember. That way you'll discover how old you are. No knowing how it'd turn out the way you guys age.'

The sand behind me stirred. I thought, A little Nip fisherman has come to investigate what these two *gaijin* are doing on his property.

My next thought: But such people don't carry bayonets and don't stick them in your back just beside the column that carries the spinal fluid. They don't grunt. They don't start to frisk you.

Very slowly I raised my hands and began to turn round. On my left, Kobi did the same.

A torch shone in my face. It was one of Yamaguchi's guards. Standing there stolidly, same boots and puttees, same drab uniform, same webbing, same kepi as when I'd seen him two days ago. What was different was the bayonet. He flicked it at me, pointed up the hill.

I pointed at my bare feet, said, 'I'll never get there without boots.'

He came very close. His breath was like a latrine, green onions mainly. He smiled evilly, jabbed with his rifle butt for me to look down. As I did, he leaned back on the heels of his leather army boots so I could see the whole range of hobnails and toe plates. I understood immediately. He had only to stamp on my foot and I'd never need boots again. 'Only joking,' I said and we set off. The other soldier had got Kobi's sabre out of its scabbard and was swishing at the bamboo to see how sharp it was.

I said to Kobi, 'If Yamaguchi were dead, they wouldn't bother with this. They'd just chuck us into the sea.'

'Such an honourable, peaceful society,' he said, which I told him was a piece of sarcasm he'd already used once.

Sixty

THAT WAS hell, that march. Kobi offered me his own boots and I'd readily have taken them and added the deed to the list of his IOUs had the guards not stepped in and prevented us. No halting, they said. When Kobi tried to get the boots off as he walked, it was the same, no stopping till we got there. They'd decided that because I'd arrived barefoot on the scene, therefore I should be barefoot when they handed me over. For anything different they'd have needed a direct order.

Thinking about this, and to take my mind off the agony of walking, I said to Kobi over my shoulder, 'It's worth remembering. If you tell a Nip to do something, he'll go on doing it till you tell him to stop.'

For these few words I was upbraided roughly by my guard, but it got me a little further forward – physically, that is, while I was considering whether or not it was true – and about half an hour later we crossed the bund road and got onto a better class of path. The night had thinned: dawn wasn't a million miles away. I can't say that I recognised any particular part of the landscape but after a while the general layout began to look familiar: it had to be Yamaguchi's house we were approaching. Then there it was above us, a long range of solid blackness with a tiny speck of light at one end.

Kobi called out something cheerful but I was in no mood to respond. My feet were wrecked, I was hungry, I was thirsty, I was angry. I thought, I've come through the most vicious revolution in the history of mankind, I've walked through a mile of fire and strode out the other side, that's what I've done. Blistered and limping maybe but with the vital functions intact.

Against all the odds I'd reached Japan and gone about setting myself up afresh as a steady wholesome chap And now? First, dumped in a leper colony to rot, then marched off at bayonet point like a man condemned.

Was I going to be like goddamned Tantalus or goddamned Sisyphus and have to go back to square one every time I thought I'd got clear, was that what life had in store for me?

For heaven's sake! I'd be as well off back in Russia. I could speak the lingo. I knew how their minds worked. I had my gold store. Let things settle down, and in a year or two I could go back and pay some Red gangster to wipe my dossier clean. Everyone had a price, they'd be no different. Then I'd look for work. The old-fashioned style of brainy Russian would have cleared out. I'd be able to pick and choose. The Academy of Sciences would throw open its doors to me. 'Welcome,' they'd say, 'welcome, Comrade Doig! On which continent would you care to work this year?'

It was worth considering.

For instance, what would the value of my gold be to Lenin rather than to someone like Yamaguchi who lived three thousand miles away?

Would he be an honest man to deal with?

A small knot of pleasure formed in my mind. Lenin, honest? A man could walk five miles pondering a question like that and feel no discomfort.

Late one night he'd be sitting there in the Kremlin smoothing away at his pink pate and worrying about how to make ends meet when suddenly the telephone would squawk and the deep, financially important voice of his Treasurer would say, 'Only the Japs can save us now, and a man they have called Charlie Doig. He alone knows where the gold is hidden. They've asked for ten million roubles as an advance. How shall I answer, Comrade?'

I stopped dead, the guard bumping into me.

Lenin, who knew everything about skimping and scraping from his days in exile, would say, 'Even a hundred is too much.' It'd be his instant reaction. It was what he'd say without even a pause, but was it what he'd think?

I got a jab in the back from a bayonet and I knew immediately how it would work.

The evil third party, never long absent from Russia and now monitoring Lenin's conversations from a nearby cubbyhole thick with the scent of cheap tobacco and stolen pomade, would draw back a corner of the maroon curtain and whisper hoarsely to his boss, 'Get hold of that man Doig and torture him till he tells. Pay nothing, Comrade Lenin, nothing at all.'

And Lenin would say, 'My opinion too, one hundred per cent.'

That's what would happen if I returned. They'd torture my balls off. I'd be screaming before they started, would tell them everything. I'd be a dead duck in double quick time.

I looked wearily upwards, to Little Paradise. What could be the purpose of my life?

But that's a question that needs to be well primed before an answer can be attempted and I was still at the first stage when we reached the house. The soldiers led us round to the back part. We passed through a gate into Yamaguchi's vegetable garden and got onto a mud path, which was good for my feet. In front of us was a circular building made of wood. At floor level it had small paper windows with a bluish tinge from the candlelight within. At the top it was all glass, like a lighthouse.

A lantern was hanging outside the door.

I said to the soldiers, to Kobi, to everyone who might be involved in this trial of strength, 'That's it. Journey's end. The prisoner is withdrawing his cooperation.' I sat down, leaning against the building. I stretched out my legs and waggled my torn and bloody toes.

How would a plump, middle-aged bourgeois have coped if God had picked him out of a bunch and said, This is why I gave you life, so you could somehow get from St Petersburg to Vladivostok to Nagasaki and on the way learn about proper hardship, not just balancing the company books?

He'd have prayed. He'd have told his wife what God had said. He'd probably have got as far as the railway station. But by now he'd be long dead, destroyed by men more purposeful than him.

So I was lucky this had happened to me when I was young. I should be grateful to someone, shouldn't be maundering and whining.

Kobi said, 'This had better be enjoyable.'

I said, 'But at least we're not dead,' to which he didn't respond.

Then our guards were handing us over to another soldier, obviously their officer. They babbled away at him. One of them took a hoe and made a sketch in the earth. It was being explained where we'd been found.

The officer looked us up and down – saw the condition of my feet – gave the soldiers merry hell. He rapped out an order. One of them ran off to the house and after a couple of minutes returned with a serving woman and a bowl of warm water. She picked my feet up and placed them in the bowl as if they were vegetables. I grinned at Kobi, saying, 'This is the eighth wonder of the world.' She dried me off, getting right between my toes, and gave me a pair of house slippers.

Smiling, the officer bowed and indicated I should enter the lighthouse. I said, 'Only with my pal,' and looking round there he was behind me, ready and waiting, his sabre restored.

The door had a sort of toggle latch – a strip of leather tied round a wooden peg. The officer unwound it, pretending to get weary at the number of turns he had to make, trying to be funny, I suppose, to compensate us for our bad treatment.

I said to Kobi, 'We're back in clover, Genghis. I can smell it.'

Alluding to the officer, he said, 'What's wrong with him? Is he that feeble he can't open a door?'

I remembered how it had been when Hijo got us to leave the boat before he did. I smiled at the officer and indicated he should lead the way.

There was only one room in that building, which was clearly where Yamaguchi's gardeners worked, and only two people in the room.

Yamaguchi rose, came over to me and bowed. 'Thank God!'

I pointed at my feet. 'God yes, but not your men. They're a rough crowd.'

He rounded on the officer, who went outside and gave our guards another dressing-down.

I said to Yamaguchi, 'But they were only doing what they were told to do – they probably expected a reward for finding us. Anyway, here we are . . .' I paused, wondering how to say politely, and where the fuck were you with the rescue team? But he beat me to it.

'Thank God! I say again, Thank God! Thank God! If you hadn't got out today, on the priest's boat, you never would have. The lepers would have caught you one night, when at last you had to sleep, held you down and infected you. I can tell you're clean. There's no fear in your face. You can never hide fear. What Hijo did was evil and cruel. He paid my boatman money to say nothing, but it is to me that Kenji is loyal, not to my cousin Sato. I was vigorous with my enquiries, you can be sure of that.'

'Hijo said you wished me to inspect another boat for spruce beetle.' I sat down beside him on a hard wooden chair. 'Why didn't you send a boat for us as soon as you knew what had happened?'

Kobi, who'd stayed beside the door bristling with suspicion, gave out a cry and ran past us.

Yamaguchi said to me, 'I'll answer your question in a minute. Let us watch this. Let us see how your man deals with the typhus doctor.'

Sixty-one

In the far corner of the gardeners' building was a well with a brick parapet no more than two feet high. Rearing above it was a thick bamboo rise-and-fall shaft for raising water.

Yamaguchi winked at me – raised his head and called out, 'Where are you hiding, doctor? Can't see you anywhere. No need to be shy. You're among friends, you know that.'

Kobi looked down into the well, turned and grinned at me, every tooth in his head showing. He knelt down. Hands on the parapet, leaning forward, he very deliberately took aim and spat. He glanced around for something to throw at Hijo – thought better of it, and went over and eyed the mechanism for bringing up the water, which was physics at its simplest: when the gardeners needed water, they raised one end of the shaft so that at the other end a bucket was lowered into the well. To raise the bucket, they pressed their end of the shaft down and the bucket rose. But now there was no bucket at the end, only Hijo.

Yamaguchi, watching Kobi figure out the possibilities, said to me, 'The answer to your question is this: I could have taken a boat to rescue you but no one would have come. People would rather kill themselves than set foot in a leper colony. Even the navy itself would have refused to help. Every five years, regular as clockwork, the people of Nagasaki petition the Emperor to remove the lepers to some other island. It is true, believe me. Alone, I could have done nothing. So you had to do it by yourselves and you had to do it on that one boat, the priest's. You did well, Doig-san. You are a most resourceful man. All that Sato said about you is true.'

I was thinking about this, not one bit impressed, when from the far side of the room, Kobi said accusingly, 'He's standing on the bottom, that's no punishment.'

Yamaguchi said, 'Wait till I have him hauled up, then you'll see.'

Leaning towards Yamaguchi, I said, 'Why do you speak so evenly about your cousin when he's been trying to have you killed?'

'Because it's not in my interest to think of him in a hostile way. Any family member is preferable to an outsider in a business, however unpleasant or stupid he may be. With family you know the boundaries of their minds, also the reach of their energy. Another thing you should consider is this: that the power of soldiers has a quite different character to the power of merchants like myself. If the Kingdom of Eastern Siberia is to succeed, I need his power. Last, I know him inside out and have done so since he first tried to kill me. Nothing that he can do will surprise me. Therefore he can do me no harm.'

It made sense. I said for him to continue.

'The moment you appeared at my door, I smelt trouble. Why does this fellow bring Hijo? I asked myself. Then I understood, he'd been sent by my cousin to keep an eye on you. So from the very first, I was on my guard. You remember, when we met at my woodland pavilion? For about five minutes I was very watchful indeed. And so were my guards, who were in the trees above us. Had you made the slightest move against me, you would have been shot down instantly.'

I said ruefully, 'I'm just not the secret agent type.'

He laughed, making his narrow eyes narrower and causing deep vertical furrows to appear in his cheeks. 'My dear Doig-san, I could tell that within a very short space of time. You are a man who fights his enemies in the open, not in the dark with a dagger. It's written all over your face. And when, only a day later, you saved Mimi, I knew for an absolute certainty not only that you were no foe of mine but also that you could never be.'

He made me a sitting-down bow. 'Let us consider the slate cleaned, in both directions. Now we shall raise the doctor from the semi-dead.'

He shouted an instruction – the officer hurried in and bowed. Yamaguchi waved him to the well. 'Bring him up now, please.'

294

Kobi stood back, arms folded across his chest.

The officer queried something with Yamaguchi, who said to me, 'He asked, did I want him brought up the whole way? I said no, a little at a time.'

Slowly Hijo was hoisted up, slowly his face rose above the brick parapet, hair plastered to the sides of his skull like a black bathing cap. He'd been bound to a stake, and the stake had been hooked to the rope.

He halted, twirling a little, as the officer took a new grip. Then his ascent resumed. Kobi took a step forward and inspected him as one might inspect the corpse of a rare mammal.

The officer glanced at Yamaguchi, who said thoughtfully, 'Another yard, why not.'

Hijo's long white neck pleading for the noose, the four silver pens in his display pocket with the Emperor's medal still in place below them, the rope gripping his chest – then the rest of him appeared, drenched, as the water cascaded back into the well. He continued to twirl as if turning to face an audience, now to the right, now to the left. He was wearing the same dark suit that he'd worn at the timber ceremony, when I'd taken Mimosa for a swim.

His hands appeared over the parapet – seemed to wave at us, maybe in pain, for his fingertips were skinned and bloody. The officer hitched up the rope and prodded at him with a pole to stop him twirling.

He blinked a lot, then stared out at us with an air of truculence.

I said to Yamaguchi, 'He still knows best.'

'That sort of man always does. But it's a mistake to treat the jury like idiots when they can have you dead within an hour. He'll soon discover that.'

'And now?' I said.

'I thought it would be interesting to see what your servant does. He will have a great hatred for the man who tried to infect him with leprosy.'

'He's not the only one,' I said.

Kobi's sabre coming out of its sheath hissed round the room like forty thousand snakes. He put the hilt to his lips and kissed it. I said to Yamaguchi, 'That's what he does before a killing.'

Kobi went over to the well. His face was about level with Hijo's navel. He turned to us and gave a hand signal to drop him a bit. Yamaguchi barked out an order. 'I said to the soldier, "OK, but first take him up and then drop him quickly, that'll be amusing."'

I said, 'You could break his jaw on the parapet. Look at the way he's swinging.'

'What of it? To knock his teeth out would be to do him a service. You're too soft, Doig-san, that's your trouble.' He shook his head. 'Those Bolsheviks you've killed, why, you just browned the pack. Rat-tat-tat and they all dropped dead. It's when you have a single man and he's looking straight at you that you have to find hardness in your soul. You once had Glebov alone in the forests – and let him go. Soft! Soft!'

'Will you kill Hijo?'

'Of course.'

'Not send him back to Sato, as a warning?'

'That will not happen.'

'You won't hand him over to the police?'

'You don't understand. This man has tried to kill you. He may try to kill me next. Or he may even turn against my cousin. What do you do with a splinter in a wound? You pull it out and burn it, then and there. Everyone knows you don't need to have an operation in hospital just to remove a splinter. It's the same with this man. I don't say it's justice in the purest sense, but it's efficient.' He paused. 'In most other respects, our societies are very different, the Russian and the Japanese. But on this point we agree: never give a rat a second chance. Now watch him being dropped.'

The doctor was hanging at the very top of the shaft, swaying like a pendulum, peering down into the well.

The officer had the rope hitched round a cleat and was watching Yamaguchi, several coils of rope loose in his hand.

'Now!' said Yamaguchi and brought his fist down hard on his thigh.

It happened as I thought: his fall wasn't plumb in line with the well and his jaw smacked against the parapet. Because he was so undershot it was his upper jaw and his ghastly yellow teeth that took the damage. It was hard to say on account of the blood pouring down his face, but I didn't see how his nose could have avoided being smashed up. He hung there for a moment, making no noise, and then plummeted into the well while the officer, who'd released more of the rope than he'd intended to, got control of it again.

Yamaguchi rebuked the officer, and Hijo started his second ascent.

Up came his head and shoulders. His mouth opened hideously, Christ it must have hurt, everything smashed to blazes – but he didn't scream, not once. Then his little white hands appeared, scrabbling furiously at the bricks, like a mole's. Defiantly he stared over at us.

I said, 'Sato must have paid him well enough.'

Yamaguchi said, 'I think there's more to it than that. Go and see if he'll speak to you.'

I went over to the well. Hijo's lower face was pulp, splintered bones sticking out of the mess at all angles. I could easily have believed he'd been struck in the mouth by a canister of shot. I said, 'Before you die, tell me if there was some great purpose behind taking us to the leper island.'

I turned my head so I didn't have to look into his mouth when he replied.

The answer came in whistling gasps, as if his breath was getting out of another hole somewhere. 'I wished to discover for certain whether leprosy is one of the contagious diseases. You are large and strong. If you caught it, I would regard it as proof. I was going to return at monthly intervals to assess you. My belief . . .'

He started to choke. I put my ear closer to his mouth. 'Yes?'

'My belief . . .'

'Say it, man.'

At last it came out with a splatter of blood, '. . . is that leprosy is caused by eating rotten fish.'

I said, 'And if I'd caught the disease?'

'I would be proved wrong. My career would be at an end.'

'As would my life.'

'That is not a question, Mr Doig.'

Impatiently Kobi elbowed me out of the way. He had the soldier lean over and grab one of Hijo's wrists. He showed the man how he wanted Hijo's hand placed, flat on the parapet with his fingers over the edge.

He said to Hijo, 'Your fingertips are like those of a leper.'

Hijo said, 'I've had to keep clawing at the walls to prevent myself being drowned. That animal there' – he nodded at the officer – 'is not a scientist. He is too stupid to know what the nation would lose if I drowned.'

Kobi said, 'What do you think of me? How stupid am I?'

Hijo blinked. 'I have nothing more to say. Let us proceed.'

Sixty-two

HOW SHOULD one feel when a man who's been prepared to commit one to a lingering death is on the point of execution? Should one get Christlike and plead for forgiveness? Should one pray for his ascending soul? Deny the justice of the act? Rejoice?

Yamaguchi's accusation of softness had stung me. I'd had Glebov to myself. To revenge the death of Lizochka I'd decided to cut off his eyelids. I'd had my cut-throat razor poised, just an inch above his left eye, which was blue with tiny red worm-threads in the white. Kobi had lashed him to a tree so he couldn't flinch.

It hadn't been my plan to kill him. I'd wanted him to live for ever and never be able to close his eyes to sleep.

But then I stayed my hand. Why? Because there'd crept out of my imagination the image of his severed eyelids on the palm of my hand and I'd thought, Those eyelashes, will they be soft like Lizochka's? Will they tickle? Will they blink at me as their lives depart? This reasoning, if such it can be called, proved more powerful than my wish to see Glebov dead. It was why I'd spared him.

Yamaguchi had heard about it – from Cyn, I supposed, via Sato. It was why he'd called me soft.

'But I shot my wife. That's not soft.' Standing beside the well, I turned and spoke harshly to Yamaguchi.

He looked at me appraisingly, didn't budge in his chair. I was coming to the end of my tether. His face, which was anyway long and narrow, seemed like a white splinter in which his eyes were set as vertical slits. 'Yes,' he said gently. Everything else

299

that was happening in the room came to a standstill for me. His tomahawk face, the eyes black as jet, the ponytail, the sober grey robes, the authority of the man, it was all on top of me, like a puzzle that I'd rather finish tomorrow. 'Yes,' he said, 'and it's time you chose another one.'

Suddenly, and from so unexpected a quarter that we instantly stopped speaking, a diversion entered that grim room. Had it been an elephant, we'd have only glanced at it. But the sun, the first of the day, blasting through the clerestory, was like an ambush by a thousand knights clad in bright armour. Everyone had been thinking in terms of the night, of candles, of Hijo going off to the black hole in the sky. But now there was sun, and with it the certainty of life continuing.

'Spare him,' I said to Yamaguchi.

He called Kobi to him. He said, 'Your master wishes that this man's life be spared. What is your opinion?'

'Any man who tries to kill me should himself be killed. There are no exceptions. It is the law of my forefathers.'

Yamaguchi shrugged at me. 'He is right, it is how it should be.'

Kobi bowed to Yamaguchi, he bowed to me. He returned to the well. The officer still had hold of Hijo's hands.

Kobi jerked at them so that the wrists were on the parapet. He stood back. He picked his sabre off the parapet and raised it above his head. The sun caught on the blade, sent jags of brilliant light through the smoky room.

He said to Hijo, 'Stick out your fingers.'

Hijo pulled back his shoulders. He said, 'What I did was not worthy of my Emperor. I deserve to die.' Then he stiffened his fingers.

The sabre fell. The white fingers and the top joints of his thumbs dropped onto the floor.

Kobi booted them out of the way. Hunkering down, looking straight into the doctor's bloody face, he said, 'Now you know what it's like to have stumps for fingers. Now you're the one who's got leprosy.'

Hijo's eyes closed and his head dropped. Maybe he'd fainted.

'Ha!' shouted Kobi, and from his full height, going up on tiptoes, his face terrible with anger, he brought the sabre down.

The severed rope flew up into the rafters. Hijo's head toppled sideways onto his shoulder, then rolled into the well. His corpse slithered out of our sight. The sun dulled as the first clouds of the day began to form.

Yamaguchi rose. 'It is over. Justice has been done. We shall go to the baths now, Doig-san.'

Sixty-three

WE WENT to the front of the house so that any hostile spirits emanating from Hijo could be batted away by the guardian dragon. We strolled past it and past the fountain, its spray dazzling in another early-morning burst of sunshine. How long ago was it that I'd first set foot here? Hijo had remained with the rickshaw puller halfway up the hill. I'd wandered off into the pleasure grounds. Was it only three days ago? So much in so short a time, was it possible?

I said, 'You've changed my life. Had you purchased the bird skin, I'd be on a steamer to America by now.'

'You're glad you stayed, yes?'

I said I was, which was the truth. It was impossible with a man such as Yamaguchi to do other than speak one's mind.

The spray from the fountain was so bewitching that I lingered admiring it. I wouldn't have minded a seat on the veranda and taking my time. But he said it would be a mistake: I should keep going until I dropped. I said I'd had a bit of sleep on the boat. He said that three or maybe four hours out of every twenty-four were all he needed himself. He could sleep during the day, he could sleep on his boat, he could sleep standing up – it was how he was made, he said.

And then suddenly he spun round, and catching me completely off guard, said, 'Your gold is more interesting than your bird. You'd be a fool to think otherwise.'

It stopped me dead in my tracks.

He said, 'Soon it'll be the only gold left in Russia. That can only mean one thing.'

But I'd just sifted through my life and reached a settlement with myself as to my achievements. The gold hadn't made it anywhere near the list. Whereas my Lala bird . . . I said sarcastically, 'I beg your pardon?'

'The Bolsheviks'll have to sell their gold, every last bar of it. Then what'll they do for money?'

'I beg your pardon but it took a mile of barges to carry only half of it – the big Volga barges. From where we're standing – past the fountain, past the dragon, keep going a bit, a hundred and twenty feet or more to each barge. That's a lot of gold. There were twenty-eight tons in my barge alone.'

He said, 'Forgive me, but on these matters I have more information than you. The Bolsheviks are selling and will continue to sell because they've nothing else with which to buy weapons. Aircraft, bombs, rifles, ammunition. Cars, locomotives, rolling stock. What for? To hunt down and kill those who disagree with them. Believe you me, they'll have to sell everything they can lay their hands on.'

'Russia is a wealthy country. I'm Russian, I know.'

'They will sell. Memorise those words, Doig-san. *They will sell*. Their enemies'll press them, they'll get desperate, they'll grab at anything. And there is another aspect to it. The Emperor has passed a law forbidding the export of gold from Japan. Ah, Sato's told you that already . . . But our trading contacts in Siberia have always been paid in gold. We've said, we're doing our best but it takes time to find spare gold. Now they're screaming their heads off. Let me say it again, your gold is having a most profitable sleep beneath the Volga. Your bird is good. But the gold is better.'

We halted in front of the big brass doors. The patter of house slippers sounded within. The doors swung open. It was the same ancient manservant as before.

We started down the long hall. Yamaguchi said casually, 'These early clouds – it will rain sometime today and wash everything away. You, as a Westerner, believe it a sin to have had that man killed. I, as a Japanese, do not. He deserved it, he expected it, he was ready. My soldiers will dispose of him and I'll send a cable to my cousin that Dr Hijo has taken a fever and died. He'll know what I mean. His American Countess too, if she has any sense.'

I started to say something about Cyn and the abundance of her practical, hard-earned sense but Yamaguchi's mind had moved on. 'I've engaged a young lady to look after us in the baths. Her name is Sayo. "Yo" means "night" and "Sa" is a prefix we use to make the next part sound nice and tender. Which she is, Doig-san, which she is! Sayo is my best bath girl. You'll surely learn some new and interesting words from her . . . Let me say now, that in order to be of the greatest use to me, you'll have to learn Japanese to a very high standard. Then you'll have three good languages. English, Russian, Japanese. It's my belief they'll be the three most powerful languages in the world for the next hundred years.'

He halted abruptly. 'Could your servant lead someone to the exact spot where you sank the barge?'

I looked him up and down. 'First we were talking about Sayo, then my language skills and now it's the gold. Which is it to be?'

'The subject changed.'

'So could my answer. For the moment it's this: Kobi might be able to take you there if he wanted to.'

'You wrote down your cross-bearings?'

'They are written in my head.'

'Ah so, that could have been done better.'

We resumed walking. The wood in a house is always the same temperature as the air in it. The dark, long-grained planking was deliciously cool beneath my bare feet, and solid and reassuring.

I said, 'Are we going to the baths or are we talking business?'

'It's impossible to separate the two in my country.'

After a few more paces I said, 'What would you pay me for my gold?'

That surprised him. His eyeballs disappeared into the corners of his eyes. For a second nothing showed.

I said, 'As it is. Underwater.'

His eyes floated back into place and he said smoothly, 'Sight unseen, of course, so a smaller value would pertain.'

'But you have your informants. Don't they know everything?'

'That is an excellent riposte. In Japan we have a proverb, "Think quickly, act slowly."'

'In Russia we also have proverbs. This is one of them: "The bear had no right to eat the cow but the cow shouldn't have been in the wood."'

'What are you saying to me?'

'That the sight of a man being executed has woken me up. Only three days after I arrive in your country an attempt is made to kill me. Now you want to know where my gold is. I'm not a fool twice running.'

'You're misunderstanding me. We say of someone like you, "He can't see the fish for the weeds." In this instance, the fish is the fact that gold will soon have vanished within Russia and the value of what's left will increase dramatically.'

'You are wrong, Yamaguchi-san. The fish is resting on the bed of the Volga, in the middle of territory controlled by the Bolsheviks, that is the fundamental issue here.'

'Did I not tell you before that the Volga needs dredging? So we shall see about your gold when Mr Lenin starts to panic – when the time is appropriate.'

'With my permission,' I said.

'But how could it be otherwise? We must trust each other, Doig-san, or our relationship will never be secure. Now we shall bathe.'

He clapped his hands and Sayo came tripping out from behind a screen, obviously having been waiting for this moment. She was wearing a severe white tunic down to her knees and had bare legs and feet. Her countenance was pretty and pleasing, her movements gracious – the nursing type, that was my immediate thought.

I said, 'Good thing Hijo didn't scream back there. Miss wouldn't be looking so cheerful if she'd heard him.'

'Our Sayo is experienced in the ways of man,' Yamaguchi said and took me by the arm.

We walked down the corridor, the girl a yard behind us. When we got to the end we turned left – the other way led to his office.

A heavy wooden door was in front of us. The girl pattered past with quick steps, opened the door and bowed us into a changing room with wooden walls and a heated floor, everything warm and steaming. She asked Yamaguchi if she should help me get undressed. He said she should, and she came to me demurely, nothing showy about her procedures. I must have stunk, but she took it in her stride – measured me up with her eye once she'd got me naked and selected for me a nice blue cotton loincloth thing. She indicated she wanted to wash my feet before anything else, which I was glad to let her do, even though they'd been washed only a couple of hours before. She pulled up a wooden three-legged stool and raised my left foot by the heel, cupping her hand round its horny ball.

I smiled at her. She smiled back – knees clamped, white tunic creased to perfection, the genuine nursing article.

A thousand years ago a whore in Burma had done the same, on a boat in a lake, by the glim of one little oil dipper – in the era of Goetz and innocence.

As the memory flashed through my mind, I said, 'No one can say I haven't lived a full life.' Yamaguchi translated it for her. She smiled pleasantly and continued with her job.

Like all of them, not much in the way of tits, which I suppose is bad manners to mention. But a lovely little slip of a thing overall, with gorgeous eyes. And was her fingernail tickling the sole of my foot, was that what it was doing?

'Oh boy, I could make my home in here, this is the ticket all right after a leper colony.'

Yamaguchi chuckled. 'As you can tell, she is far from having the manners of a geisha. But do we want singing and sorcery and courtly games and ladies with mountains of lacquered hair? Is that what Doig-san will want? I asked myself. No, I said, when he gets off the island and returns victorious, he will be like other men and want to have a woman handy who will praise him and stroke him, a proper normal woman. Praise is always top of the list for men.'

'Praise me, kiss me, fuck me, the chant of the conquering hero. No need to translate that one. She knows what I'm on about.'

My loincloth was starting to flicker, like a marmot's nose when it comes out of its winter burrow and sees that all the joys of life are still available.

He said, 'Now she has removed the worst of the dirt, she'll take us next door and go over you inch by inch with the scraper. Then we'll have a long hot soak and talk things over.'

He raked me up and down as I stood up. 'You will be the father of mighty men, Doig-san!'

Sixty-four

THE SOAKING tub was heart-shaped. Yamaguchi lay in one ventricle, I in the other, like marine creatures basking. His body was paler than his face, was neat, slim and muscled, with a light covering of black hair.

The steam rose like thin smoke. There were no windows. Everything was made of a dark wood that glistened with beads of moisture.

He said, 'This is the second thing we have in common with the Russians. One, we place little value on human life; two, we enjoy our baths. Sayo will bring you some sake in a moment. It will all be for you. Drinking affects my brain. Ah, here she is . . . Just look at that! Feast your eyes on her, Doig-san!'

Through the wisps of steam there glided Sayo, no longer my nurse, but lithe and gleaming, naked except for a twist of black cord strung round her hips and a scrap of black cloth where you'd expect. Her dark hair flowed over her shoulders.

Dark hair, dark eyes, dark navel, dark nipples staring at me as she bowed. Dark trim, everything dark and golden in the swirling steam.

Yamaguchi told her to carry on – said it more gruffly than I would have.

She came to my side – knelt – set down her tray and proffered the flask of sake. Her long cusped fingers parted like lips to display the beauty of the chinaware. With her eyebrows she said, 'How much shall I pour?'

I replied, 'To the brim.'

Those breasts – as she poured, leaning slightly forward – so smooth, so tight, so beguiling. I laid my head sideways so I could watch every little undulation, every quiver. I had only to stretch out my hand. Or my tongue. I could be like a humming-bird hawkmoth. *Macroglossum*. Mr Moth with his big long tongue.

'Hurry, hurry,' I whispered in Russian, 'or you'll have me dancing on the ceiling.'

From the other side of the bath Yamaguchi said, 'The sake is from our own rice. I can't tell you how often they polish it, anyway a lot. In Japan this quality is called *daiginjo*. It is the best. Like the girl. Everything I'm now giving you is the best.'

The nose of the sake was deep and pungent. I took a long sip, squeezing it between my lips – said lazily, 'What exactly is it that you want from me, Yamaguchi-san?'

He replied, equally lazily, 'Would you believe me if I told you?'

Somehow, don't ask me how, that firing back of a question in reply to my own rankled. Since meeting Sato I'd got used to the obliqueness of the Japanese manner and their politeness and hypocrisy – it was all tied up together. But now – it was pathetic to say he hadn't been able to come and rescue us because all Japanese were afraid of lepers. He employed thousands. Every means of intimidation known to man was available to him. He could have press-ganged a crew and taken a private army to the island. Beaten the lepers to pulp. Had us off in five minutes. But he hadn't. So what was his game?

Running this through my mind, I got nervous on top of being annoyed. I was getting out of my depth. It was time to seek firmer shores.

Jerking upright – looking down at him floating so indolently: 'Listen, *hojo*, I've said it before but I'm not your sort. I'm a foot taller than any of you, my hands are huge, I can't sit cross-legged, I swig my tea as a horse would and I'm tired of all this bowing. That's for a start—'

'There's more?' he said mildly.

'The rice has made me constipated. I need more to eat than pellets of seaweed. Next: whenever I say what I'm thinking, you all look shocked, as if I'd farted. Is there something wrong with speaking one's mind? When I ask a question, I expect an answer, not another question thrown back at me . . . Honey, Sweetheart, whatever your name is, just leave the drinks tray and go for a walk, would you? Fucky-fucky some other time . . . So why are you being so goddamn nice to me? – that's what I want to know. Is it the gold, can it really be as simple as that? You know what I'm thinking—'

I'll tell you what it was that stopped me dead – it was Sayo. She'd shimmered round to the end of the tub, folded her hands over her pudenda in such a way as to enclose and slightly compress her breasts, and bowed to us. Being a rude Westerner, a mere *gaijin*, I can't adequately describe the effect of this for you, I just don't have the words for that sort of aesthetic. Think of the fruits, think of pert, glistening berries, think of wanting to get rootling and snuffling into every corner of the sweetie shop like a pig on the rampage, that's as close as I can get. Christ, I thought, how does any Japanese man ever get to his work if they all have wives like Sayo? It was no wonder the population had risen by a million.

I cried out, 'See what I mean? Can't she just vanish into the steam without all this fuss? I mean, does she bow when you've screwed her?'

'Sometimes,' Yamaguchi said, still smiling, still drifting around without a worry in the world. 'That's because I please her. I don't know about her other clients. She can be very dismissive about certain of them. Think of Sayo as another lesson in our Japanese ways.'

'Oh?'

'Our best-looking women are particular, Doig-san, that's the lesson. You need to be careful with them. Don't take them at face value, that's a good place to start.'

I could feel the drink going to my head. I couldn't remember when I'd last had anything solid to eat. The sake, Sayo and her neat, tight buttocks mincing away through the steam, Yamaguchi lolling in the tub and obviously after something – I had to keep my wits about me. Where was the trap? Was it in view yet? Did I want to hang around to find out?

I seized the flask of sake and emptied it into the tub.

'Very wise when you've nothing in your belly. Even though it was the best in the whole of Kyushu.'

'Whoever wants it can come and drink my bathwater,' I said.

'I'm getting out – of the bath, the house, Japan. This whole set-up smells. It's been going on ever since I bumped into Sato. Bogey-bogey business is what the Countess called it and boy, was she right. It's not who I am. I'm Charlie Doig and I've been on the run for two years, day in, day out. I kill, I screw, I survive, that's who I am. You show me a better way of winning and I'll change, become all delicate.' I was standing at the edge of the tub looking down at him. 'I'm not pretty. Look at me, look at the scars. Does it surprise you after what I've been through? And what's more, those twenty-eight tons of gold belong to me. You want them, you come to me, not I to you. Now I'm going to get Kobi and when I've done that we'll go.'

By go, I meant go to the bank, get steamer tickets to the US, and go – vamoose, up sticks, quit the land of lepers.

A new thought came to me. 'And look here, buddy boy *hojo*, that Countess dame of Sato's may be a bit too much in love with complicated routines and conspiracies and stuff like that, but she's a top-class lady at heart. So you make sure she doesn't get treated like shite by cousin Sato. I know what happens to woman number two in your country. Dough, that's what she'll need.' I paused. He swished some water over his stomach with a fancy-looking dipper, said nothing, just watched me. 'Plus she's got a great fanny,' I said, and having said it, found it was the end of my speech. 'Where'll I find my clothes?'

He was like a sealion flopping around down there. I knew he was doing it just to give himself time to think. Eventually he flicked back his hair and said, 'Doig-san, the day is dawning. Let us leave the shadows of the night behind us. For whatever I said, I apologise. I am an honourable man. I wish you luck with the gold. I wish you luck finding a woman who is sensible, who will still be attractive in thirty years, who will give you healthy, interesting children. I wish you luck in everything. But before you leave my house, would you say goodbye to my Mimi? You saved her life. To depart without allowing her to resolve the debt would be an ungracious act.'

I said time and tide never waited, said I wanted to get on my way, said I'd be glad to see the back of Japan – spoke oafishly to him and only as an afterthought said, OK, I'd go and see her as long as we made it snappy.

He rose dripping from the tub.

'That is a sign of your family's nobility, that you can oblige a man who is old enough to be your father.'

'OK, but I need my clothes.'

He shouted for Sayo, who glided out of the steam just as before. He spoke to her and then, 'I regret that your clothes were considered inappropriate in my house. They have been removed and burned. It is another error for which I must apologise. However . . . one must always try to wring a profit from a disadvantage . . . would you, would you consider wearing a Japanese costume when you go to Mimi?'

He stood back from me to take my measure. 'A kimono would sit well on a man of your build and character. You would look impressive. You would look like an oriental tsar, Doig-san.'

There he was at it again, deflecting my rudeness, in fact turning it back on me so that I felt the crassness of my words with more force than he ever had.

Shame rose in a wave and struck at me. I bowed my head – naked, I bowed to him and went down so low I was staring at my balls. I wasn't faking it. I'd behaved unworthily and I knew it. Head still down, I said I deeply regretted the words I'd just spoken.

'That is sufficient,' he said gently and, putting an arm round my shoulder, eased me upright. Then he urged me to take a cold plunge, which he said would really set me up for the day. 'However you choose to spend it – after you've had a long rest, that is. The pavilion is the best place. It is where Mimi will be at this time of day. My friend Hana will watch over you both.'

'And then I'll collect Kobi and we'll leave,' I said.

'Of course! But first you must sleep. And your servant too. What will such a man do in America, I wonder' – which he said musingly, taking a towel from Sayo.

'To become a cowboy is his latest dream,' I said.

'Ah yes, an American cowboy, as in the magazines,' then he wandered off into the steam while Sayo towelled me dry, chattering away about something to do with kimonos. She took me by the hand and led me back to the changing room, where I got into long blue cotton drawers and a cotton undershirt. She eyed me, indicated that once I had a kimono on, I should stand straight and not slouch like a typical *gaijin*. I said I was knackered. She gave me a steely look and led me down the corridor to another room. Stopping at the door, she said that only men were allowed in: it was time for *sayonara*. She knocked, she bowed, she left me, flicking her bottom as she went.

Sixty-five

Y AMAGUCHI SAID, 'Wearing a kimono is not a matter of choosing a nice colour and putting it on. It's you, the wearer, who brings life to the garment, not the other way round. For those who have eyes, it displays all a man's character.'

From the chest I'd picked long baggy culottes, which they called *hakama*, of plum blue with a wavy vertical silver thread, like fish ascending a waterfall. Yamaguchi and the dresser (who was the same old man who'd answered the door) applauded my choice – manly, majestic, perfect for the spring season, they said.

I flaunted myself in the full-length mirror. I thrust my knee forward, I whipped the fishes back and forth, tried it for pockets and failed, laughed, snarled, grimaced at my reflection, wondered aloud to Yamaguchi whether a light grey kimono would go with the blue – and took five of my largest strides across the room to make sure that the function was still possible.

He said, 'Doig-san has become a new man. That is what a kimono can do.'

Spinning round in a whirl of blue, grinning, I said to him, 'So what is this costume telling you about my character? In your opinion. Be bold.'

'In my opinion,' he said thoughtfully, stroking his chin. 'In my opinion . . . to be candid? Without stirring up your anger again?'

I put my hands on my hips, strutted, tossed my fingers up and clacked them – castanets. 'Yes, candid. I can take it.'

'And of course you are leaving Japan, so we can both say what we think.'

'Of course.'

'In which case I would say that this *hakama*, which let us remember is only half the dress, reveals a man who possesses, in equal proportions, determination, vanity and generosity.' He paused. 'Impatience also. Impulsiveness also.' He paused again. 'This man is no savage, that much is absolutely certain.'

I let the flounces subside. 'Generosity?'

'The great are generous,' he said.

'No courage?'

He smiled. 'I don't detect it in this *hakama*. But I know it's there. I've seen it, on the dockside.'

I said purring, 'I like the dress. There's freedom in it.' Then I leapt – did the splits – slapped my hands against my thighs in mid-air. An afternoon visit with my father to the Ballets Russes, just before he died, that was where that came from.

'Doig-san, please! If you are to carry yourself off as a gentleman, you must allow yourself only small controlled movements. A woman in a kimono, when drinking tea, will use her left hand as a tray. Remember that image and adjust your behaviour accordingly. You are not an acrobat, you are not marching into battle, you are going to pay your respects to a young unmarried lady.'

'Will she give me something to eat?'

'Of course, if you are pleasant in her company.' He stepped back to get a fuller look at me. 'Oh, Doig-san, how my little Mimi's heart will sing! She has been a romantic ever since she learned how to read. It is for her that I do everything. Yumi just rushed away the moment she heard what Hijo had done to you. "Leprosy!" she exclaimed – and was gone in an instant.'

'No benefit of the doubt? No wait and see?'

'She counts the money in my businesses. She cannot allow herself even to think about doubt.'

'How do you know I haven't got leprosy? It's possible. The old man could have brushed against me. Maybe the germs were present on something I touched. You don't know.'

He said, 'Dr Hijo was of the opinion that it's caused by eating bad fish. You heard him say that.'

'But we don't *know*.'

He said, 'You may not, but I do. If you'd done anything, if

you'd made any contact with a leper, it would show in your face. There would be fear. But I see no fear in you. Once my men told me which boat you'd come back in, I knew your entire story. I have searched you inside and out for the disease – and found nothing. It's one of the reasons we went to the bath. Would I let you near my daughter if I thought you unclean?'

'And if you'd thought I was carrying the disease?'

'You'd be dead by now. We have discussed this state of mind already. Shall we move forward?'

The dresser had laid out a number of kimonos for me to choose from. Yamaguchi's voice stroked at my ear: 'Not the grey, not for you. Grey is for pilgrims and pageboys and young ladies. Why don't we try this dark green *tsumugi* one? Spun silk, *oshima tsumugi*, one of our very finest materials. It is perfect for informal occasions.'

I had to check on that. It seemed to me my visit to Mimosa was turning into a pageant.

'But of course it's informal! She'll be practising her flute at this hour, as she always does. What could it be other than informal? If you were proposing marriage, the costume would be quite different. Also if you were hoping to make love to her.'

'How would I say that?' I asked laughing.

'*Tomarokk* is one of our words. It means, "Shall we spend the night?" We are very frank about these matters. A lady expects pleasure as much as a man. Why ever not? But she is my Mimi and my number-one daughter, and you, Mr Russian Barbarian, will do well to remember that.'

It was decided that I didn't need a proper *obi*, that a straightforward sash round my waist would do just as well. I chose a rose one, with dragons chasing each other round it in black-and-gold thread.

Yamaguchi clapped me, his hands above his head. 'Dragons for top-quality performance all round. And look at the way the sewing lady has taken the breath of each one and joined them into our numeral for eight. You cannot do better than eight for luck. All Japanese pray for an eight when playing games.'

We went out onto the terrace. The clouds were still high. The sun had lost its early brilliance and settled down to a steady, cheerful glow. It was one of those balmy lemon-coloured days when insects go giddy with the scents and everything grows like wildfire.

I said to him, 'So I'll need luck, will I?'

His Jurassic face split into five thousand more cracks. 'Every man going to meet a pretty girl needs luck. Now let me see how those sandals suit you. It's vital that your costume has allure, that it swings and rustles and says interesting things. And that depends in the first instance on how you walk. You must tread firmly, but with a spring in your step to demonstrate optimism. Show me . . . turn your feet out a little more. No, not like a duck! Watch me – so! You have strong tendons in your heels. That's good, that's good! Only virile men have virile feet. Ladies know that very well. They always look at a man's feet before any other part of him.'

He stepped back to see how I looked. 'Oh, Doig-san, there is a magnificence about you that I cannot describe. Your height, your bearing, the colours of your costume . . . we should change your name, Doig is so stern. Now go to Mimi. A son must meet a daughter.'

It stopped me dead. I was dazed by lack of sleep, by the busyness of spring, by the hum of the foraging bees, by the unexpected sweetness of living. And now this – 'Say that again,' I said, which he did.

I hooked my thumbs into my rose dragon-chasing sash—

'No! Not that! You've spoilt everything!'

He came and fussed around and got me all straight again. With his hands on my shoulders and looking straight into my eyes, he said, 'The son I never had.'

He said it with such simplicity and calmness – his face was lit by an inner glow. I couldn't move. It was as if I was standing in a pan of cobbler's glue. He waved me towards the walkway of box bushes that led down the hill to the pleasure grounds. 'Go! Go to her!'

He was wearing the same blue kimono in which I'd first met him, old, comfortable, a little worn at the cuffs. An assignation was being offered to me – the sound of her flute was rising from below like some exquisite vapour – I could have been gone there, swoosh, faster than an arrow from the notch. But nothing was working in my feet. We could only stand and stare at each other.

'Go!' he shouted. 'What are you waiting for?'

I went to him, I put my arms around him and I crushed him against me. It was extraordinary to have such a feeling of love, which was in the range of a child's love for a parent. I kissed him in the Russian way, which made him blush. He said, 'True happiness cannot be understood. It is like a bird. No one can say on which tree it will alight. Now go, please, before I weep.'

I went, feet turned out as instructed. All around me heavenly star shells of love were bursting, for Pushkin, my mother, Lizochka, for little Joseph, for Cyn, Kobi, Yamaguchi, for everyone I'd broken bread with or lain against. I could think of no exclusions. I took them all in my arms, I smiled upon them, I sang to them, I entertained only the noblest thoughts about love.

Sixty-six

BELOW ME, the flute babbled like a stream as it squeezes between two rocks. Exhilarated by the turn in my fortune, I strode down the grassy avenue flashing my costume to left and right so that the birdies sank in alarm to the bottom of their nests and the butterflies scattered like handfuls of confetti.

I looked up to God to render thanks to Him for bringing me out of the valley of evil. 'You're a proper brick,' I said, and not so far away a bush warbler came in on cue, *hoh-hokekyo, hoh-hokekyo.*

How could I ever have intended to kill a man such as Yamaguchi – and for such a low reward? No more heads on poles, that'd be my policy in future. If the question ever arose of retaliation against Sato, I'd have nothing to do with it. A benefit could be worked from the knowledge that he'd conspired to have his cousin assassinated. No benefit could be had from killing him.

Directly over my head, in a great sweep of blue, was a gash of last night's moon, white as a scar.

What was she playing now? Ought I to know it? Were her lips getting pursy and tired waiting for me? Did she have a pretty little speech ready? Did she know I had to catch a boat?

The path curved round and down. The pavilion was below. Scarlet timbers, turquoise tiles, dragons with bulging eyes crouching on the ridge beams – her guardians, snapping their tails as they kept watch for stinkers like me.

She was standing in the centre, the flute sticking sideways out of her head – as it appeared to me looking from above. Not petite like Sayo but not large either. When I said before that she

319

was sturdy, I was wrong, she was too tall for that. She was of a goodly shape, let me put it like that – held herself well, proudly, staunchly, her father's daughter. Of course the last time I'd seen her she'd been sopping wet, which gives a false impression of anyone. Now she was as she chose to be, wearing a kimono of the purest softest grey you could ever hope to see. It was like dawn, and around her waist was the other part of dawn, the sheer pink silk of her *obi*. Not a girl, not a woman, but a lady, a lady with style.

Mimosa pudica, the sensitive plant.

Her music stand, which was in the shape of a lyre, was facing in my direction. She wanted to see me descend the path – to have ample notice of my coming so that she could collect herself.

She saw me or sensed my movement, must have – looked up – bowed, awkwardly, holding her flute before her with both hands. My heart went out to her. I, who have felt awkward being polite for as long as I can remember, knew how she was feeling.

Don't put it down for my sake, lady, that's the spirit! Bend the rules, do whatever suits you, I don't care!

I called down, 'I've kept you, I'm sorry. I was in the baths – your father was getting me dressed – there were matters to be seen to.' No need to say anything about the execution of Hijo.

She said back – a strong clear voice, unembarrassed, not a simpering, bowing voice at all: 'Are you hungry?'

'Am I hungry!' I stopped in my tracks.

'A little hungry? Or maximum?'

'My belly's howling like a dog,' and I bounded forward, round the last bend in the path and took the steps up to the pavilion in one great leap.

She said, 'Did my father not instruct you about the importance of not exposing your legs?'

'I have great legs. I'm not ashamed of them. What shames me is my hunger. I could eat an old woman.'

'I have something better,' she said, and going over slid back the paper screens of the enclosed part of the pavilion. The aroma of cooking smote me and my knees went slack.

'See,' she said, and, lifting the cover of a red lacquer dish, showed me three grilled bream laid out on a bed of pine needles. 'See,' she said, and, lifting another cover, showed me rice that was white as snow, and another one of gingko nuts in a celadon bowl that was the colour of heaven in spring, and another one of *zenzai*, their thick, sweet, red-bean broth, and another one and another one – twenty or thirty dishes altogether, each one beautifully finished. On a separate table were a flask of sake and four different sizes of cup.

She asked me which one I wanted. I said the largest. She took the smallest for herself. We raised our cups – '*Kanpai!*'

I said, 'It'll go straight to my head. I'm as empty as a can.'

She said, 'Me too. I just wanted to impress you.'

But I still had a sip, a good long one. I said, 'It's different drinking with a woman.'

'In what sense?' It was exactly how she spoke. Not curtly but effectively.

'To drink with a man is like solving a problem to which you already know the answer. With a woman there's a whole range of possibilities and angles of thought, only some of which have been disclosed beforehand. It's different.'

'My father and I are the same. Drink doesn't suit us.'

Her cheeks coloured – ever so little, exquisitely. She dropped her head and said in a low voice, 'I mean *our* father.'

I put my hand beneath her elbow and held her. 'Does that make you unhappy? We didn't talk about it. It was a great rush of emotion for each of us. Then he sent me down here, to you.'

She looked into my eyes. As I've mentioned already, hers were a fantastic shade of brown – umber, toffee, like a nightingale's eggs. She said, 'Everything about my father makes me happy. As for me – you saved my life. I have obligations to you that are deep inside me. They are serious. We can only complete a discussion of them over a long period.'

I said, 'Yes, but that wasn't the question. It was whether you're happy to share your father with me.'

She said, 'He feels that by saving my life you saved his also. That is the nature of the love between us. Shall we eat, Doig-san?'

To do honour to my pantaloons I sat cross-legged. She hunkered down at the other end of the table, propped on her heels.

From the hem of her kimono and rising up and up to breathe its golden dust over her bosom was a dragon, stitched in a green that was exactly the colour of the new gingko leaves.

I raised my cup to her. 'We share a taste in dragons.'

'To auspicious meetings,' she said.

Her hair was jet black and as strong as ivy. She had a camellia flower somewhere above her right ear. She sat upright, very correctly, taking small mouthfuls with the greatest delicacy. Bet she wants to let rip, I said to myself, she's no goody-goody, look at the humour round her mouth. Meanwhile I'd got hold of the soup ladle and was sweeping the dishes towards me with it and guzzling everything that took my fancy, scooping the stuff into my mouth like a gorilla.

After a bit of this she said, 'Make as much mess as you want.'

Glancing up, I caught the remains of a smile on her face. I said, 'Pardon me, but it's been a day and a half since I ate anything.'

She waited on me, removing dishes from the table that I didn't like and making sure I had enough of those that I did.

Scarcely a word passed between us. Something was pending. We both knew it.

Halfway through Hana tried to climb into the pavilion. She must have smelt the red-bean cakes. Mimosa whished her out – resumed her seat. I said to her, 'Which of us is the older person?'

'You are the older one,' she replied. 'So whatever you say has virtue, that's how it is in this country.'

That was all we said.

We had green tea, shared a warm cloth for our hands, and rose.

I said, 'Let's settle our business.'

She said. 'Though I am the younger person, allow me to correct you. Let us commence our business is what you should have said.'

Sixty-seven

S HE TOOK me by the hand. In the centre of the pavilion she pointed upwards, into the roof. Hanging there, painted red, was another lucky eight. She said, 'Wait. A man must be comfortable in order to talk sense.'

She went into the lunch room and returned lugging a low wooden chair, like the nursing chair Mother hung on to in our flat in the Tverskaya. I filled it and more, bum almost on the ground, knees sticking up like fence posts. She knelt opposite – folded her kimono smooth over her thighs – fiddled her camellia bloom straight – shook a fan out of her sleeve with an elegant movement of the wrist and dropped her hands into her lap as if to say, 'You go first.'

I'd started to speak of her father when suddenly she tapped me on the foot with her fan. 'That matter is settled so far as the three of us are concerned – that is, my father, you and myself. My sister Yumi has a different attitude towards you.'

'What do you think? Have I got leprosy or not?'

'I agree with my father. If you'd been touched by any of them, the fear would show in your face. There is no fear. Therefore you are clean. Yumi is a problem for my father and me to deal with. As for the financial arrangements for an adopted son, that is up to my father alone.'

I said, 'I'm not a greedy man. Perhaps I should have paid more attention to the money. But I haven't. It's how I am.'

She smiled at me quite beautifully. Not prettily, not sensually, but honestly – which went with her strong, open face. I said, 'You look so like your father.'

The smile lingered, raising up her cheeks and making little

mounds of them like pies. She said, 'But there are other questions besides that of Yumi.'

The food was making me drowsy. I climbed out of the chair awkwardly and lay on the tatami mat staring up at the lucky eight, which was shaped something like a star. 'There are always other questions,' I said.

She said in a lower voice, 'These are private questions.'

I looked at her from beneath my lashes. She took the bloom from behind her ear and started to roll its stem between her fingers, back and forth, back and forth. She hunched her shoulders – cleared her throat in an artless way, no dainty stuff behind the hand. 'Doig-san, here are some of them. You must promise me that you'll answer truthfully. Do you?'

'I do.'

Then without anything girlish by way of a preliminary, she said, 'Could you ever like me in the way men like women?'

That I had not been expecting. I said, 'Yes.' When a woman asks you a question like that, only one answer is possible.

'Could you trust me? Could you father children with me?'

That was exactly how she said it, this game, glorious lady. On her hunkers, the fan lying half closed in front of her, the white bloom held upright in her lap, steady as a rock. Not a trace of embarrassment on her long pagan face. One could see immediately who her father was, just from the slant of her eyes. But hers, when they got to the top, had something his didn't: a tiny downward fold that gave her face the potential for great sadness. And for graveness, as now, when she was looking at me with the corners of her mouth also a little downturned.

It was the moment to have withdrawn had I wanted to. To have returned the compliment she paid me and holding her by the eye laid out my reasons in a firm, clear manner for wishing to go no further.

But I had no such reasons. I lay there on the mat and looked up at her with amazement.

Her face not changing, she went on, 'You've held me in your arms, so here are some further questions. Am I fat enough? Does the idea of my breasts excite you? Is my hair the right length for you? My teeth, what of them? Is my neck long enough for you? Japanese men regard the neck as especially significant

324

in their lovemaking. Unless you wish to say something very contrary, you need only give me a general answer now.'

I rolled forward and knelt opposite her, our knees almost touching. I picked up her fan and laid it across her wrist. I said, 'You are a completely extraordinary woman.'

'Does your breath come faster to think about me naked?' She pushed out her bosom – not coquettishly, absolutely not. She'd asked a question and was helping me answer it, that was all.

I shook my head in wonderment. I took the bloom from her and put it aside. Then I picked her two hands – her two narrow fine-boned hands – out of her lap and said, 'What are you proposing, Mimi?'

'The moment you complete the formalities of adoption with my father, you'll be entering the clan of Yamaguchi. The gates will close behind you and you'll find yourself in a sort of prison. There'll be no escape. It's how it is in our Japanese society.'

She paused to see how I'd take it. I said nothing.

She said, 'It will be interesting for you to begin with but after a while you will feel that everyone is watching you, that you have lost the power to express yourself as you wish. That is how it is with me: a question of freedom. It is why I learned your kind of music, in order to escape to a foreign land for at least two hours in every day. So this is my proposal. That I give you my family position and my body. You know what these two things mean in our class in Japan? Everything, they mean everything. I am offering to you all that we consider most estimable. In return you would give me your strength, your foreignness, your children – and your luck. I would become part of you and your life, wherever it might take us. That is my proposal.'

Her fingers tightened on mine. 'I wanted to make this declaration before we see our father, when matters relating to your position in our family are bound to be discussed. My sister will also desire to be present. If you wish to refuse me, now is the time. Otherwise sleep, and then we can talk again.'

I said, 'Play something for me.'

I lay back on the tatami mat, folded my hands behind my head and stared up at the lucky eight. Closing my eyes, I said to Lizochka, 'Stop whatever it is you're doing up there, take a look at Mimi and tell me what you think. This instant. Urgent.'

But there was no answer.

I said, 'You've never let me down before. Remember Smolny, when I had to get off the steps in a hurry? The night Lenin took over? When I expected to be shot at every step I took? You helped me then. So come on, old girl, be a pal and do it again.'

But there was still no answer.

Mimosa was cleaning the spit out of her flute with her back to me. I said to her, 'You know that I killed my wife?'

Turning, she said, 'I know. I know also that she asked you to.'

Again I looked up at the lucky eight. Every man needs a woman if he's to prosper and that's a fact larger than a continent. But was she the one?

At that moment Lizochka called to me from a very great distance, 'I'm sorry, I was busy just then. But first you must describe her for me. Her appearance, her physique, her breeding and so on. I can't help you otherwise.'

Mimi was standing over me holding her flute.

I said to Lizochka, 'Not so loud, she's right beside me.'

Lizochka said, 'So that's her! My goodness, a foreign lady! You surprise me, Charlenka. But don't worry, I'll keep my voice down. Now tell me, has she a body for childbearing?'

'Yes,' I said.

'Has she a sweet nature?'

'Yes,' I said. 'A bold mind and a sweet nature, like yours, the best combination that can exist in a woman.'

'Have you seen her mother?'

'She's been dead for a long time.'

Lizochka sighed, a faraway rustle, like snow against the windowpane. 'That's a pity. It would have been better to see how the mother turned out. But one can't have everything . . . dear me, the things you ask of a girl!' Then more briskly, 'Oh, Charlie darling, do it and give me happiness! Make a home, have children, live quietly. Stop struggling so much, it was always your weakest point. What's her name?'

'Mimi.'

'Wonderful! I see her more clearly now. So much more

handsome than that other woman you were after. She was a slapper pure and simple.'

Do it, said my healing heart, she's a strong safe woman, she'll be an adventure for you, right up to the very end.

Do it, said Hana, trying to steal into the pavilion again, do it, said the birdies, do it, said the bees looking back over their shoulders, do it, they all said in chorus, do it like we do, for contentment only.

I said to Mimi, 'I'm not one for small matters, and that's the truth of it. If it's just low stuff you want from your man, fetching and carrying, that sort of thing, don't look at me' – which I said severely, maybe scowling, so as to concentrate her mind. There are times when one gets drawn too deeply into something at the very start, gets trapped in it and needs a fright to make one jump clear. Men and women, it happens to us both.

She said modestly, 'We could do things together, maybe?'

'Like what?' I said, as a test of her spirit.

'Might we conquer the world?' she said, now with flames in her eyes.

'Why not?' I said.

She put down her flute and knelt before me. 'I would be your number-one woman? No Countess, no others?'

Lizochka chuckled, and I said to her from the corner of my mouth, 'I know what you're thinking. You're thinking that Doig is done. Well, you just keep your big nose out of this.'

I shoved my face close to Mimi's. 'What, no others, eh?' – it came out growling and unhappy. She recoiled, a cloud sweeping across her face – dismay, disappointment, the crushing of her pride, I saw all of them in that one instant. And suddenly, in the most immediate and irresistible manner, like an electric shock in the pit of one's stomach, I knew that Lizochka was right: I had come to the end of something, not temporarily as in a postponement but in a way that was both vital and conclusive. It was the end, not just of an episode, not of a chapter, but of an entire story, that of my Russian inheritance.

I bowed to Mimi. I laid my hand across my heart. 'No others,' I said, 'Doig is done.'

A slow smile covered her face, in which there was neither triumph nor conceit, nor any emotion in which deception could have made a home. Joy, it was all I saw, the joy of a woman binding herself to a man.

I stretched out my hand to touch her face. She caught it and held it. Then she lay down beside me in the pavilion, in the glade, in the sweet air of spring.